MARVEL

GUARDIANS OF THE GALAXY

AN AWESOME MIX

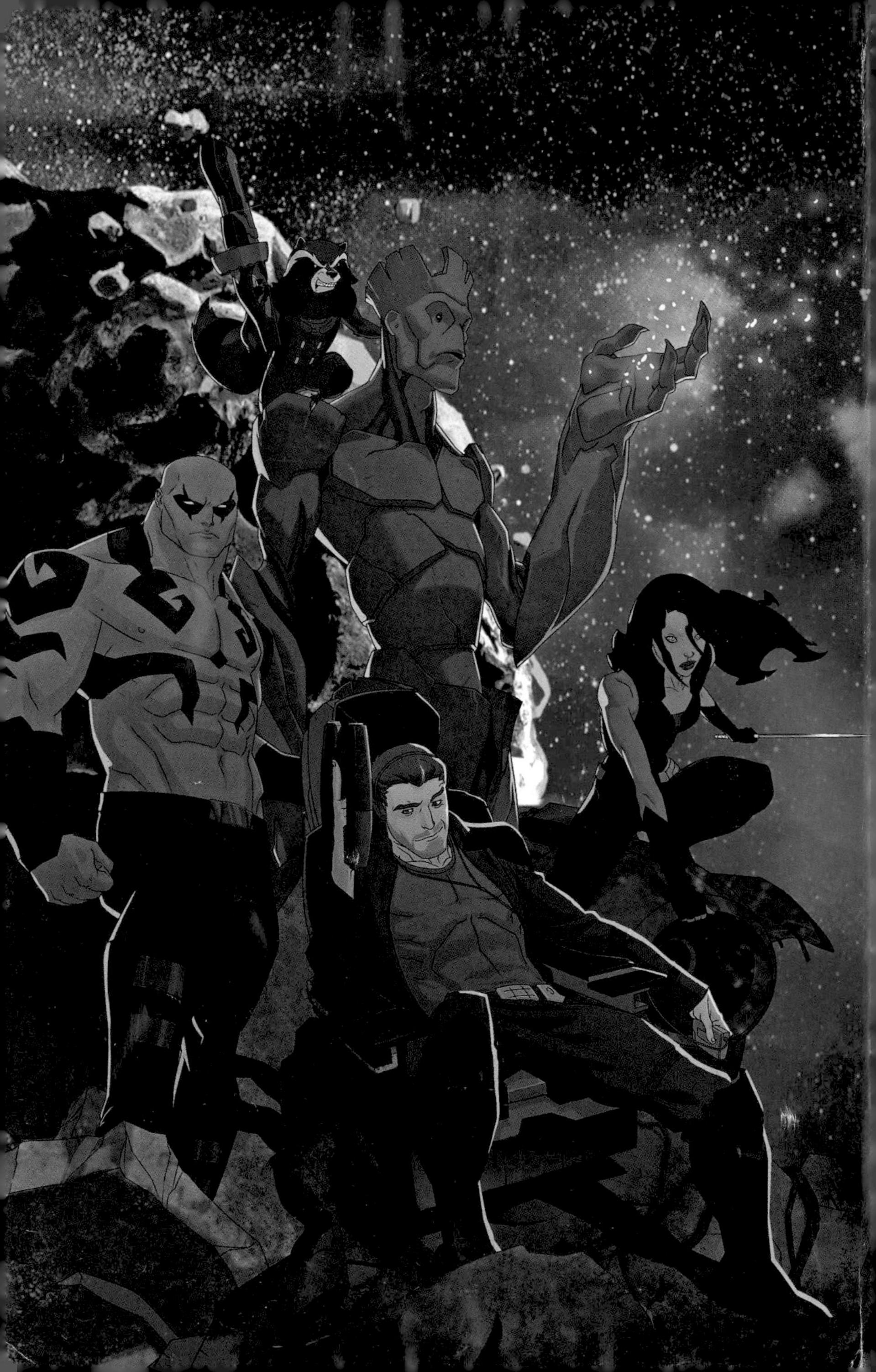

MARVEL

GUARDIANS OF THE GALAXY

MARVEL UNIVERSE GUARDIANS OF THE GALAXY (2015A) #1-4

WRITERS: **MAIRGHREAD SCOTT** (#1-2),
PAUL ALLOR (#3) & **JOE CARAMAGNA** (#4)
ARTIST: **ADAM ARCHER**
COLOR ARTISTS: **ANDY ELDER** (#1)
& **CHARLIE KIRCHOFF** (#2-4)
LETTERER: **VC'S JOE CARAMAGNA**
EDITORS: **SEBASTIAN GIRNER** & **JON MOISAN**
SENIOR EDITOR: **MARK PANICCIA**

MARVEL UNIVERSE GUARDIANS OF THE GALAXY (2015B) #3, #5, #9

BASED ON THE TV SERIES WRITTEN BY
STEVE MELCHING & **DAVID McDERMOTT**
DIRECTED BY **JAMES YANG**
ART BY **MARVEL ANIMATION STUDIOS**
ADAPTED BY **JOE CARAMAGNA**
SPECIAL THANKS TO **HANNAH MACDONALD** & **PRODUCT FACTORY**
EDITOR: **MARK BASSO**
SENIOR EDITOR: **MARK PANICCIA**

COLLECTION EDITOR: **JENNIFER GRÜNWALD**
ASSISTANT EDITOR: **CAITLIN O'CONNELL**
ASSOCIATE MANAGING EDITOR: **KATERI WOODY**
EDITOR, SPECIAL PROJECTS: **MARK D. BEAZLEY**
VP PRODUCTION & SPECIAL PROJECTS: **JEFF YOUNGQUIST**
SVP PRINT, SALES & MARKETING: **DAVID GABRIEL**
HEAD OF MARVEL TELEVISION: **JEPH LOEB**
RESEARCH: **JESS HAROLD**

EDITOR IN CHIEF: **AXEL ALONSO**
CHIEF CREATIVE OFFICER: **JOE QUESADA**
PRESIDENT: **DAN BUCKLEY**
EXECUTIVE PRODUCER: **ALAN FINE**

GUARDIANS OF THE GALAXY: AN AWESOME MIX. Contains material originally published in magazine form as MARVEL UNIVERSE GUARDIANS OF THE GALAXY (2015A) #1-4; and MARVEL UNIVERSE GUARDIANS OF THE GALAXY (2015B) #3, #5 and #9. First printing 2017. ISBN# 978-1-302-90933-8. Published by MARVEL WORLDWIDE, INC., a subsidiary of MARVEL ENTERTAINMENT, LLC. OFFICE OF PUBLICATION: 135 West 50th Street, New York, NY 10020. Copyright © 2017 MARVEL No similarity between any of the names, characters, persons, and/or institutions in this magazine with those of any living or dead person or institution is intended, and any such similarity which may exist is purely coincidental. Printed in the U.S.A. DAN BUCKLEY, President, Marvel Entertainment; JOE QUESADA, Chief Creative Officer; TOM BREVOORT, SVP of Publishing; DAVID BOGART, SVP of Business Affairs & Operations, Publishing & Partnership; C.B. CEBULSKI, VP of Brand Management & Development, Asia; DAVID GABRIEL, SVP of Sales & Marketing, Publishing; JEFF YOUNGQUIST, VP of Production & Special Projects; DAN CARR, Executive Director of Publishing Technology; ALEX MORALES, Director of Publishing Operations; SUSAN CRESPI, Production Manager; STAN LEE, Chairman Emeritus. For information regarding advertising in Marvel Comics or on Marvel.com, please contact Vit DeBellis, Integrated Sales Manager, at vdebellis@marvel.com. For Marvel subscription inquiries, please call 888-511-5480. **Manufactured between 8/25/2017 and 9/26/2017 by SHERIDAN, CHELSEA, MI, USA.**

10 9 8 7 6 5 4 3 2 1

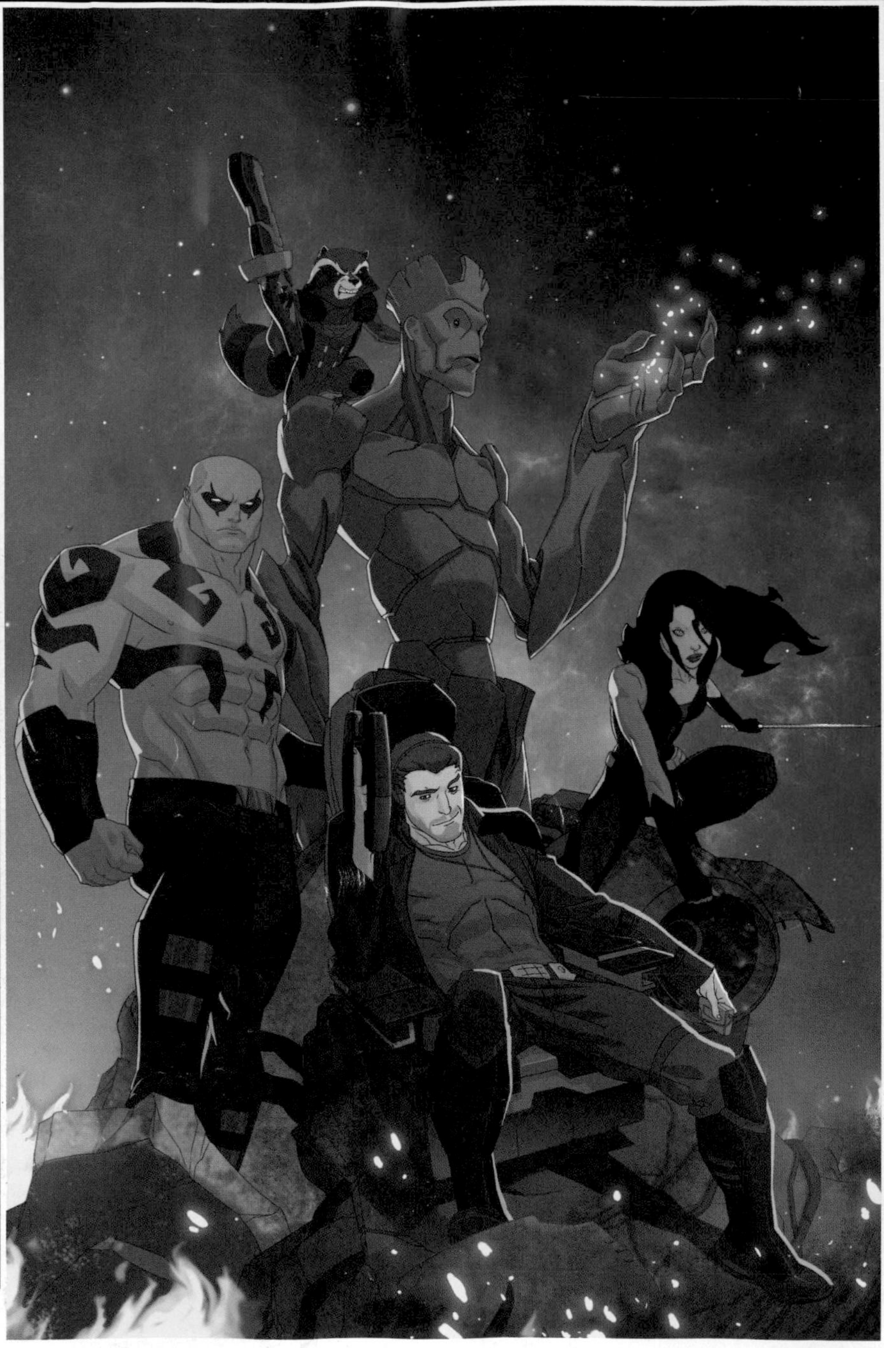

1 "SO VERY YOUNG"

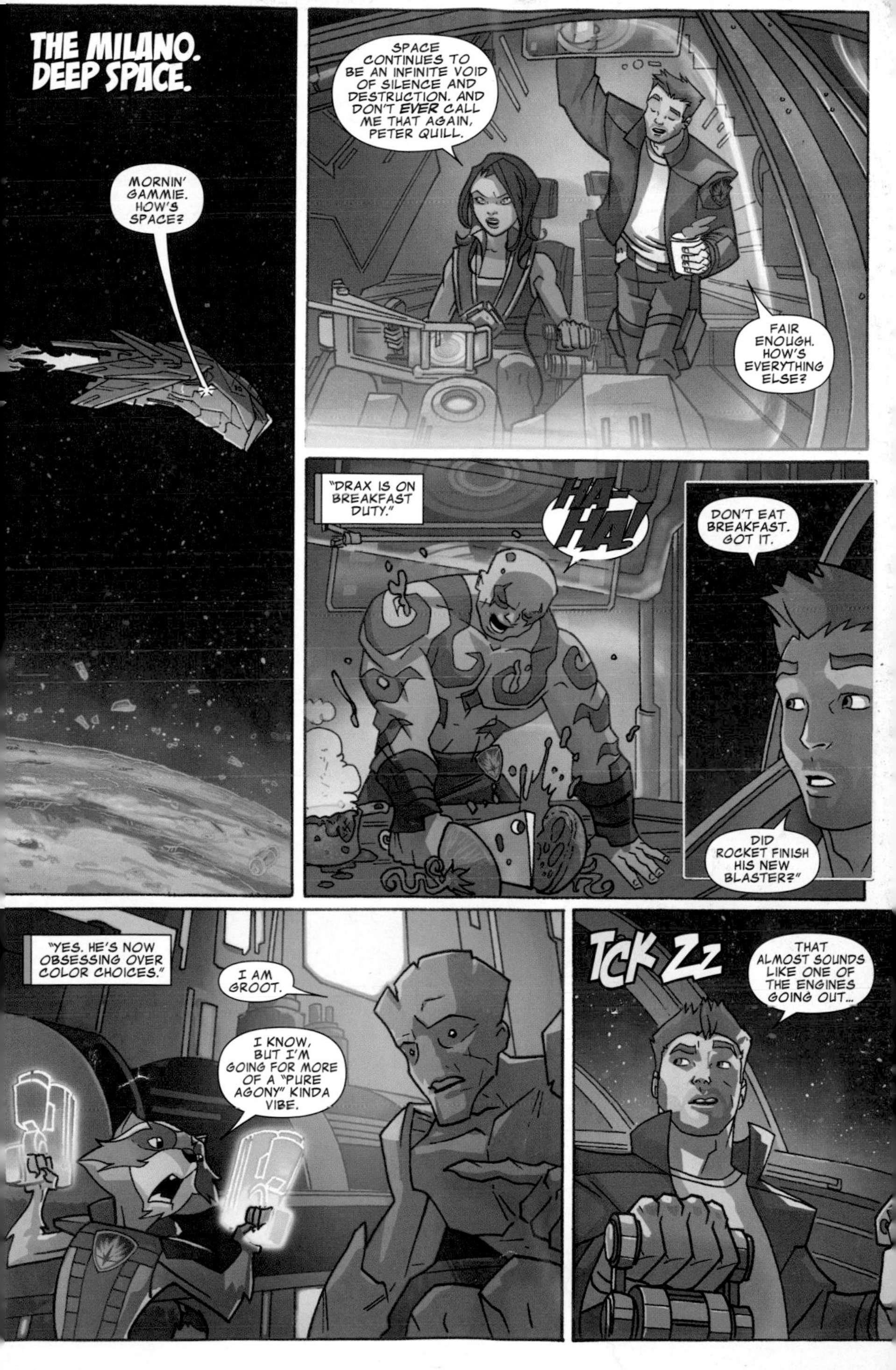
THE MILANO. DEEP SPACE.
MORNIN' GAMMIE. HOW'S SPACE?
SPACE CONTINUES TO BE AN INFINITE VOID OF SILENCE AND DESTRUCTION. AND DON'T EVER CALL ME THAT AGAIN, PETER QUILL.
FAIR ENOUGH. HOW'S EVERYTHING ELSE?
"DRAX IS ON BREAKFAST DUTY."
HA-HA!
DON'T EAT BREAKFAST. GOT IT.
DID ROCKET FINISH HIS NEW BLASTER?"
"YES. HE'S NOW OBSESSING OVER COLOR CHOICES."
I AM GROOT.
I KNOW, BUT I'M GOING FOR MORE OF A "PURE AGONY" KINDA VIBE.
TCK Zz
THAT ALMOST SOUNDS LIKE ONE OF THE ENGINES GOING OUT...

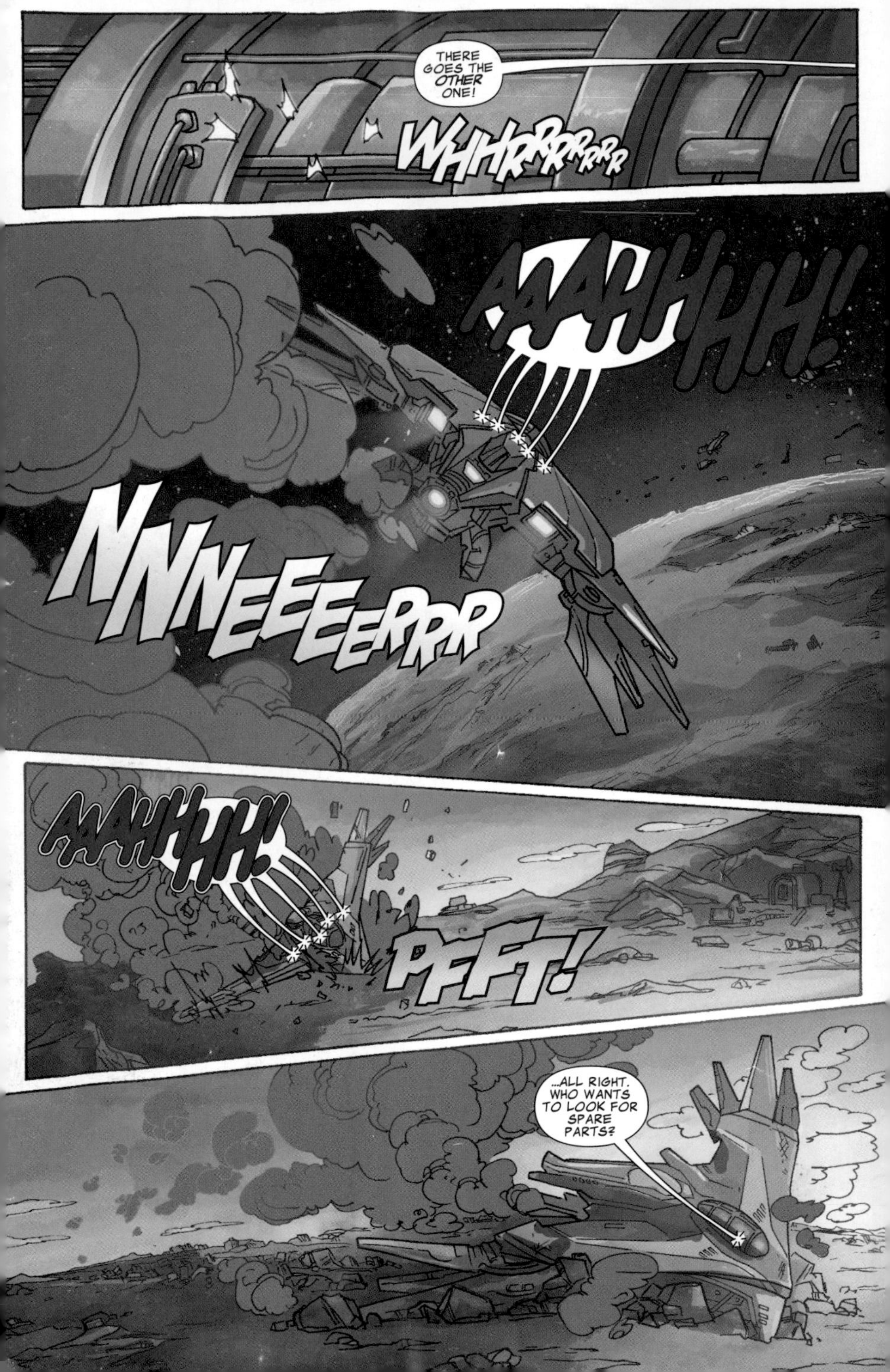
THERE GOES THE OTHER ONE!
WHHRRRRRRR
AAAHHHHH!
NNNEEEEERRR
AAAHHHH!
PFFT!
...ALL RIGHT. WHO WANTS TO LOOK FOR SPARE PARTS?

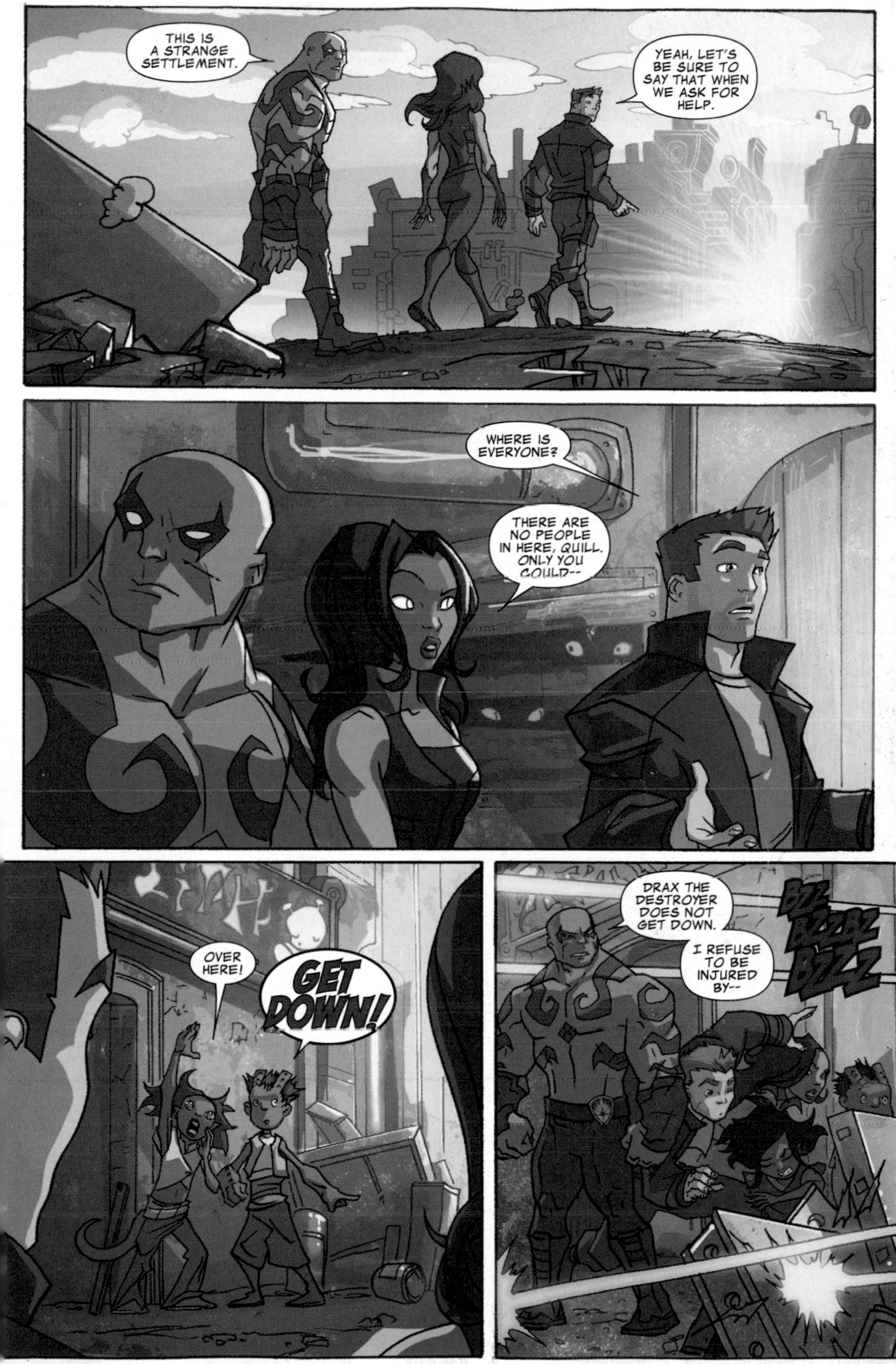
THIS IS A STRANGE SETTLEMENT.
YEAH, LET'S BE SURE TO SAY THAT WHEN WE ASK FOR HELP.
WHERE IS EVERYONE?
THERE ARE NO PEOPLE IN HERE, QUILL. ONLY YOU COULD--
OVER HERE!
GET DOWN!
DRAX THE DESTROYER DOES NOT GET DOWN.
I REFUSE TO BE INJURED BY--
BZZ BZZBZ BZZZ

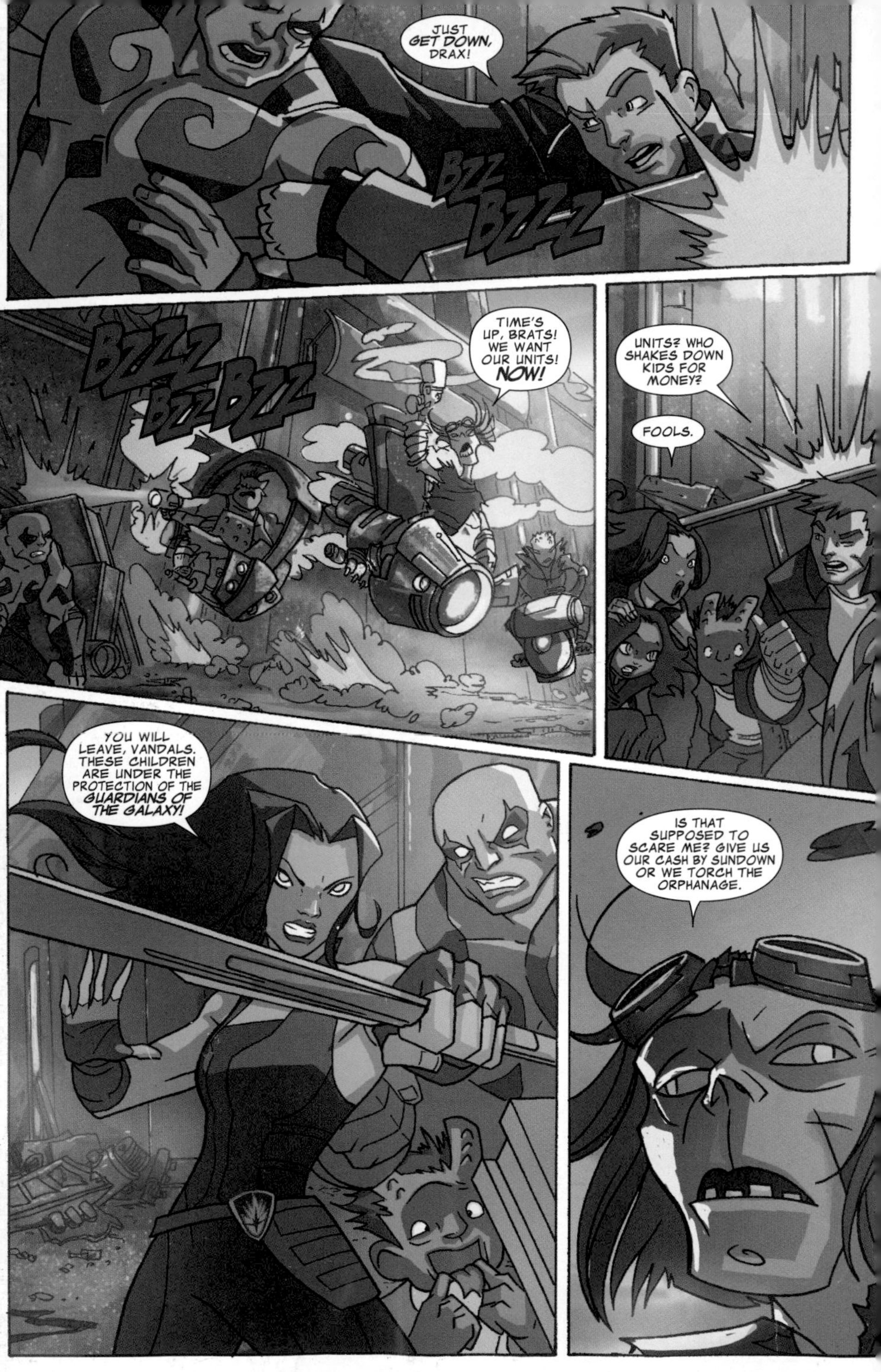
JUST GET DOWN, DRAX!
BZZ BZZZ
BZZZZ BZZ BZZZ
TIME'S UP, BRATS! WE WANT OUR UNITS! NOW!
UNITS? WHO SHAKES DOWN KIDS FOR MONEY?
FOOLS.
YOU WILL LEAVE, VANDALS. THESE CHILDREN ARE UNDER THE PROTECTION OF THE GUARDIANS OF THE GALAXY!
IS THAT SUPPOSED TO SCARE ME? GIVE US OUR CASH BY SUNDOWN OR WE TORCH THE ORPHANAGE.

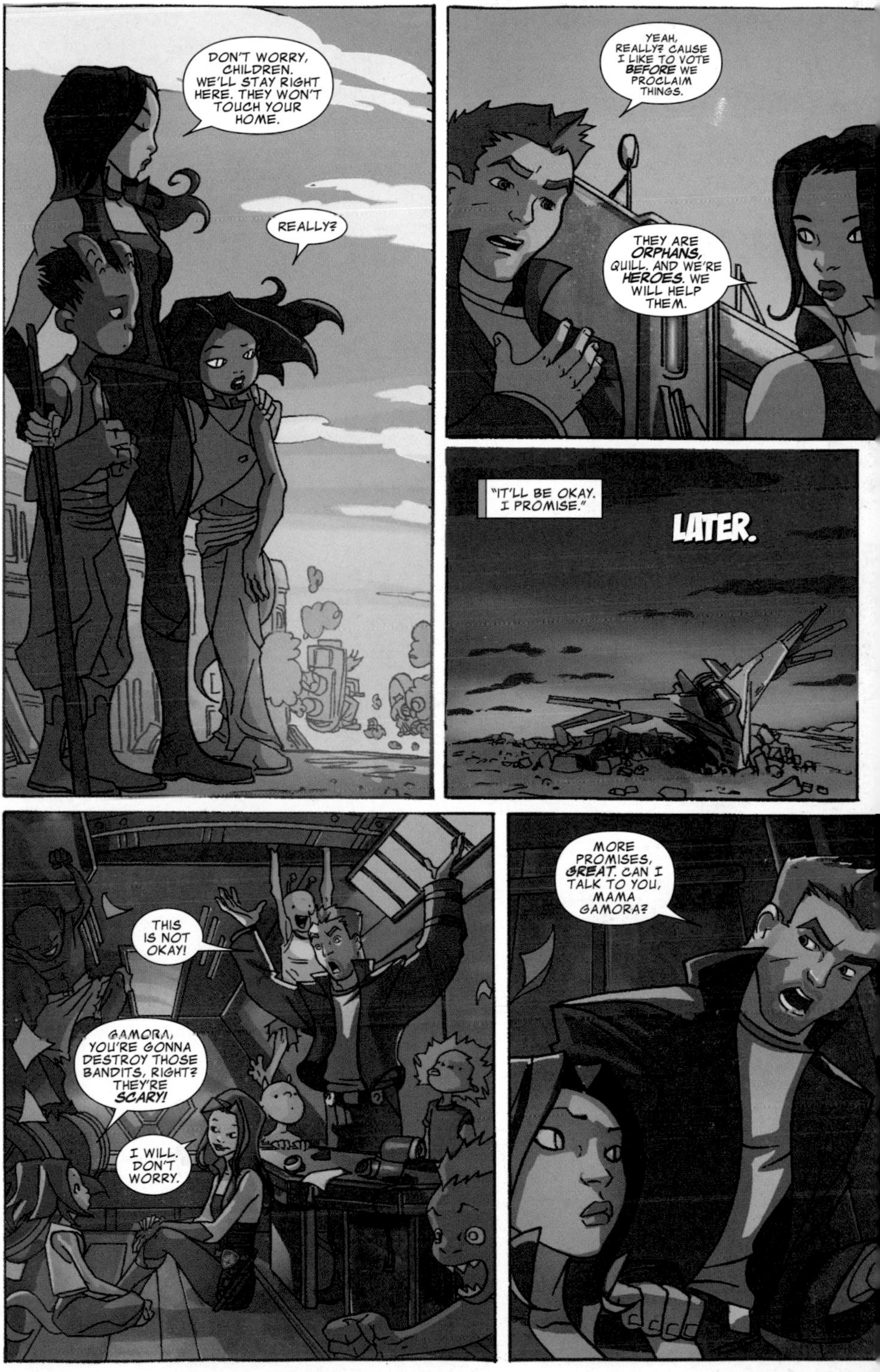
DON'T WORRY, CHILDREN. WE'LL STAY RIGHT HERE. THEY WON'T TOUCH YOUR HOME.
REALLY?
YEAH, REALLY? CAUSE I LIKE TO VOTE BEFORE WE PROCLAIM THINGS.
THEY ARE ORPHANS, QUILL. AND WE'RE HEROES. WE WILL HELP THEM.
"IT'LL BE OKAY. I PROMISE."
LATER.
THIS IS NOT OKAY!
GAMORA, YOU'RE GONNA DESTROY THOSE BANDITS, RIGHT? THEY'RE SCARY!
I WILL. DON'T WORRY.
MORE PROMISES, GREAT. CAN I TALK TO YOU, MAMA GAMORA?

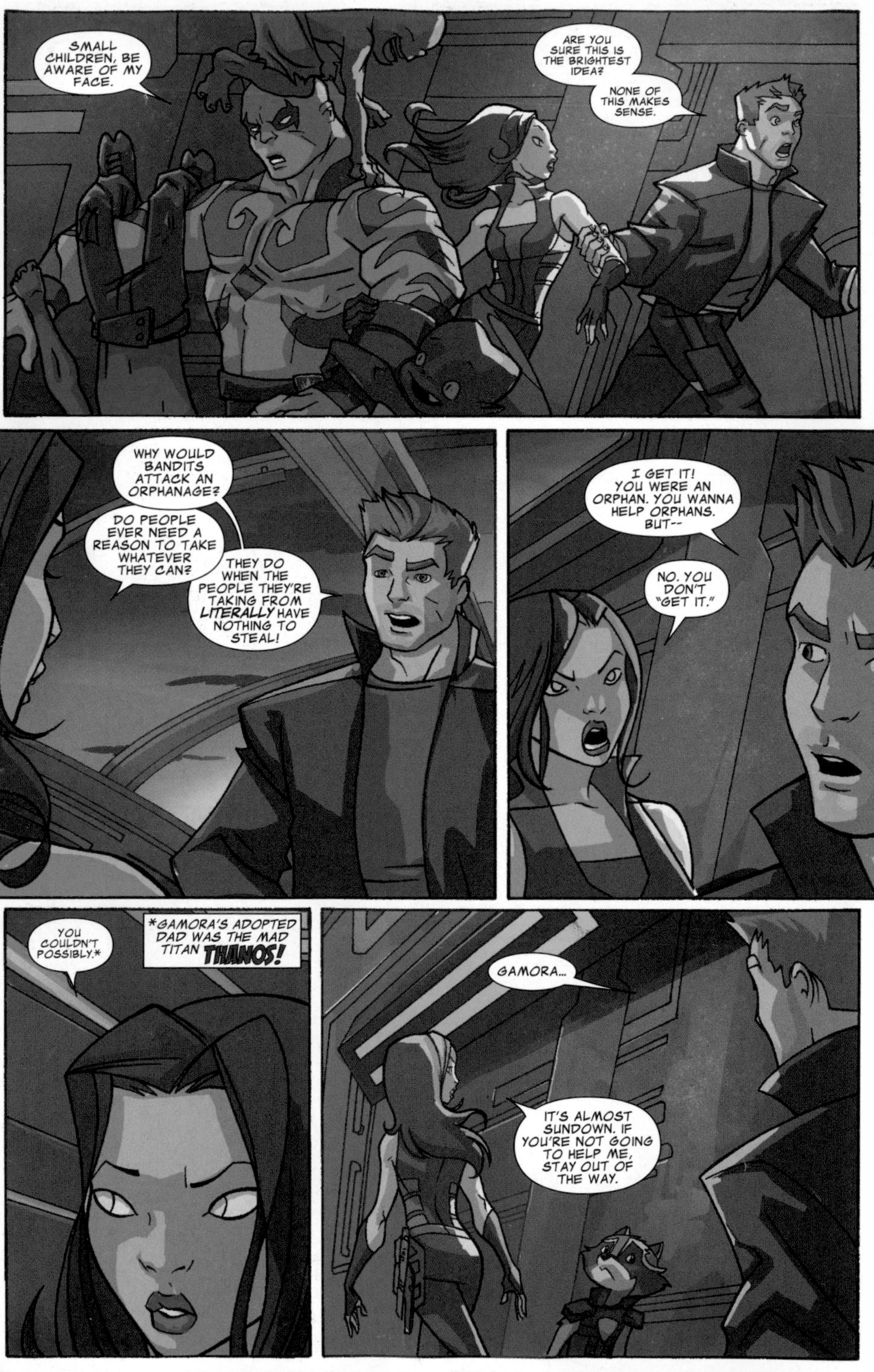
SMALL CHILDREN, BE AWARE OF MY FACE.
ARE YOU SURE THIS IS THE BRIGHTEST IDEA?
NONE OF THIS MAKES SENSE.
WHY WOULD BANDITS ATTACK AN ORPHANAGE?
DO PEOPLE EVER NEED A REASON TO TAKE WHATEVER THEY CAN?
THEY DO WHEN THE PEOPLE THEY'RE TAKING FROM LITERALLY HAVE NOTHING TO STEAL!
I GET IT! YOU WERE AN ORPHAN. YOU WANNA HELP ORPHANS. BUT--
NO. YOU DON'T "GET IT."
YOU COULDN'T POSSIBLY.*
*GAMORA'S ADOPTED DAD WAS THE MAD TITAN THANOS!
GAMORA...
IT'S ALMOST SUNDOWN. IF YOU'RE NOT GOING TO HELP ME, STAY OUT OF THE WAY.

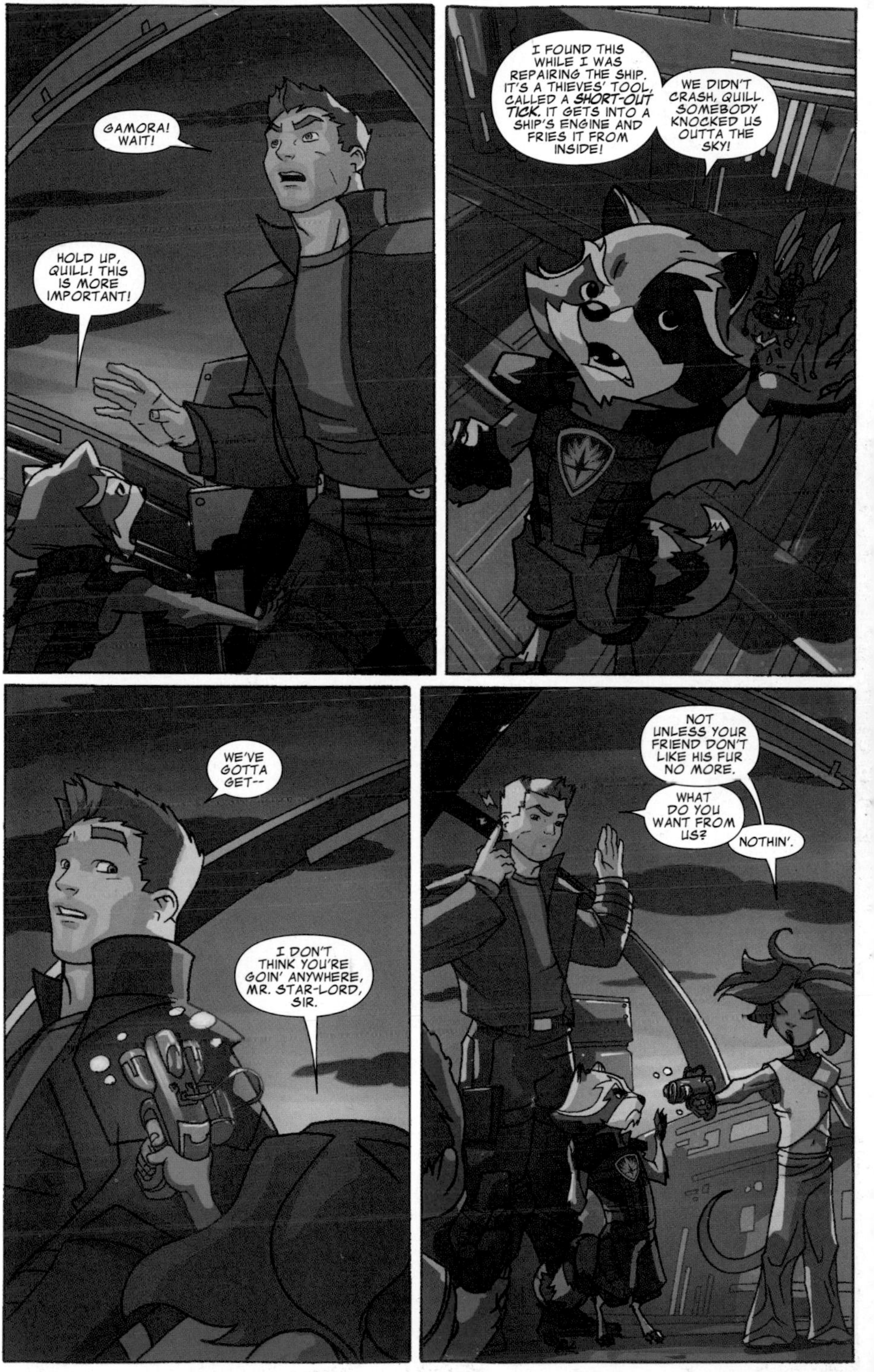
GAMORA! WAIT!
HOLD UP, QUILL! THIS IS MORE IMPORTANT!
I FOUND THIS WHILE I WAS REPAIRING THE SHIP. IT'S A THIEVES' TOOL, CALLED A SHORT-OUT TICK. IT GETS INTO A SHIP'S ENGINE AND FRIES IT FROM INSIDE!
WE DIDN'T CRASH, QUILL. SOMEBODY KNOCKED US OUTTA THE SKY!
WE'VE GOTTA GET--
I DON'T THINK YOU'RE GOIN' ANYWHERE, MR. STAR-LORD, SIR.
WHAT DO YOU WANT FROM US?
NOTHIN'.
NOT UNLESS YOUR FRIEND DON'T LIKE HIS FUR NO MORE.

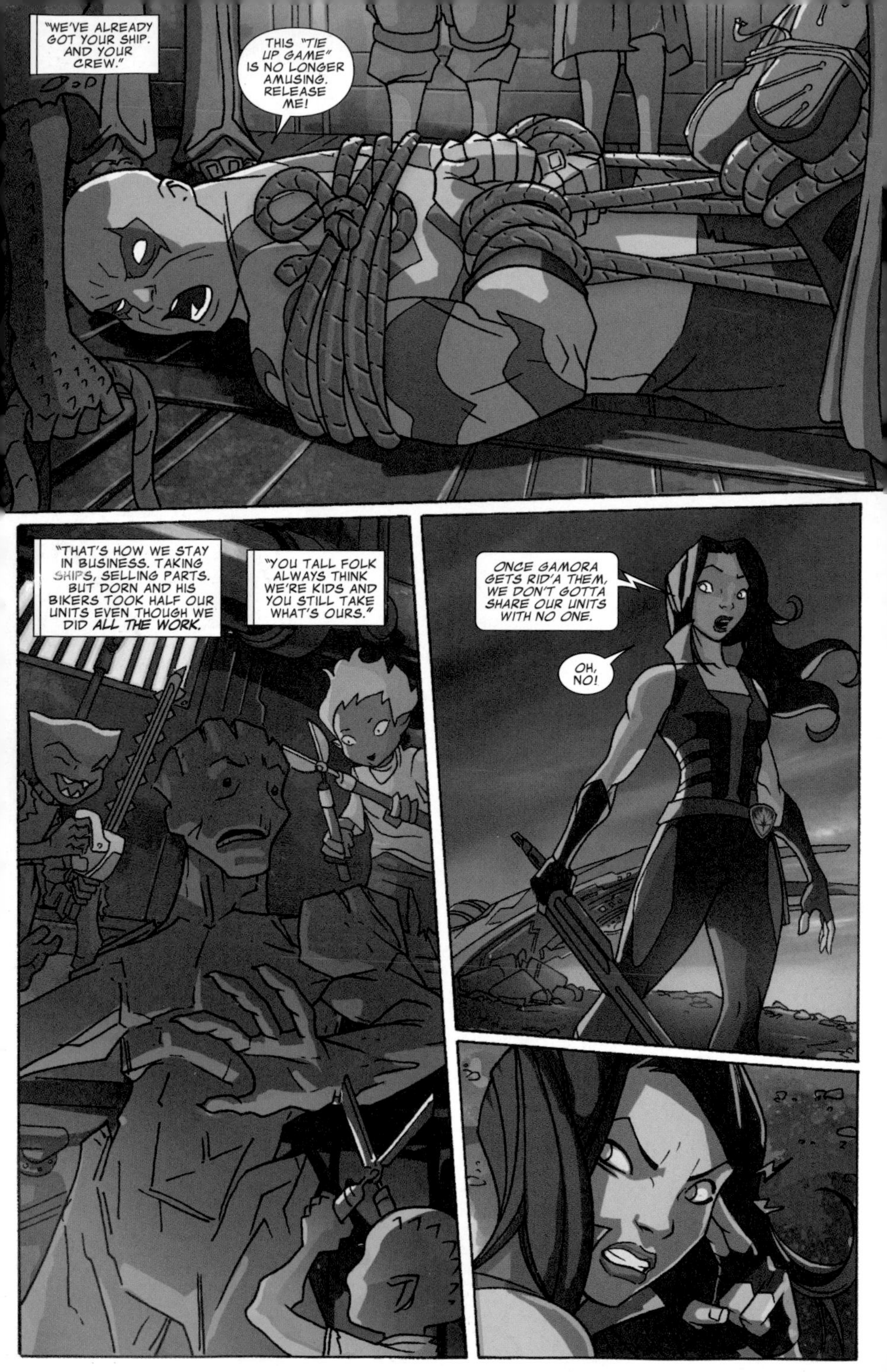
"WE'VE ALREADY GOT YOUR SHIP. AND YOUR CREW."
THIS "TIE UP GAME" IS NO LONGER AMUSING. RELEASE ME!
"THAT'S HOW WE STAY IN BUSINESS. TAKING SHIPS, SELLING PARTS. BUT DORN AND HIS BIKERS TOOK HALF OUR UNITS EVEN THOUGH WE DID ALL THE WORK.
"YOU TALL FOLK ALWAYS THINK WE'RE KIDS AND YOU STILL TAKE WHAT'S OURS."
ONCE GAMORA GETS RID'A THEM, WE DON'T GOTTA SHARE OUR UNITS WITH NO ONE.
OH, NO!

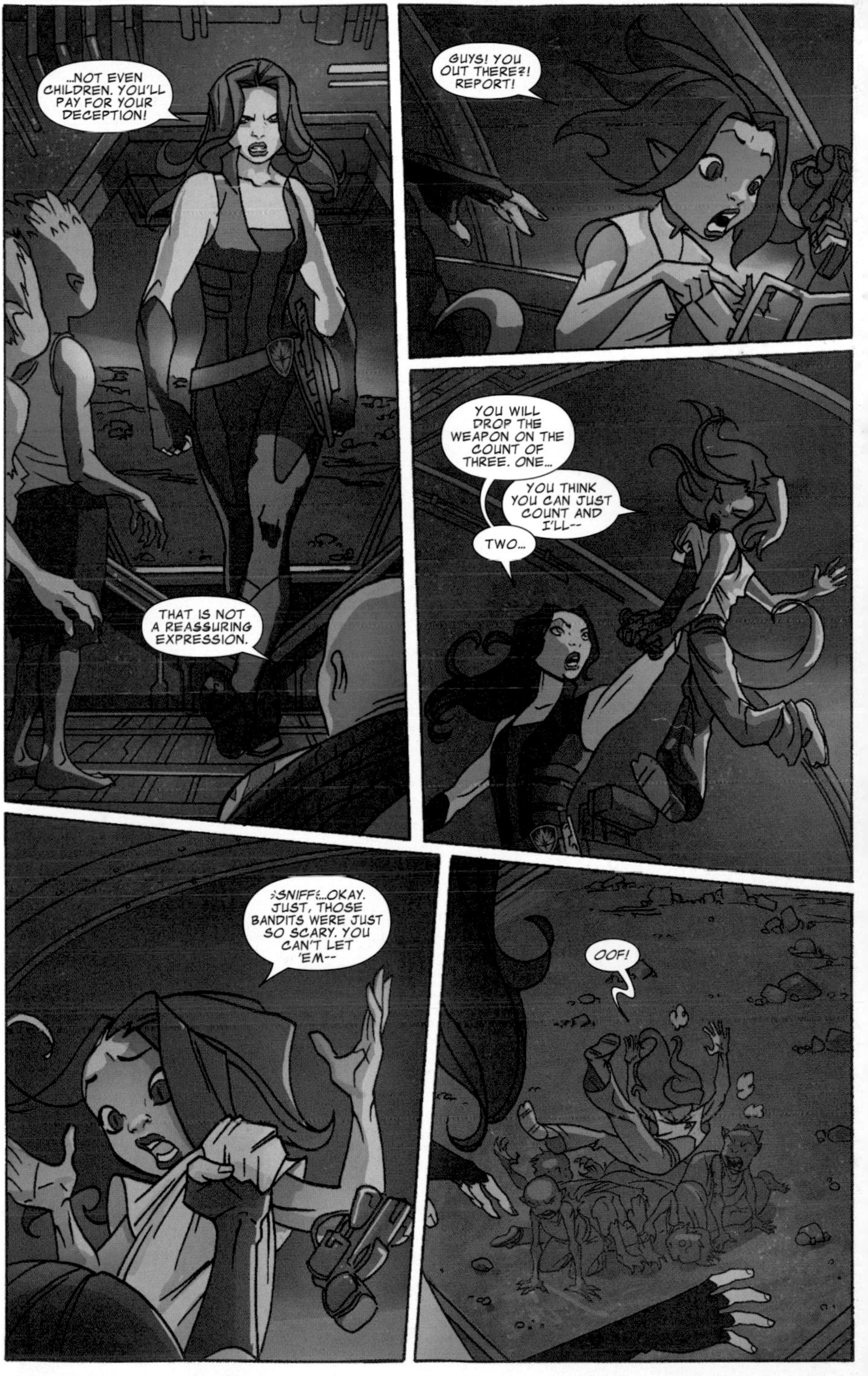
...NOT EVEN CHILDREN. YOU'LL PAY FOR YOUR DECEPTION!
THAT IS NOT A REASSURING EXPRESSION.
GUYS! YOU OUT THERE?! REPORT!
YOU WILL DROP THE WEAPON ON THE COUNT OF THREE. ONE...
YOU THINK YOU CAN JUST COUNT AND I'LL--
TWO...
SNIFF ...OKAY. JUST, THOSE BANDITS WERE JUST SO SCARY. YOU CAN'T LET 'EM--
OOF!

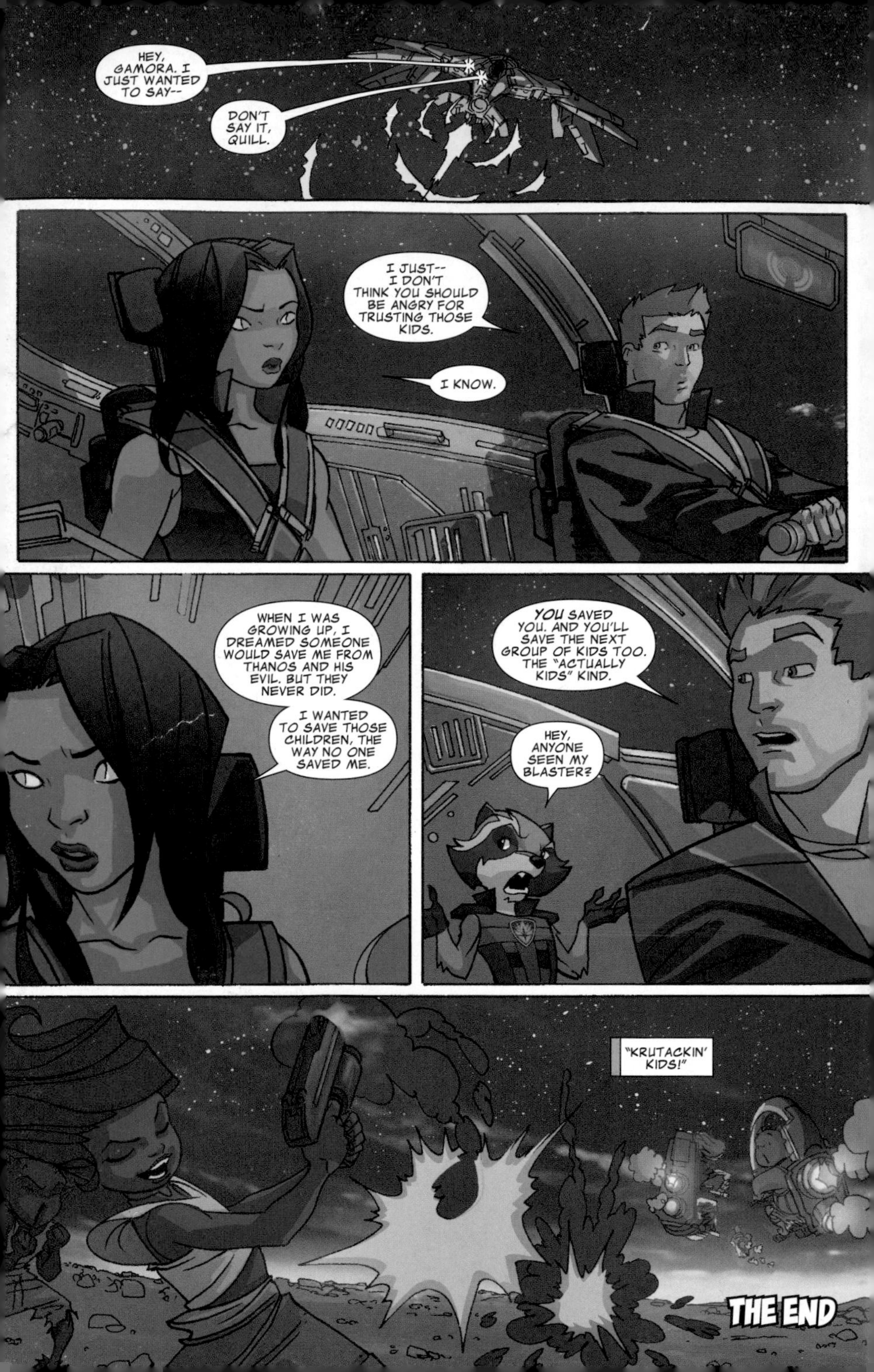
HEY, GAMORA. I JUST WANTED TO SAY--
DON'T SAY IT, QUILL.
I JUST-- I DON'T THINK YOU SHOULD BE ANGRY FOR TRUSTING THOSE KIDS.
I KNOW.
WHEN I WAS GROWING UP, I DREAMED SOMEONE WOULD SAVE ME FROM THANOS AND HIS EVIL. BUT THEY NEVER DID.
I WANTED TO SAVE THOSE CHILDREN, THE WAY NO ONE SAVED ME.
YOU SAVED YOU. AND YOU'LL SAVE THE NEXT GROUP OF KIDS TOO. THE "ACTUALLY KIDS" KIND.
HEY, ANYONE SEEN MY BLASTER?
"KRUTACKIN' KIDS!"
THE END

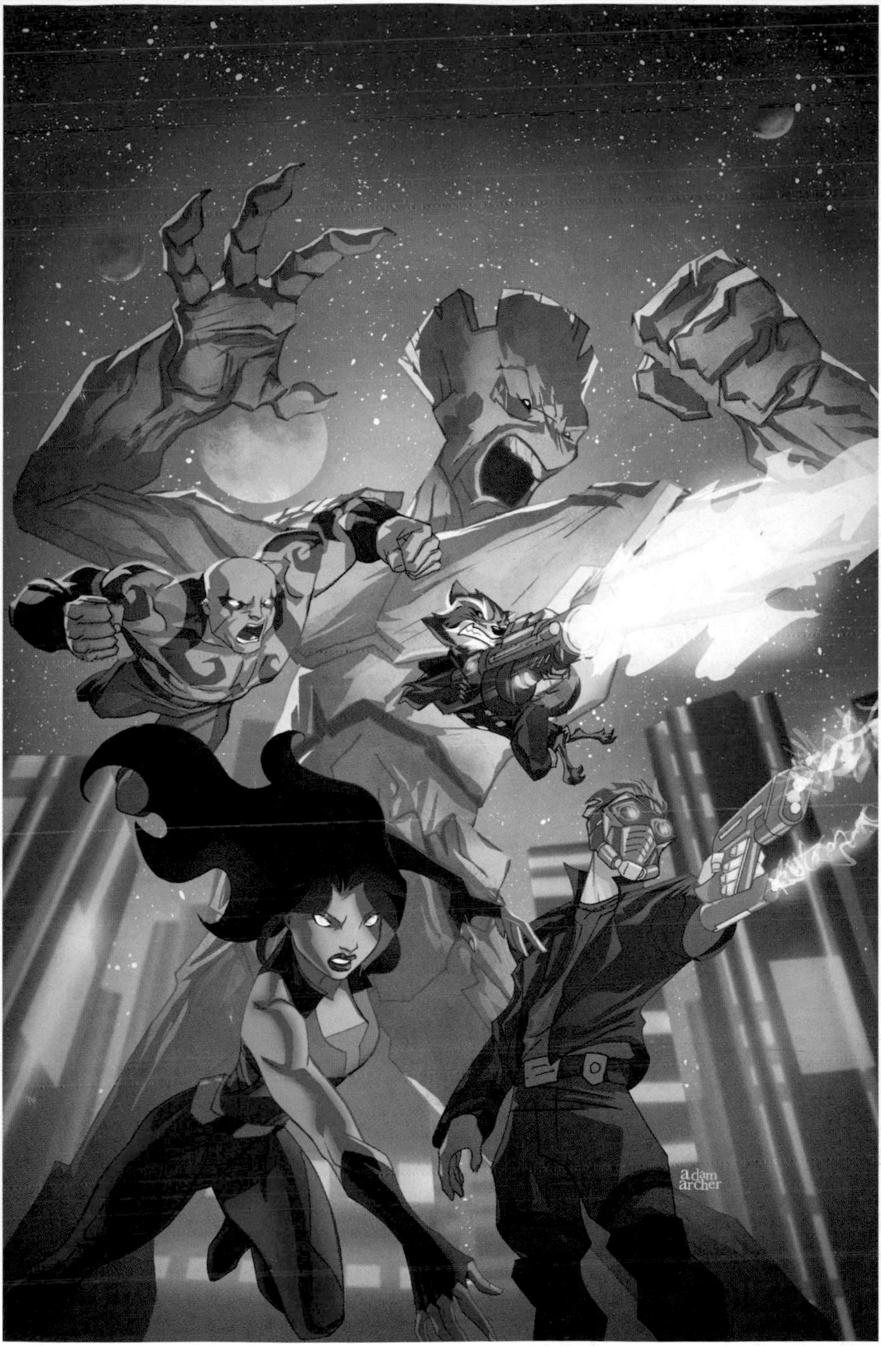
adam
archer

"SHOW AND TELL" **2**

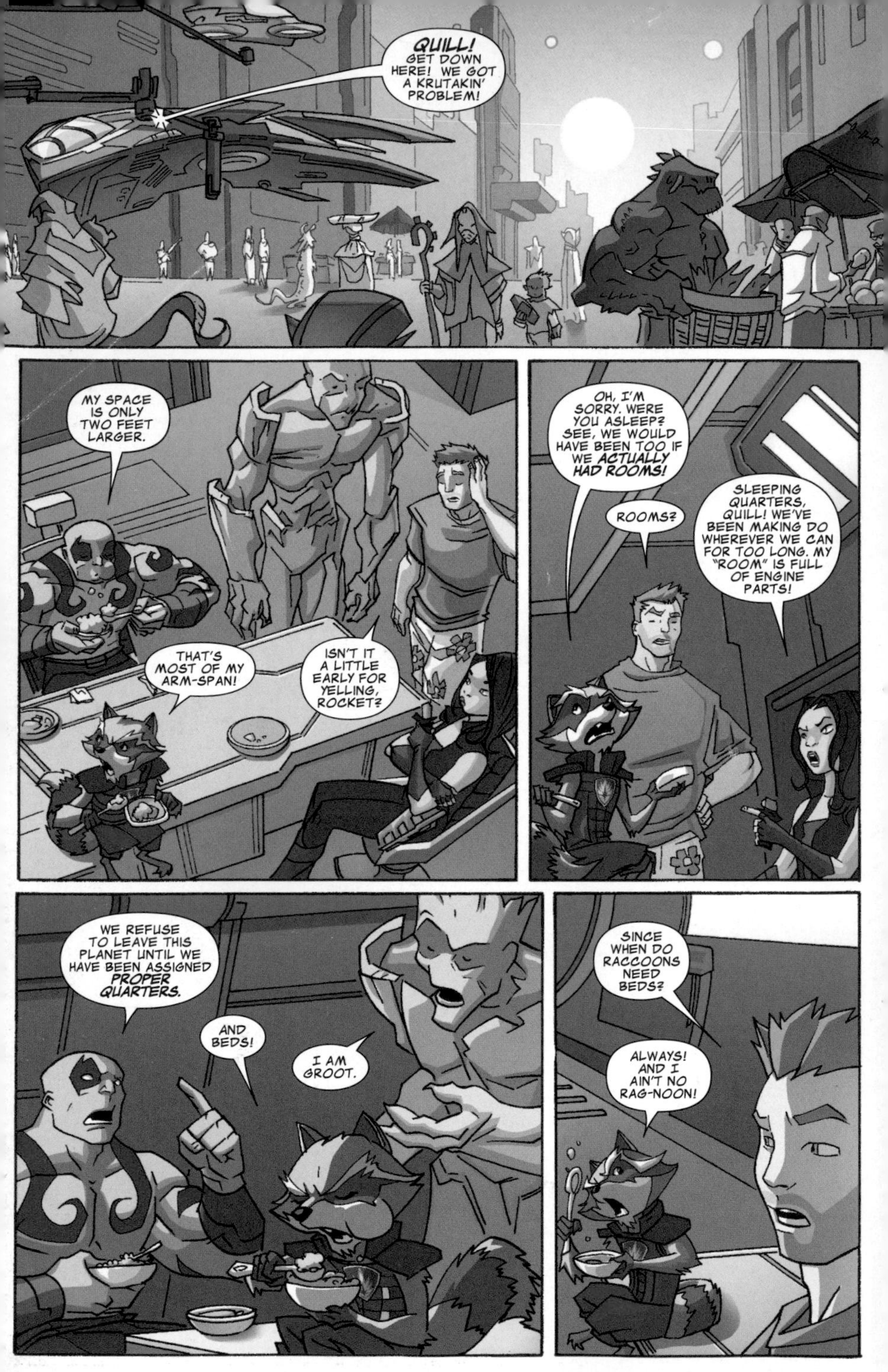
QUILL! GET DOWN HERE! WE GOT A KRUTAKIN' PROBLEM!
MY SPACE IS ONLY TWO FEET LARGER.
THAT'S MOST OF MY ARM-SPAN!
ISN'T IT A LITTLE EARLY FOR YELLING, ROCKET?
OH, I'M SORRY. WERE YOU ASLEEP? SEE, WE WOULD HAVE BEEN TOO IF WE ACTUALLY HAD ROOMS!
ROOMS?
SLEEPING QUARTERS, QUILL! WE'VE BEEN MAKING DO WHEREVER WE CAN FOR TOO LONG. MY "ROOM" IS FULL OF ENGINE PARTS!
WE REFUSE TO LEAVE THIS PLANET UNTIL WE HAVE BEEN ASSIGNED PROPER QUARTERS.
AND BEDS!
I AM GROOT.
SINCE WHEN DO RACCOONS NEED BEDS?
ALWAYS! AND I AIN'T NO RAG-NOON!

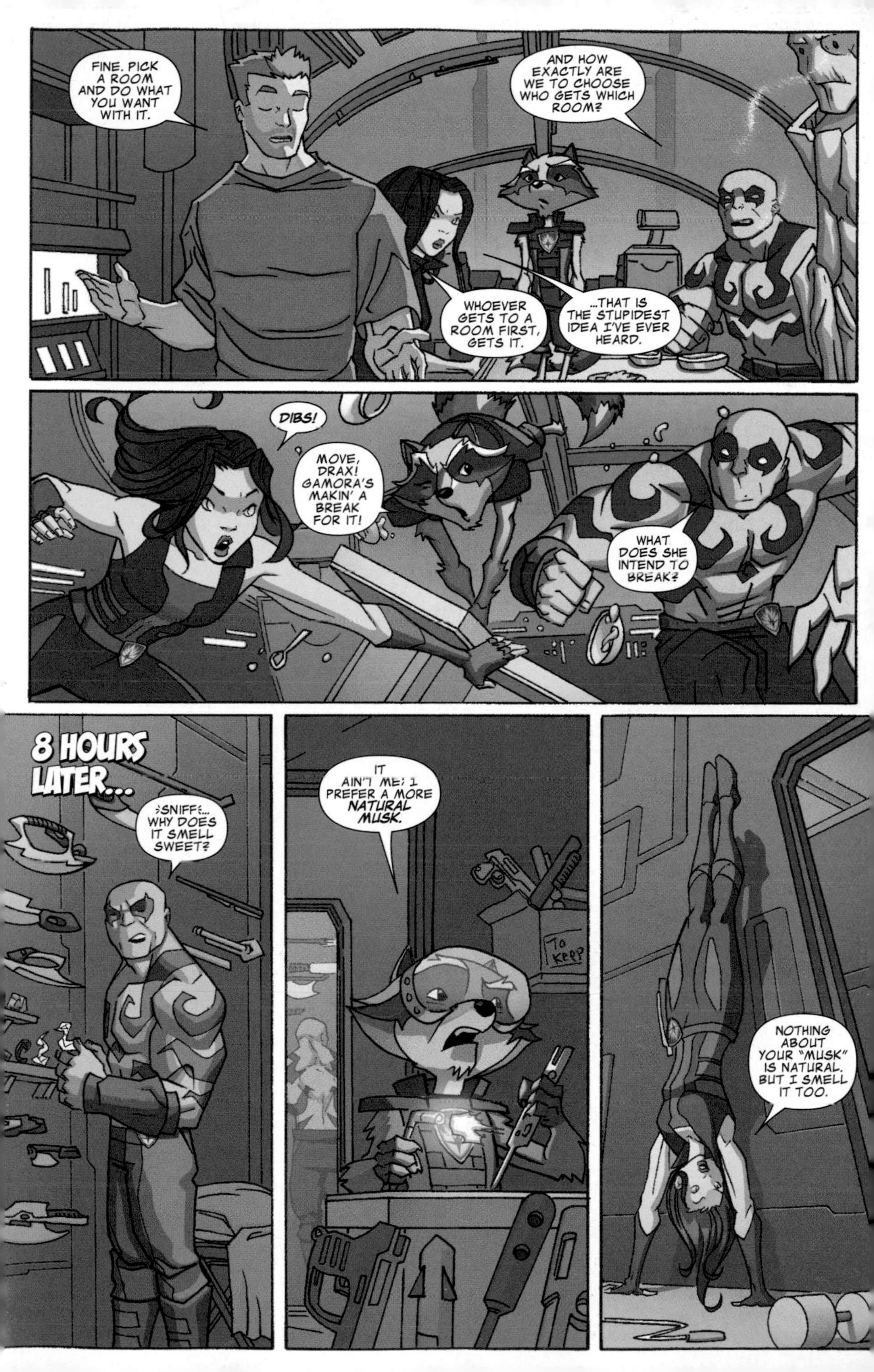
FINE. PICK A ROOM AND DO WHAT YOU WANT WITH IT.
AND HOW EXACTLY ARE WE TO CHOOSE WHO GETS WHICH ROOM?
WHOEVER GETS TO A ROOM FIRST, GETS IT.
...THAT IS THE STUPIDEST IDEA I'VE EVER HEARD.
DIBS!
MOVE, DRAX! GAMORA'S MAKIN' A BREAK FOR IT!
WHAT DOES SHE INTEND TO BREAK?
8 HOURS LATER...
SNIFF... WHY DOES IT SMELL SWEET?
IT AIN'T ME; I PREFER A MORE NATURAL MUSK.
TO KEEP
NOTHING ABOUT YOUR "MUSK" IS NATURAL. BUT I SMELL IT TOO.

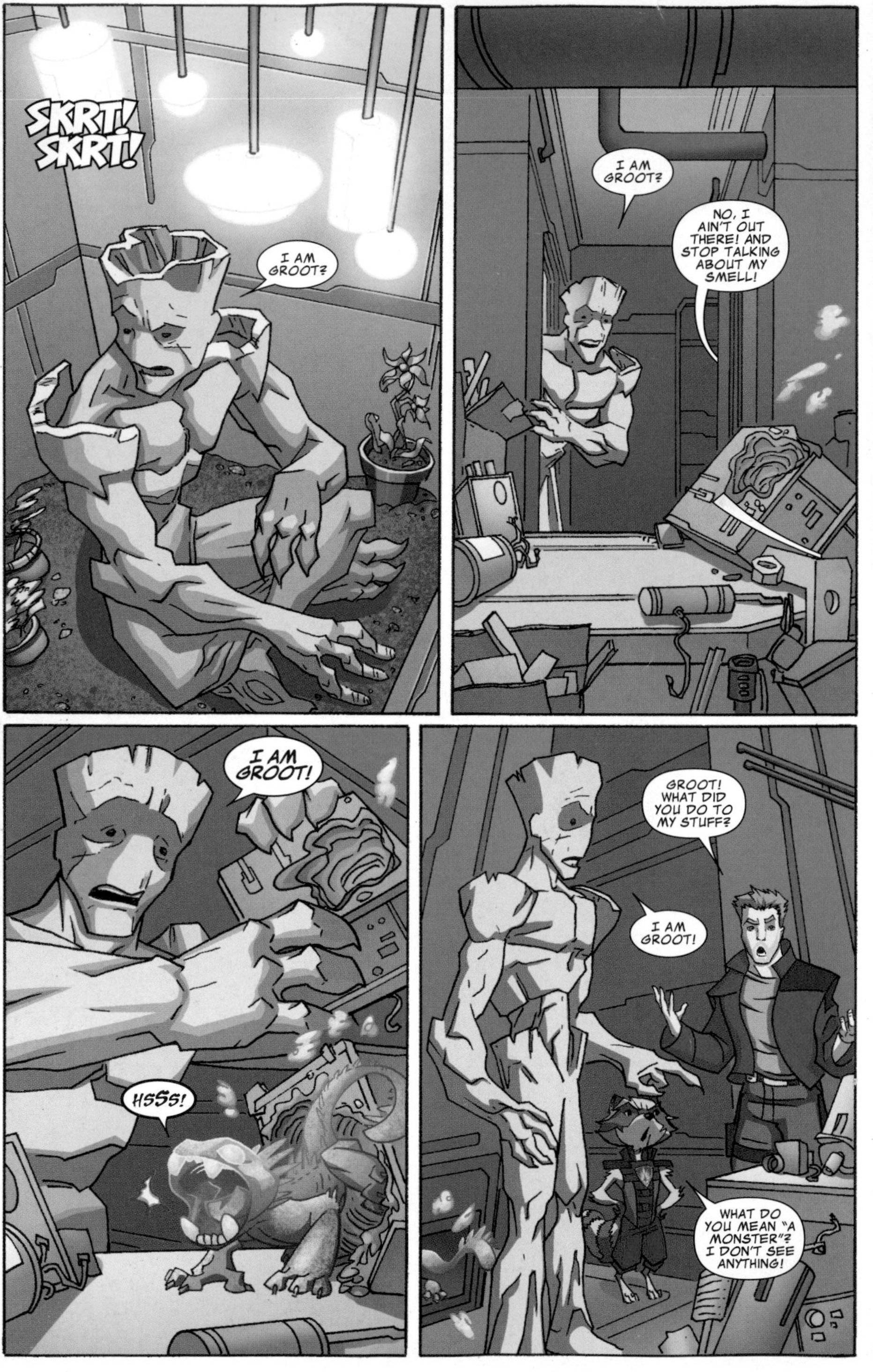
SKRT! SKRT!
I AM GROOT?
I AM GROOT?
NO, I AIN'T OUT THERE! AND STOP TALKING ABOUT MY SMELL!
I AM GROOT!
HSSS!
GROOT! WHAT DID YOU DO TO MY STUFF?
I AM GROOT!
WHAT DO YOU MEAN "A MONSTER"? I DON'T SEE ANYTHING!

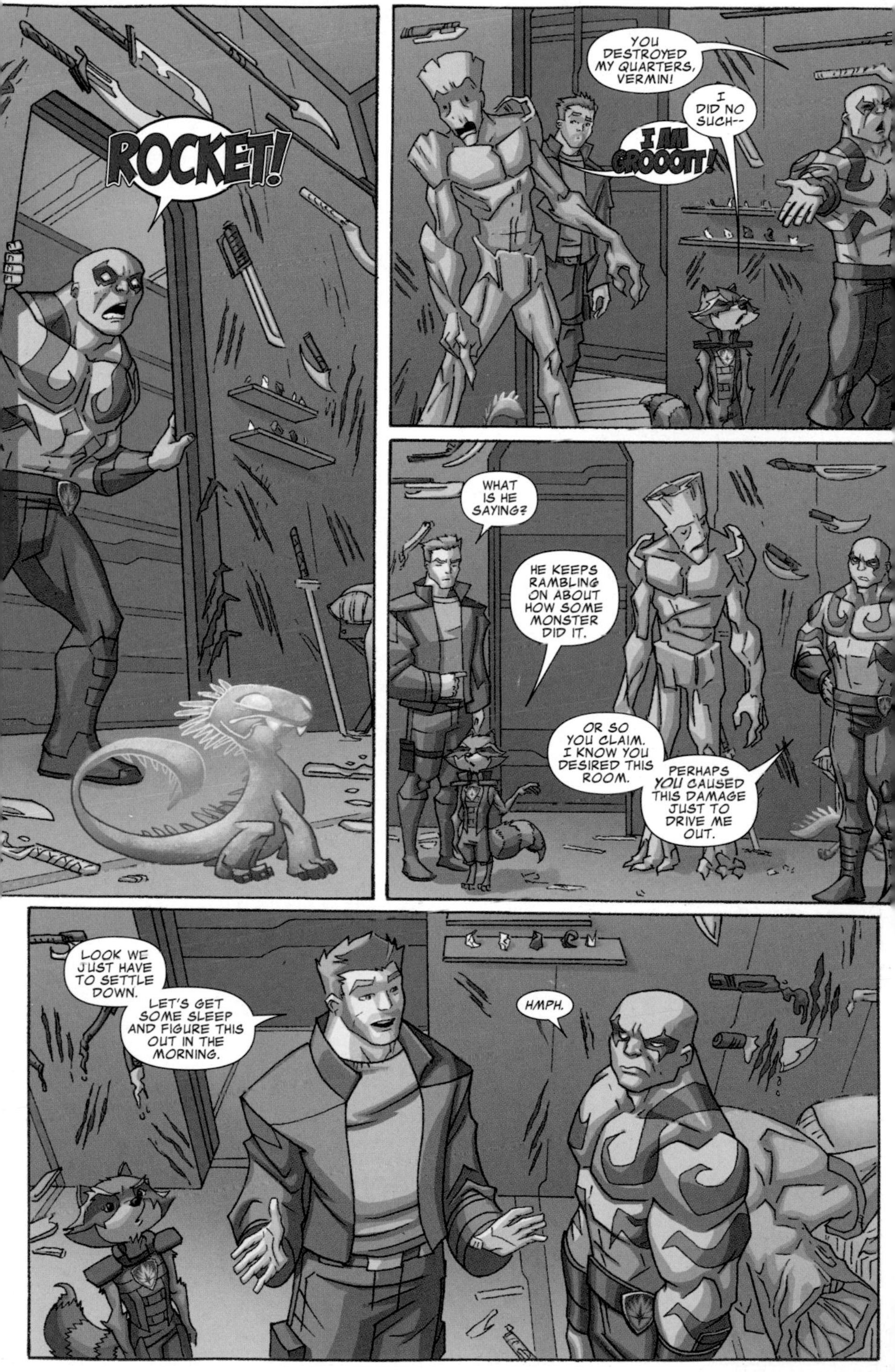
ROCKET!
YOU DESTROYED MY QUARTERS, VERMIN!
I DID NO SUCH--
I AM GROOOTT!
WHAT IS HE SAYING?
HE KEEPS RAMBLING ON ABOUT HOW SOME MONSTER DID IT.
OR SO YOU CLAIM. I KNOW YOU DESIRED THIS ROOM.
PERHAPS YOU CAUSED THIS DAMAGE JUST TO DRIVE ME OUT.
LOOK WE JUST HAVE TO SETTLE DOWN.
LET'S GET SOME SLEEP AND FIGURE THIS OUT IN THE MORNING.
HMPH.

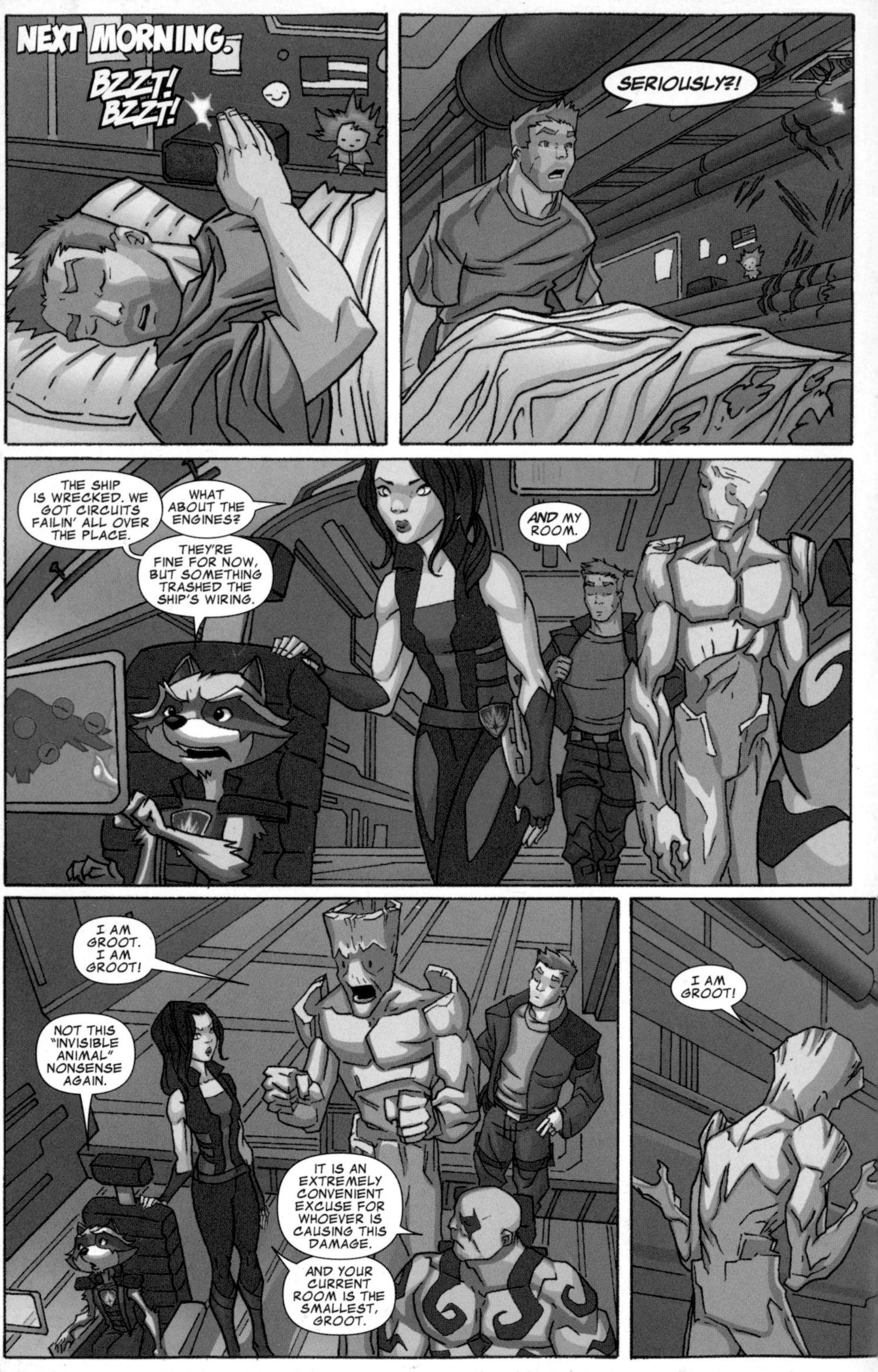
NEXT MORNING...
BZZT! BZZT!
SERIOUSLY?!
THE SHIP IS WRECKED. WE GOT CIRCUITS FAILIN' ALL OVER THE PLACE.
WHAT ABOUT THE ENGINES?
THEY'RE FINE FOR NOW, BUT SOMETHING TRASHED THE SHIP'S WIRING.
AND MY ROOM.
I AM GROOT. I AM GROOT!
NOT THIS "INVISIBLE ANIMAL" NONSENSE AGAIN.
IT IS AN EXTREMELY CONVENIENT EXCUSE FOR WHOEVER IS CAUSING THIS DAMAGE.
AND YOUR CURRENT ROOM IS THE SMALLEST, GROOT.
I AM GROOT!

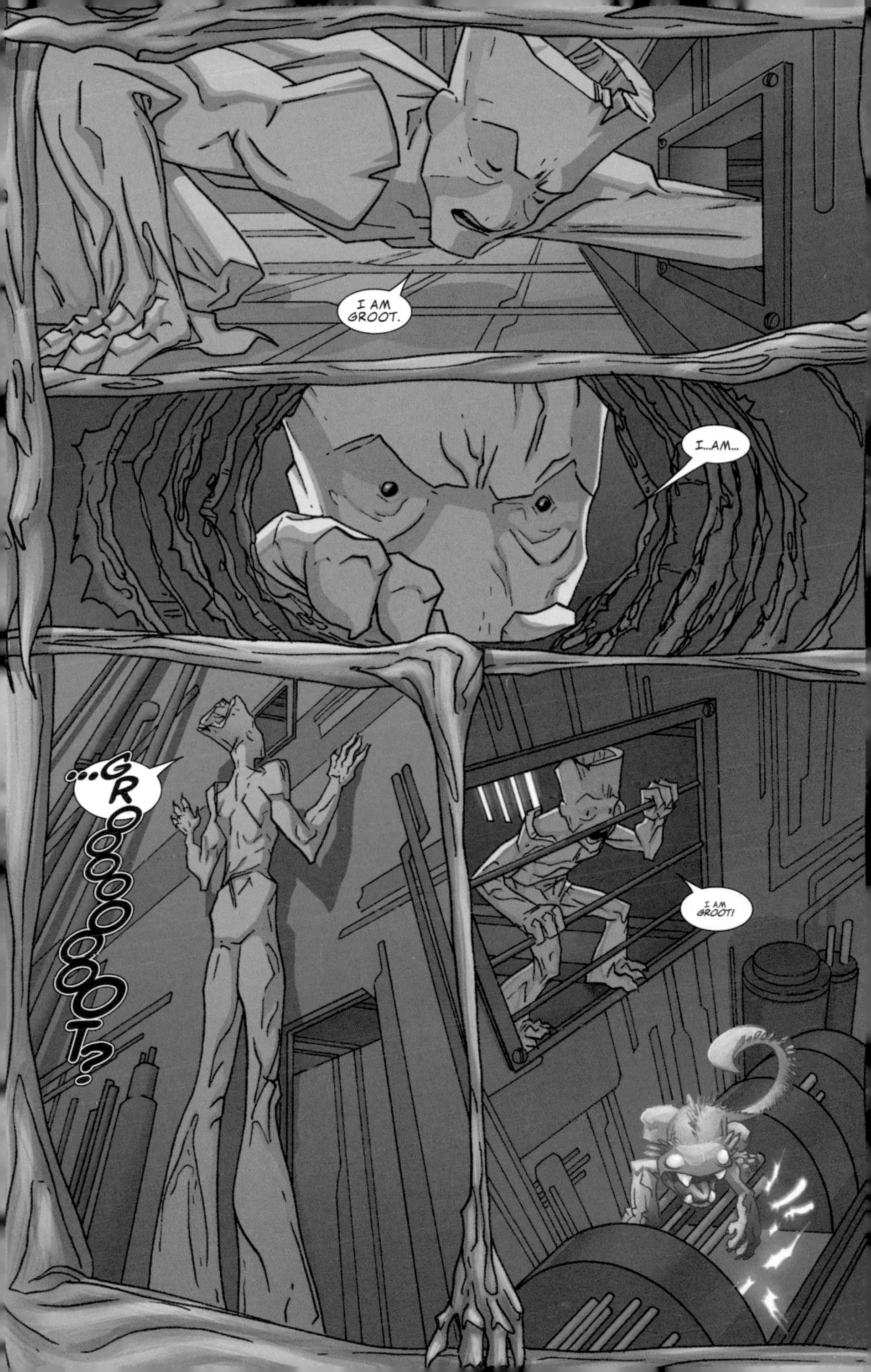
I AM GROOT.
I...AM...
...GROOOOOOOOT?
I AM GROOT!

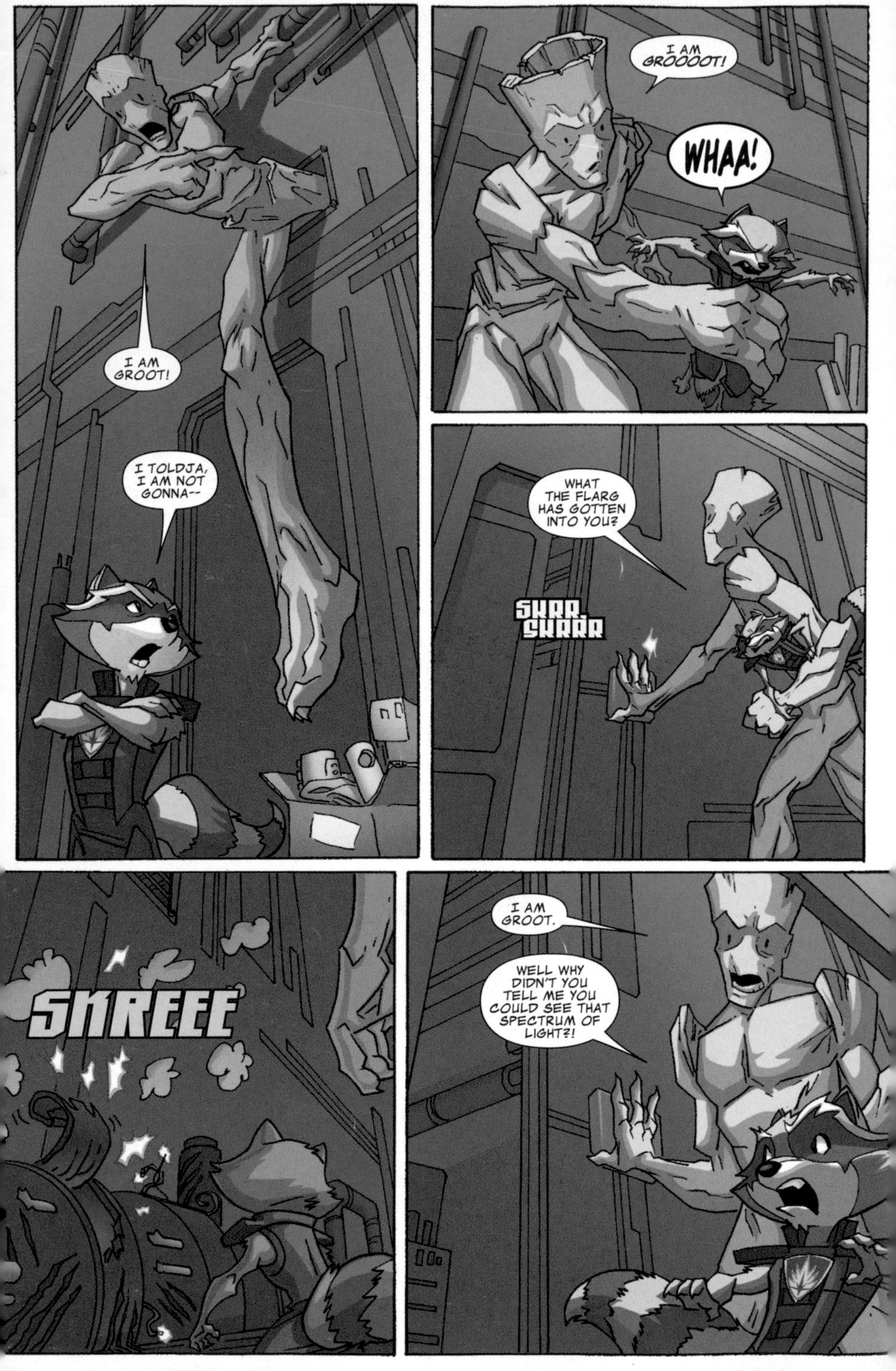

I AM GROOT!
I TOLDJA, I AM NOT GONNA--
I AM GROOOOT!
WHAA!
WHAT THE FLARG HAS GOTTEN INTO YOU?
SKRR SKRRR
SKREEE
I AM GROOT.
WELL WHY DIDN'T YOU TELL ME YOU COULD SEE THAT SPECTRUM OF LIGHT?!

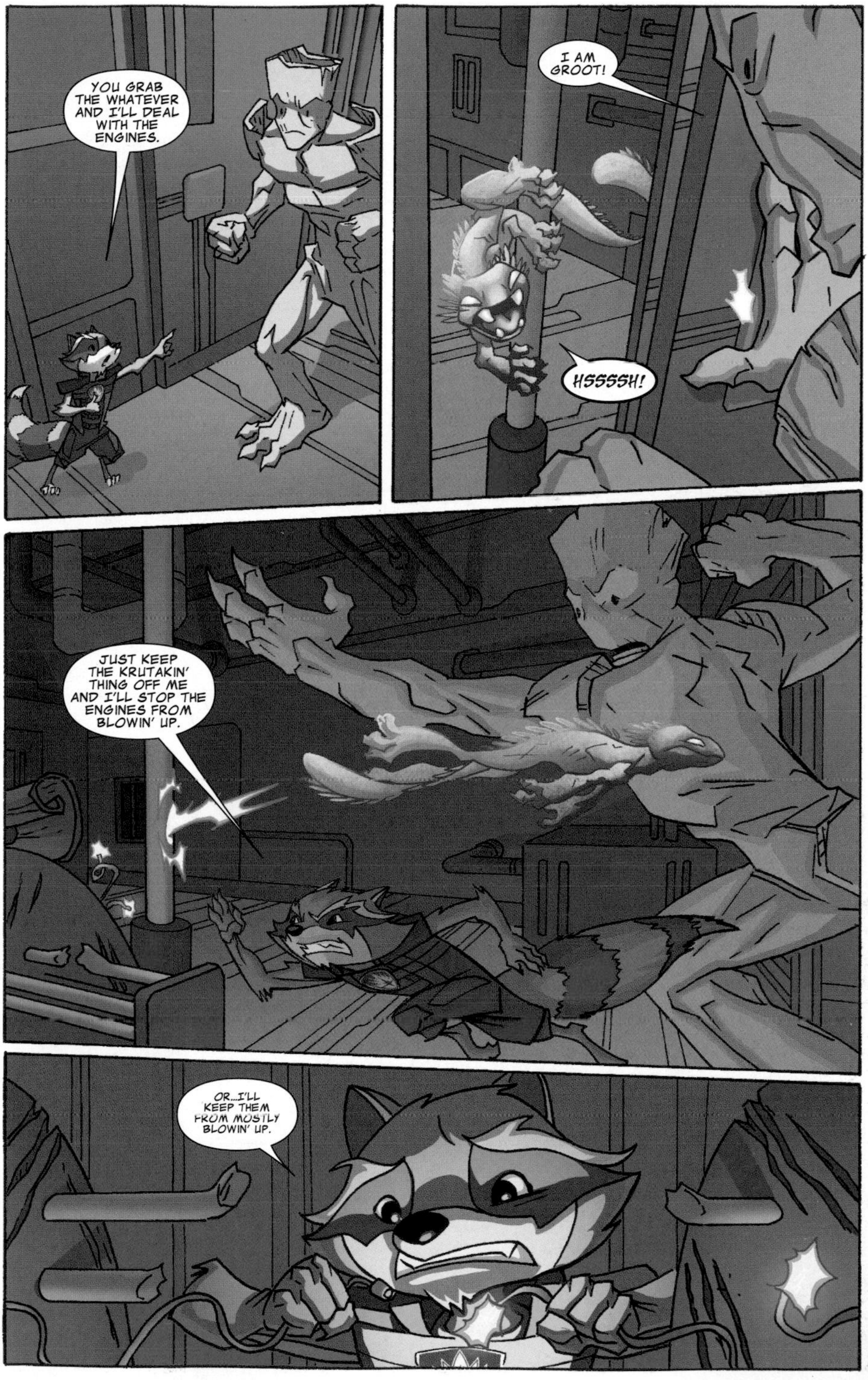
YOU GRAB THE WHATEVER AND I'LL DEAL WITH THE ENGINES.
I AM GROOT!
HSSSSH!
JUST KEEP THE KRUTAKIN' THING OFF ME AND I'LL STOP THE ENGINES FROM BLOWIN' UP.
OR...I'LL KEEP THEM FROM MOSTLY BLOWIN' UP.

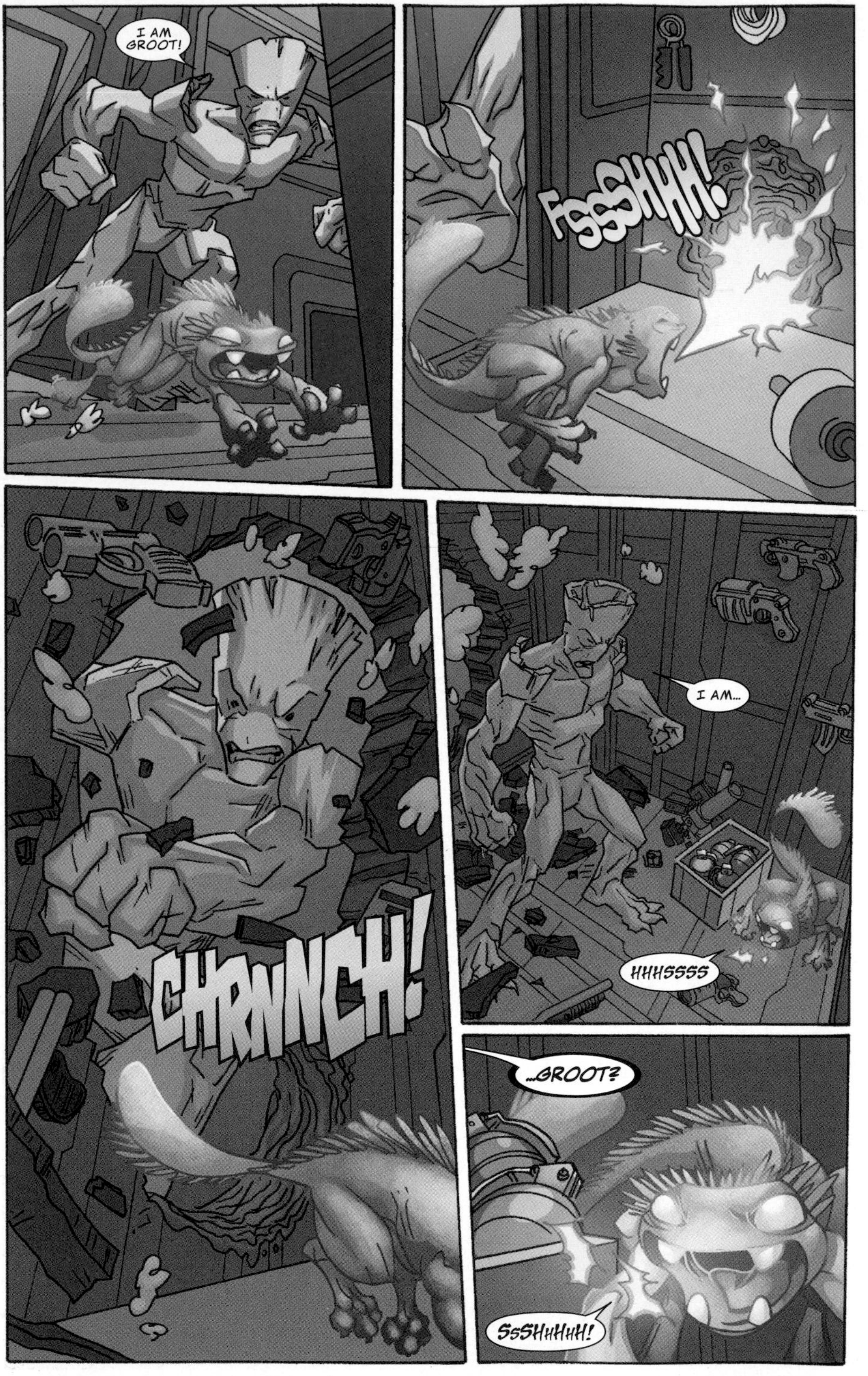
I AM GROOT!
FSSSHHH!
CHRNNCH!
I AM...
HHHSSSS
...GROOT?
SSSHHHHH!

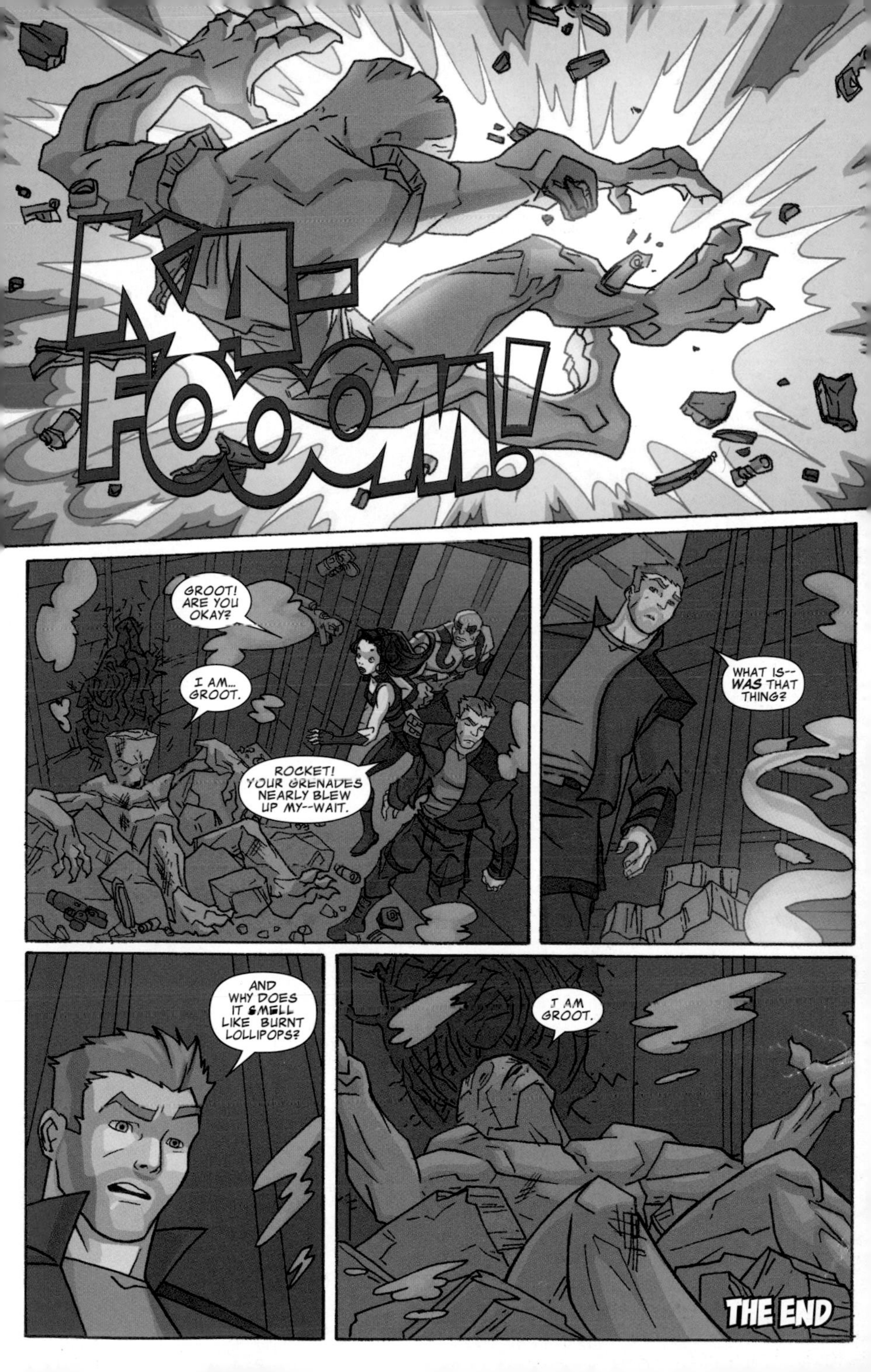
KA-FOOOM!
GROOT! ARE YOU OKAY?
I AM... GROOT.
ROCKET! YOUR GRENADES NEARLY BLEW UP MY--WAIT.
WHAT IS-- WAS THAT THING?
AND WHY DOES IT SMELL LIKE BURNT LOLLIPOPS?
I AM GROOT.
THE END

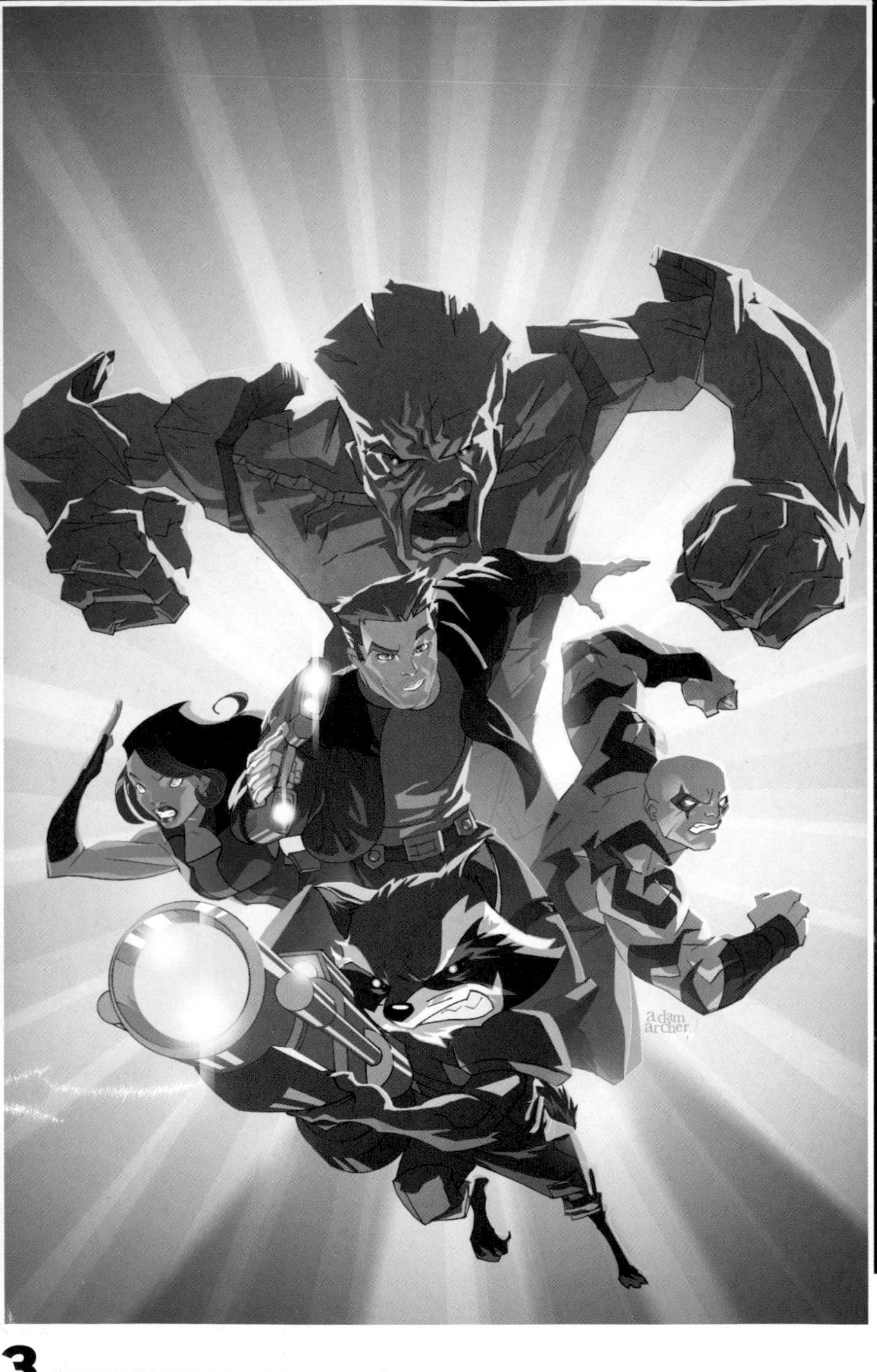
adam
archer

3 "GESUNDHEIT, HANG ON TIGHT!"

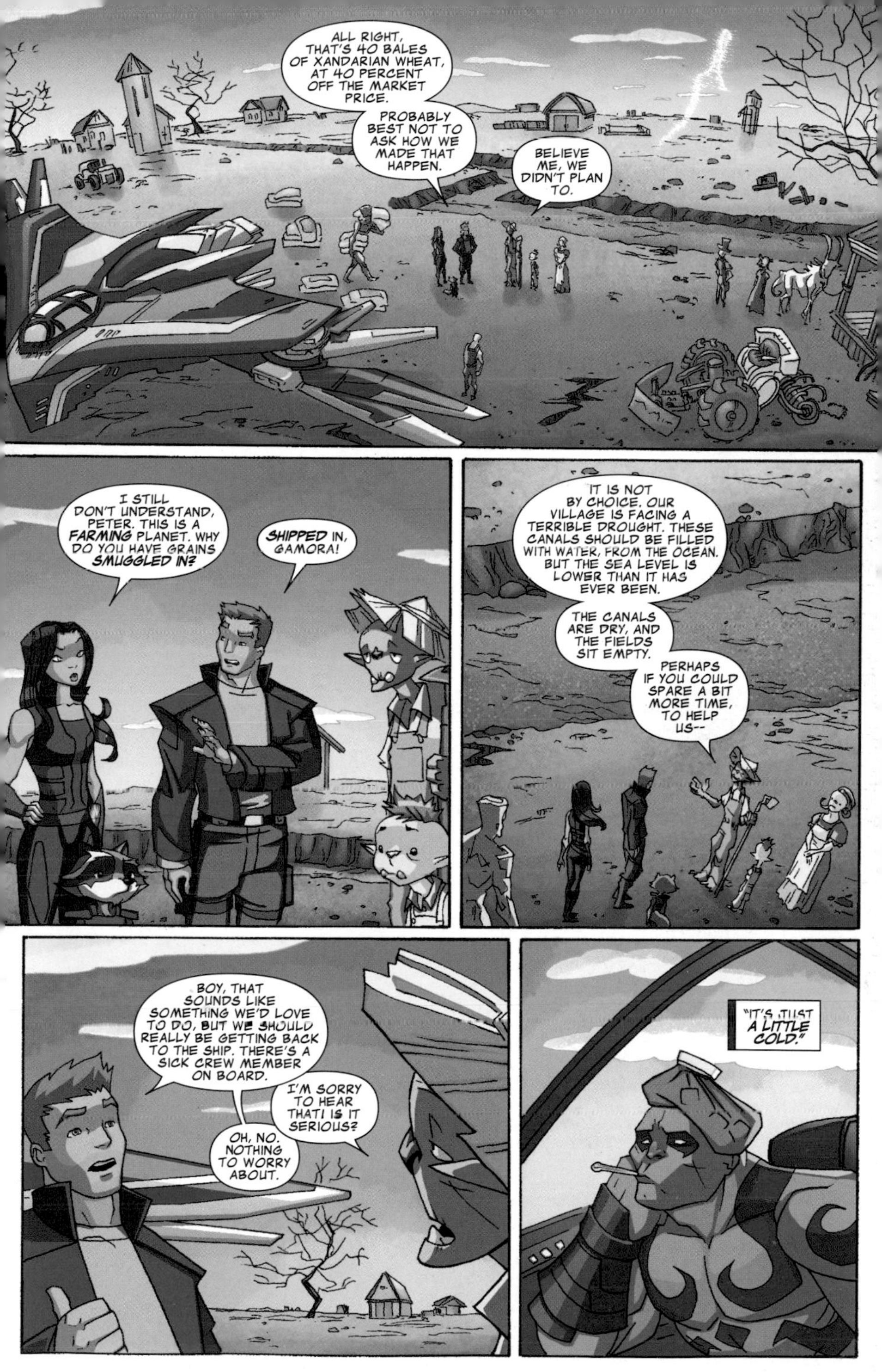
ALL RIGHT, THAT'S 40 BALES OF XANDARIAN WHEAT, AT 40 PERCENT OFF THE MARKET PRICE.
PROBABLY BEST NOT TO ASK HOW WE MADE THAT HAPPEN.
BELIEVE ME, WE DIDN'T PLAN TO.
I STILL DON'T UNDERSTAND, PETER. THIS IS A FARMING PLANET. WHY DO YOU HAVE GRAINS SMUGGLED IN?
SHIPPED IN, GAMORA!
IT IS NOT BY CHOICE. OUR VILLAGE IS FACING A TERRIBLE DROUGHT. THESE CANALS SHOULD BE FILLED WITH WATER, FROM THE OCEAN. BUT THE SEA LEVEL IS LOWER THAN IT HAS EVER BEEN.
THE CANALS ARE DRY, AND THE FIELDS SIT EMPTY.
PERHAPS IF YOU COULD SPARE A BIT MORE TIME, TO HELP US--
BOY, THAT SOUNDS LIKE SOMETHING WE'D LOVE TO DO, BUT WE SHOULD REALLY BE GETTING BACK TO THE SHIP. THERE'S A SICK CREW MEMBER ON BOARD.
I'M SORRY TO HEAR THAT! IS IT SERIOUS?
OH, NO. NOTHING TO WORRY ABOUT.
"IT'S JUST A LITTLE COLD."

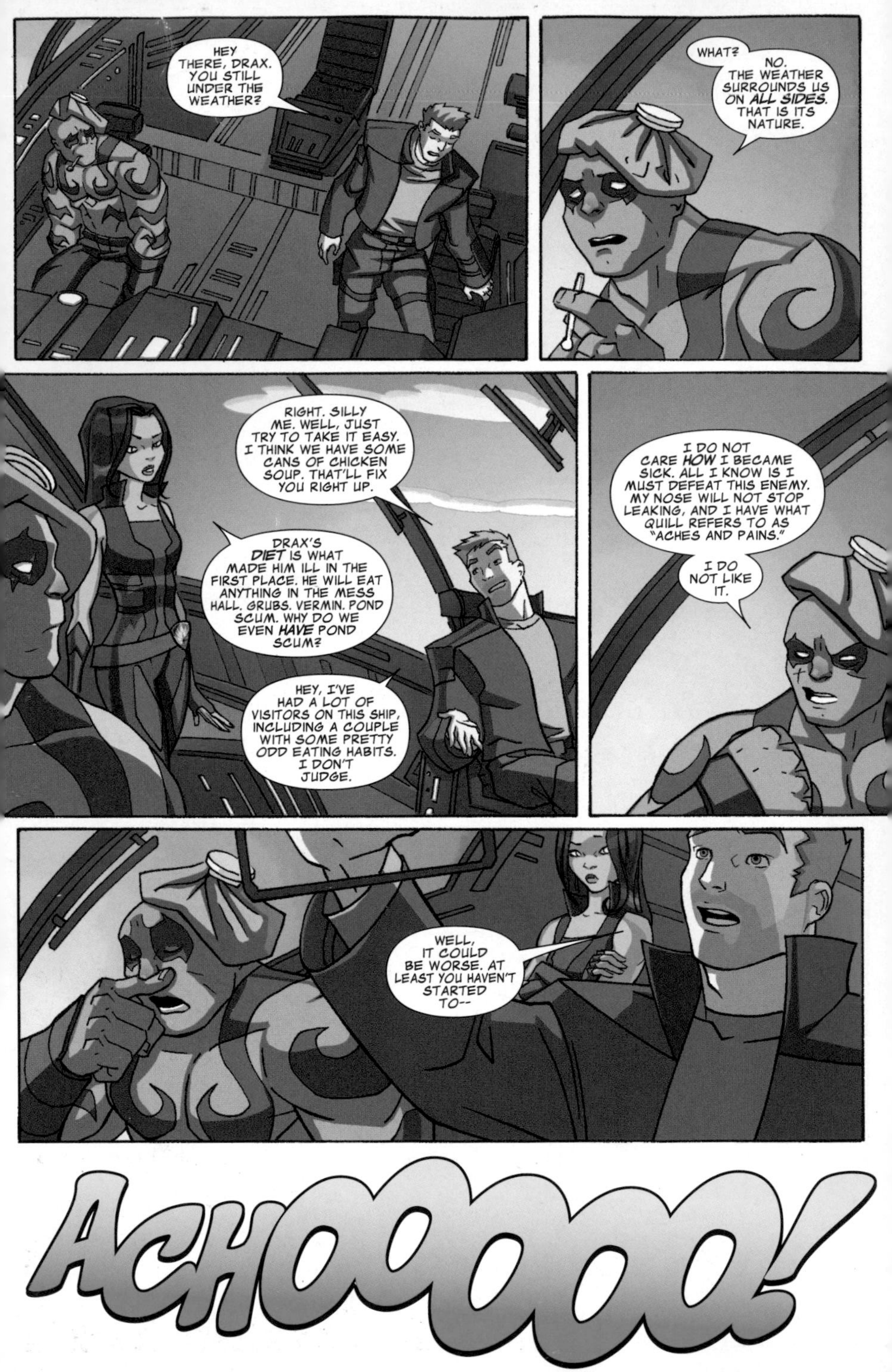
HEY THERE, DRAX. YOU STILL UNDER THE WEATHER?
WHAT?
NO. THE WEATHER SURROUNDS US ON ALL SIDES. THAT IS ITS NATURE.
RIGHT. SILLY ME. WELL, JUST TRY TO TAKE IT EASY. I THINK WE HAVE SOME CANS OF CHICKEN SOUP. THAT'LL FIX YOU RIGHT UP.
DRAX'S DIET IS WHAT MADE HIM ILL IN THE FIRST PLACE. HE WILL EAT ANYTHING IN THE MESS HALL. GRUBS. VERMIN. POND SCUM. WHY DO WE EVEN HAVE POND SCUM?
HEY, I'VE HAD A LOT OF VISITORS ON THIS SHIP, INCLUDING A COUPLE WITH SOME PRETTY ODD EATING HABITS. I DON'T JUDGE.
I DO NOT CARE HOW I BECAME SICK. ALL I KNOW IS I MUST DEFEAT THIS ENEMY. MY NOSE WILL NOT STOP LEAKING, AND I HAVE WHAT QUILL REFERS TO AS "ACHES AND PAINS."
I DO NOT LIKE IT.
WELL, IT COULD BE WORSE. AT LEAST YOU HAVEN'T STARTED TO--
ACHOOOOO!

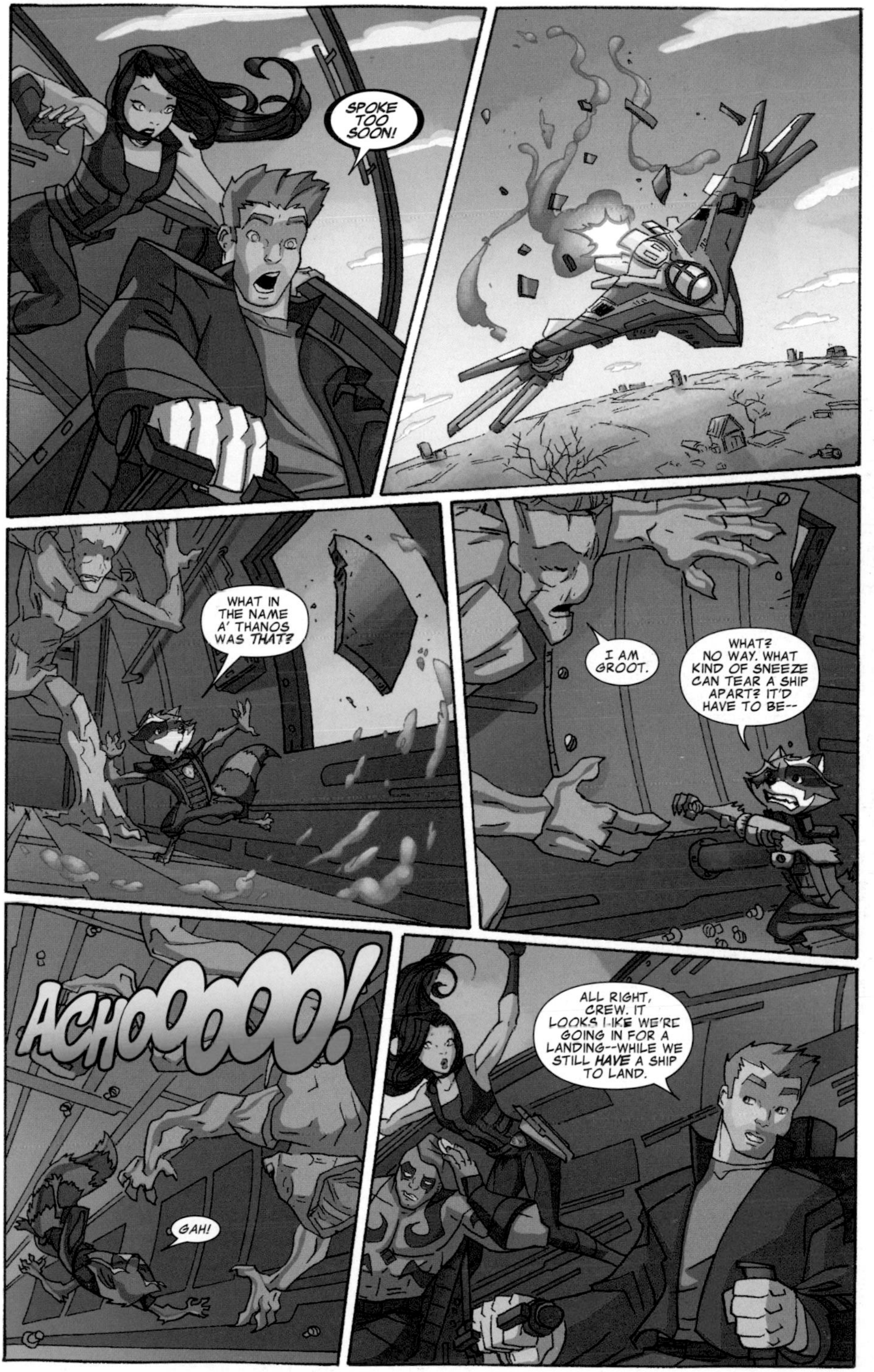
SPOKE TOO SOON!
WHAT IN THE NAME A' THANOS WAS *THAT*?
I AM GROOT.
WHAT? NO WAY. WHAT KIND OF SNEEZE CAN TEAR A SHIP APART? IT'D HAVE TO BE--
ACHOOOOO!
GAH!
ALL RIGHT, CREW. IT LOOKS LIKE WE'RE GOING IN FOR A LANDING--WHILE WE STILL *HAVE* A SHIP TO LAND.

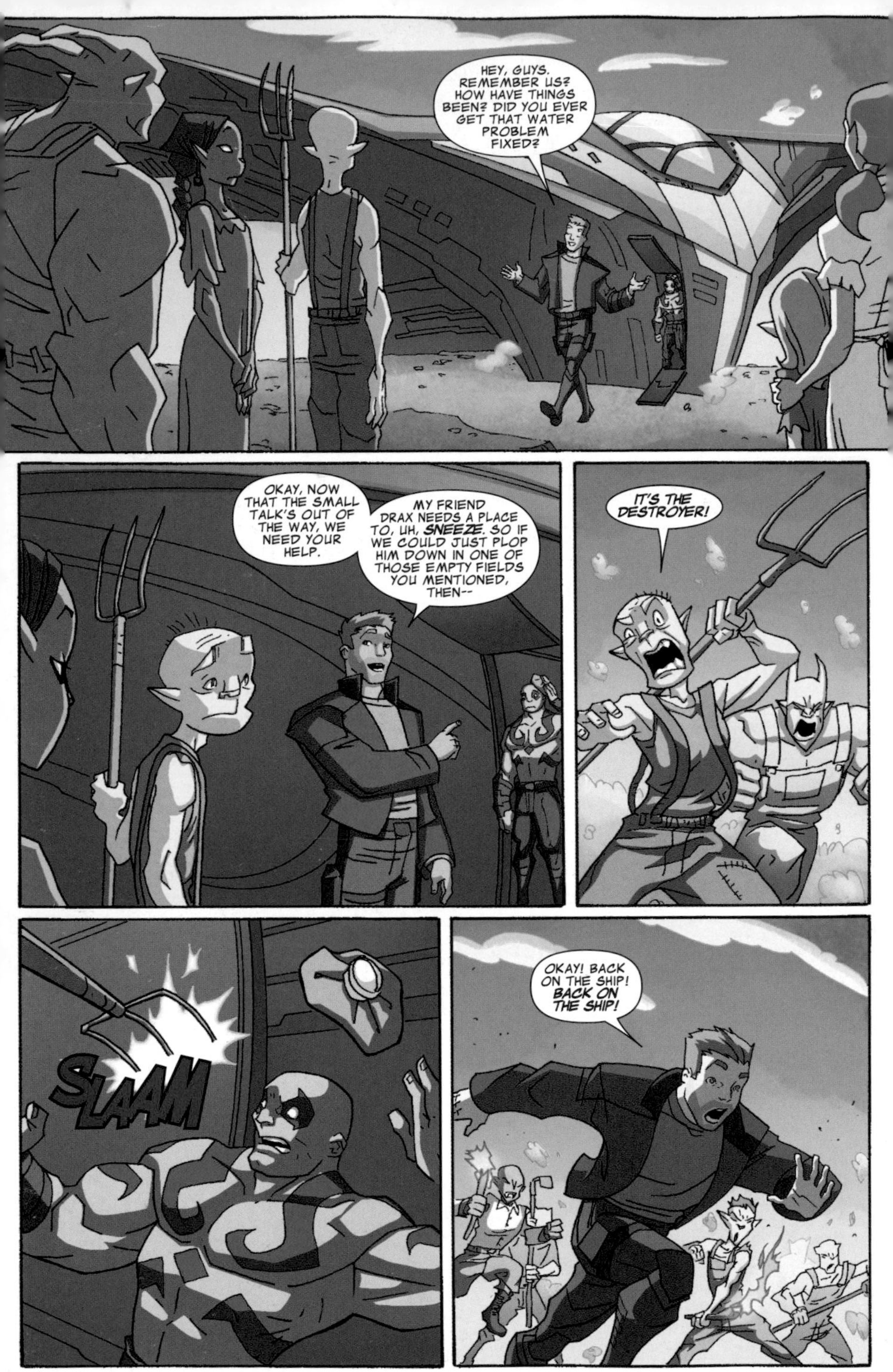

HEY, GUYS. REMEMBER US? HOW HAVE THINGS BEEN? DID YOU EVER GET THAT WATER PROBLEM FIXED?
OKAY, NOW THAT THE SMALL TALK'S OUT OF THE WAY, WE NEED YOUR HELP.
MY FRIEND DRAX NEEDS A PLACE TO, UH, ***SNEEZE***. SO IF WE COULD JUST PLOP HIM DOWN IN ONE OF THOSE EMPTY FIELDS YOU MENTIONED, THEN--
IT'S THE DESTROYER!
SLAAM
OKAY! BACK ON THE SHIP! ***BACK ON THE SHIP!***

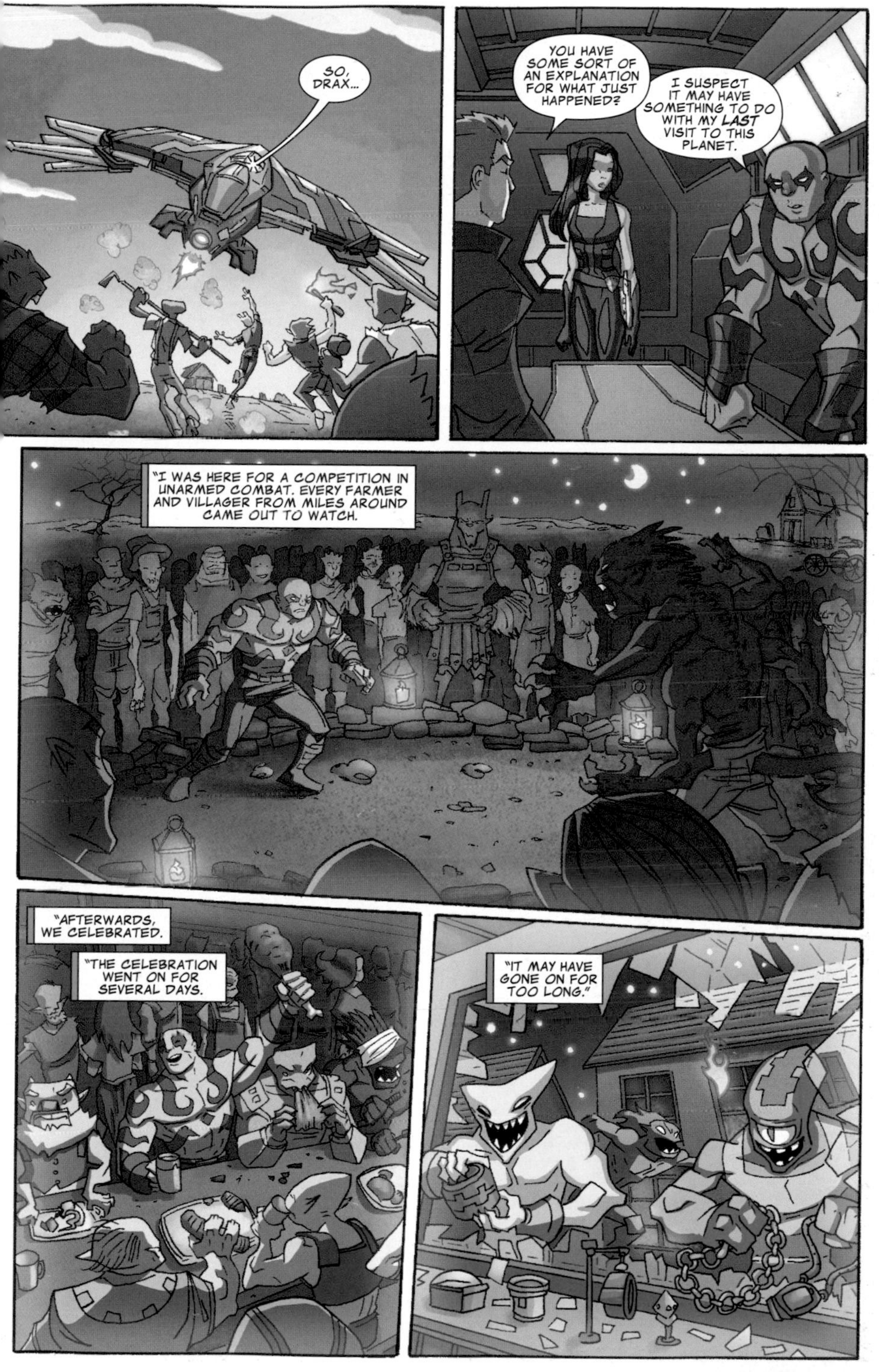

SO, DRAX...
YOU HAVE SOME SORT OF AN EXPLANATION FOR WHAT JUST HAPPENED?
I SUSPECT IT MAY HAVE SOMETHING TO DO WITH MY LAST VISIT TO THIS PLANET.
"I WAS HERE FOR A COMPETITION IN UNARMED COMBAT. EVERY FARMER AND VILLAGER FROM MILES AROUND CAME OUT TO WATCH.
"AFTERWARDS, WE CELEBRATED.
"THE CELEBRATION WENT ON FOR SEVERAL DAYS.
"IT MAY HAVE GONE ON FOR TOO LONG."

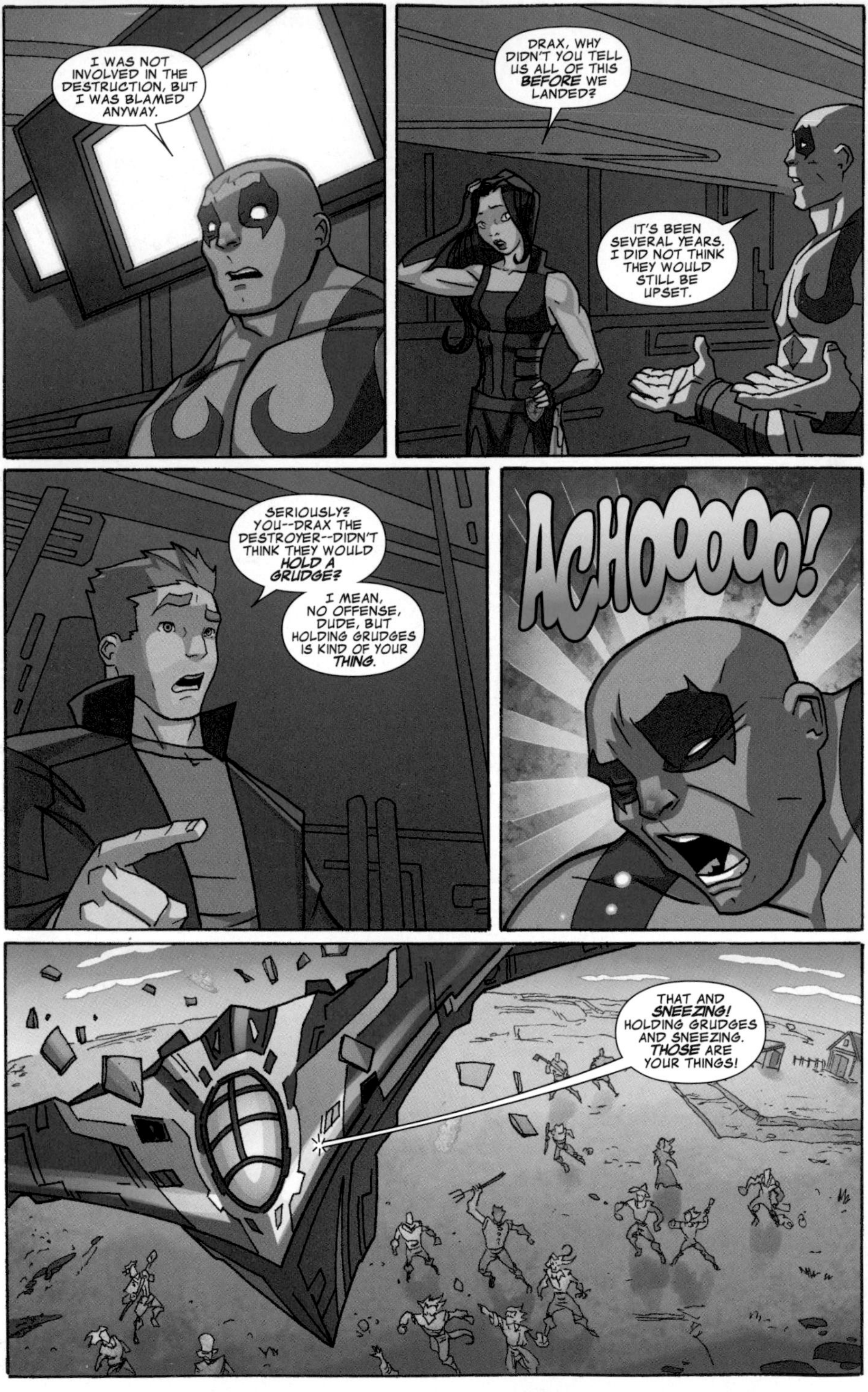
I WAS NOT INVOLVED IN THE DESTRUCTION, BUT I WAS BLAMED ANYWAY.
DRAX, WHY DIDN'T YOU TELL US ALL OF THIS BEFORE WE LANDED?
IT'S BEEN SEVERAL YEARS. I DID NOT THINK THEY WOULD STILL BE UPSET.
SERIOUSLY? YOU--DRAX THE DESTROYER--DIDN'T THINK THEY WOULD HOLD A GRUDGE?
I MEAN, NO OFFENSE, DUDE, BUT HOLDING GRUDGES IS KIND OF YOUR THING.
ACHOOOOO!
THAT AND SNEEZING! HOLDING GRUDGES AND SNEEZING. THOSE ARE YOUR THINGS!

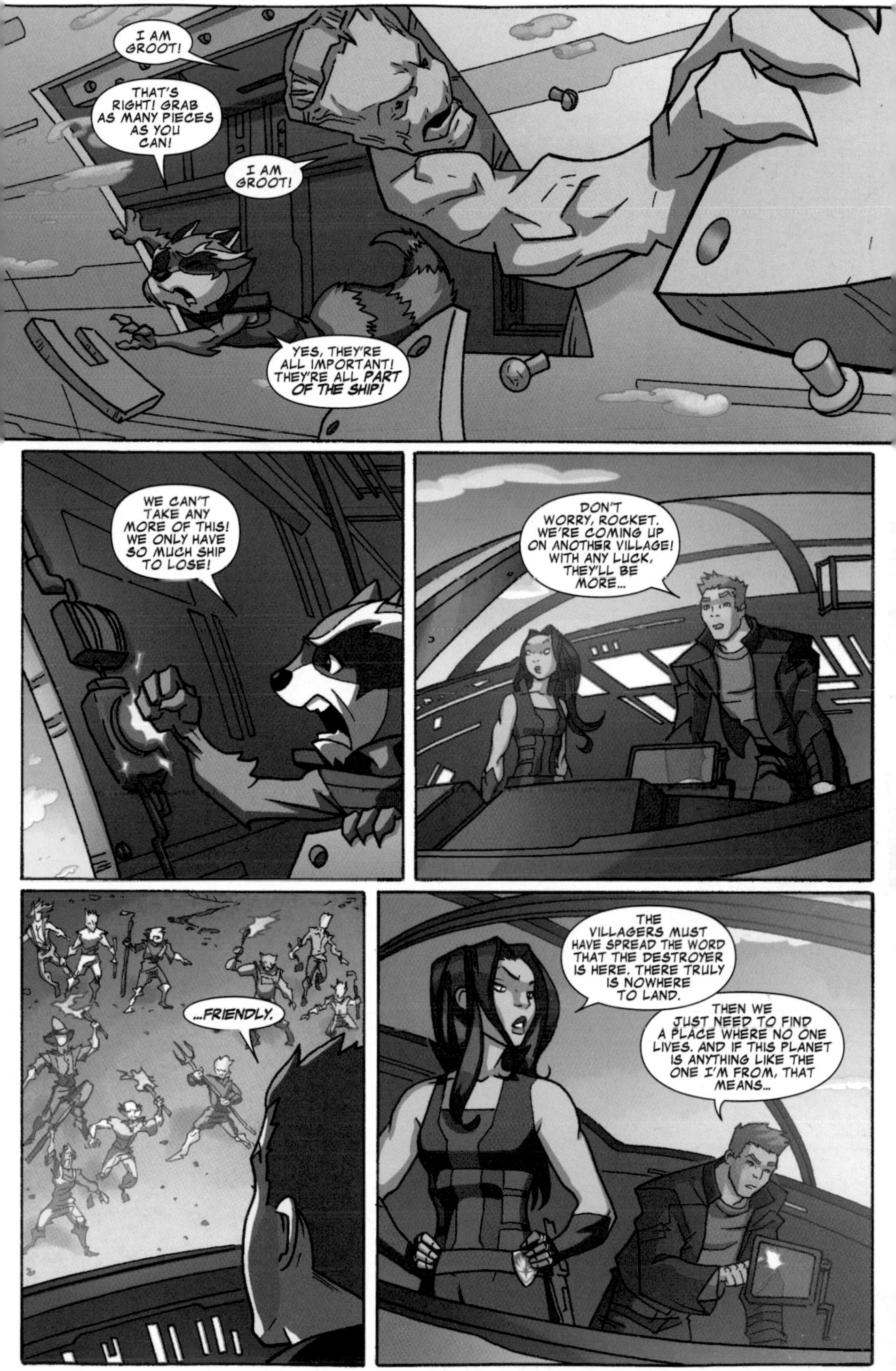
I AM GROOT!
THAT'S RIGHT! GRAB AS MANY PIECES AS YOU CAN!
I AM GROOT!
YES, THEY'RE ALL IMPORTANT! THEY'RE ALL *PART OF THE SHIP!*
WE CAN'T TAKE ANY MORE OF THIS! WE ONLY HAVE SO MUCH SHIP TO LOSE!
DON'T WORRY, ROCKET. WE'RE COMING UP ON ANOTHER VILLAGE! WITH ANY LUCK, THEY'LL BE MORE...
...*FRIENDLY.*
THE VILLAGERS MUST HAVE SPREAD THE WORD THAT THE DESTROYER IS HERE. THERE TRULY IS NOWHERE TO LAND.
THEN WE JUST NEED TO FIND A PLACE WHERE NO ONE LIVES. AND IF THIS PLANET IS ANYTHING LIKE THE ONE I'M FROM, THAT MEANS...

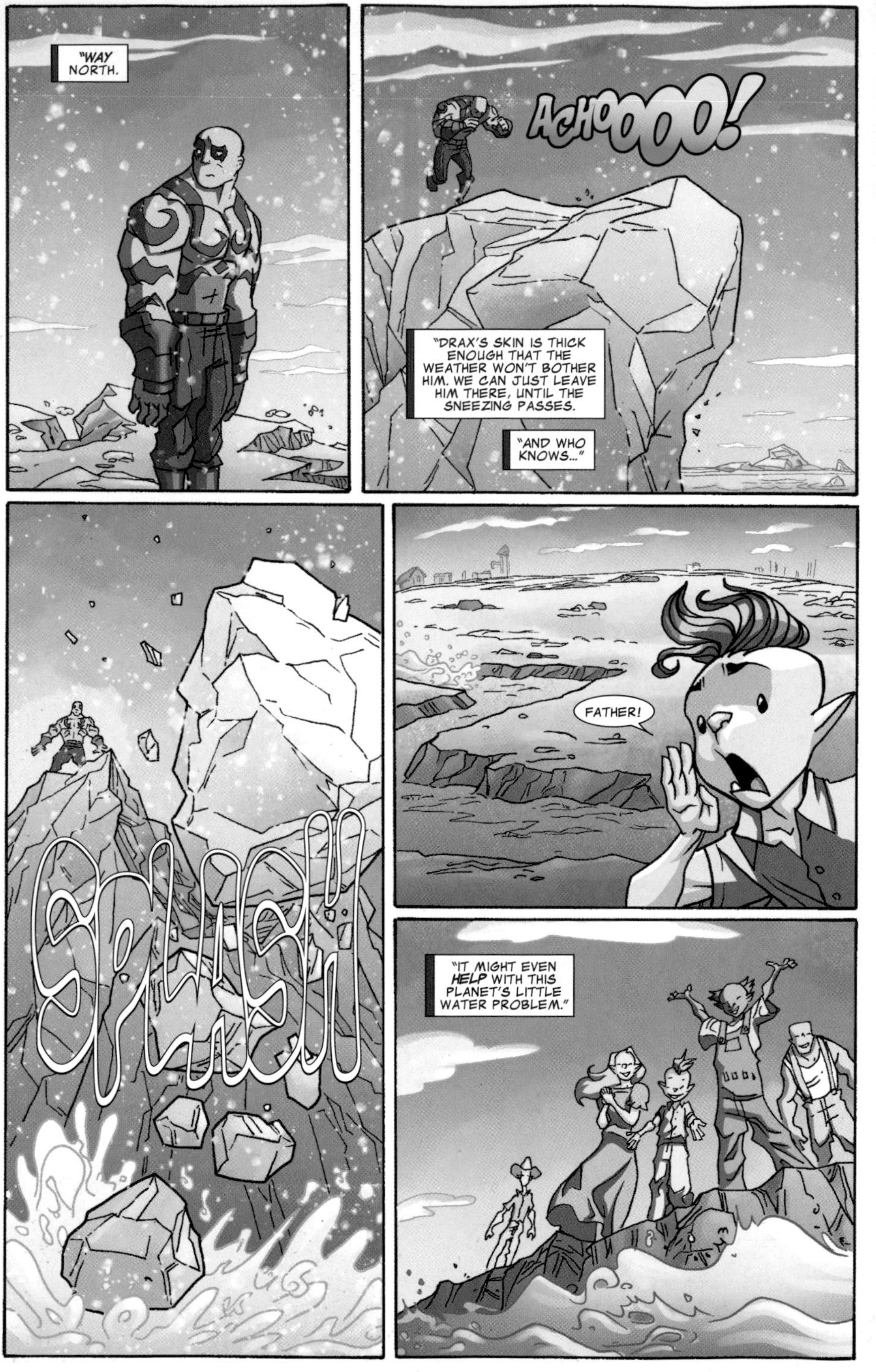
"WAY NORTH.
ACHOOOOO!
"DRAX'S SKIN IS THICK ENOUGH THAT THE WEATHER WON'T BOTHER HIM. WE CAN JUST LEAVE HIM THERE, UNTIL THE SNEEZING PASSES.
"AND WHO KNOWS..."
SPLASH!
FATHER!
"IT MIGHT EVEN HELP WITH THIS PLANET'S LITTLE WATER PROBLEM."

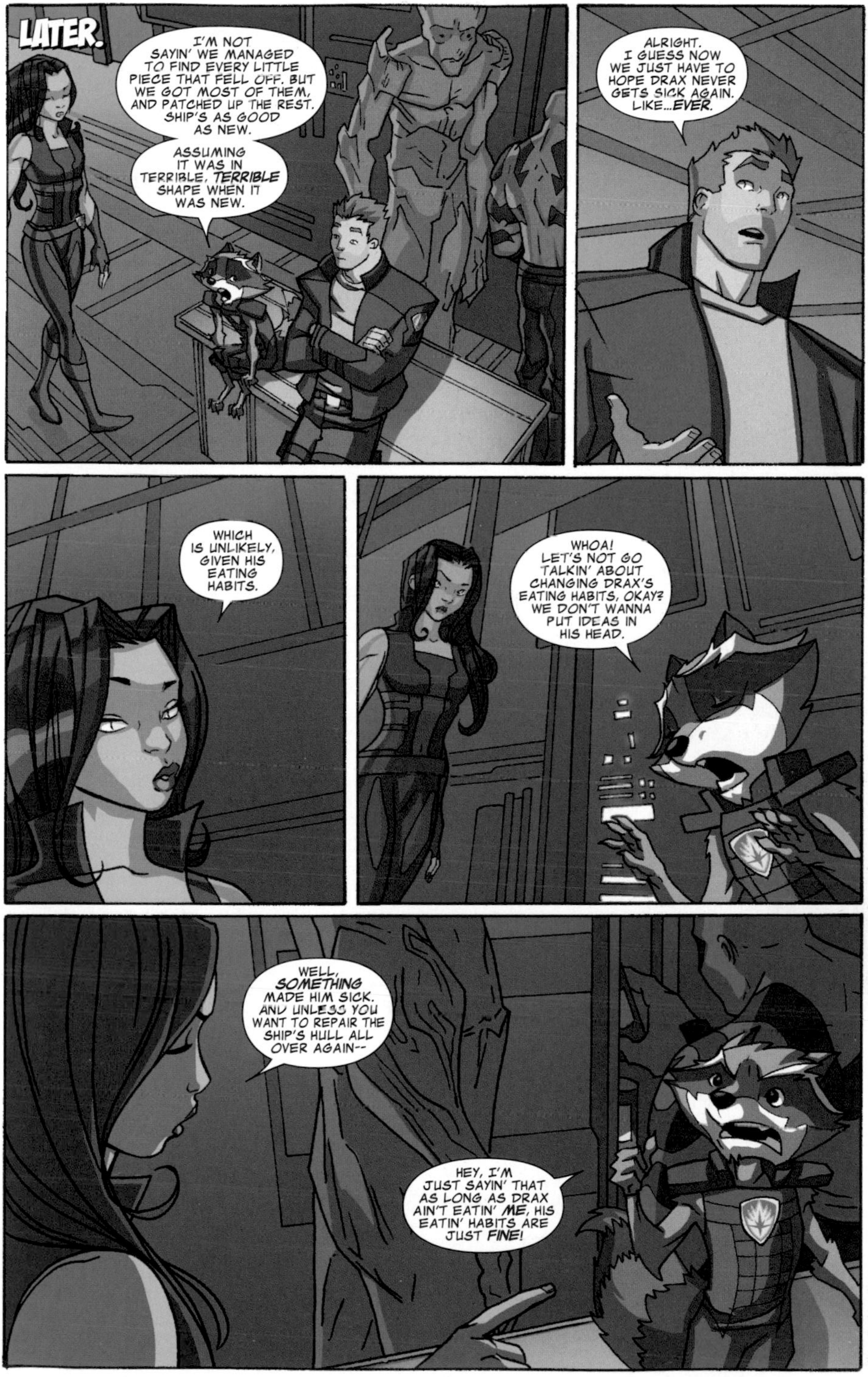
LATER.
I'M NOT SAYIN' WE MANAGED TO FIND EVERY LITTLE PIECE THAT FELL OFF. BUT WE GOT MOST OF THEM, AND PATCHED UP THE REST. SHIP'S AS GOOD AS NEW.
ASSUMING IT WAS IN TERRIBLE, TERRIBLE SHAPE WHEN IT WAS NEW.
ALRIGHT. I GUESS NOW WE JUST HAVE TO HOPE DRAX NEVER GETS SICK AGAIN. LIKE...EVER.
WHICH IS UNLIKELY, GIVEN HIS EATING HABITS.
WHOA! LET'S NOT GO TALKIN' ABOUT CHANGING DRAX'S EATING HABITS, OKAY? WE DON'T WANNA PUT IDEAS IN HIS HEAD.
WELL, SOMETHING MADE HIM SICK. AND UNLESS YOU WANT TO REPAIR THE SHIP'S HULL ALL OVER AGAIN--
HEY, I'M JUST SAYIN' THAT AS LONG AS DRAX AIN'T EATIN' ME, HIS EATIN' HABITS ARE JUST FINE!

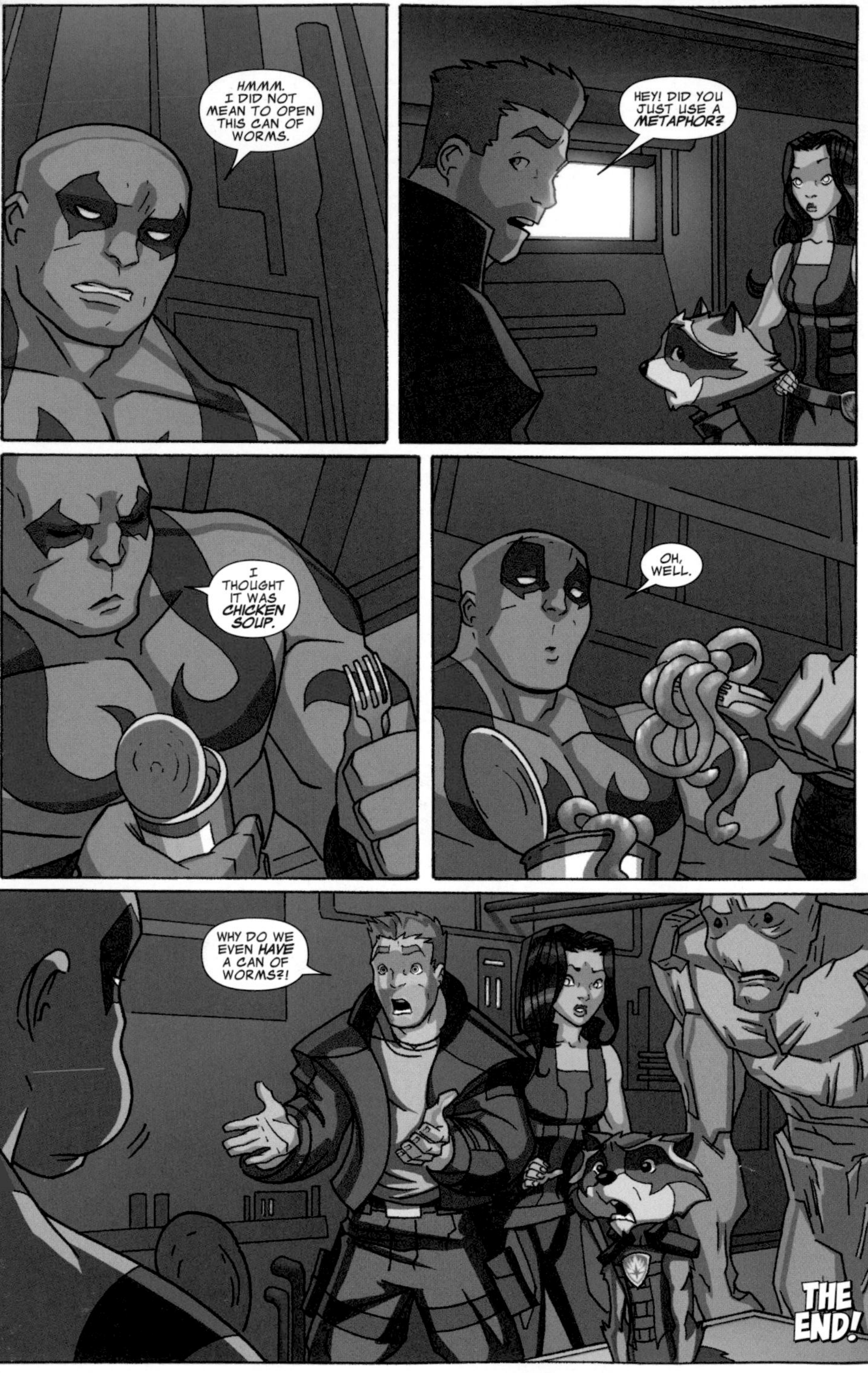
HMMM. I DID NOT MEAN TO OPEN THIS CAN OF WORMS.
HEY! DID YOU JUST USE A METAPHOR?
I THOUGHT IT WAS CHICKEN SOUP.
OH, WELL.
WHY DO WE EVEN HAVE A CAN OF WORMS?!
THE END!

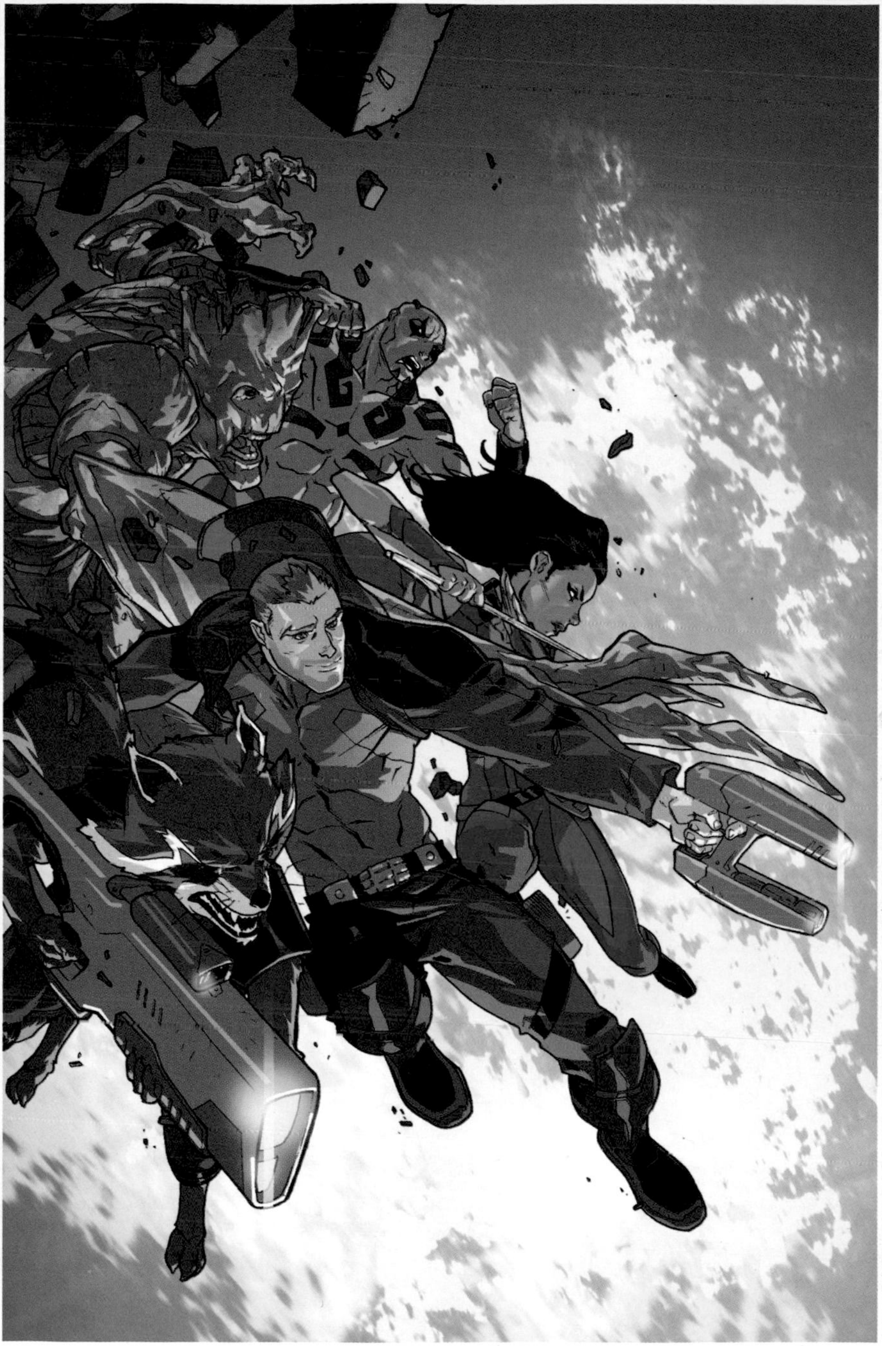

"ALL HAIL KING GROOT!" **4**

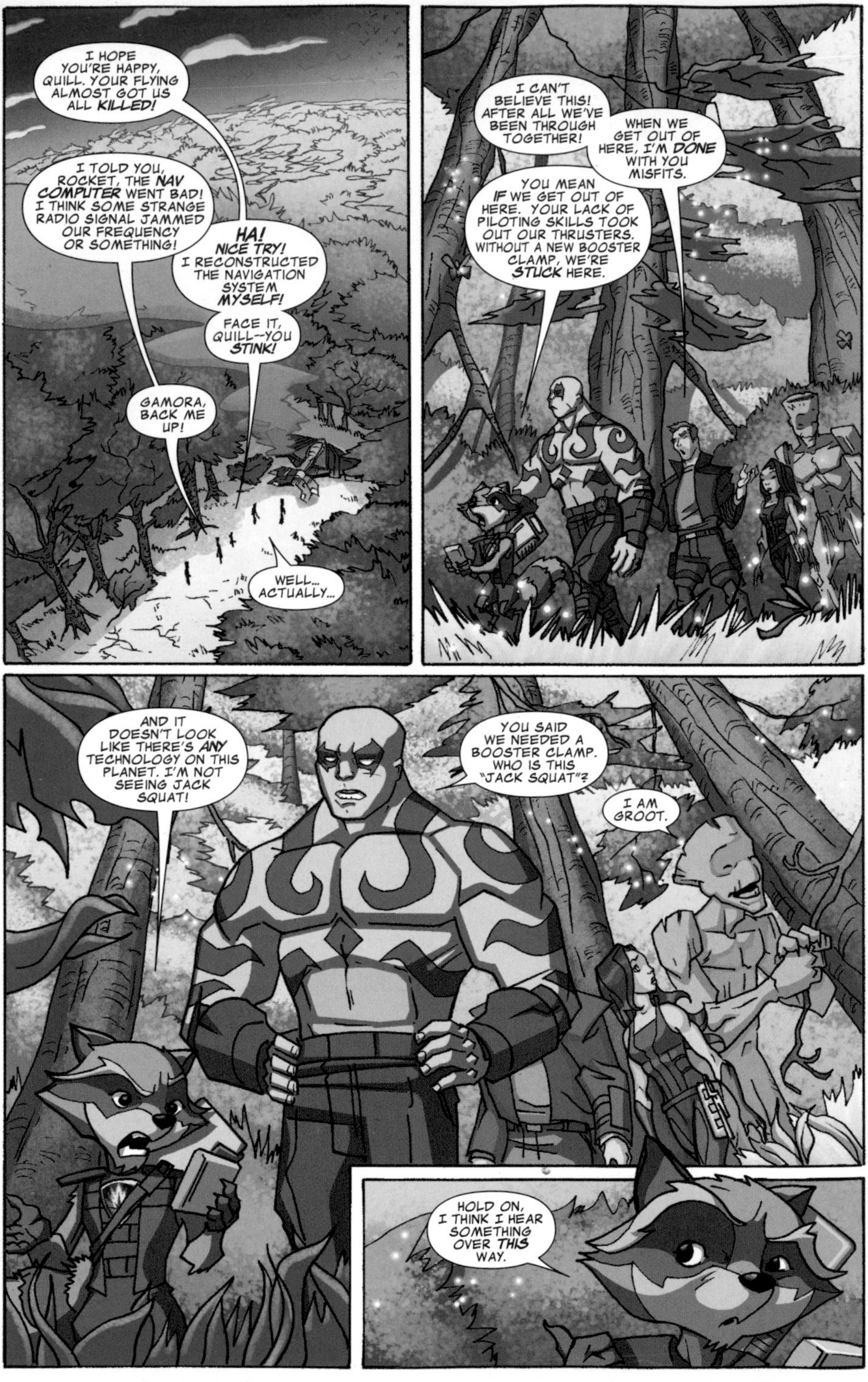
I HOPE YOU'RE HAPPY, QUILL. YOUR FLYING ALMOST GOT US ALL KILLED!
I TOLD YOU, ROCKET, THE NAV COMPUTER WENT BAD! I THINK SOME STRANGE RADIO SIGNAL JAMMED OUR FREQUENCY OR SOMETHING!
HA! NICE TRY! I RECONSTRUCTED THE NAVIGATION SYSTEM MYSELF!
FACE IT, QUILL--YOU STINK!
GAMORA, BACK ME UP!
WELL... ACTUALLY...
I CAN'T BELIEVE THIS! AFTER ALL WE'VE BEEN THROUGH TOGETHER!
WHEN WE GET OUT OF HERE, I'M DONE WITH YOU MISFITS.
YOU MEAN IF WE GET OUT OF HERE. YOUR LACK OF PILOTING SKILLS TOOK OUT OUR THRUSTERS. WITHOUT A NEW BOOSTER CLAMP, WE'RE STUCK HERE.
AND IT DOESN'T LOOK LIKE THERE'S ANY TECHNOLOGY ON THIS PLANET. I'M NOT SEEING JACK SQUAT!
YOU SAID WE NEEDED A BOOSTER CLAMP. WHO IS THIS "JACK SQUAT"?
I AM GROOT.
HOLD ON, I THINK I HEAR SOMETHING OVER THIS WAY.

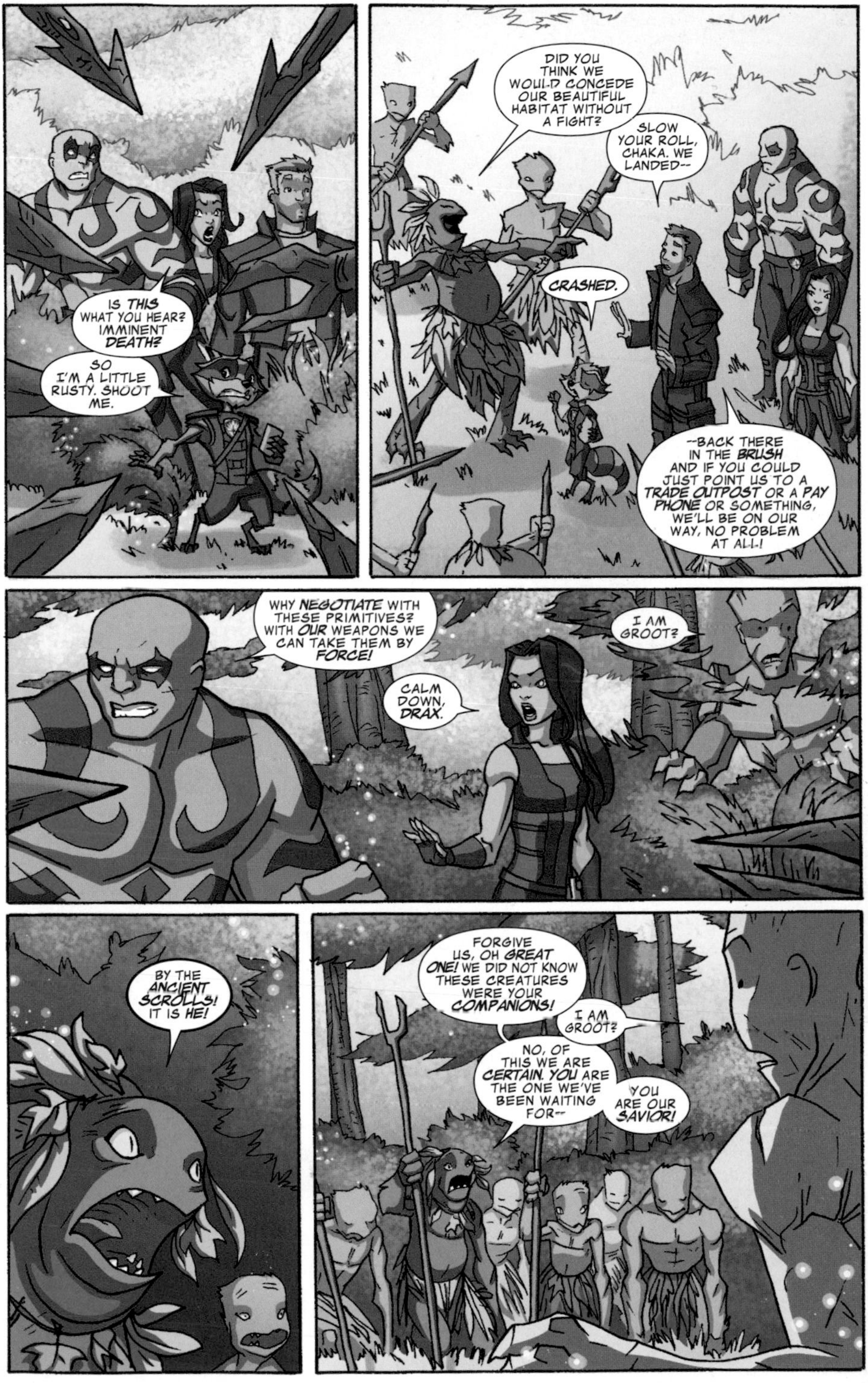
IS THIS WHAT YOU HEAR? IMMINENT DEATH?
SO I'M A LITTLE RUSTY. SHOOT ME.
DID YOU THINK WE WOULD CONCEDE OUR BEAUTIFUL HABITAT WITHOUT A FIGHT?
SLOW YOUR ROLL, CHAKA. WE LANDED--
CRASHED.
--BACK THERE IN THE BRUSH AND IF YOU COULD JUST POINT US TO A TRADE OUTPOST OR A PAY PHONE OR SOMETHING, WE'LL BE ON OUR WAY, NO PROBLEM AT ALL!
WHY NEGOTIATE WITH THESE PRIMITIVES? WITH OUR WEAPONS WE CAN TAKE THEM BY FORCE!
CALM DOWN, DRAX.
I AM GROOT?
BY THE ANCIENT SCROLLS! IT IS HE!
FORGIVE US, OH GREAT ONE! WE DID NOT KNOW THESE CREATURES WERE YOUR COMPANIONS!
I AM GROOT?
NO, OF THIS WE ARE CERTAIN. YOU ARE THE ONE WE'VE BEEN WAITING FOR--
YOU ARE OUR SAVIOR!

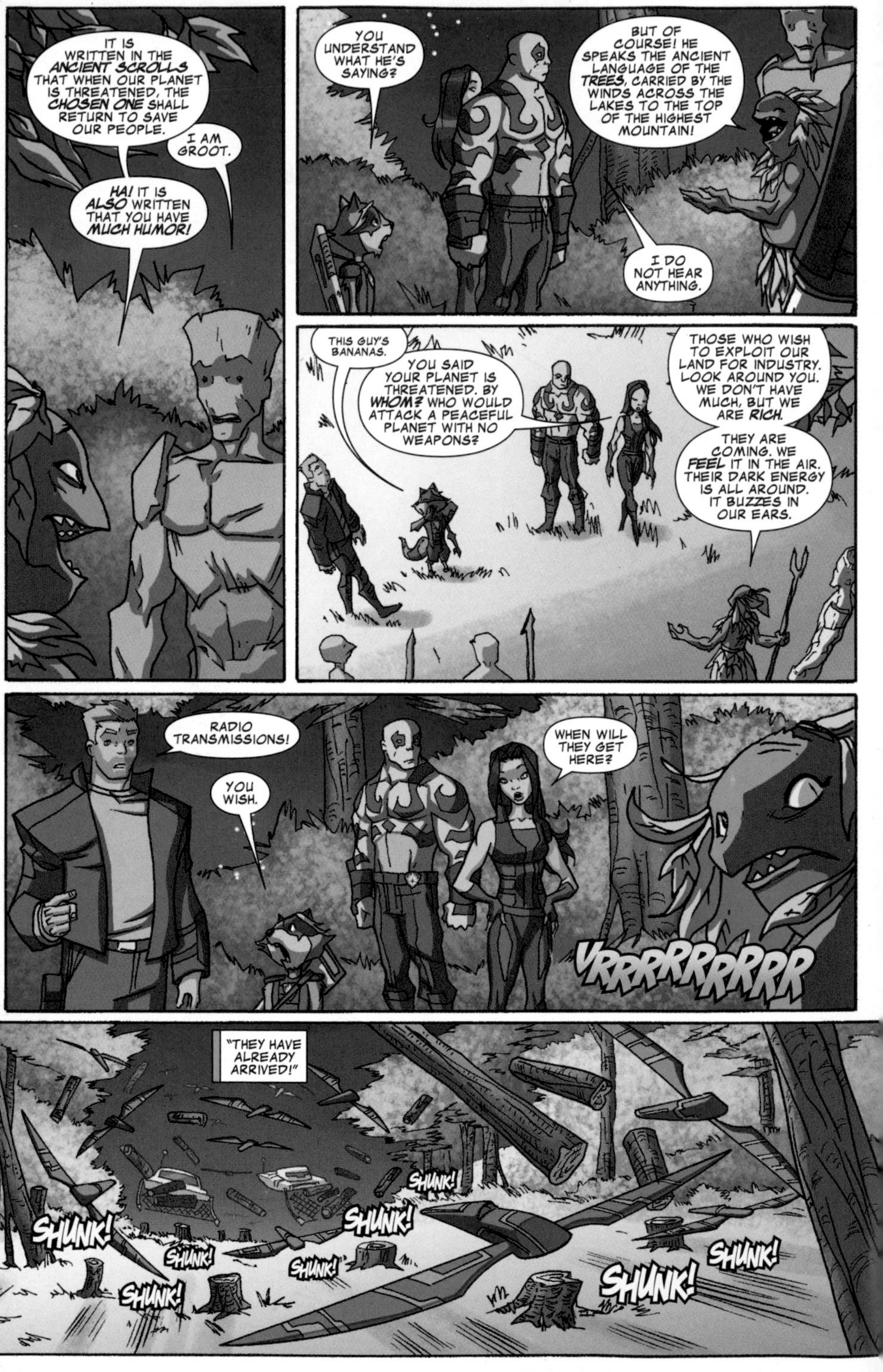
IT IS WRITTEN IN THE ANCIENT SCROLLS THAT WHEN OUR PLANET IS THREATENED, THE CHOSEN ONE SHALL RETURN TO SAVE OUR PEOPLE.
I AM GROOT.
HA! IT IS ALSO WRITTEN THAT YOU HAVE MUCH HUMOR!
YOU UNDERSTAND WHAT HE'S SAYING?
BUT OF COURSE! HE SPEAKS THE ANCIENT LANGUAGE OF THE TREES, CARRIED BY THE WINDS ACROSS THE LAKES TO THE TOP OF THE HIGHEST MOUNTAIN!
I DO NOT HEAR ANYTHING.
THIS GUY'S BANANAS.
YOU SAID YOUR PLANET IS THREATENED. BY WHOM? WHO WOULD ATTACK A PEACEFUL PLANET WITH NO WEAPONS?
THOSE WHO WISH TO EXPLOIT OUR LAND FOR INDUSTRY. LOOK AROUND YOU. WE DON'T HAVE MUCH, BUT WE ARE RICH.
THEY ARE COMING. WE FEEL IT IN THE AIR. THEIR DARK ENERGY IS ALL AROUND. IT BUZZES IN OUR EARS.
RADIO TRANSMISSIONS!
YOU WISH.
WHEN WILL THEY GET HERE?
VRRRRRRRRR
"THEY HAVE ALREADY ARRIVED!"
SHUNK!
SHUNK!
SHUNK!
SHUNK!
SHUNK!
SHUNK!
SHUNK!
SHUNK!

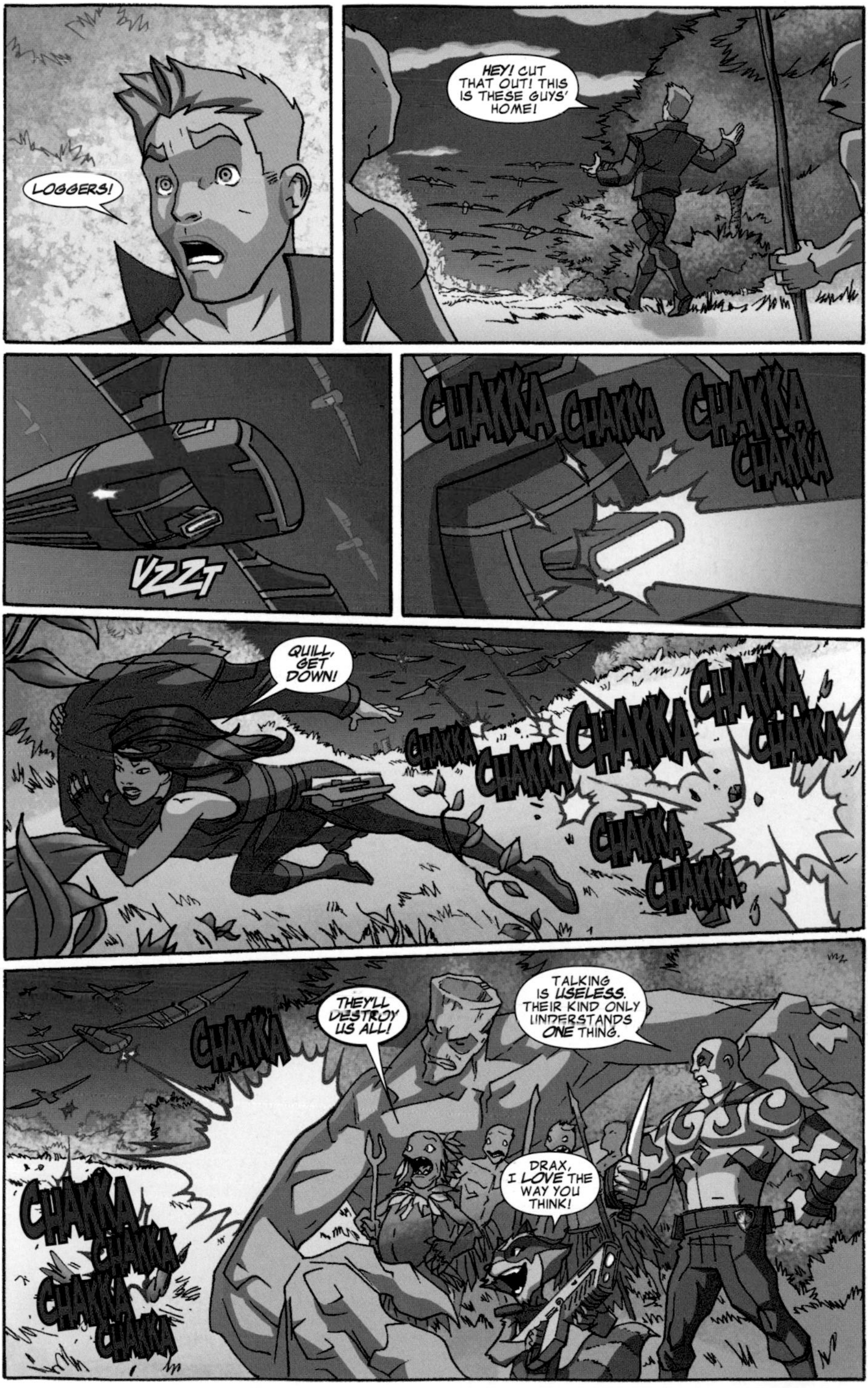
LOGGERS!
HEY! CUT THAT OUT! THIS IS THESE GUYS' HOME!
VZZT
CHAKKA CHAKKA CHAKKA CHAKKA
QUILL, GET DOWN!
CHAKKA CHAKKA CHAKKA CHAKKA CHAKKA CHAKKA CHAKKA
CHAKKA
THEY'LL DESTROY US ALL!
TALKING IS USELESS. THEIR KIND ONLY UNDERSTANDS ONE THING.
DRAX, I LOVE THE WAY YOU THINK!
CHAKKA CHAKKA CHAKKA CHAKKA

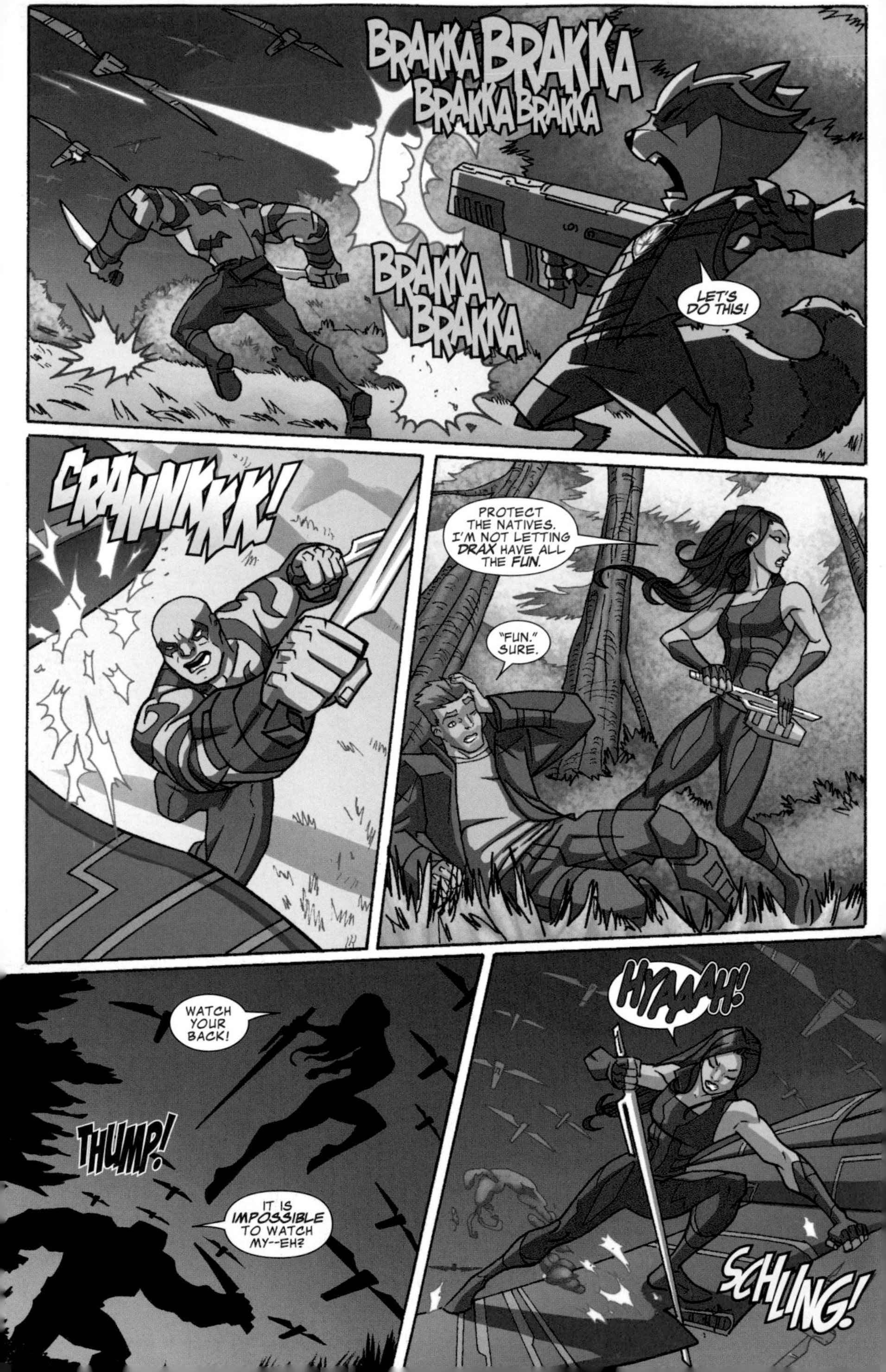
BRAKKA BRAKKA
BRAKKA BRAKKA
BRAKKA BRAKKA
LET'S DO THIS!
CRANKKK!
PROTECT THE NATIVES. I'M NOT LETTING DRAX HAVE ALL THE FUN.
"FUN." SURE.
WATCH YOUR BACK!
THUMP!
IT IS IMPOSSIBLE TO WATCH MY--EH?
HYAAAH!
SCHLING!

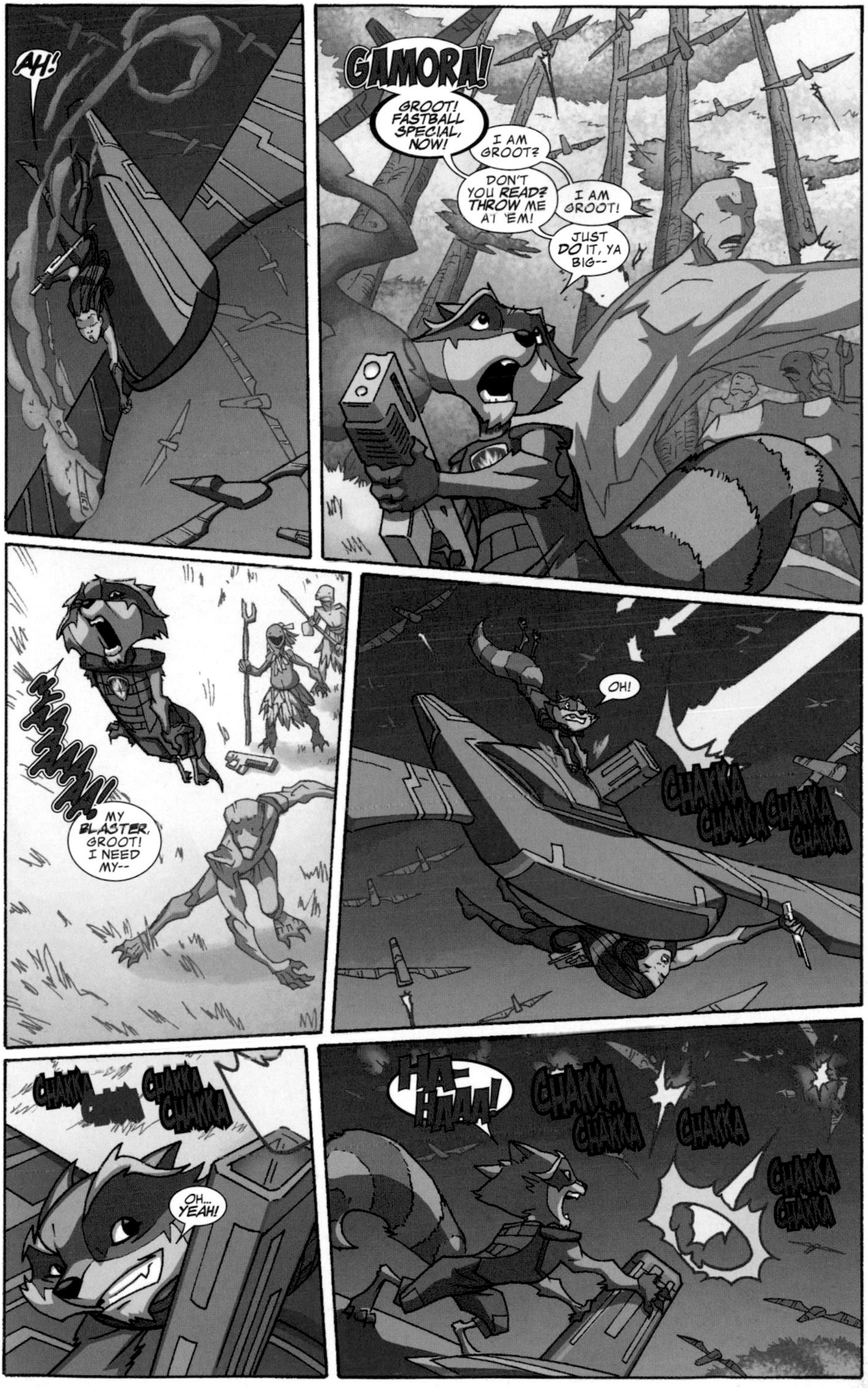

AH!
GAMORA!
GROOT! FASTBALL SPECIAL, NOW!
I AM GROOT?
DON'T YOU READ? THROW ME AT 'EM!
I AM GROOT!
JUST DO IT, YA BIG--
MY BLASTER, GROOT! I NEED MY--
OH!
CHAKKA CHAKKA CHAKKA CHAKKA
CHAKKA CHAKKA CHAKKA
OH... YEAH!
HA-HAAA!
CHAKKA CHAKKA
CHAKKA
CHAKKA CHAKKA

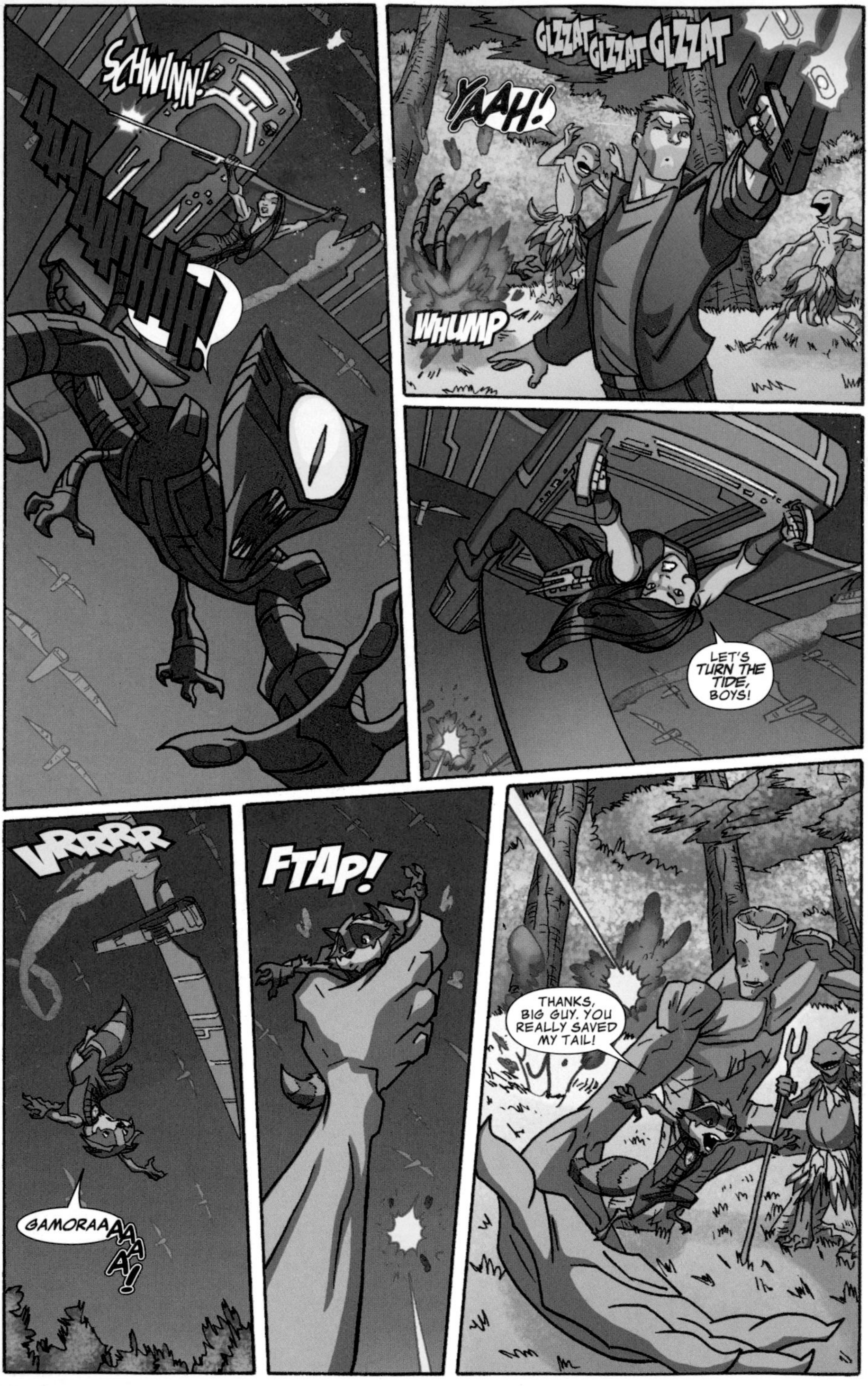
SCHWINN!
AAAAAHHHH!
GLZZAT GLZZAT GLZZAT
YAAH!
WHUMP
LET'S TURN THE TIDE, BOYS!
VRRRR
GAMORAAAAAA!
FTAP!
THANKS, BIG GUY. YOU REALLY SAVED MY TAIL!

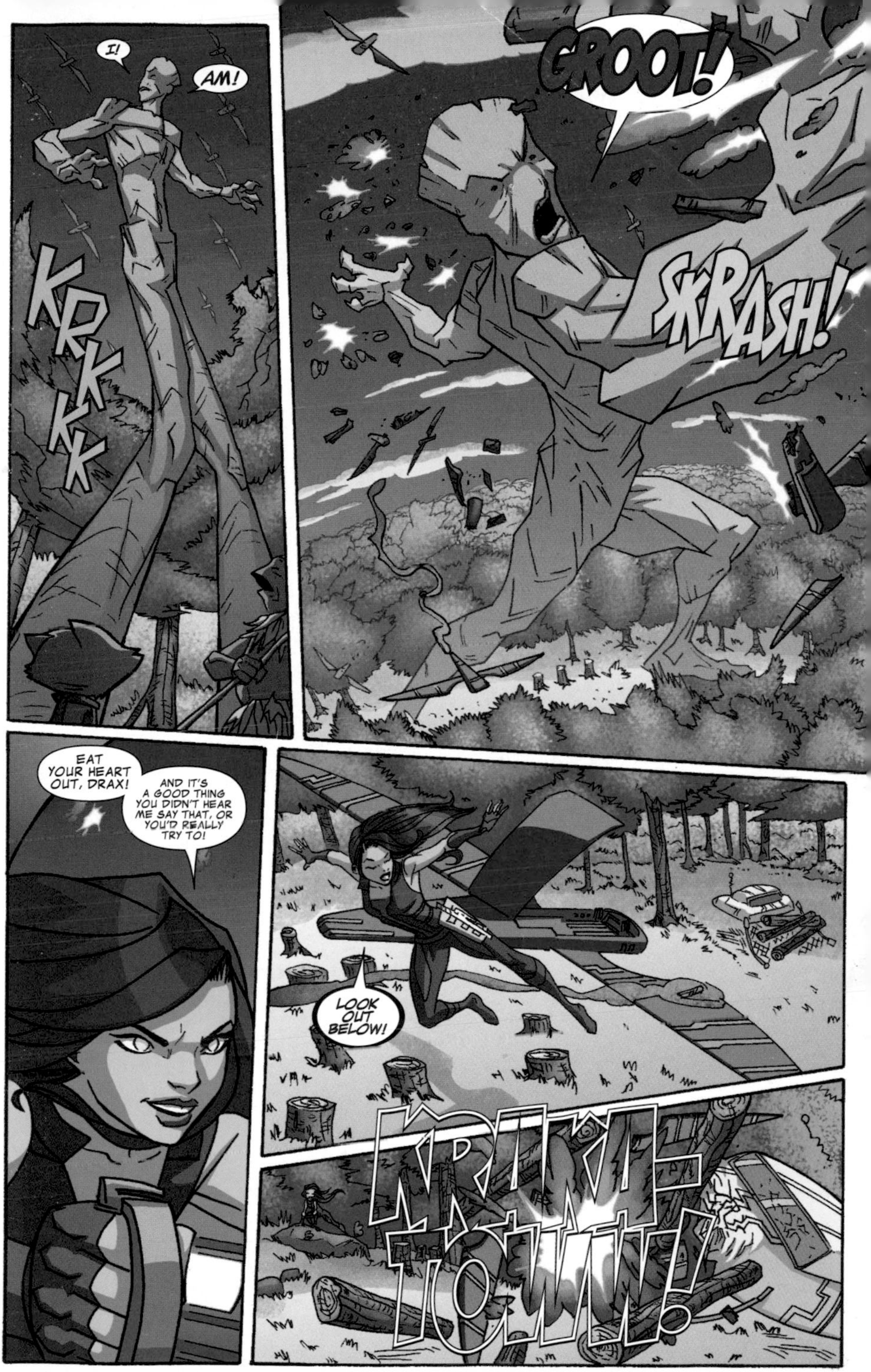

I!
AM!
KRKKKK
GROOT!
SKRASH!
EAT YOUR HEART OUT, DRAX!
AND IT'S A GOOD THING YOU DIDN'T HEAR ME SAY THAT, OR YOU'D REALLY TRY TO!
LOOK OUT BELOW!

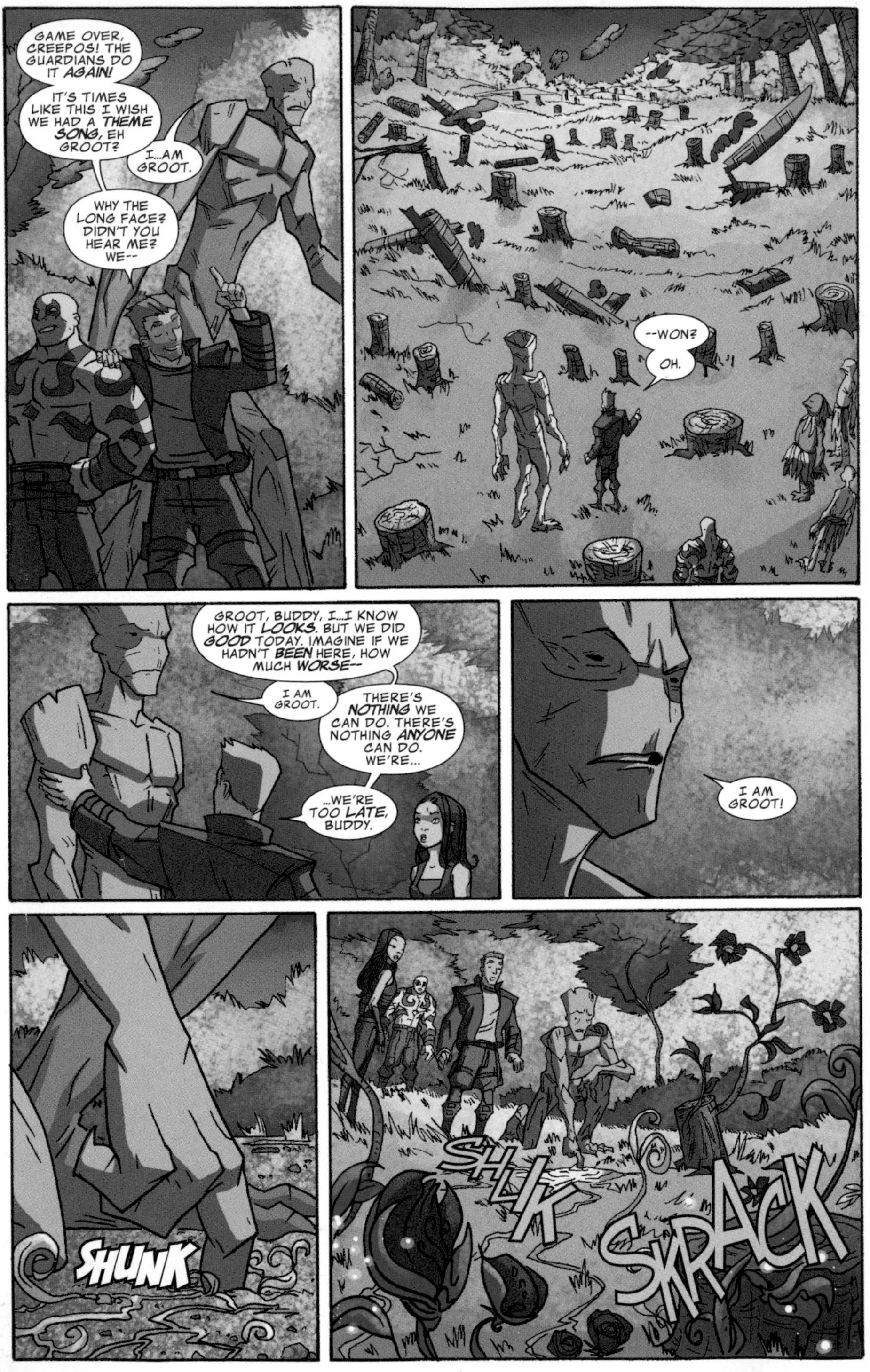
GAME OVER, CREEPOS! THE GUARDIANS DO IT AGAIN!
IT'S TIMES LIKE THIS I WISH WE HAD A THEME SONG, EH GROOT?
I...AM GROOT.
WHY THE LONG FACE? DIDN'T YOU HEAR ME? WE--
--WON?
OH.
GROOT, BUDDY, I...I KNOW HOW IT LOOKS. BUT WE DID GOOD TODAY. IMAGINE IF WE HADN'T BEEN HERE, HOW MUCH WORSE--
I AM GROOT.
THERE'S NOTHING WE CAN DO. THERE'S NOTHING ANYONE CAN DO. WE'RE...
...WE'RE TOO LATE, BUDDY.
I AM GROOT!
SHUNK
SHLIK
SKRACK

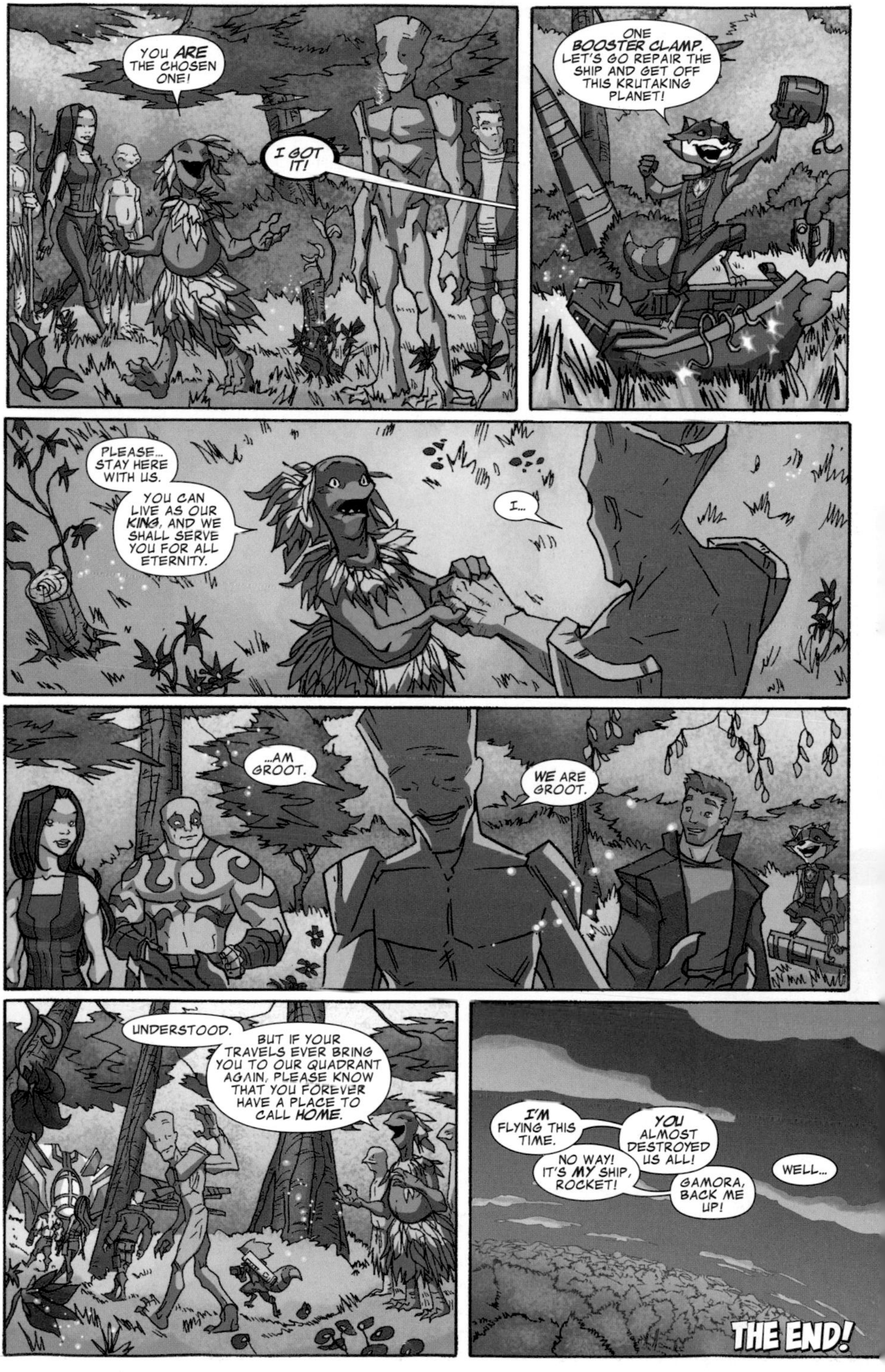
YOU ARE THE CHOSEN ONE!
I GOT IT!
ONE BOOSTER CLAMP. LET'S GO REPAIR THE SHIP AND GET OFF THIS KRUTAKING PLANET!
PLEASE... STAY HERE WITH US.
YOU CAN LIVE AS OUR KING, AND WE SHALL SERVE YOU FOR ALL ETERNITY.
I...
...AM GROOT.
WE ARE GROOT.
UNDERSTOOD.
BUT IF YOUR TRAVELS EVER BRING YOU TO OUR QUADRANT AGAIN, PLEASE KNOW THAT YOU FOREVER HAVE A PLACE TO CALL HOME.
I'M FLYING THIS TIME.
YOU ALMOST DESTROYED US ALL!
NO WAY! IT'S MY SHIP, ROCKET!
GAMORA, BACK ME UP!
WELL...
THE END!

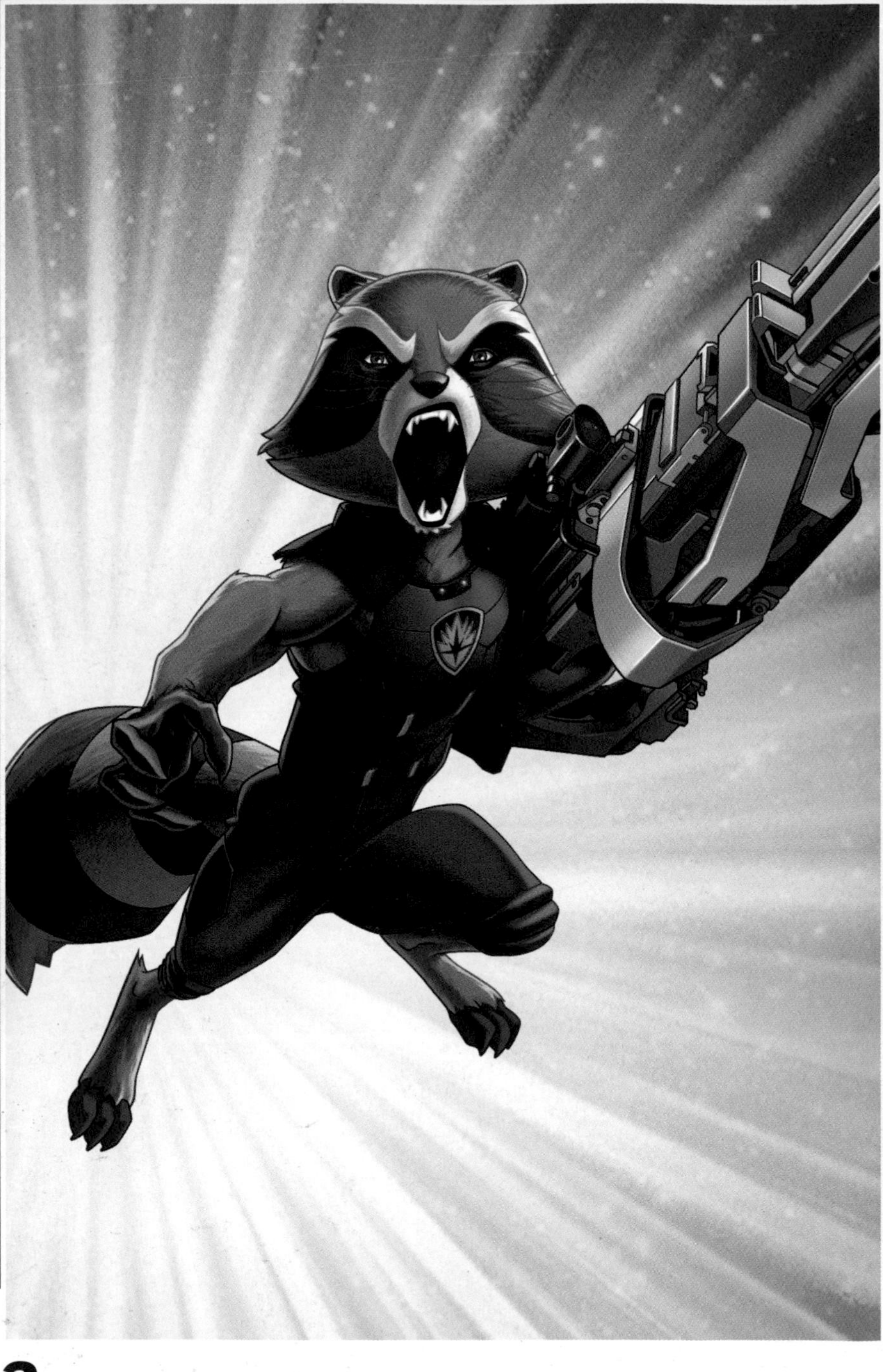

3 BASED ON **"ONE IN A MILLION YOU"**

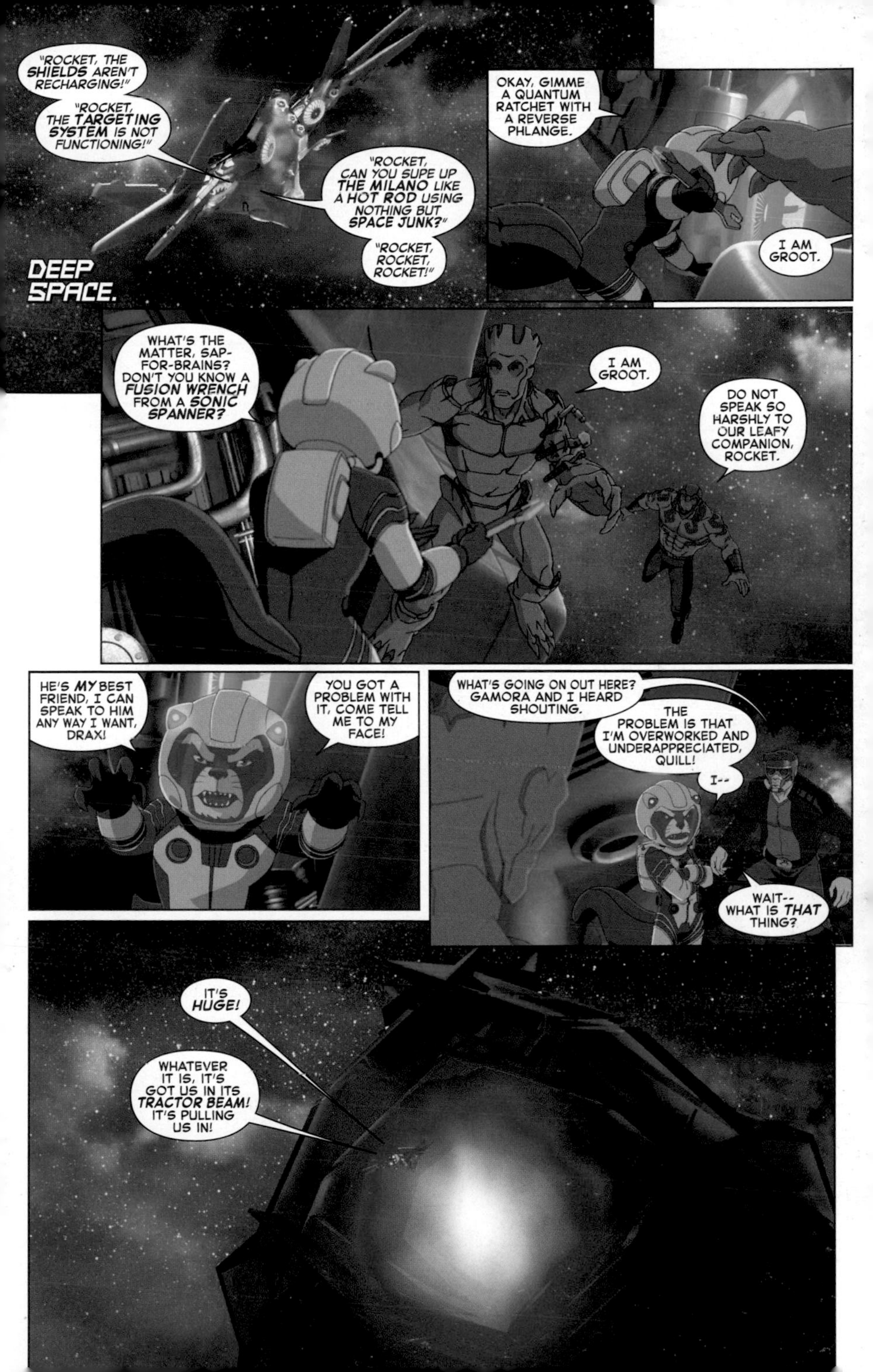
"ROCKET, THE SHIELDS AREN'T RECHARGING!"
"ROCKET, THE TARGETING SYSTEM IS NOT FUNCTIONING!"
"ROCKET, CAN YOU SUPE UP THE MILANO LIKE A HOT ROD USING NOTHING BUT SPACE JUNK?"
"ROCKET, ROCKET, ROCKET!"
DEEP SPACE.
OKAY, GIMME A QUANTUM RATCHET WITH A REVERSE PHLANGE.
I AM GROOT.
WHAT'S THE MATTER, SAP-FOR-BRAINS? DON'T YOU KNOW A FUSION WRENCH FROM A SONIC SPANNER?
I AM GROOT.
DO NOT SPEAK SO HARSHLY TO OUR LEAFY COMPANION, ROCKET.
HE'S MY BEST FRIEND, I CAN SPEAK TO HIM ANY WAY I WANT, DRAX!
YOU GOT A PROBLEM WITH IT, COME TELL ME TO MY FACE!
WHAT'S GOING ON OUT HERE? GAMORA AND I HEARD SHOUTING.
THE PROBLEM IS THAT I'M OVERWORKED AND UNDERAPPRECIATED, QUILL!
I--
WAIT-- WHAT IS THAT THING?
IT'S HUGE!
WHATEVER IT IS, IT'S GOT US IN ITS TRACTOR BEAM! IT'S PULLING US IN!

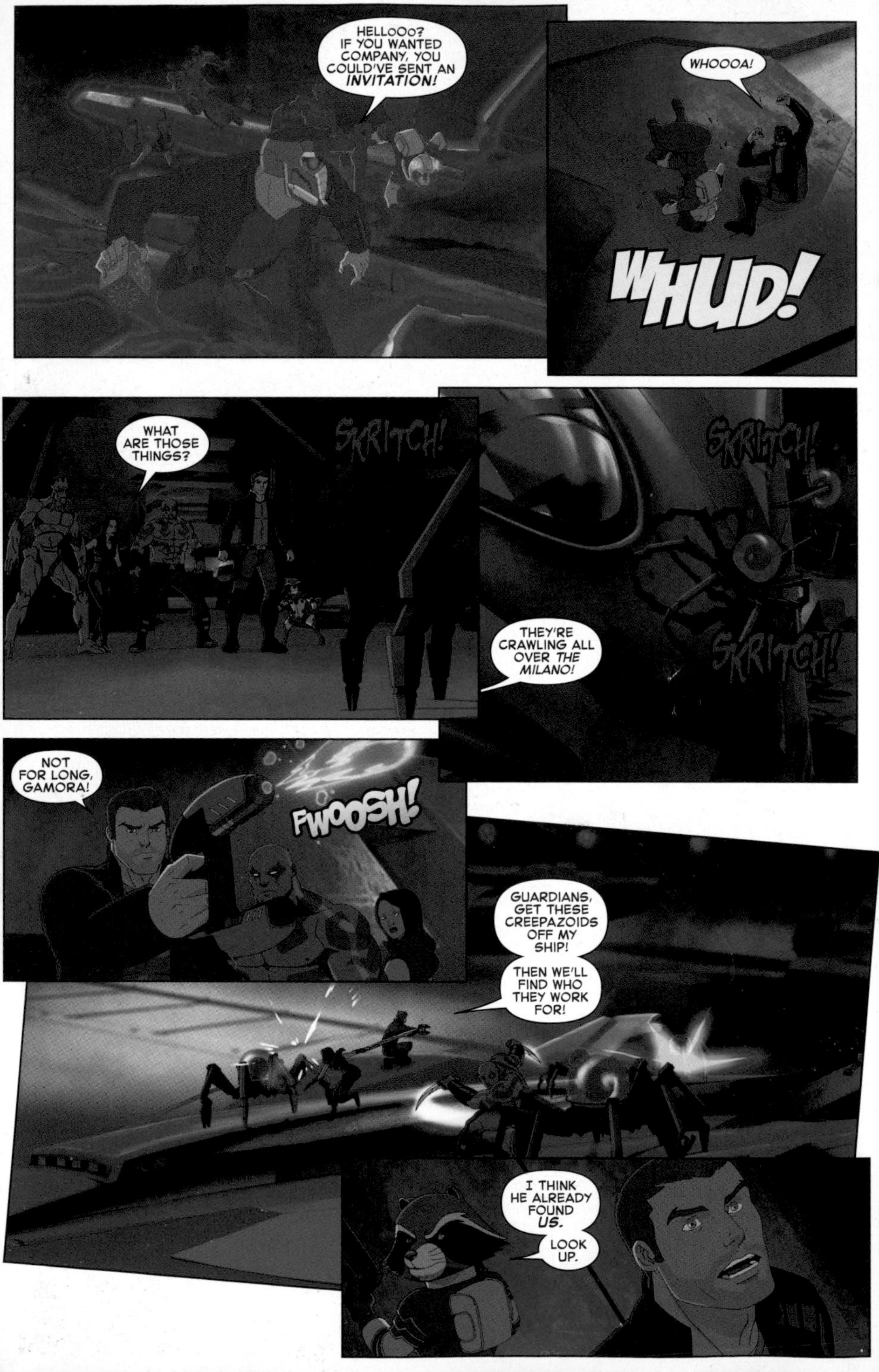
HELLOOO? IF YOU WANTED COMPANY, YOU COULD'VE SENT AN *INVITATION!*
WHOOOA!
WHUD!
WHAT ARE THOSE THINGS?
SKRITCH!
SKRITCH!
THEY'RE CRAWLING ALL OVER *THE MILANO!*
SKRITCH!
NOT FOR LONG, GAMORA!
FWOOSH!
GUARDIANS, GET THESE CREEPAZOIDS OFF MY SHIP!
THEN WE'LL FIND WHO THEY WORK FOR!
I THINK HE ALREADY FOUND *US.*
LOOK UP.

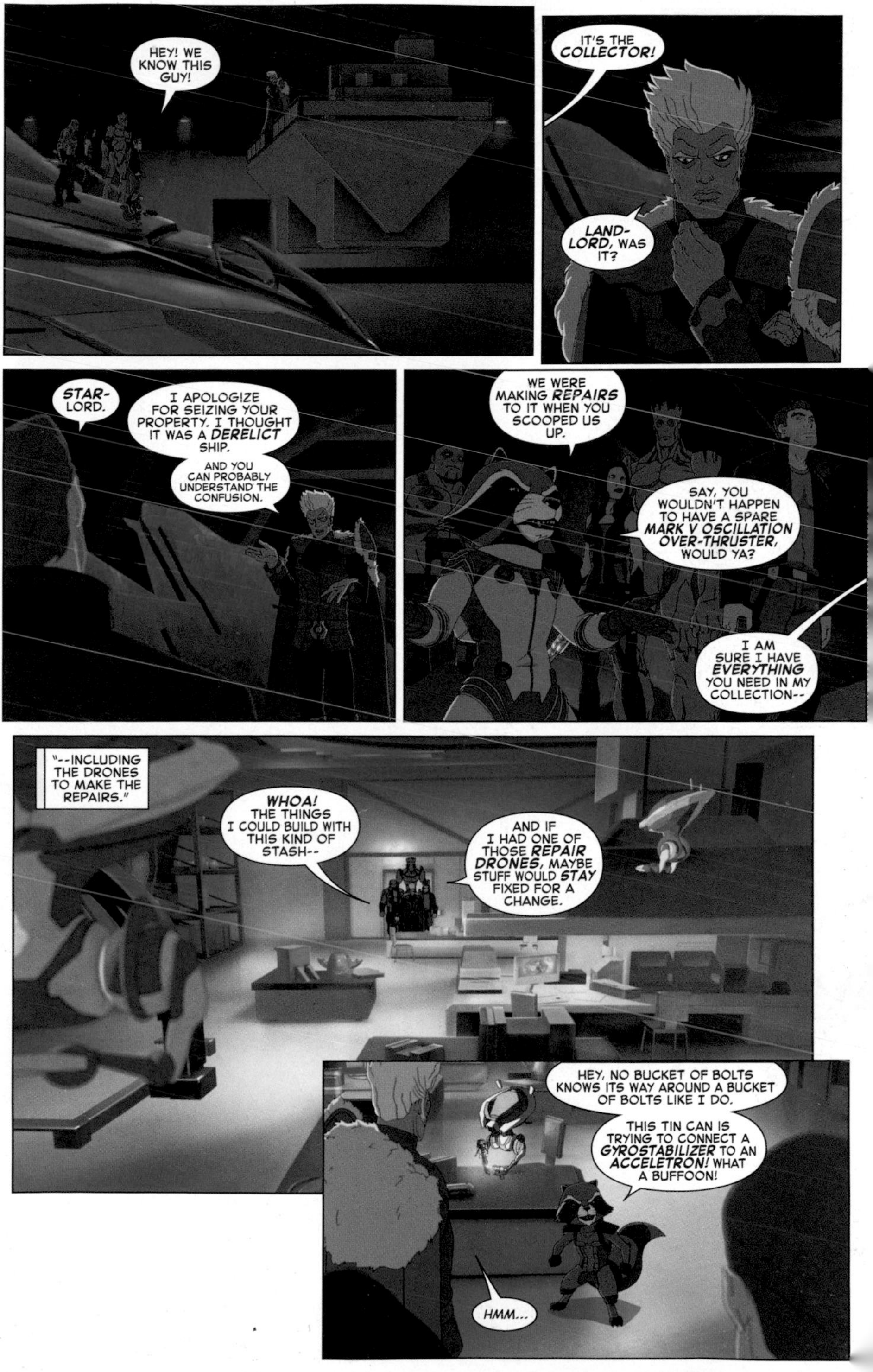
HEY! WE KNOW THIS GUY!
IT'S THE COLLECTOR!
LAND-LORD, WAS IT?
STAR-LORD.
I APOLOGIZE FOR SEIZING YOUR PROPERTY. I THOUGHT IT WAS A DERELICT SHIP.
AND YOU CAN PROBABLY UNDERSTAND THE CONFUSION.
WE WERE MAKING REPAIRS TO IT WHEN YOU SCOOPED US UP.
SAY, YOU WOULDN'T HAPPEN TO HAVE A SPARE MARK V OSCILLATION OVER-THRUSTER, WOULD YA?
I AM SURE I HAVE EVERYTHING YOU NEED IN MY COLLECTION--
"--INCLUDING THE DRONES TO MAKE THE REPAIRS."
WHOA! THE THINGS I COULD BUILD WITH THIS KIND OF STASH--
AND IF I HAD ONE OF THOSE REPAIR DRONES, MAYBE STUFF WOULD STAY FIXED FOR A CHANGE.
HEY, NO BUCKET OF BOLTS KNOWS ITS WAY AROUND A BUCKET OF BOLTS LIKE I DO.
THIS TIN CAN IS TRYING TO CONNECT A GYROSTABILIZER TO AN ACCELETRON! WHAT A BUFFOON!
HMM...

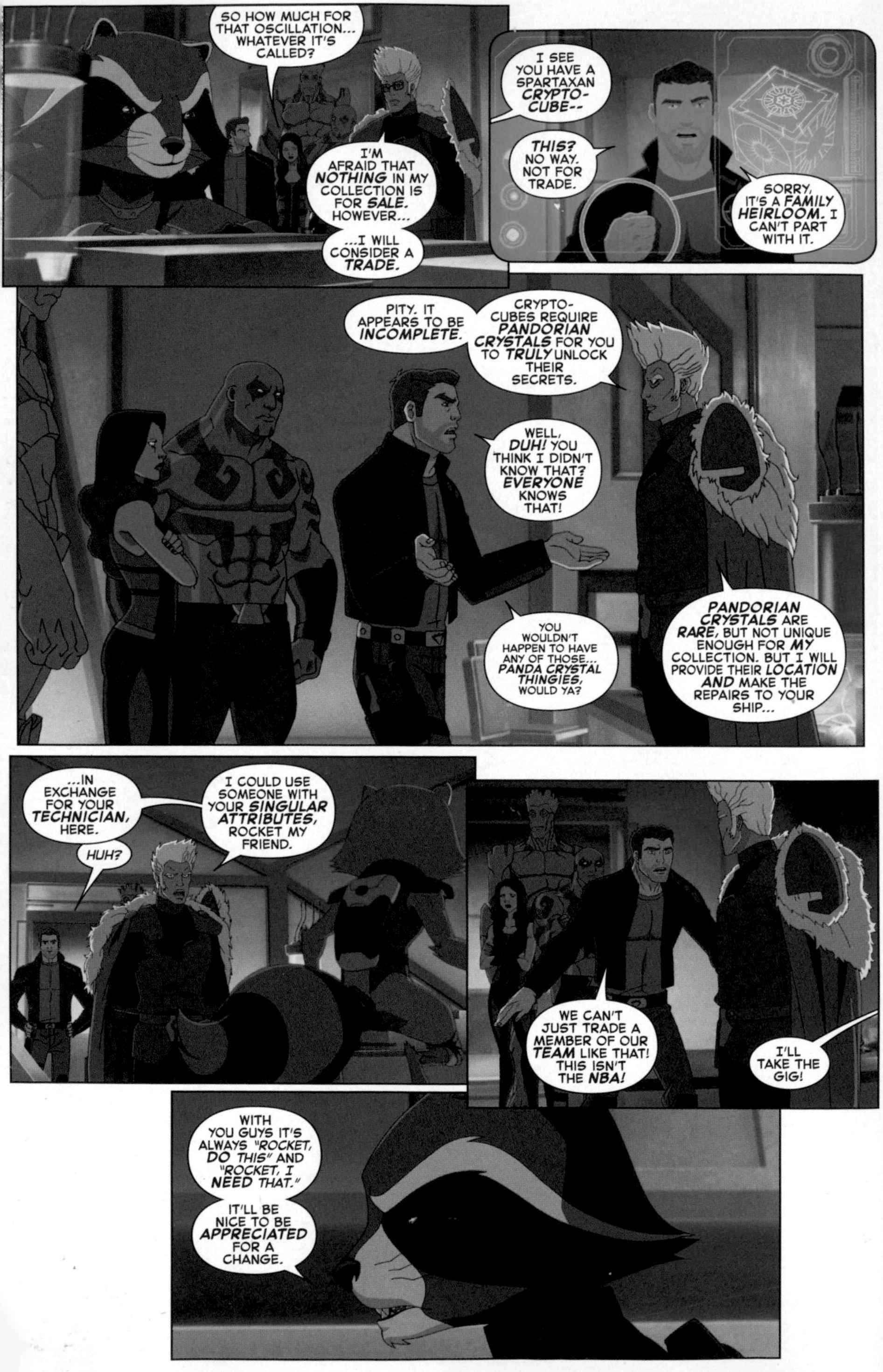

SO HOW MUCH FOR THAT OSCILLATION... WHATEVER IT'S CALLED?
I'M AFRAID THAT NOTHING IN MY COLLECTION IS FOR SALE. HOWEVER...
...I WILL CONSIDER A TRADE.
I SEE YOU HAVE A SPARTAXAN CRYPTO-CUBE--
THIS? NO WAY. NOT FOR TRADE.
SORRY, IT'S A FAMILY HEIRLOOM. I CAN'T PART WITH IT.
PITY. IT APPEARS TO BE INCOMPLETE.
CRYPTO-CUBES REQUIRE PANDORIAN CRYSTALS FOR YOU TO TRULY UNLOCK THEIR SECRETS.
WELL, DUH! YOU THINK I DIDN'T KNOW THAT? EVERYONE KNOWS THAT!
YOU WOULDN'T HAPPEN TO HAVE ANY OF THOSE... PANDA CRYSTAL THINGIES, WOULD YA?
PANDORIAN CRYSTALS ARE RARE, BUT NOT UNIQUE ENOUGH FOR MY COLLECTION. BUT I WILL PROVIDE THEIR LOCATION AND MAKE THE REPAIRS TO YOUR SHIP...
...IN EXCHANGE FOR YOUR TECHNICIAN, HERE.
HUH?
I COULD USE SOMEONE WITH YOUR SINGULAR ATTRIBUTES, ROCKET MY FRIEND.
WE CAN'T JUST TRADE A MEMBER OF OUR TEAM LIKE THAT! THIS ISN'T THE NBA!
I'LL TAKE THE GIG!
WITH YOU GUYS IT'S ALWAYS "ROCKET, DO THIS" AND "ROCKET, I NEED THAT."
IT'LL BE NICE TO BE APPRECIATED FOR A CHANGE.

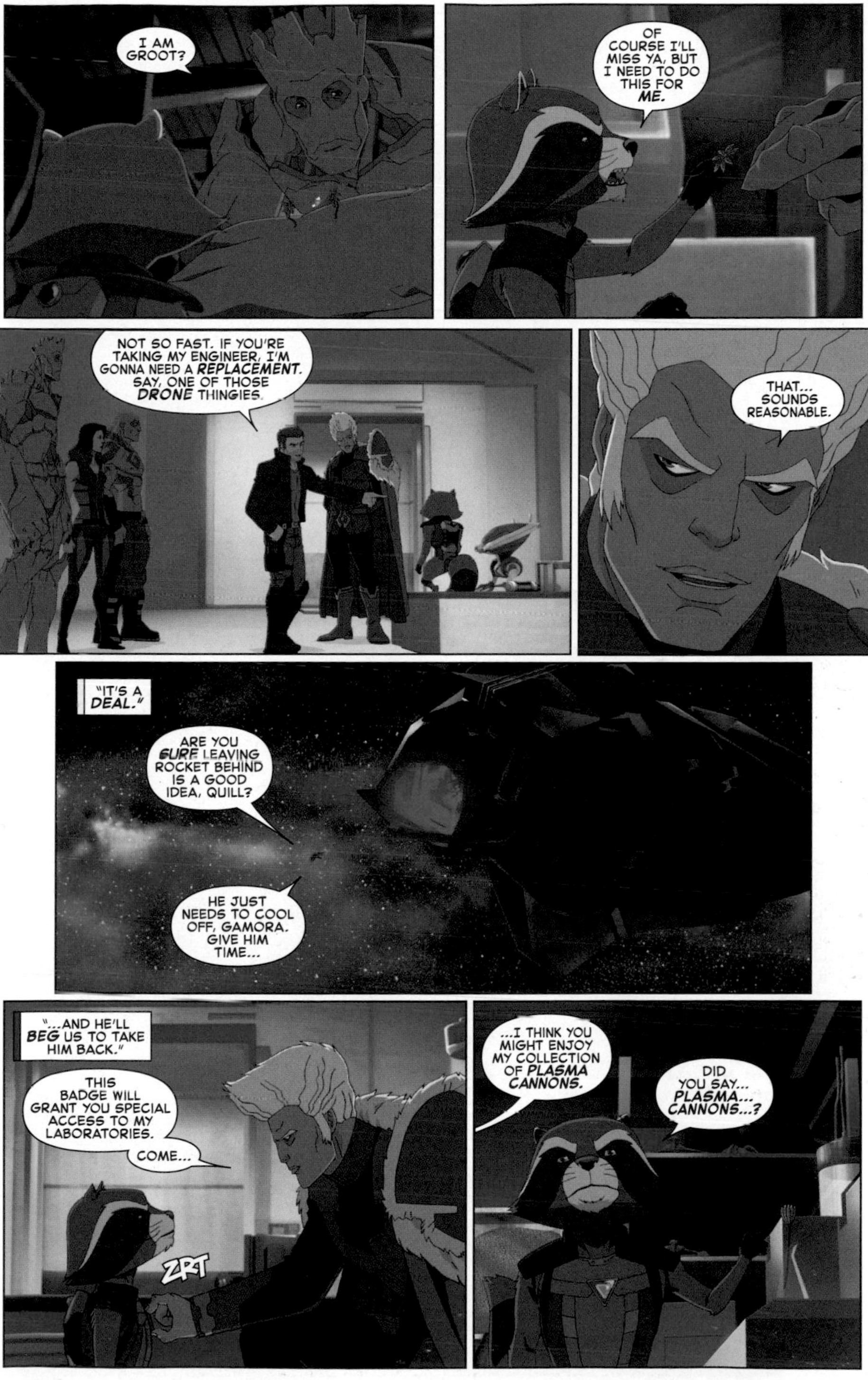
I AM GROOT?
OF COURSE I'LL MISS YA, BUT I NEED TO DO THIS FOR ME.
NOT SO FAST. IF YOU'RE TAKING MY ENGINEER, I'M GONNA NEED A REPLACEMENT. SAY, ONE OF THOSE DRONE THINGIES.
THAT... SOUNDS REASONABLE.
"IT'S A DEAL."
ARE YOU SURE LEAVING ROCKET BEHIND IS A GOOD IDEA, QUILL?
HE JUST NEEDS TO COOL OFF, GAMORA. GIVE HIM TIME...
"...AND HE'LL BEG US TO TAKE HIM BACK."
THIS BADGE WILL GRANT YOU SPECIAL ACCESS TO MY LABORATORIES.
COME...
ZRT
...I THINK YOU MIGHT ENJOY MY COLLECTION OF PLASMA CANNONS.
DID YOU SAY... PLASMA... CANNONS...?

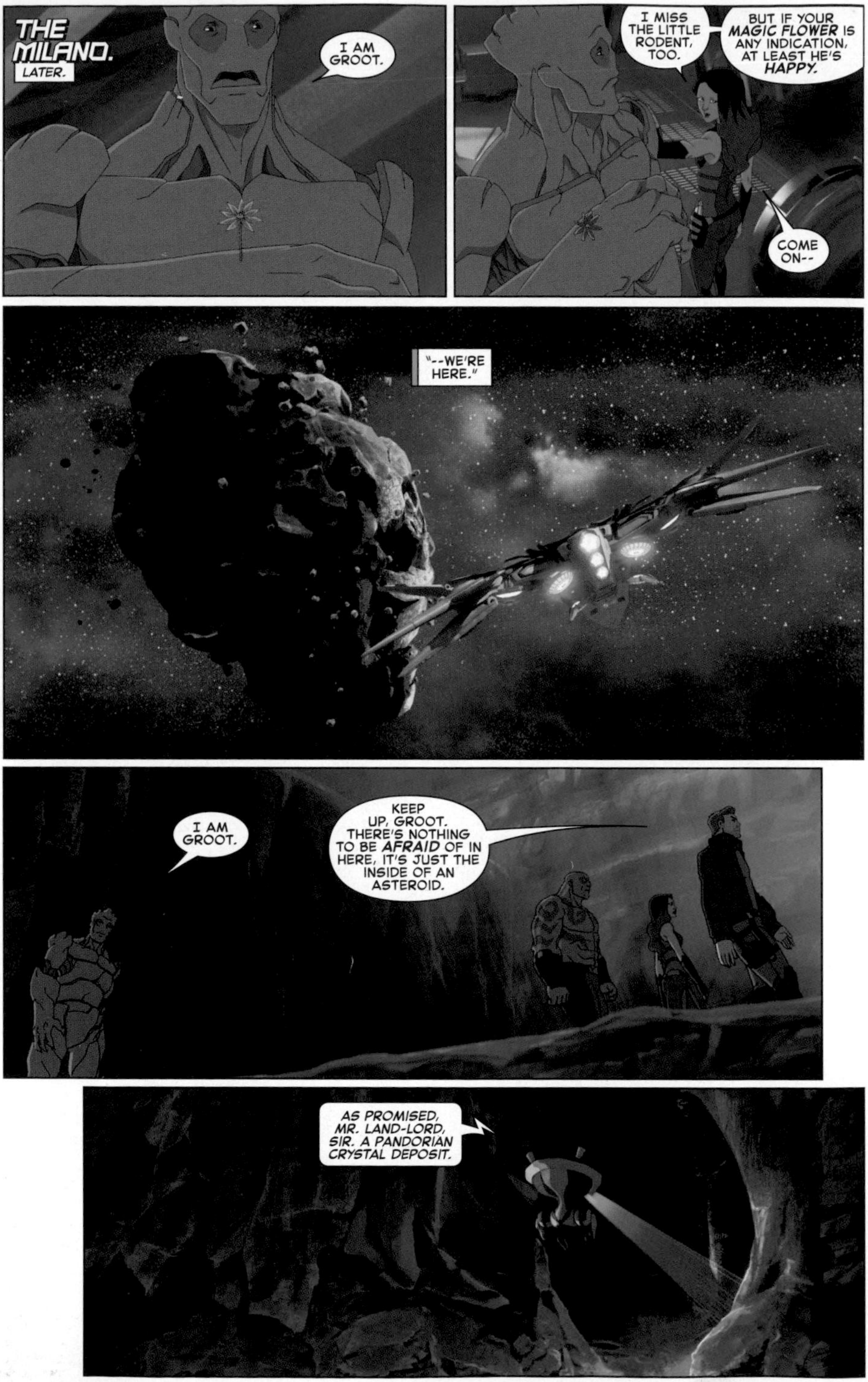
THE MILANO.
LATER.
I AM GROOT.
I MISS THE LITTLE RODENT, TOO.
BUT IF YOUR MAGIC FLOWER IS ANY INDICATION, AT LEAST HE'S HAPPY.
COME ON--
"--WE'RE HERE."
I AM GROOT.
KEEP UP, GROOT. THERE'S NOTHING TO BE AFRAID OF IN HERE, IT'S JUST THE INSIDE OF AN ASTEROID.
AS PROMISED, MR. LAND-LORD, SIR. A PANDORIAN CRYSTAL DEPOSIT.

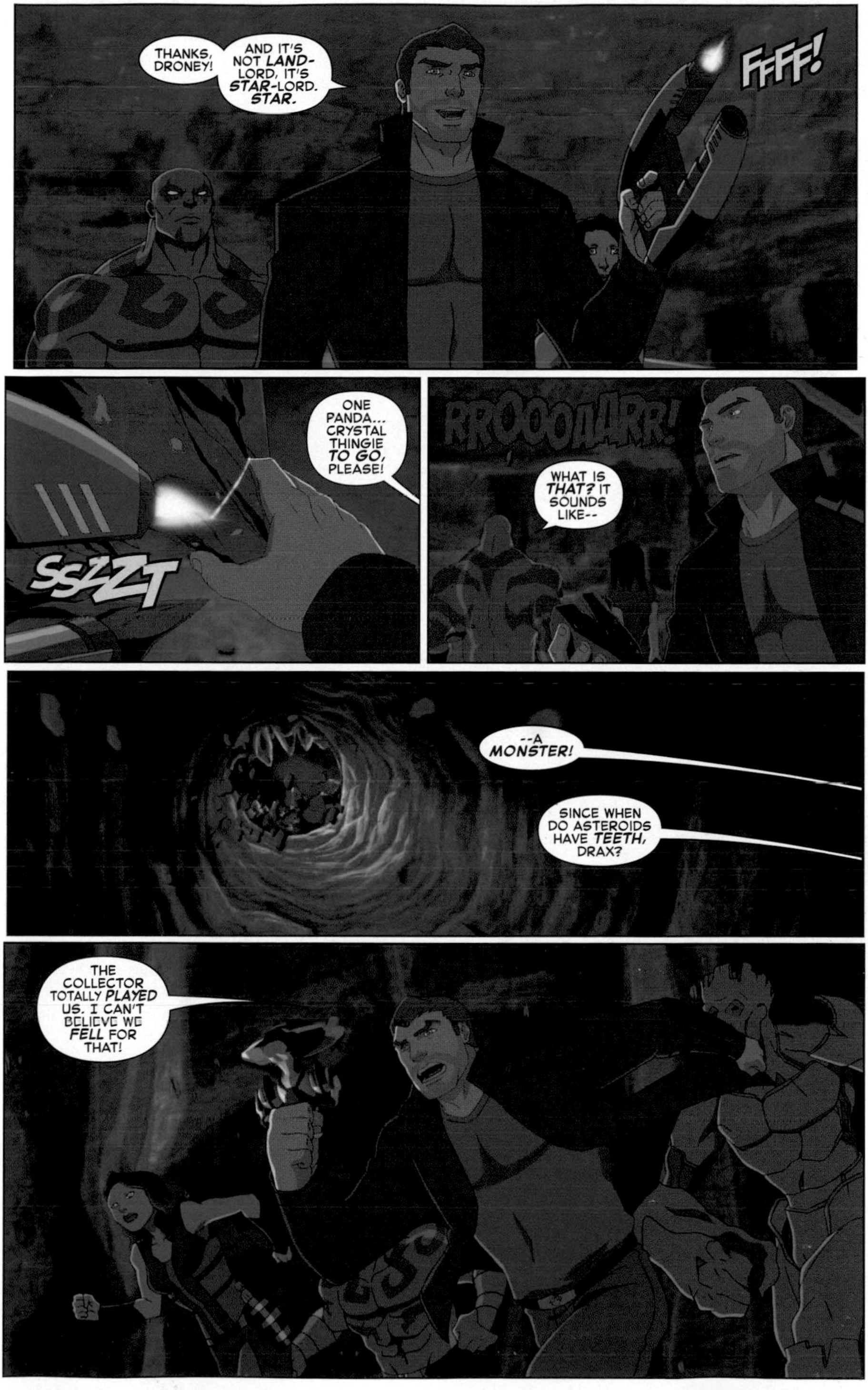
THANKS, DRONEY!
AND IT'S NOT LAND-LORD, IT'S STAR-LORD. STAR.
FFFF!
ONE PANDA... CRYSTAL THINGIE TO GO, PLEASE!
SSZZT
RROOOAARR!
WHAT IS THAT? IT SOUNDS LIKE--
--A MONSTER!
SINCE WHEN DO ASTEROIDS HAVE TEETH, DRAX?
THE COLLECTOR TOTALLY PLAYED US. I CAN'T BELIEVE WE FELL FOR THAT!

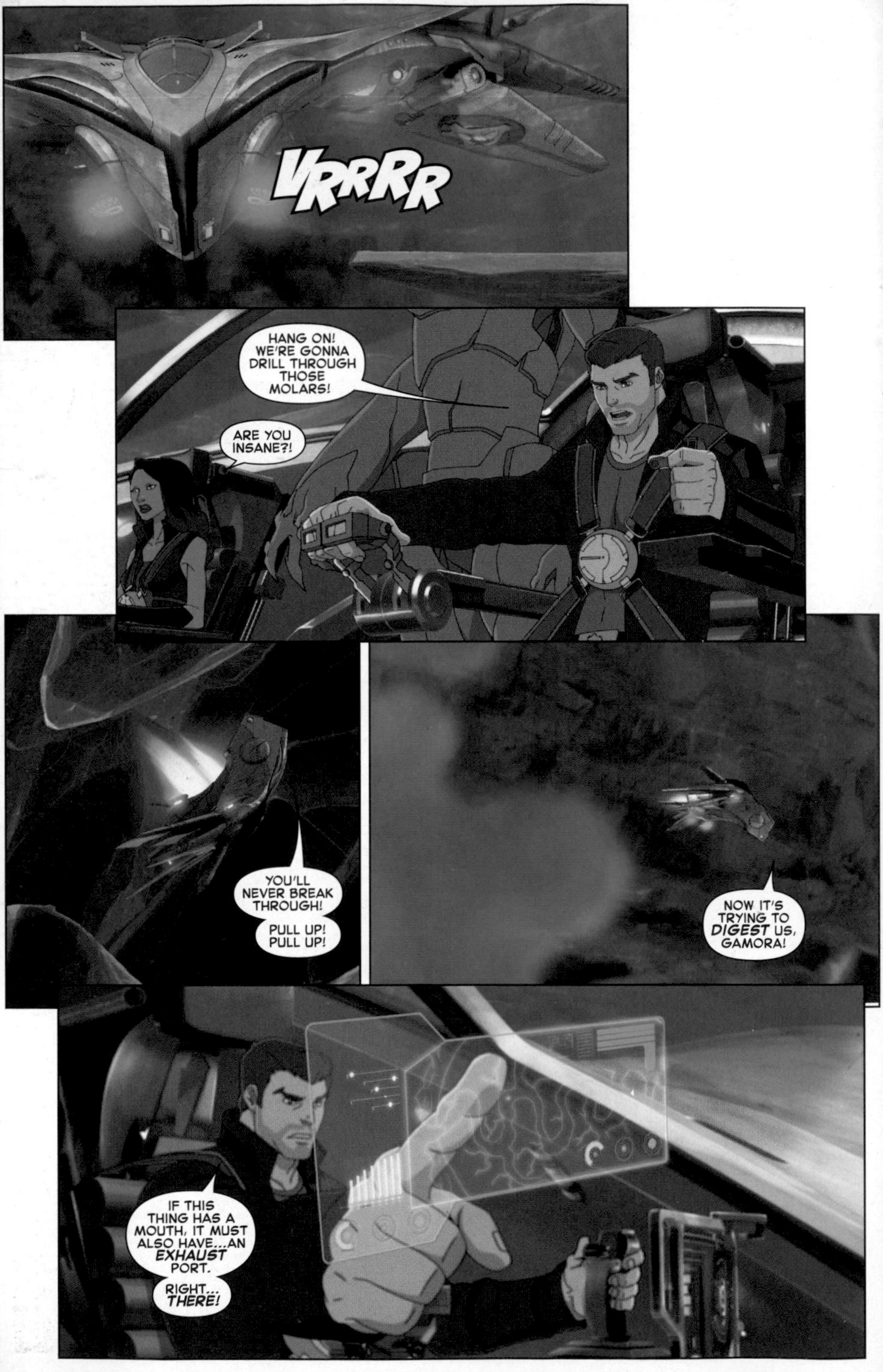
VRRRR
HANG ON! WE'RE GONNA DRILL THROUGH THOSE MOLARS!
ARE YOU INSANE?!
YOU'LL NEVER BREAK THROUGH!
PULL UP! PULL UP!
NOW IT'S TRYING TO DIGEST US, GAMORA!
IF THIS THING HAS A MOUTH, IT MUST ALSO HAVE...AN EXHAUST PORT.
RIGHT... THERE!

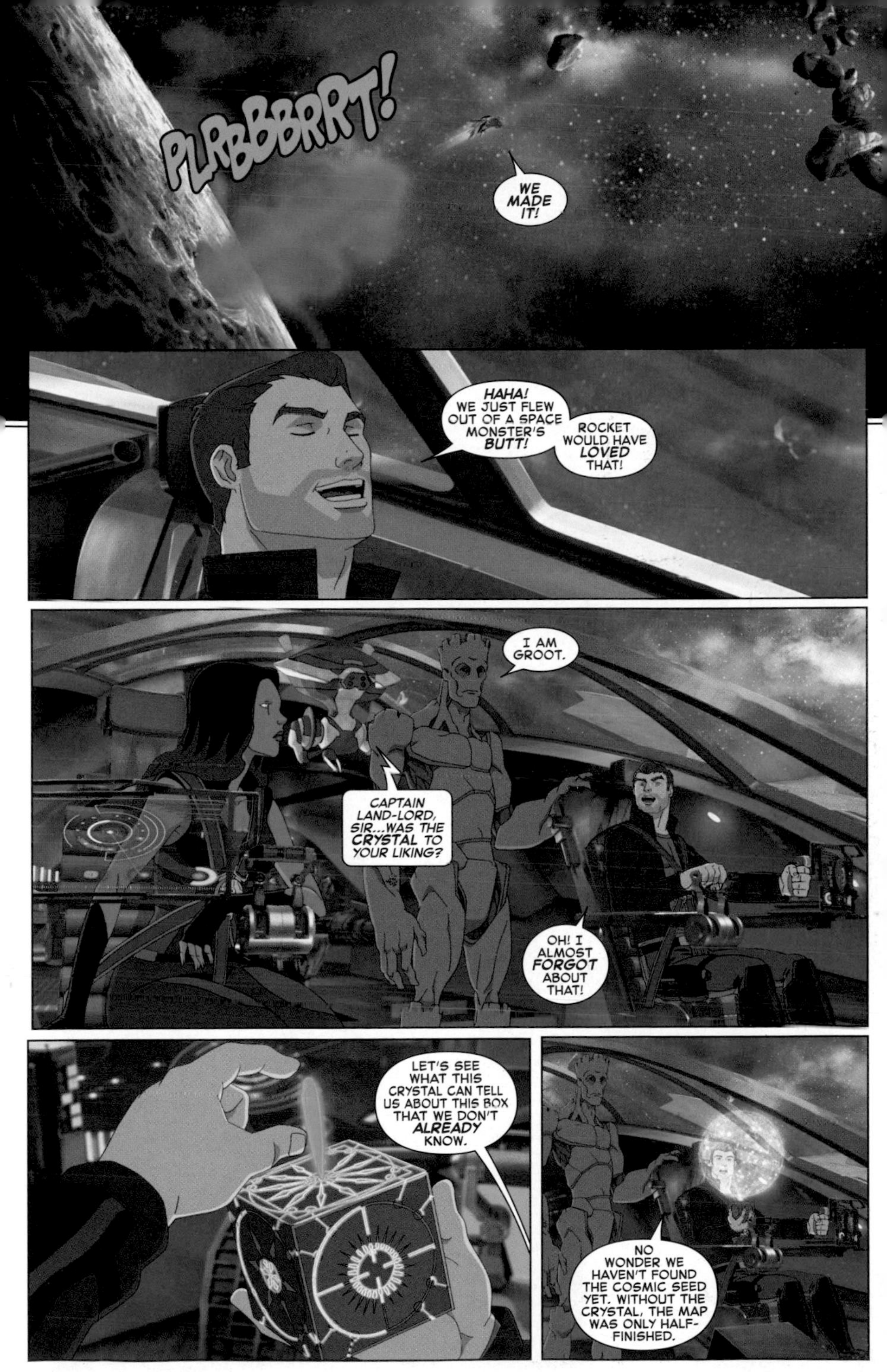
PLRBBBRRT!
WE MADE IT!
HAHA! WE JUST FLEW OUT OF A SPACE MONSTER'S BUTT!
ROCKET WOULD HAVE LOVED THAT!
I AM GROOT.
CAPTAIN LAND-LORD, SIR...WAS THE CRYSTAL TO YOUR LIKING?
OH! I ALMOST FORGOT ABOUT THAT!
LET'S SEE WHAT THIS CRYSTAL CAN TELL US ABOUT THIS BOX THAT WE DON'T ALREADY KNOW.
NO WONDER WE HAVEN'T FOUND THE COSMIC SEED YET. WITHOUT THE CRYSTAL, THE MAP WAS ONLY HALF-FINISHED.

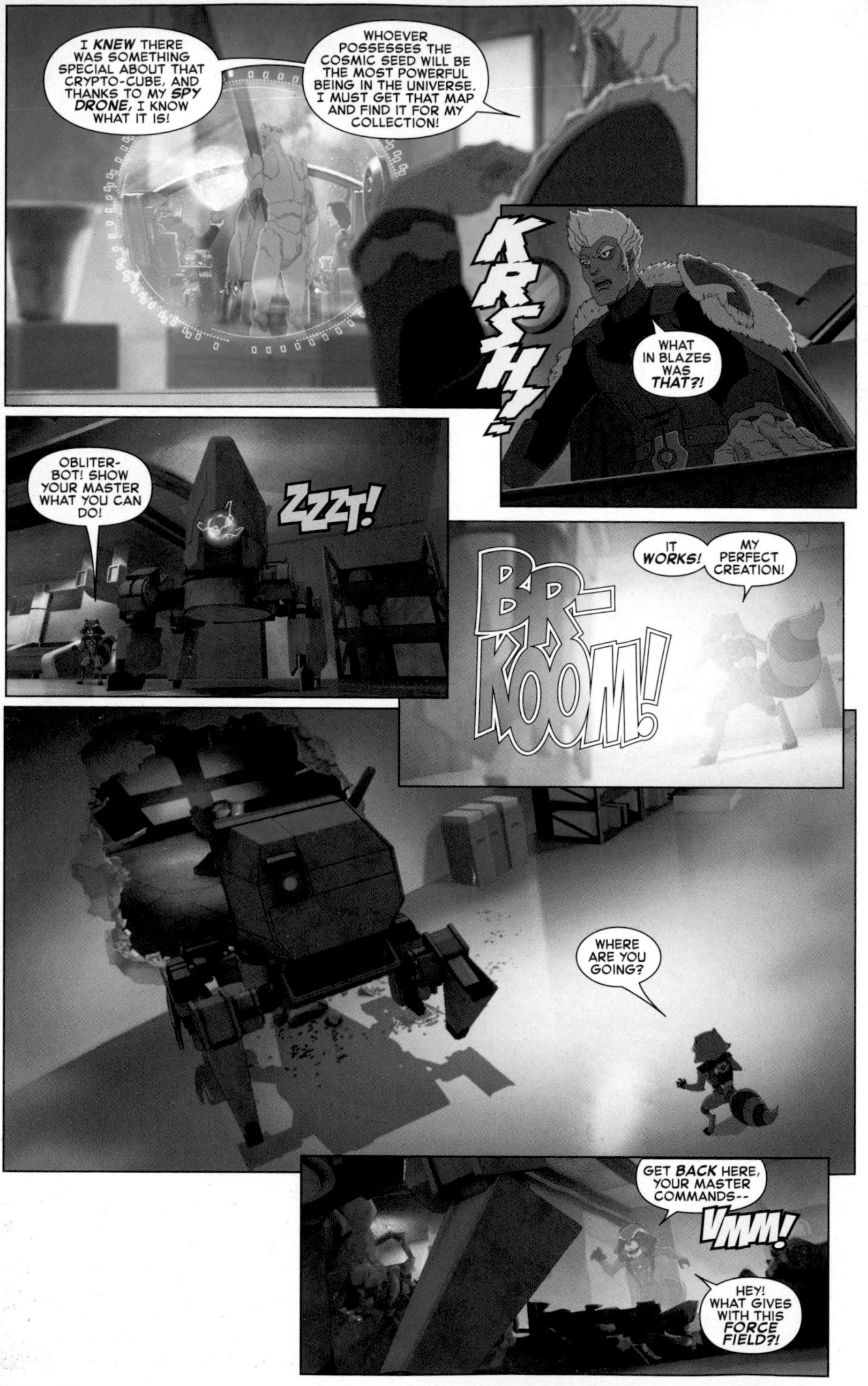
I KNEW THERE WAS SOMETHING SPECIAL ABOUT THAT CRYPTO-CUBE, AND THANKS TO MY SPY DRONE, I KNOW WHAT IT IS!
WHOEVER POSSESSES THE COSMIC SEED WILL BE THE MOST POWERFUL BEING IN THE UNIVERSE. I MUST GET THAT MAP AND FIND IT FOR MY COLLECTION!
KRSH!
WHAT IN BLAZES WAS THAT?!
OBLITER-BOT! SHOW YOUR MASTER WHAT YOU CAN DO!
ZZZT!
BR-KOOM!
IT WORKS!
MY PERFECT CREATION!
WHERE ARE YOU GOING?
GET BACK HERE, YOUR MASTER COMMANDS--
VMM!
HEY! WHAT GIVES WITH THIS FORCE FIELD?!

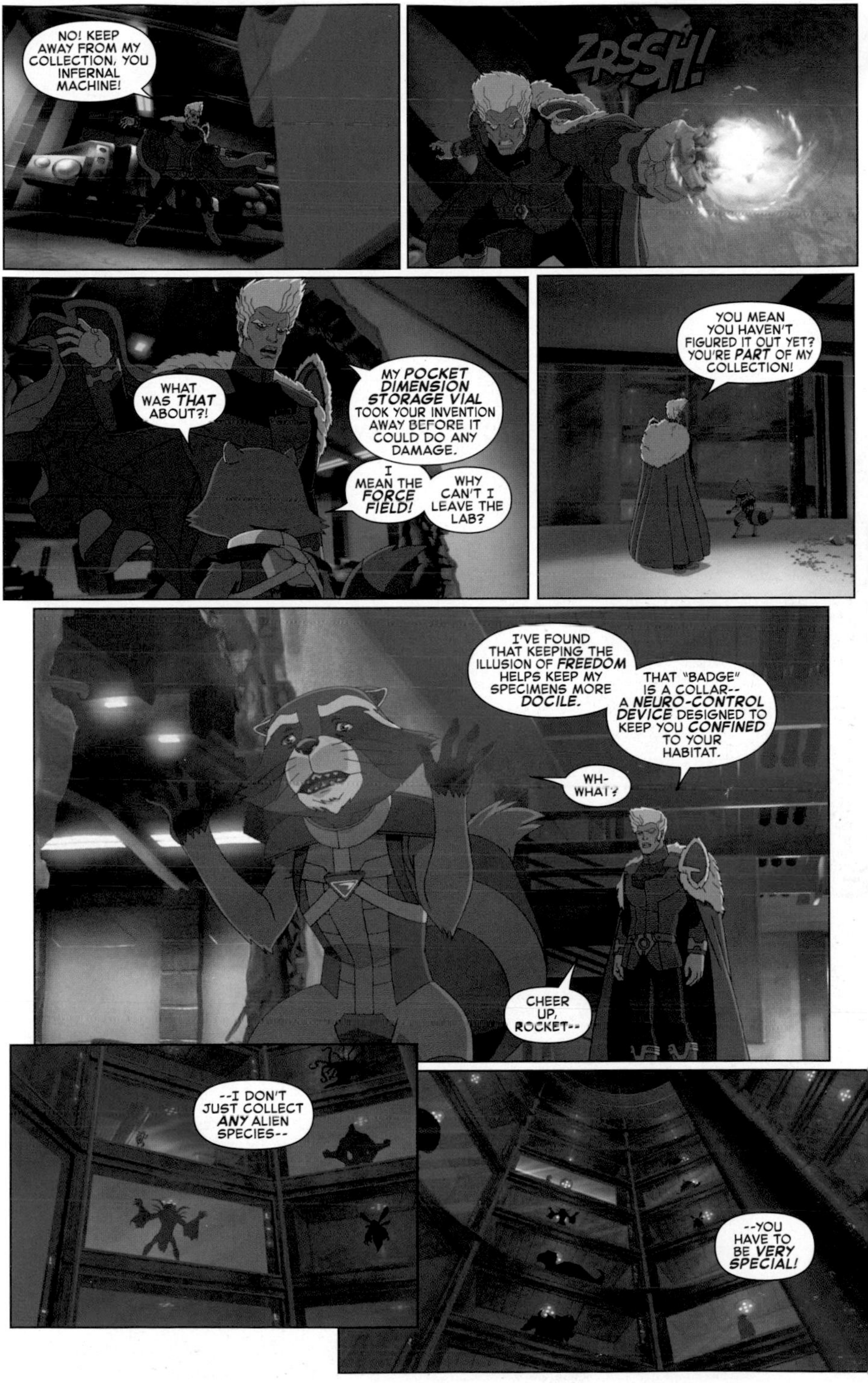
NO! KEEP AWAY FROM MY COLLECTION, YOU INFERNAL MACHINE!
ZRSSH!
WHAT WAS THAT ABOUT?!
MY POCKET DIMENSION STORAGE VIAL TOOK YOUR INVENTION AWAY BEFORE IT COULD DO ANY DAMAGE.
I MEAN THE FORCE FIELD!
WHY CAN'T I LEAVE THE LAB?
YOU MEAN YOU HAVEN'T FIGURED IT OUT YET? YOU'RE PART OF MY COLLECTION!
I'VE FOUND THAT KEEPING THE ILLUSION OF FREEDOM HELPS KEEP MY SPECIMENS MORE DOCILE.
THAT "BADGE" IS A COLLAR-- A NEURO-CONTROL DEVICE DESIGNED TO KEEP YOU CONFINED TO YOUR HABITAT.
WH- WHAT?
CHEER UP, ROCKET--
--I DON'T JUST COLLECT ANY ALIEN SPECIES--
--YOU HAVE TO BE VERY SPECIAL!

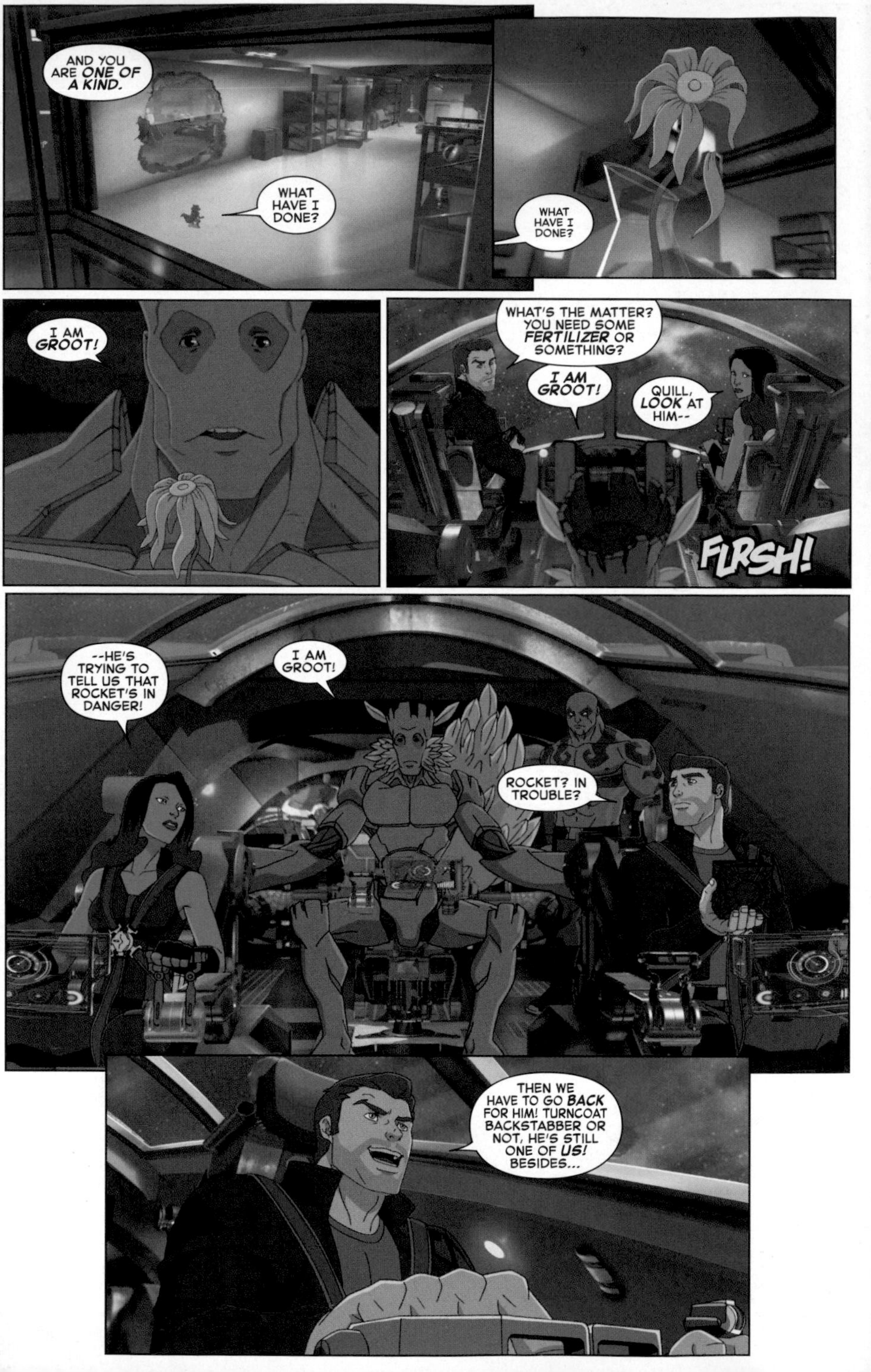
AND YOU ARE ONE OF A KIND.
WHAT HAVE I DONE?
WHAT HAVE I DONE?
I AM GROOT!
WHAT'S THE MATTER? YOU NEED SOME FERTILIZER OR SOMETHING?
I AM GROOT!
QUILL, LOOK AT HIM--
FLRSH!
--HE'S TRYING TO TELL US THAT ROCKET'S IN DANGER!
I AM GROOT!
ROCKET? IN TROUBLE?
THEN WE HAVE TO GO BACK FOR HIM! TURNCOAT BACKSTABBER OR NOT, HE'S STILL ONE OF US! BESIDES...

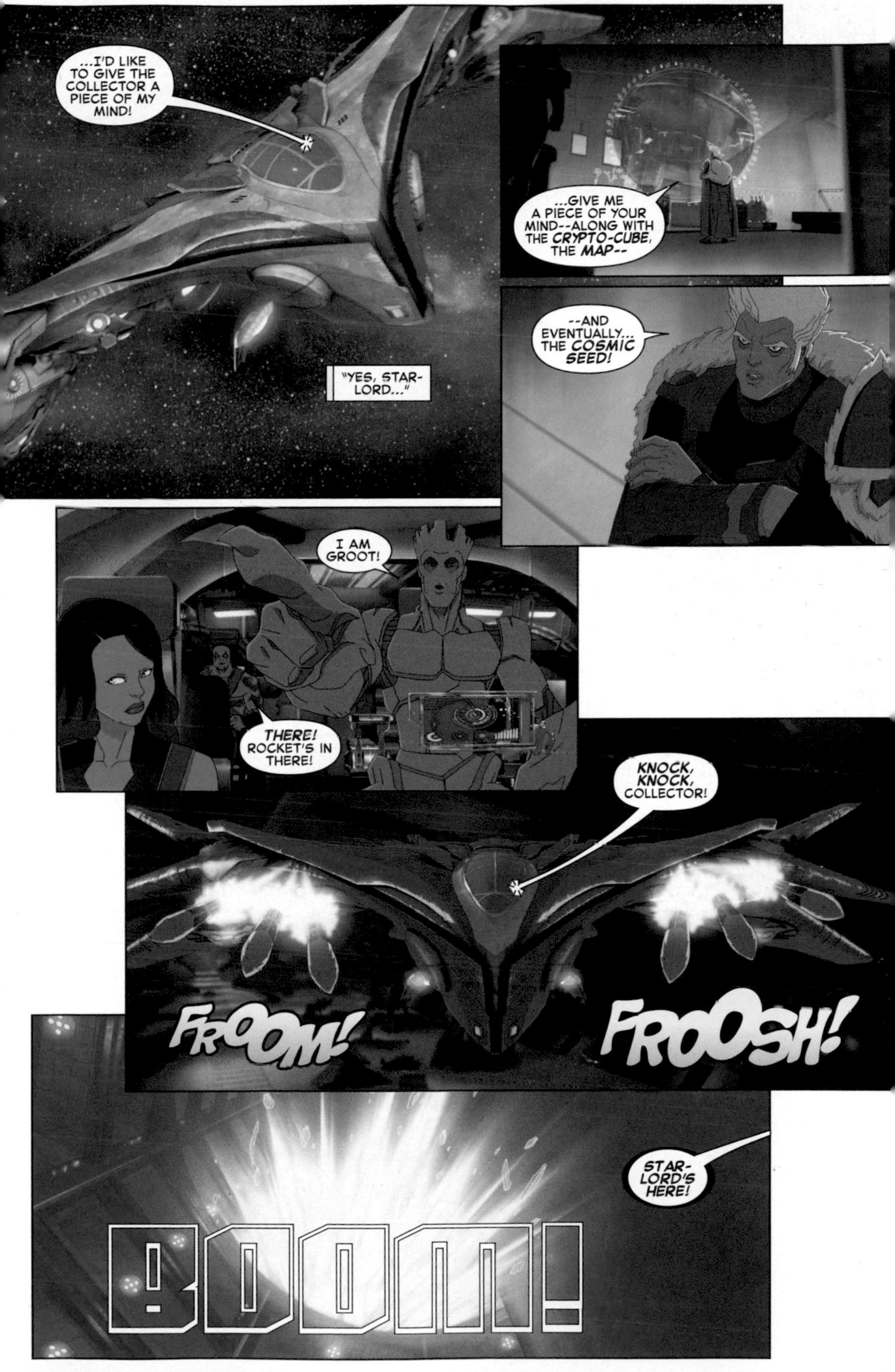
...I'D LIKE TO GIVE THE COLLECTOR A PIECE OF MY MIND!
"YES, STAR-LORD..."
...GIVE ME A PIECE OF YOUR MIND--ALONG WITH THE CRYPTO-CUBE, THE MAP--
--AND EVENTUALLY... THE COSMIC SEED!
I AM GROOT!
THERE! ROCKET'S IN THERE!
KNOCK, KNOCK, COLLECTOR!
FROOOM!
FROOSH!
STAR-LORD'S HERE!
BOOM!

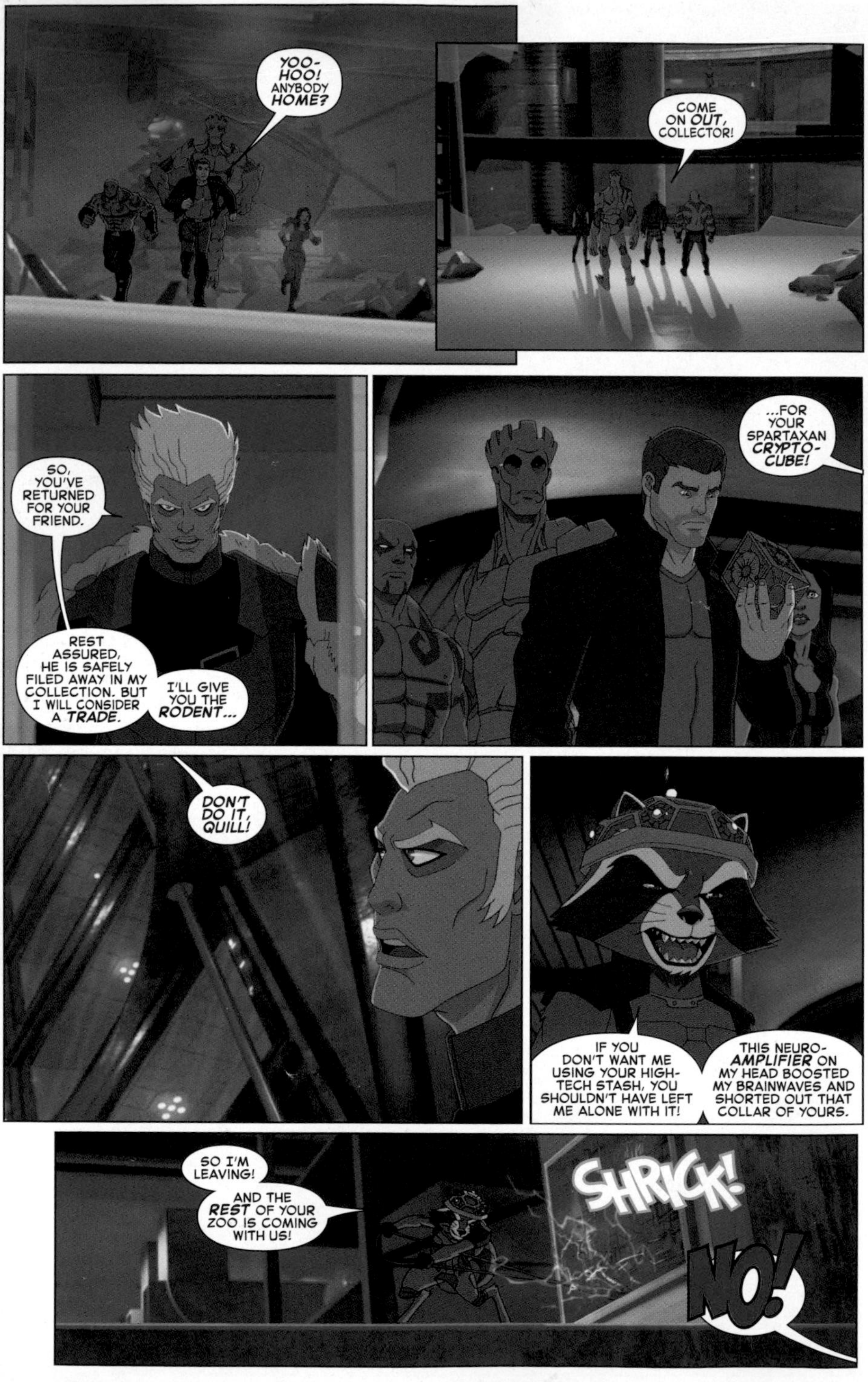
YOO-HOO! ANYBODY HOME?
COME ON OUT, COLLECTOR!
SO, YOU'VE RETURNED FOR YOUR FRIEND.
REST ASSURED, HE IS SAFELY FILED AWAY IN MY COLLECTION. BUT I WILL CONSIDER A TRADE.
I'LL GIVE YOU THE RODENT...
...FOR YOUR SPARTAXAN CRYPTO-CUBE!
DON'T DO IT, QUILL!
IF YOU DON'T WANT ME USING YOUR HIGH-TECH STASH, YOU SHOULDN'T HAVE LEFT ME ALONE WITH IT!
THIS NEURO-AMPLIFIER ON MY HEAD BOOSTED MY BRAINWAVES AND SHORTED OUT THAT COLLAR OF YOURS.
SO I'M LEAVING!
AND THE REST OF YOUR ZOO IS COMING WITH US!
SHRICK!
NO!

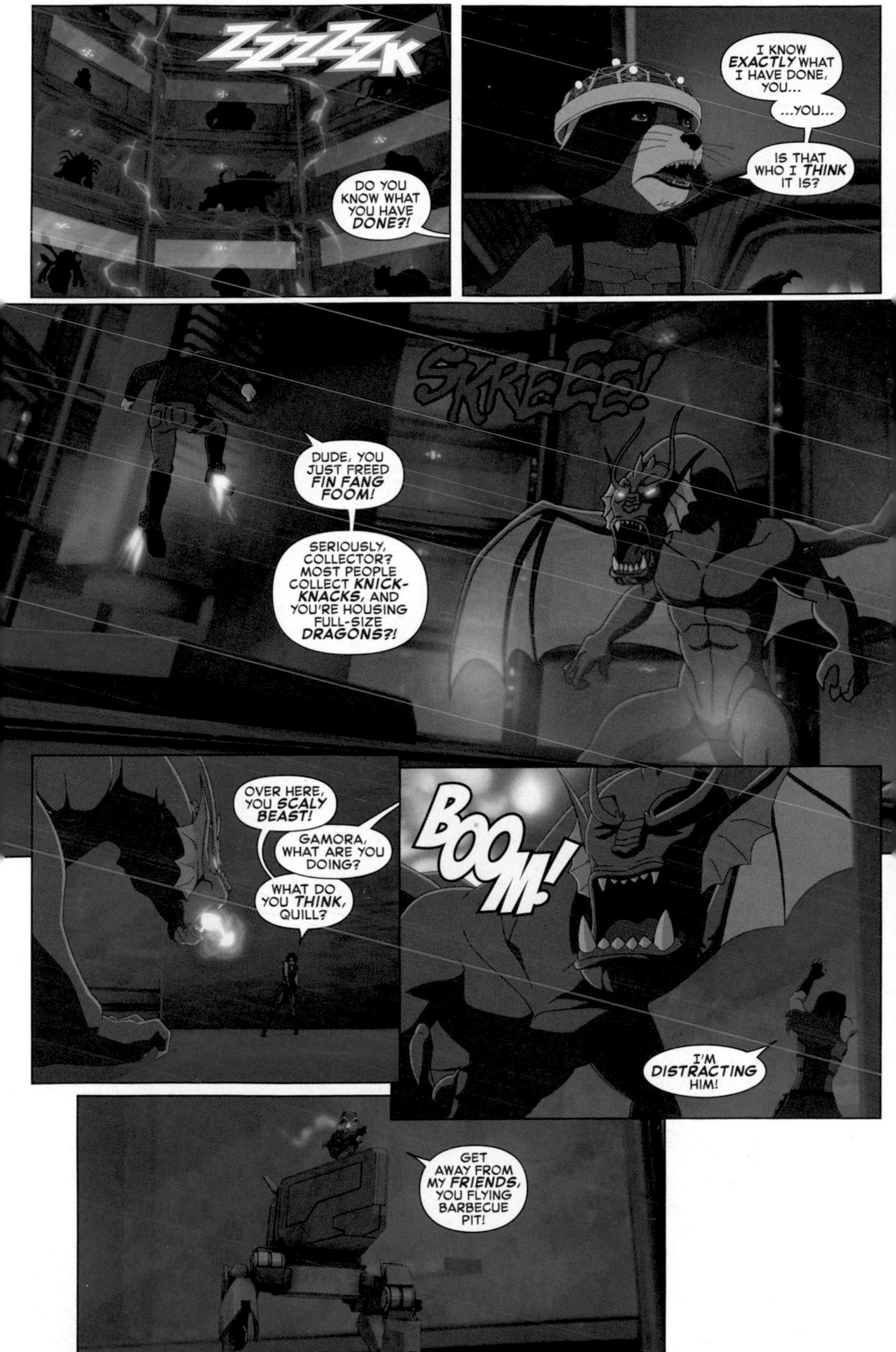
ZZZZZK
DO YOU KNOW WHAT YOU HAVE DONE?!
I KNOW EXACTLY WHAT I HAVE DONE, YOU...
...YOU...
IS THAT WHO I THINK IT IS?
SKREEE!
DUDE, YOU JUST FREED FIN FANG FOOM!
SERIOUSLY, COLLECTOR? MOST PEOPLE COLLECT KNICK-KNACKS, AND YOU'RE HOUSING FULL-SIZE DRAGONS?!
OVER HERE, YOU SCALY BEAST!
GAMORA, WHAT ARE YOU DOING?
WHAT DO YOU THINK, QUILL?
BOOM!
I'M DISTRACTING HIM!
GET AWAY FROM MY FRIENDS, YOU FLYING BARBECUE PIT!

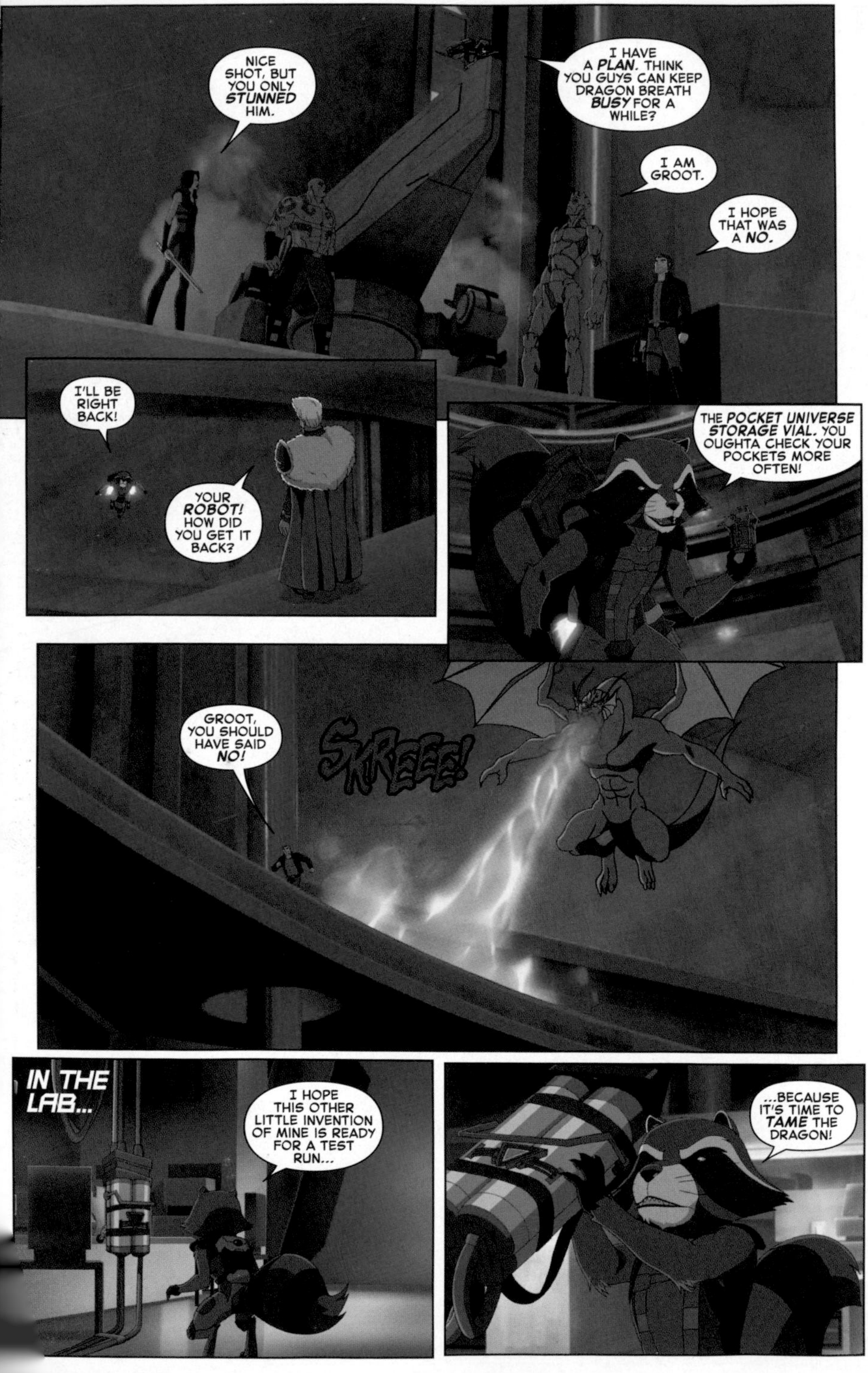
NICE SHOT, BUT YOU ONLY STUNNED HIM.
I HAVE A PLAN. THINK YOU GUYS CAN KEEP DRAGON BREATH BUSY FOR A WHILE?
I AM GROOT.
I HOPE THAT WAS A NO.
I'LL BE RIGHT BACK!
YOUR ROBOT! HOW DID YOU GET IT BACK?
THE POCKET UNIVERSE STORAGE VIAL. YOU OUGHTA CHECK YOUR POCKETS MORE OFTEN!
GROOT, YOU SHOULD HAVE SAID NO!
SKREEE!
IN THE LAB...
I HOPE THIS OTHER LITTLE INVENTION OF MINE IS READY FOR A TEST RUN...
...BECAUSE IT'S TIME TO TAME THE DRAGON!

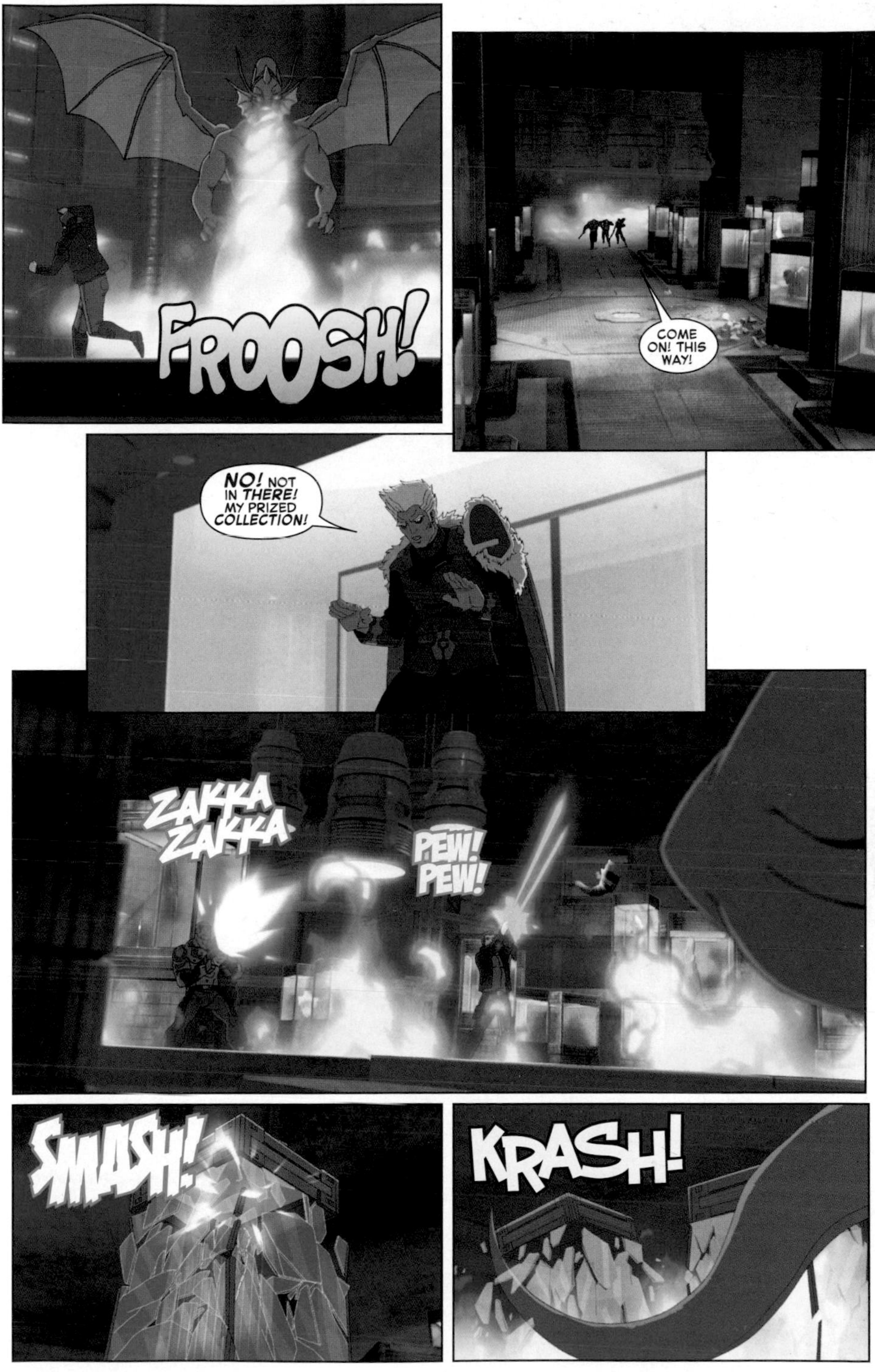
FROOSH!
COME ON! THIS WAY!
NO! NOT IN THERE! MY PRIZED COLLECTION!
ZAKKA ZAKKA
PEW! PEW!
SMASH!
KRASH!

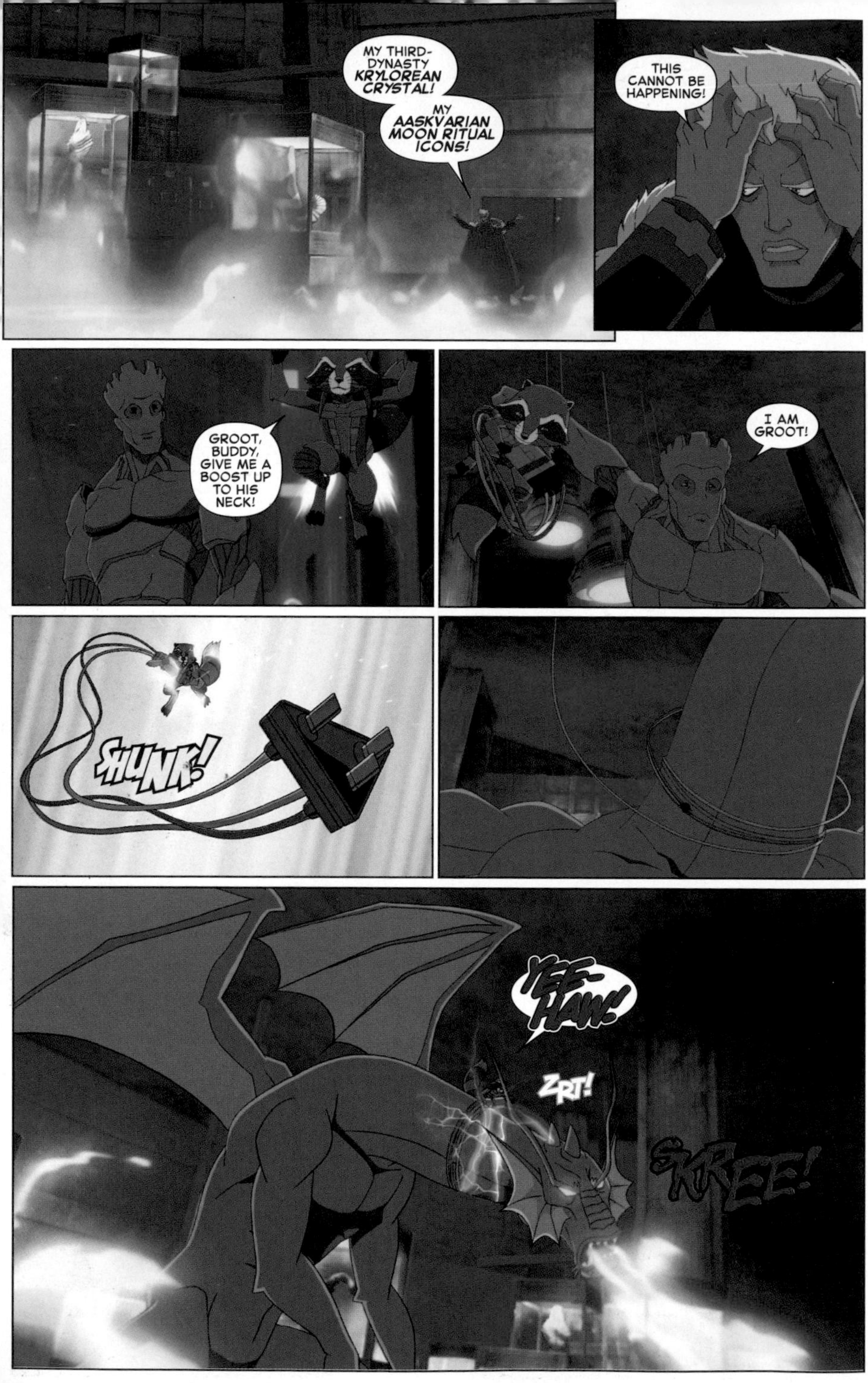
MY THIRD-DYNASTY KRYLOREAN CRYSTAL!
MY AASKVARIAN MOON RITUAL ICONS!
THIS CANNOT BE HAPPENING!
GROOT, BUDDY, GIVE ME A BOOST UP TO HIS NECK!
I AM GROOT!
SHUNK!
YEE-HAW!
ZRRT!
SKREE!

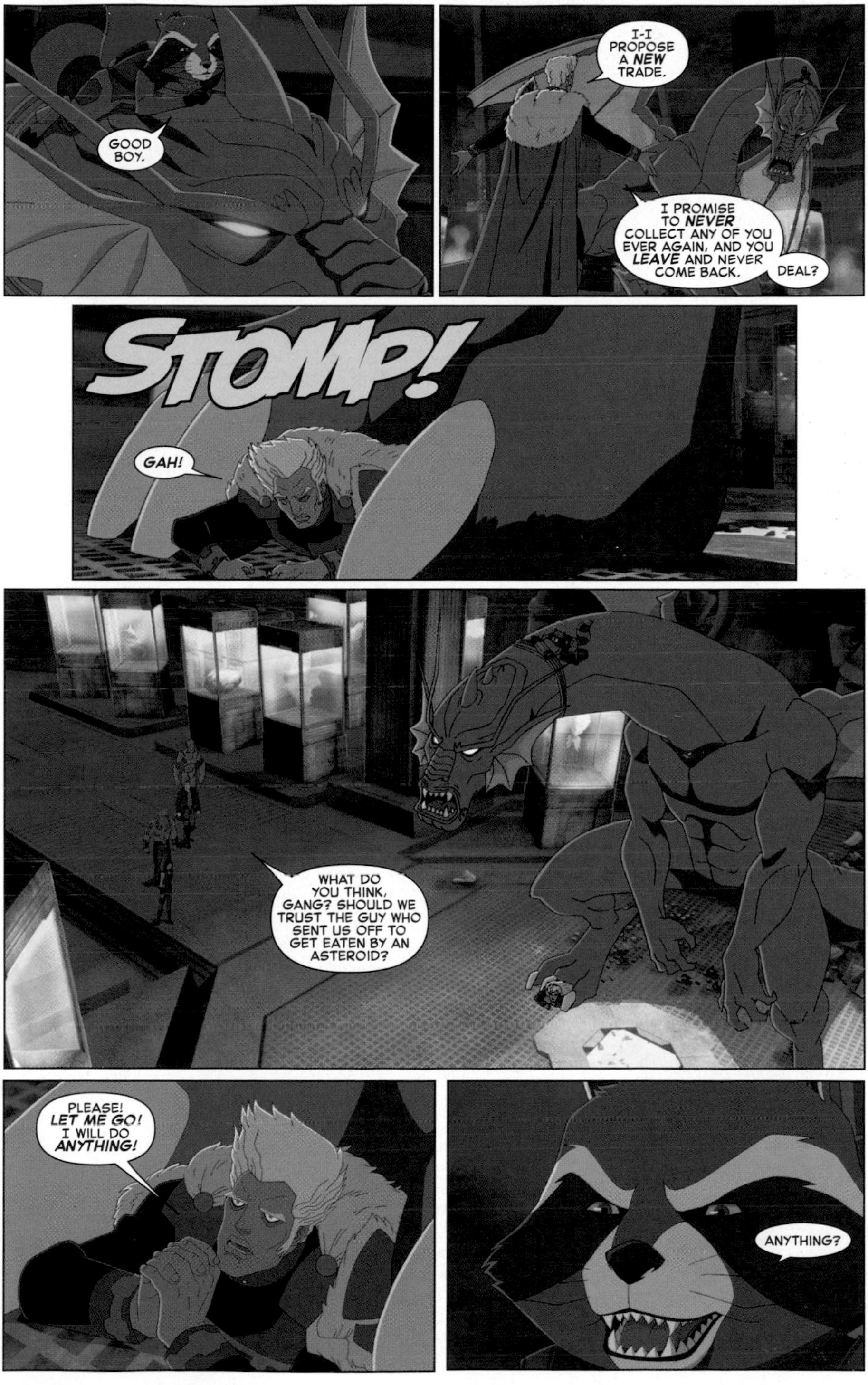
GOOD BOY.
I-I PROPOSE A NEW TRADE.
I PROMISE TO NEVER COLLECT ANY OF YOU EVER AGAIN, AND YOU LEAVE AND NEVER COME BACK.
DEAL?
STOMP!
GAH!
WHAT DO YOU THINK, GANG? SHOULD WE TRUST THE GUY WHO SENT US OFF TO GET EATEN BY AN ASTEROID?
PLEASE! LET ME GO! I WILL DO ANYTHING!
ANYTHING?

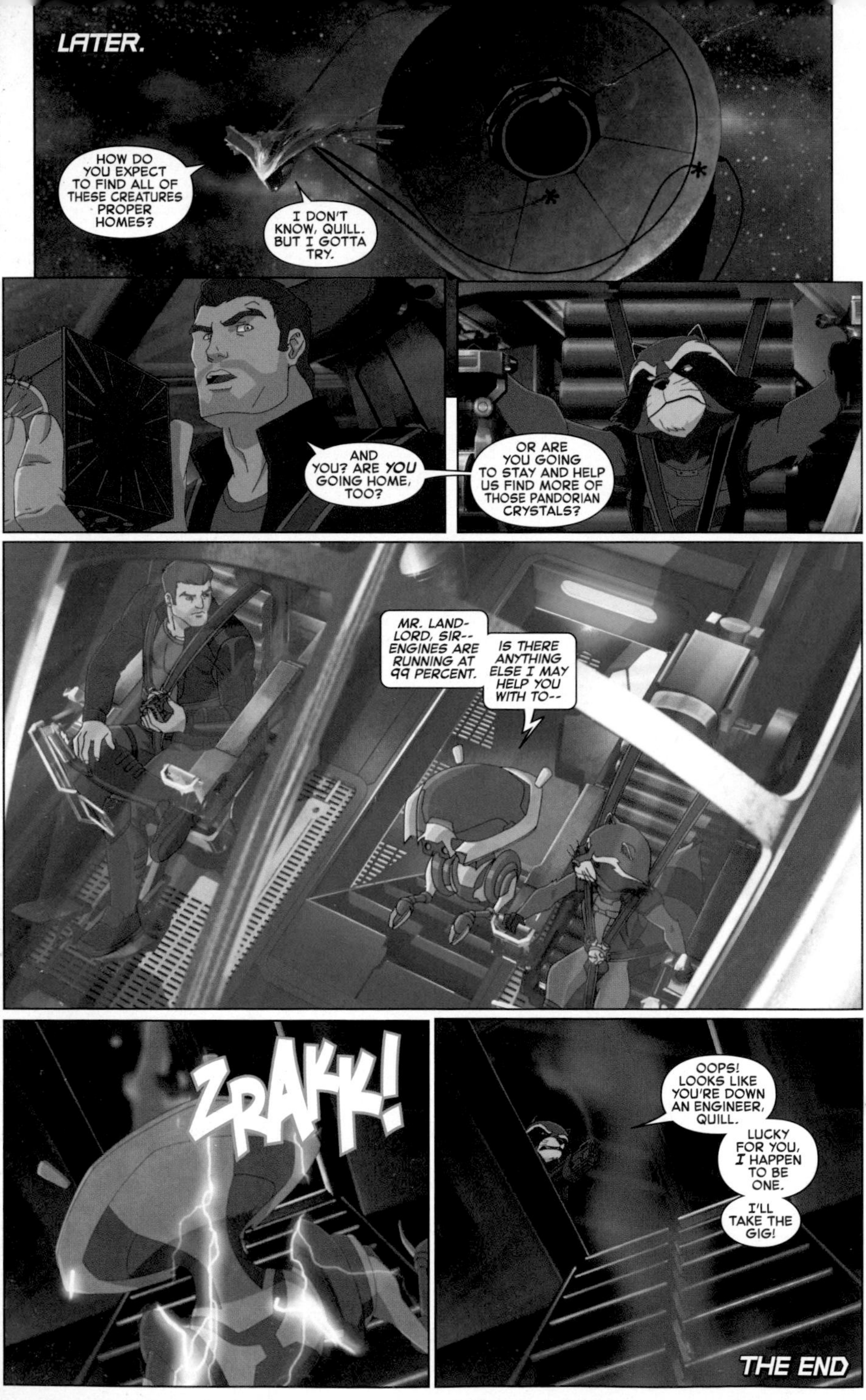
LATER.
HOW DO YOU EXPECT TO FIND ALL OF THESE CREATURES PROPER HOMES?
I DON'T KNOW, QUILL. BUT I GOTTA TRY.
AND YOU? ARE YOU GOING HOME, TOO?
OR ARE YOU GOING TO STAY AND HELP US FIND MORE OF THOSE PANDORIAN CRYSTALS?
MR. LAND-LORD, SIR-- ENGINES ARE RUNNING AT 99 PERCENT.
IS THERE ANYTHING ELSE I MAY HELP YOU WITH TO--
ZRAKK!
OOPS! LOOKS LIKE YOU'RE DOWN AN ENGINEER, QUILL.
LUCKY FOR YOU, I HAPPEN TO BE ONE.
I'LL TAKE THE GIG!
THE END

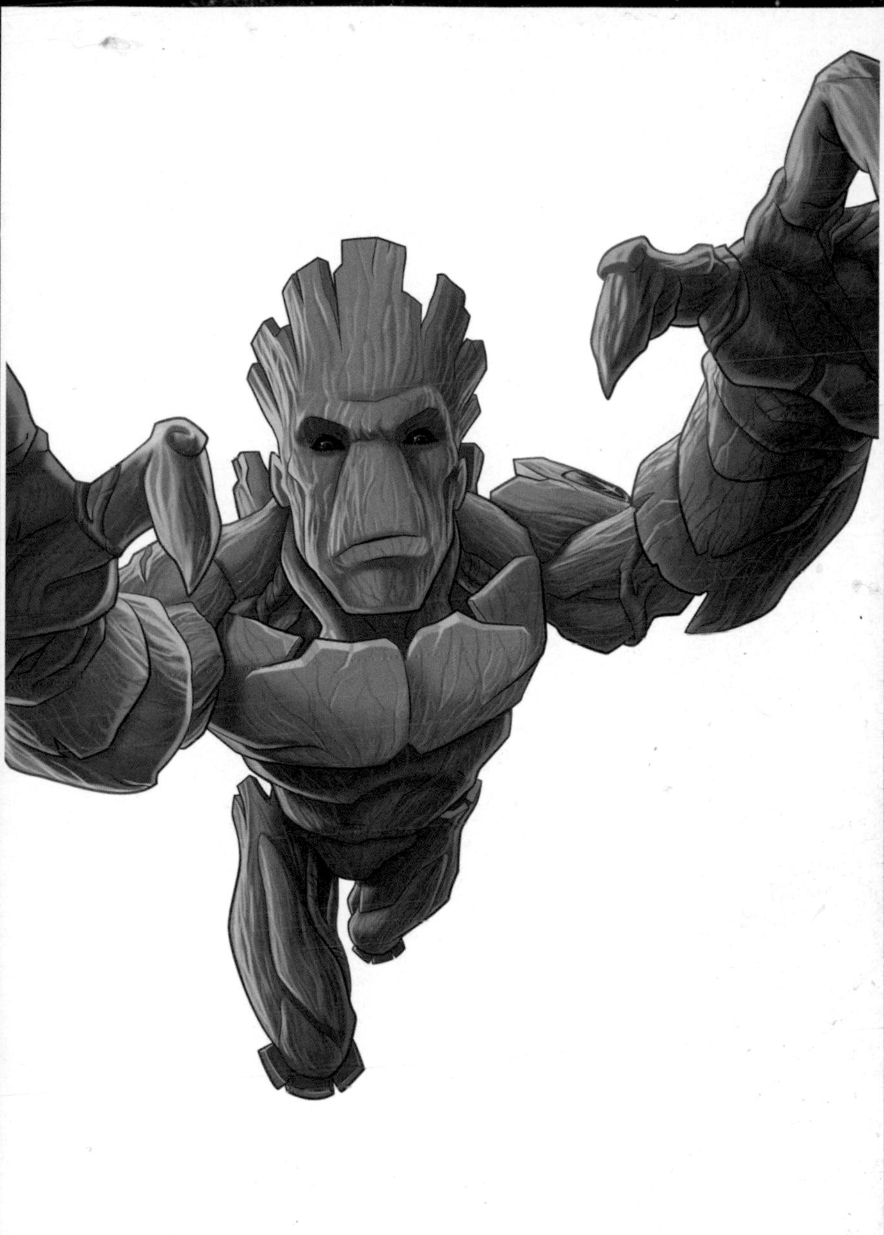

BASED ON **"CAN'T FIGHT THIS SEEDLING"** **5**

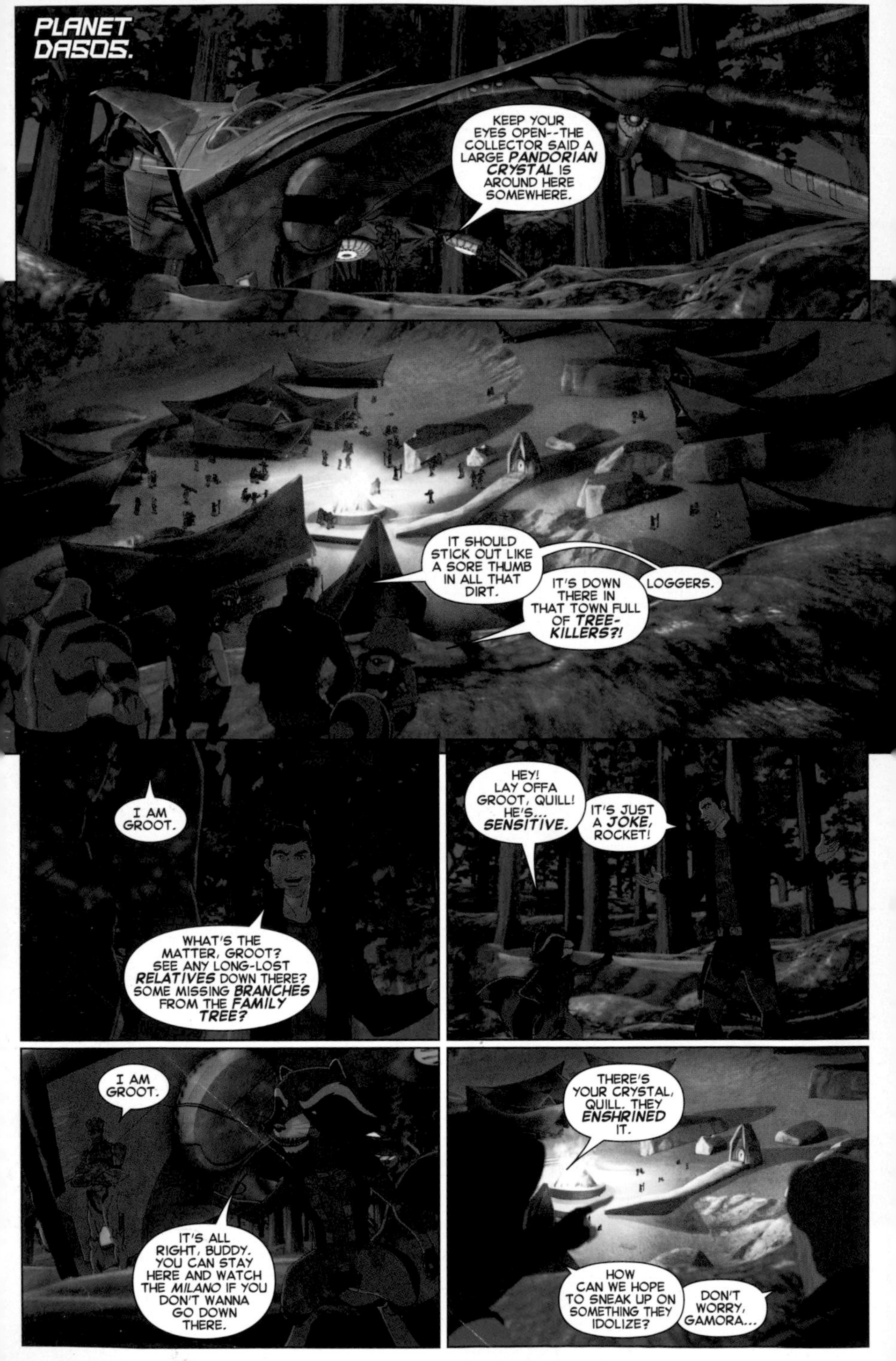
PLANET DASOS.
KEEP YOUR EYES OPEN--THE COLLECTOR SAID A LARGE PANDORIAN CRYSTAL IS AROUND HERE SOMEWHERE.
IT SHOULD STICK OUT LIKE A SORE THUMB IN ALL THAT DIRT.
IT'S DOWN THERE IN THAT TOWN FULL OF TREE-KILLERS?!
LOGGERS.
I AM GROOT.
WHAT'S THE MATTER, GROOT? SEE ANY LONG-LOST RELATIVES DOWN THERE? SOME MISSING BRANCHES FROM THE FAMILY TREE?
HEY! LAY OFFA GROOT, QUILL! HE'S... SENSITIVE.
IT'S JUST A JOKE, ROCKET!
I AM GROOT.
IT'S ALL RIGHT, BUDDY. YOU CAN STAY HERE AND WATCH THE MILANO IF YOU DON'T WANNA GO DOWN THERE.
THERE'S YOUR CRYSTAL, QUILL. THEY ENSHRINED IT.
HOW CAN WE HOPE TO SNEAK UP ON SOMETHING THEY IDOLIZE?
DON'T WORRY, GAMORA...

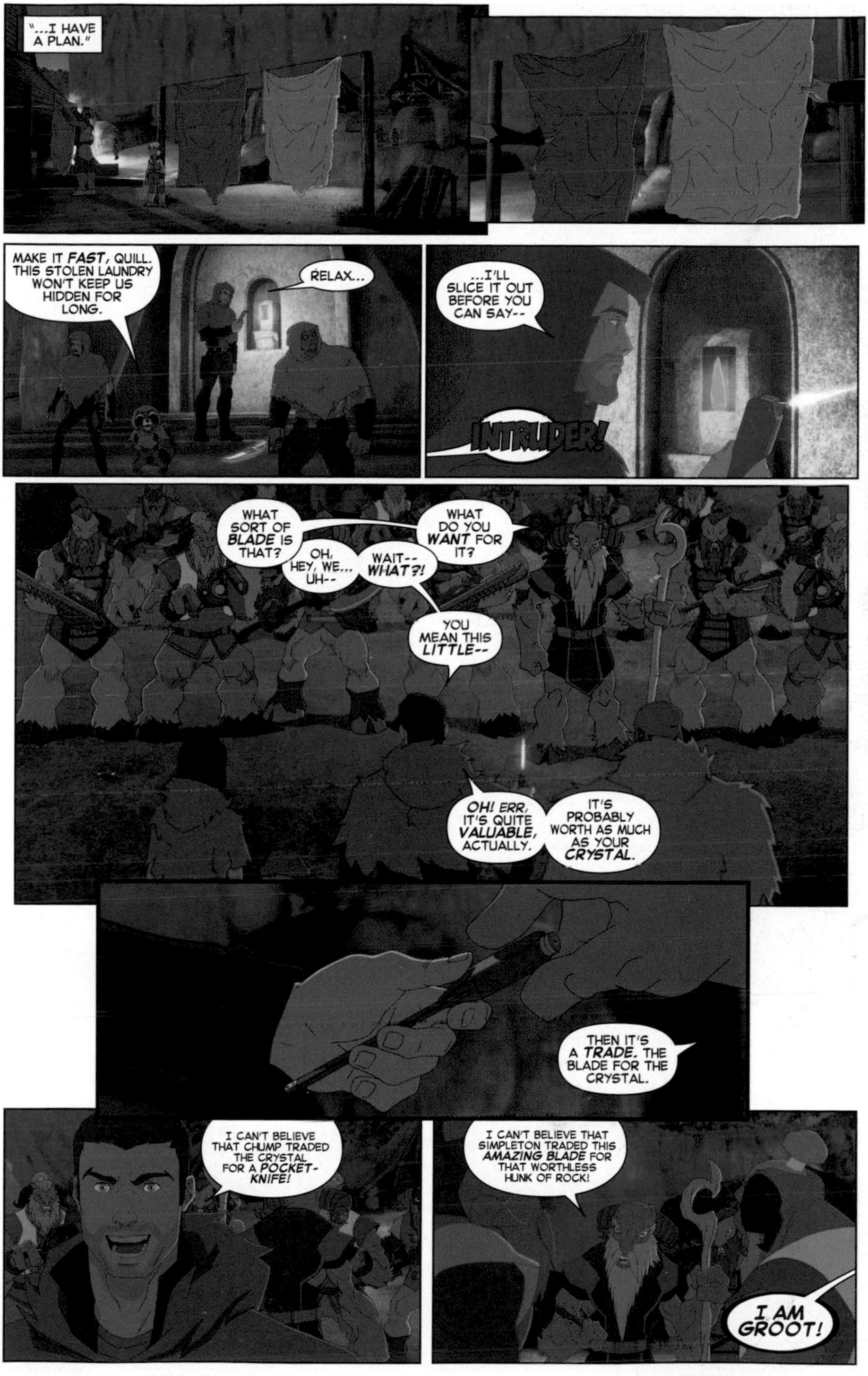
"...I HAVE A PLAN."
MAKE IT FAST, QUILL. THIS STOLEN LAUNDRY WON'T KEEP US HIDDEN FOR LONG.
RELAX...
...I'LL SLICE IT OUT BEFORE YOU CAN SAY--
INTRUDER!
WHAT SORT OF BLADE IS THAT?
OH, HEY, WE... UH--
WAIT-- WHAT?!
WHAT DO YOU WANT FOR IT?
YOU MEAN THIS LITTLE--
OH! ERR, IT'S QUITE VALUABLE, ACTUALLY.
IT'S PROBABLY WORTH AS MUCH AS YOUR CRYSTAL.
THEN IT'S A TRADE. THE BLADE FOR THE CRYSTAL.
I CAN'T BELIEVE THAT CHUMP TRADED THE CRYSTAL FOR A POCKET-KNIFE!
I CAN'T BELIEVE THAT SIMPLETON TRADED THIS AMAZING BLADE FOR THAT WORTHLESS HUNK OF ROCK!
I AM GROOT!

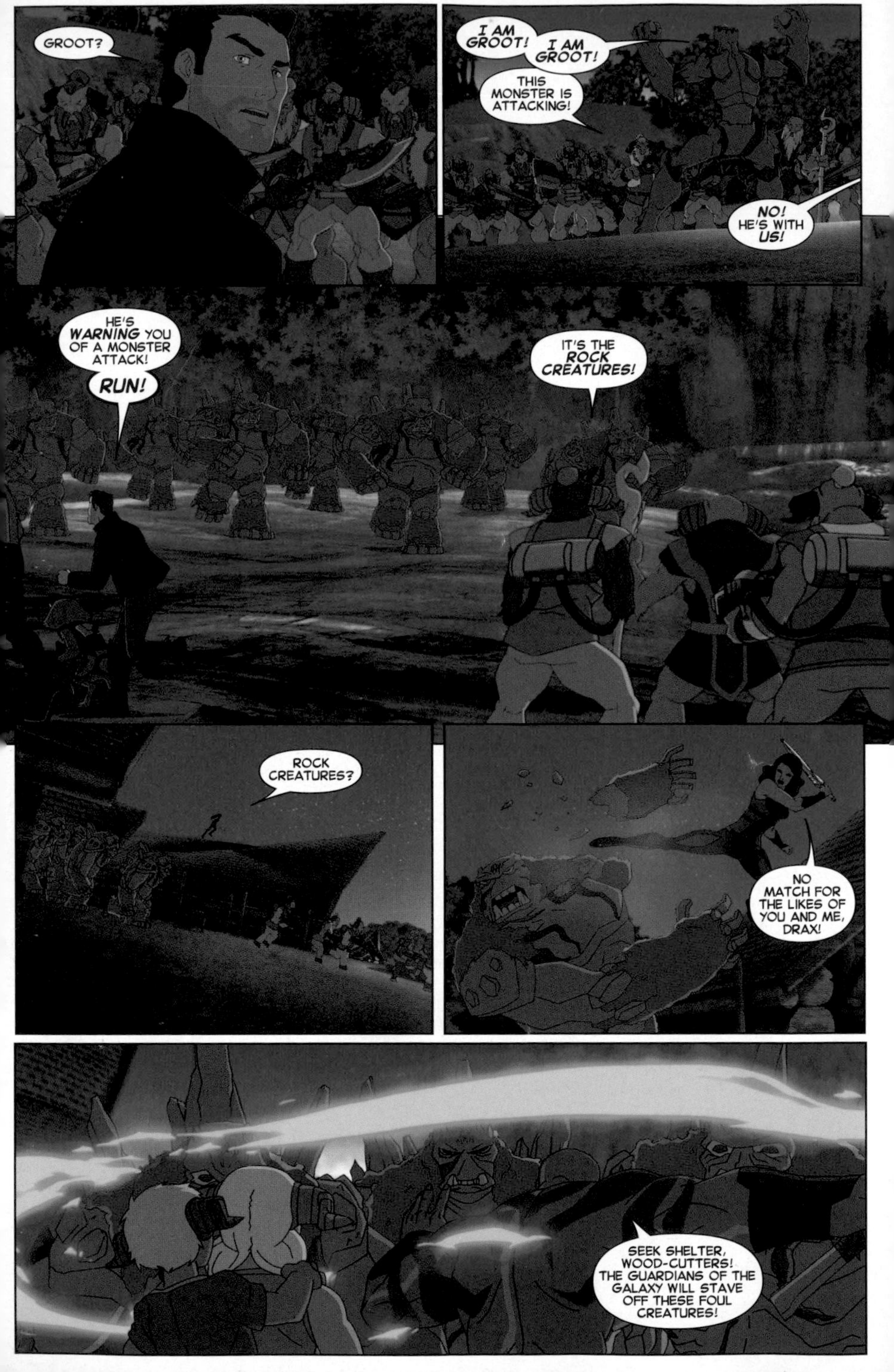
GROOT?
I AM GROOT!
I AM GROOT!
THIS MONSTER IS ATTACKING!
NO! HE'S WITH US!
HE'S WARNING YOU OF A MONSTER ATTACK!
RUN!
IT'S THE ROCK CREATURES!
ROCK CREATURES?
NO MATCH FOR THE LIKES OF YOU AND ME, DRAX!
SEEK SHELTER, WOOD-CUTTERS! THE GUARDIANS OF THE GALAXY WILL STAVE OFF THESE FOUL CREATURES!

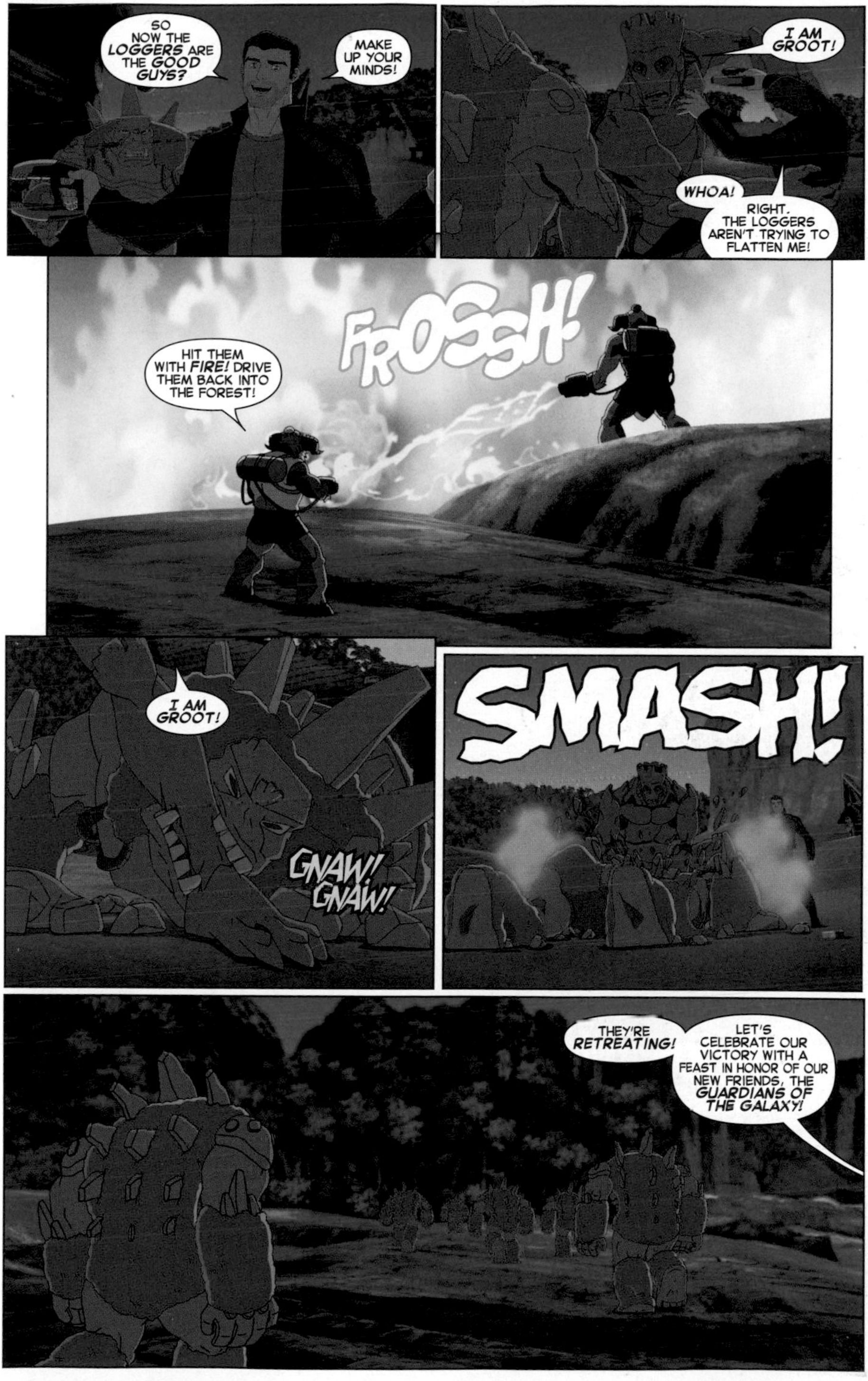

SO NOW THE LOGGERS ARE THE GOOD GUYS?
MAKE UP YOUR MINDS!
I AM GROOT!
WHOA!
RIGHT. THE LOGGERS AREN'T TRYING TO FLATTEN ME!
FROSSH!
HIT THEM WITH FIRE! DRIVE THEM BACK INTO THE FOREST!
I AM GROOT!
GNAW! GNAW!
SMASH!
THEY'RE RETREATING!
LET'S CELEBRATE OUR VICTORY WITH A FEAST IN HONOR OF OUR NEW FRIENDS, THE GUARDIANS OF THE GALAXY!

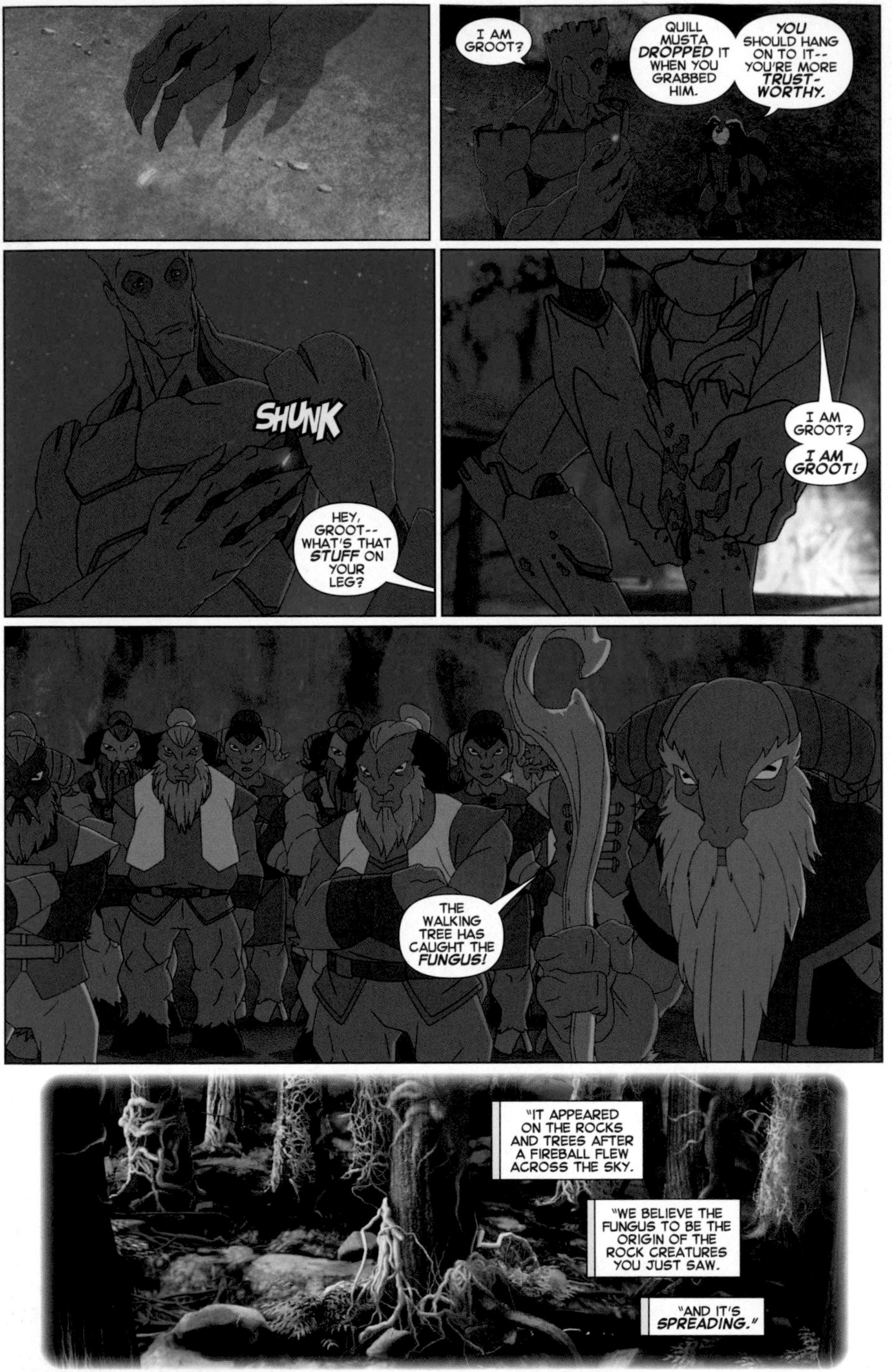
I AM GROOT?
QUILL MUSTA DROPPED IT WHEN YOU GRABBED HIM.
YOU SHOULD HANG ON TO IT--YOU'RE MORE TRUST-WORTHY.
SHUNK
HEY, GROOT--WHAT'S THAT STUFF ON YOUR LEG?
I AM GROOT?
I AM GROOT!
THE WALKING TREE HAS CAUGHT THE FUNGUS!
"IT APPEARED ON THE ROCKS AND TREES AFTER A FIREBALL FLEW ACROSS THE SKY.
"WE BELIEVE THE FUNGUS TO BE THE ORIGIN OF THE ROCK CREATURES YOU JUST SAW.
"AND IT'S SPREADING."

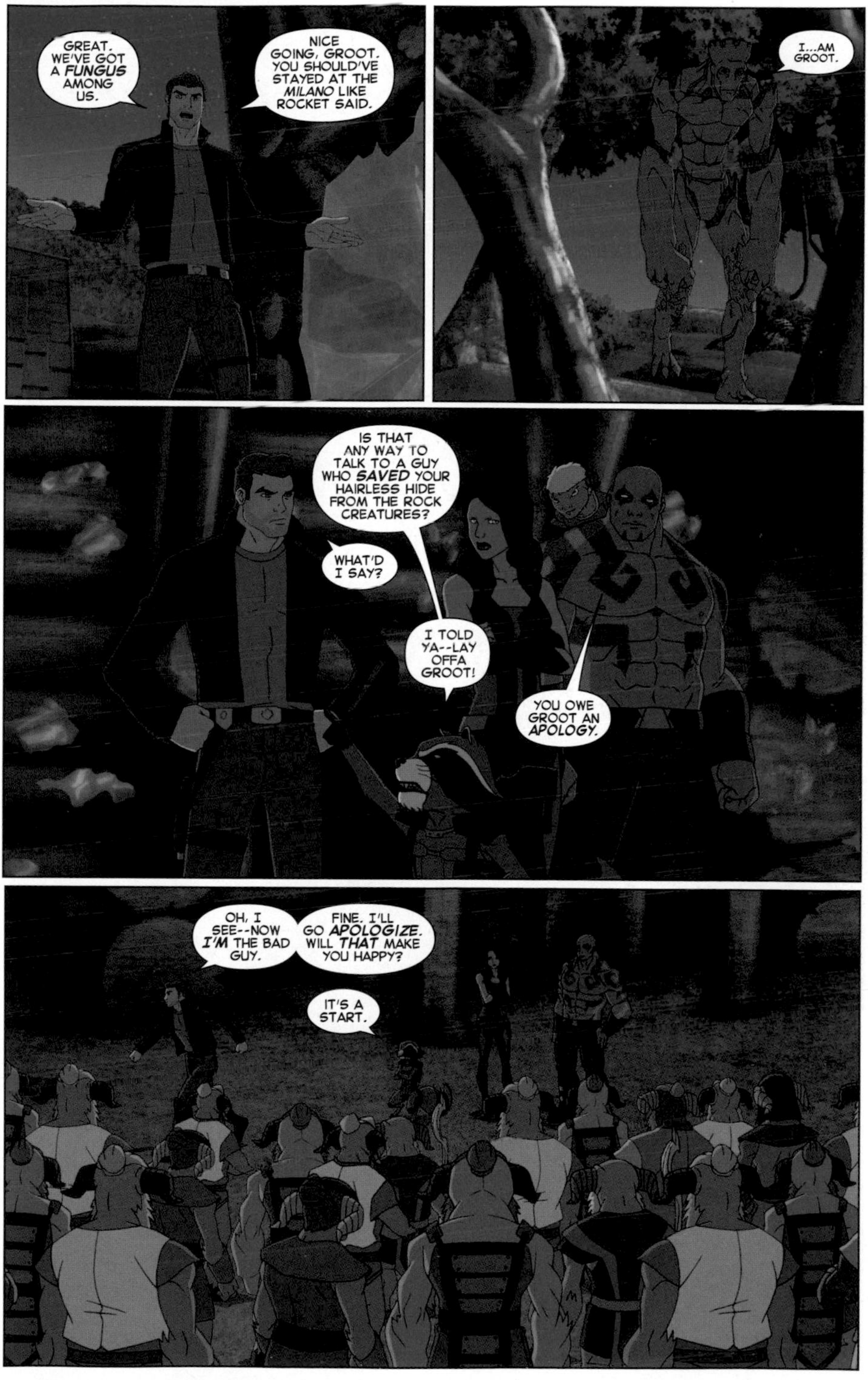
GREAT. WE'VE GOT A *FUNGUS* AMONG US.
NICE GOING, GROOT. YOU SHOULD'VE STAYED AT THE *MILANO* LIKE ROCKET SAID.
I...AM GROOT.
IS THAT ANY WAY TO TALK TO A GUY WHO ***SAVED*** YOUR HAIRLESS HIDE FROM THE ROCK CREATURES?
WHAT'D I SAY?
I TOLD YA--LAY OFFA GROOT!
YOU OWE GROOT AN *APOLOGY.*
OH, I SEE--NOW ***I'M*** THE BAD GUY.
FINE. I'LL GO *APOLOGIZE.* WILL ***THAT*** MAKE YOU HAPPY?
IT'S A START.

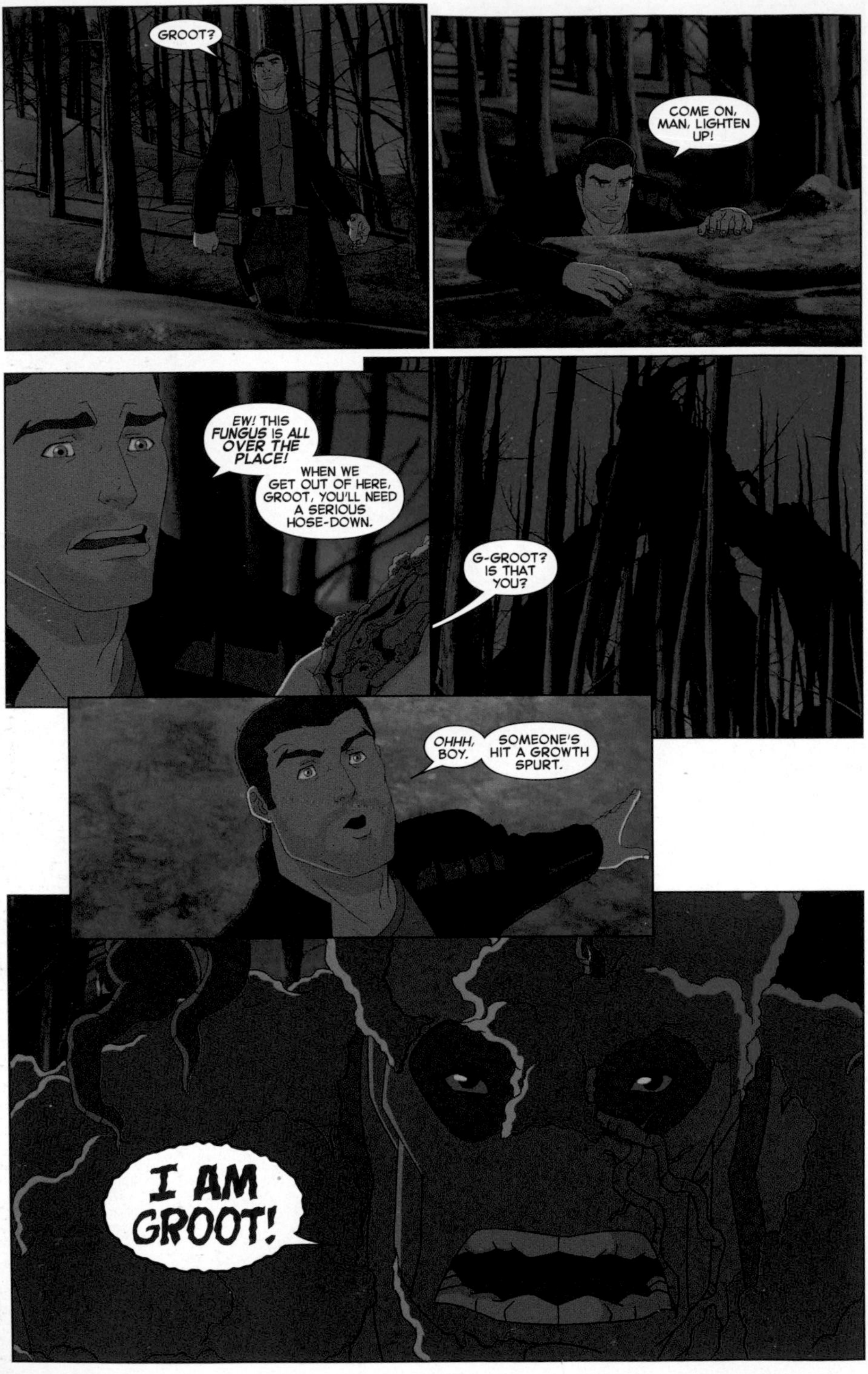
GROOT?
COME ON, MAN, LIGHTEN UP!
EW! THIS FUNGUS IS ALL OVER THE PLACE!
WHEN WE GET OUT OF HERE, GROOT, YOU'LL NEED A SERIOUS HOSE-DOWN.
G-GROOT? IS THAT YOU?
OHHH, BOY.
SOMEONE'S HIT A GROWTH SPURT.
I AM GROOT!

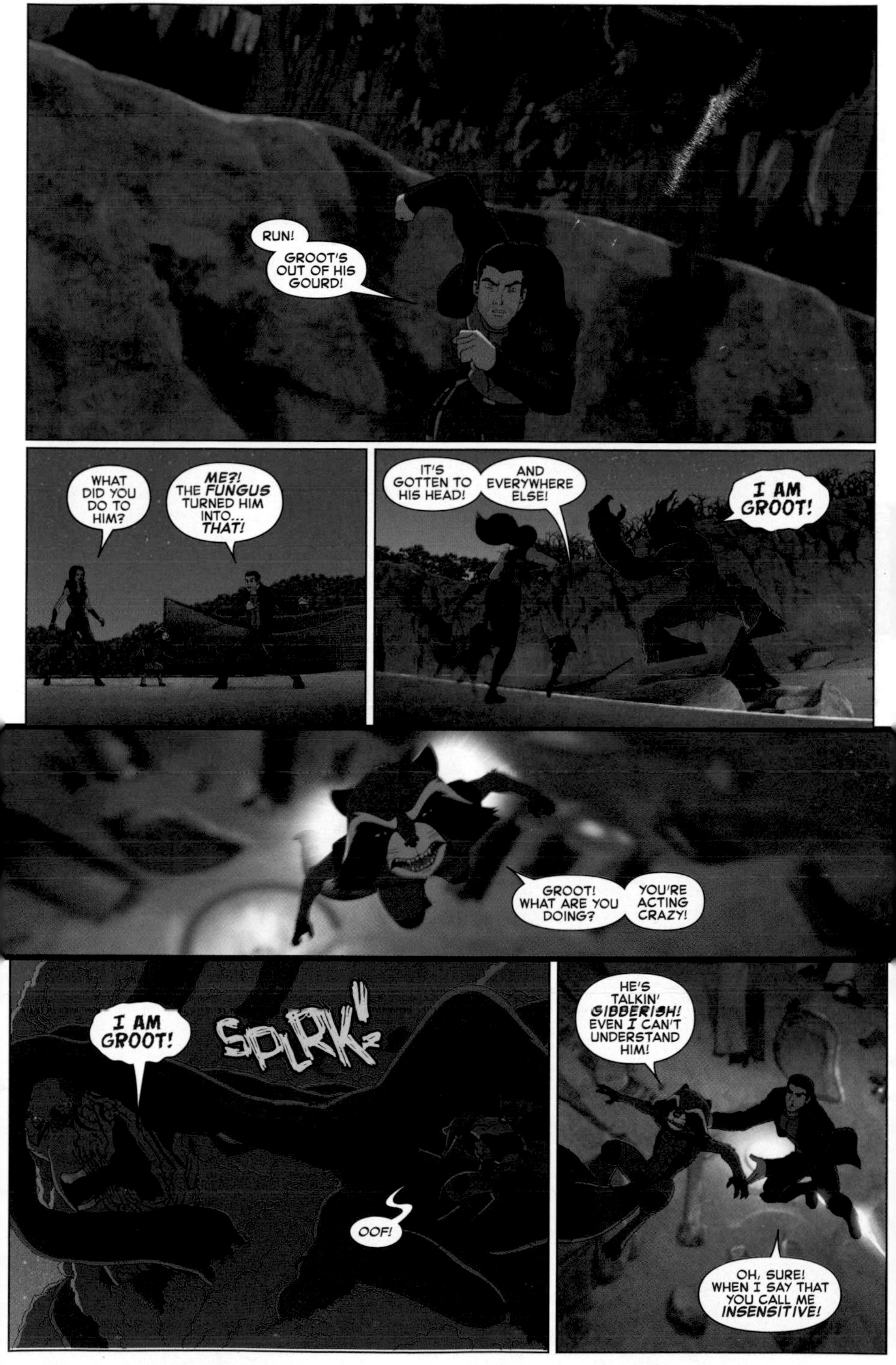
RUN!
GROOT'S OUT OF HIS GOURD!
WHAT DID YOU DO TO HIM?
ME?! THE FUNGUS TURNED HIM INTO... THAT!
IT'S GOTTEN TO HIS HEAD!
AND EVERYWHERE ELSE!
I AM GROOT!
GROOT! WHAT ARE YOU DOING?
YOU'RE ACTING CRAZY!
I AM GROOT!
SPLRK!
OOF!
HE'S TALKIN' GIBBERISH! EVEN I CAN'T UNDERSTAND HIM!
OH, SURE! WHEN I SAY THAT YOU CALL ME INSENSITIVE!

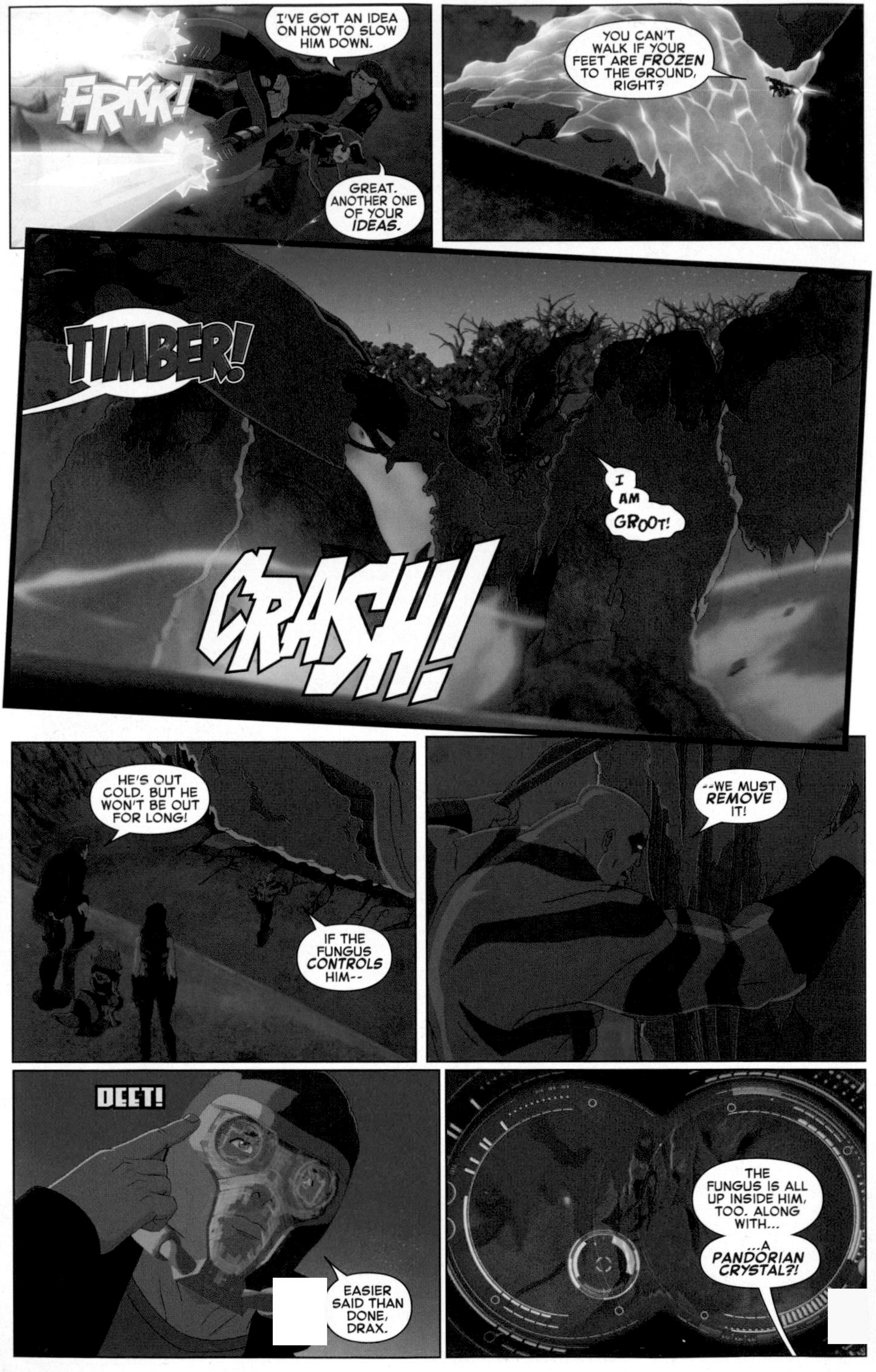

FRKK!
I'VE GOT AN IDEA ON HOW TO SLOW HIM DOWN.
GREAT. ANOTHER ONE OF YOUR IDEAS.
YOU CAN'T WALK IF YOUR FEET ARE FROZEN TO THE GROUND, RIGHT?
TIMBER!
I AM GROOT!
CRASH!
HE'S OUT COLD. BUT HE WON'T BE OUT FOR LONG!
IF THE FUNGUS CONTROLS HIM--
--WE MUST REMOVE IT!
DEET!
EASIER SAID THAN DONE, DRAX.
THE FUNGUS IS ALL UP INSIDE HIM, TOO. ALONG WITH...
...A PANDORIAN CRYSTAL?!

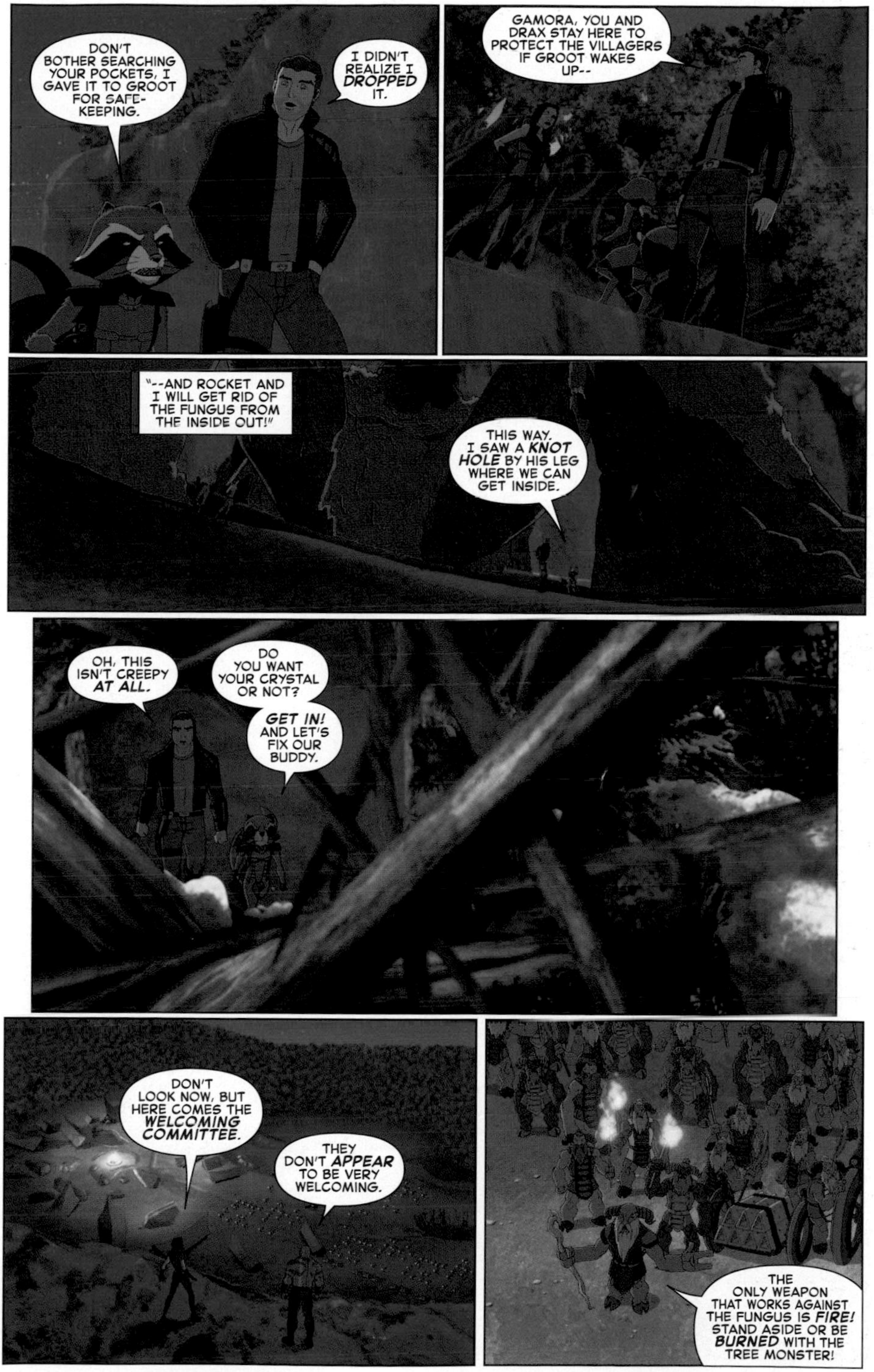
DON'T BOTHER SEARCHING YOUR POCKETS, I GAVE IT TO GROOT FOR SAFE-KEEPING.
I DIDN'T REALIZE I DROPPED IT.
GAMORA, YOU AND DRAX STAY HERE TO PROTECT THE VILLAGERS IF GROOT WAKES UP--
"--AND ROCKET AND I WILL GET RID OF THE FUNGUS FROM THE INSIDE OUT!"
THIS WAY. I SAW A KNOT HOLE BY HIS LEG WHERE WE CAN GET INSIDE.
OH, THIS ISN'T CREEPY AT ALL.
DO YOU WANT YOUR CRYSTAL OR NOT?
GET IN! AND LET'S FIX OUR BUDDY.
DON'T LOOK NOW, BUT HERE COMES THE WELCOMING COMMITTEE.
THEY DON'T APPEAR TO BE VERY WELCOMING.
THE ONLY WEAPON THAT WORKS AGAINST THE FUNGUS IS FIRE! STAND ASIDE OR BE BURNED WITH THE TREE MONSTER!

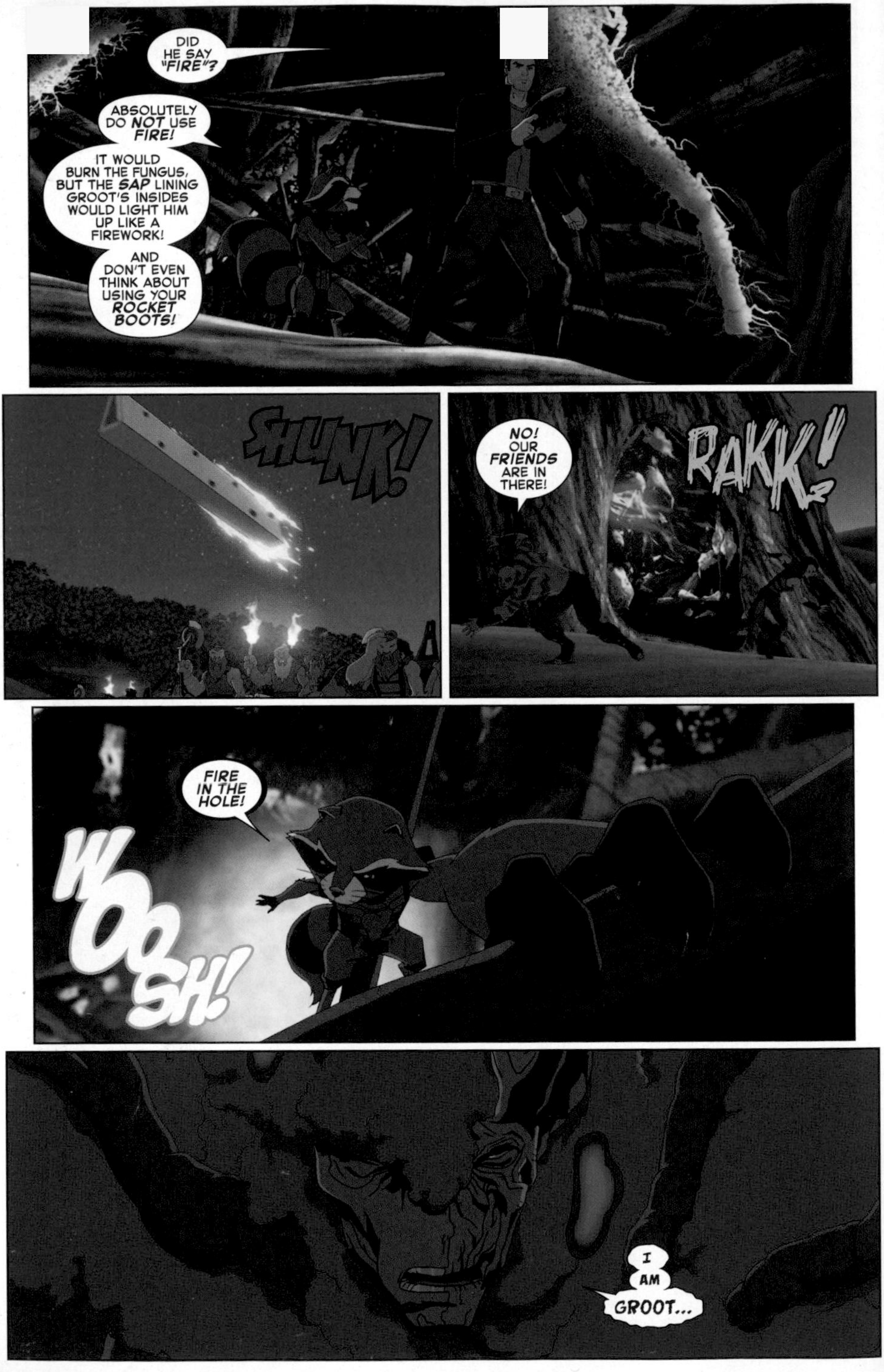

DID HE SAY "FIRE"?
ABSOLUTELY DO NOT USE FIRE!
IT WOULD BURN THE FUNGUS, BUT THE SAP LINING GROOT'S INSIDES WOULD LIGHT HIM UP LIKE A FIREWORK!
AND DON'T EVEN THINK ABOUT USING YOUR ROCKET BOOTS!
SHUNK!
NO! OUR FRIENDS ARE IN THERE!
RAKK!
FIRE IN THE HOLE!
WOOOSH!
I AM GROOT...

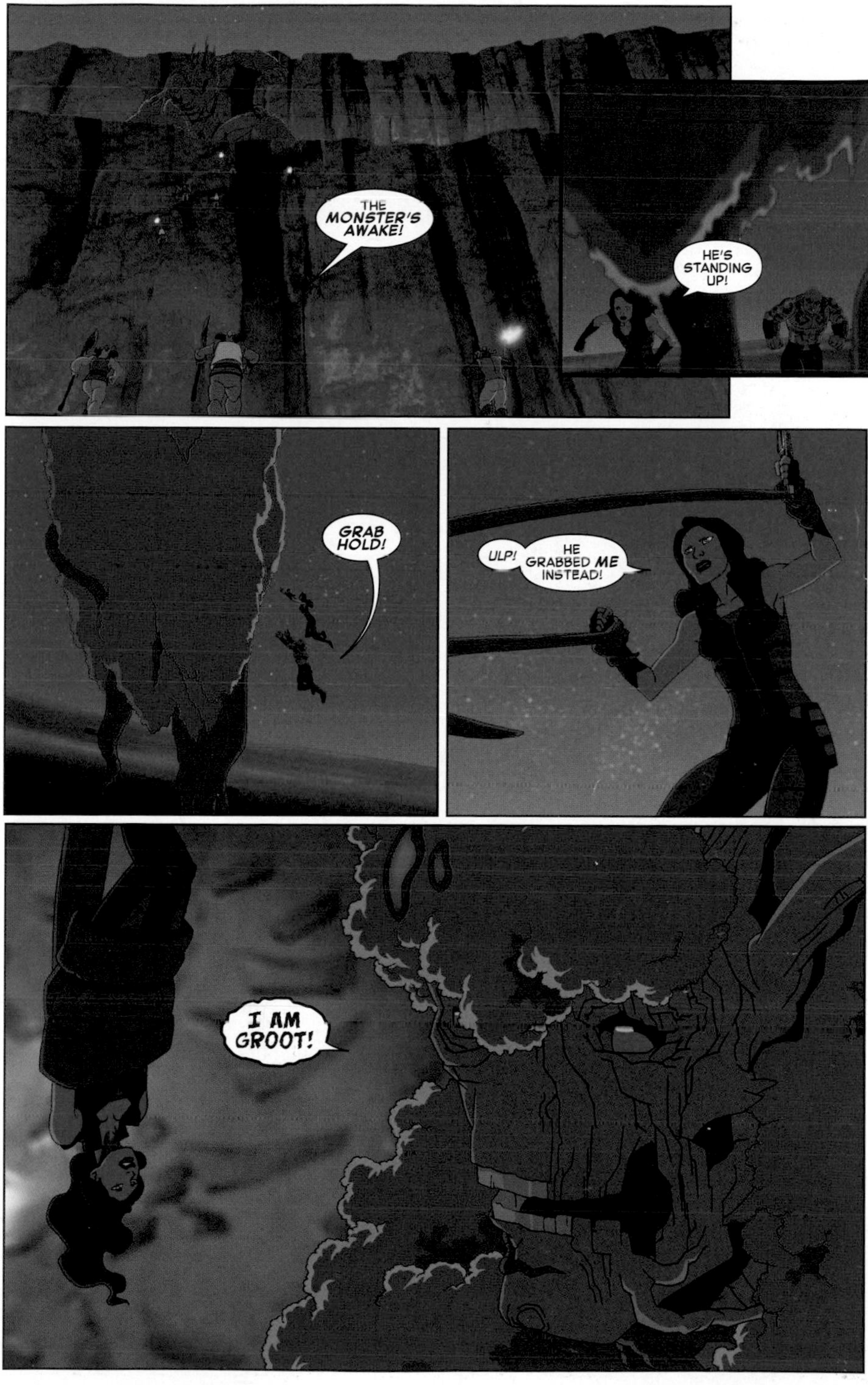
THE MONSTER'S AWAKE!
HE'S STANDING UP!
GRAB HOLD!
ULP!
HE GRABBED ME INSTEAD!
I AM GROOT!

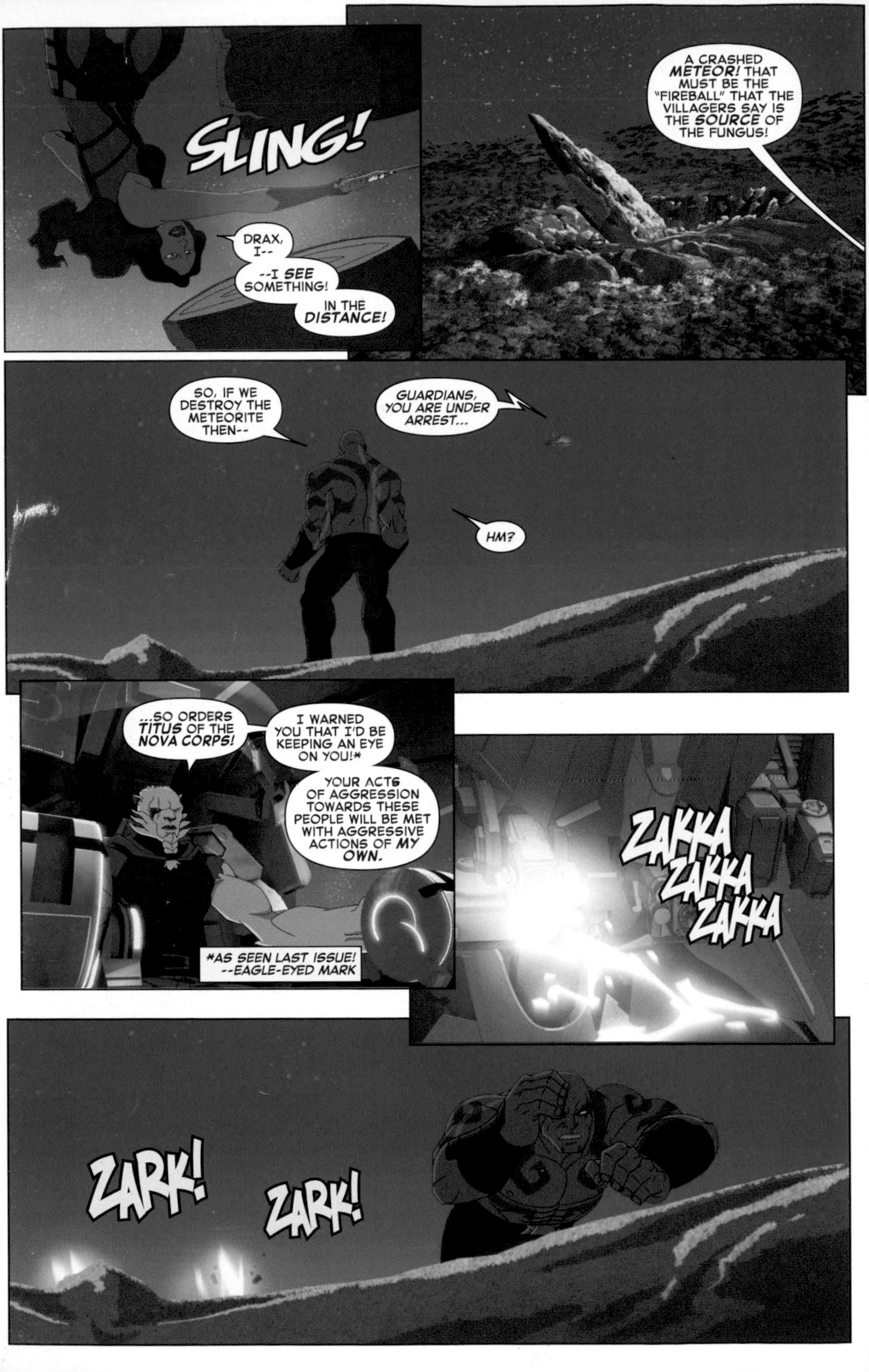
SLING!
DRAX, I--
--I SEE SOMETHING!
IN THE DISTANCE!
A CRASHED METEOR! THAT MUST BE THE "FIREBALL" THAT THE VILLAGERS SAY IS THE SOURCE OF THE FUNGUS!
SO, IF WE DESTROY THE METEORITE THEN--
GUARDIANS, YOU ARE UNDER ARREST...
HM?
...SO ORDERS TITUS OF THE NOVA CORPS!
I WARNED YOU THAT I'D BE KEEPING AN EYE ON YOU!*
YOUR ACTS OF AGGRESSION TOWARDS THESE PEOPLE WILL BE MET WITH AGGRESSIVE ACTIONS OF MY OWN.
*AS SEEN LAST ISSUE! --EAGLE-EYED MARK
ZAKKA ZAKKA ZAKKA
ZARK!
ZARK!

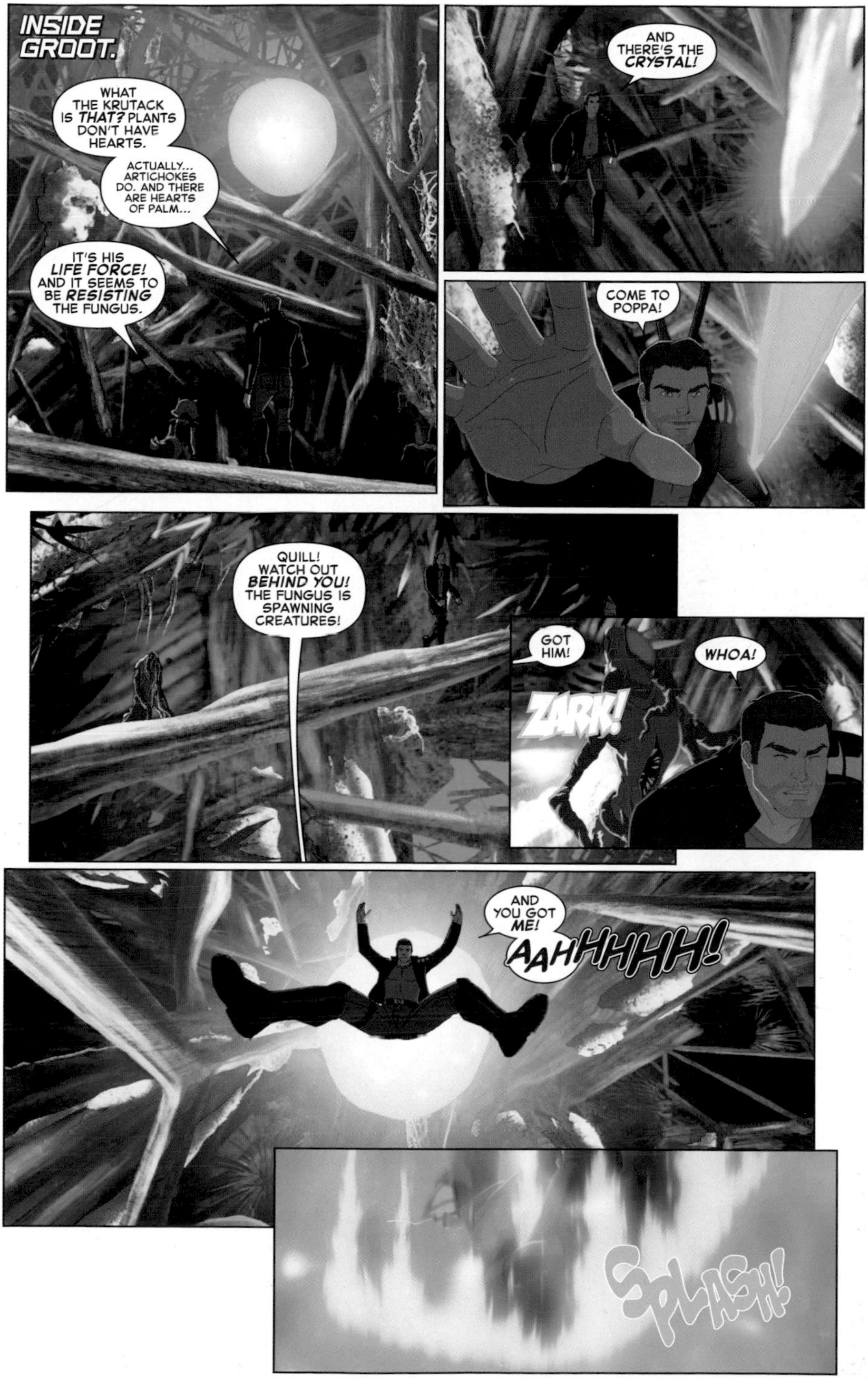
INSIDE GROOT.
WHAT THE KRUTACK IS THAT? PLANTS DON'T HAVE HEARTS.
ACTUALLY... ARTICHOKES DO. AND THERE ARE HEARTS OF PALM...
IT'S HIS LIFE FORCE! AND IT SEEMS TO BE RESISTING THE FUNGUS.
AND THERE'S THE CRYSTAL!
COME TO POPPA!
QUILL! WATCH OUT BEHIND YOU! THE FUNGUS IS SPAWNING CREATURES!
GOT HIM!
ZARK!
WHOA!
AND YOU GOT ME!
AAHHHHH!
SPLASH!

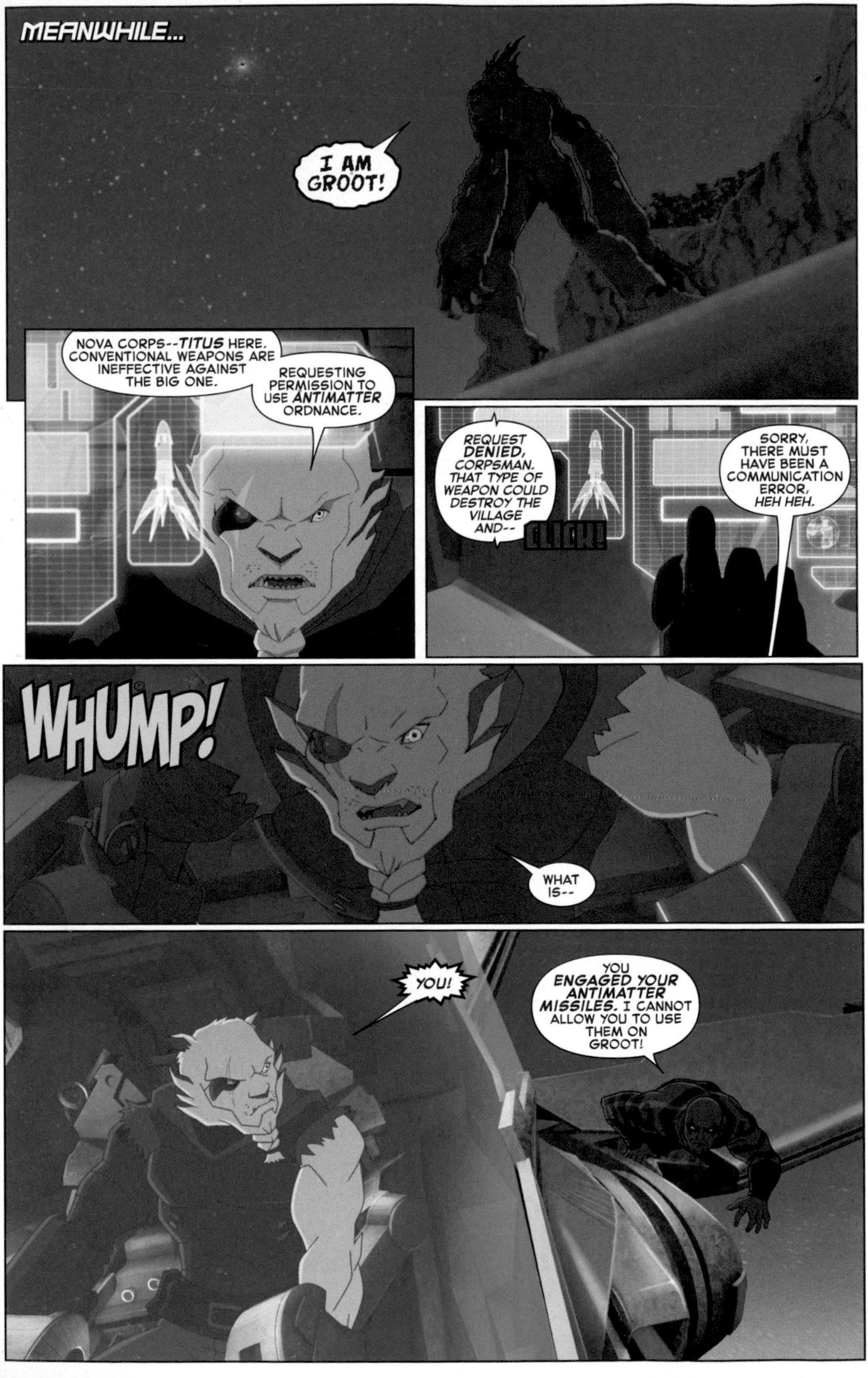
MEANWHILE...
I AM GROOT!
NOVA CORPS--TITUS HERE. CONVENTIONAL WEAPONS ARE INEFFECTIVE AGAINST THE BIG ONE.
REQUESTING PERMISSION TO USE ANTIMATTER ORDNANCE.
REQUEST DENIED, CORPSMAN. THAT TYPE OF WEAPON COULD DESTROY THE VILLAGE AND--
CLICK!
SORRY, THERE MUST HAVE BEEN A COMMUNICATION ERROR, HEH HEH.
WHUMP!
WHAT IS--
YOU!
YOU ENGAGED YOUR ANTIMATTER MISSILES. I CANNOT ALLOW YOU TO USE THEM ON GROOT!

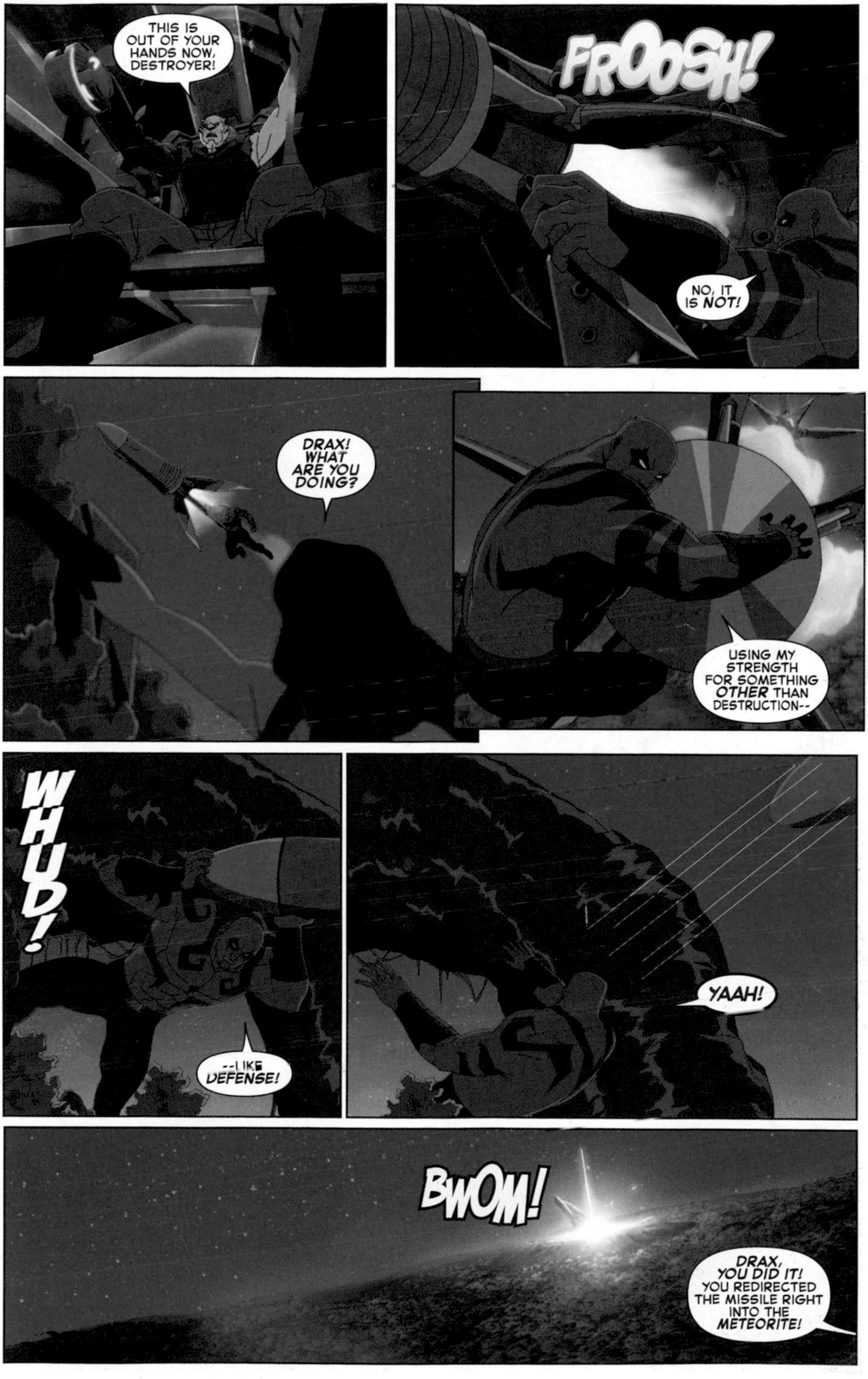
THIS IS OUT OF YOUR HANDS NOW, DESTROYER!
FROOSH!
NO, IT IS NOT!
DRAX! WHAT ARE YOU DOING?
USING MY STRENGTH FOR SOMETHING OTHER THAN DESTRUCTION--
WHUD!
--LIKE DEFENSE!
YAAH!
BWOM!
DRAX, YOU DID IT! YOU REDIRECTED THE MISSILE RIGHT INTO THE METEORITE!

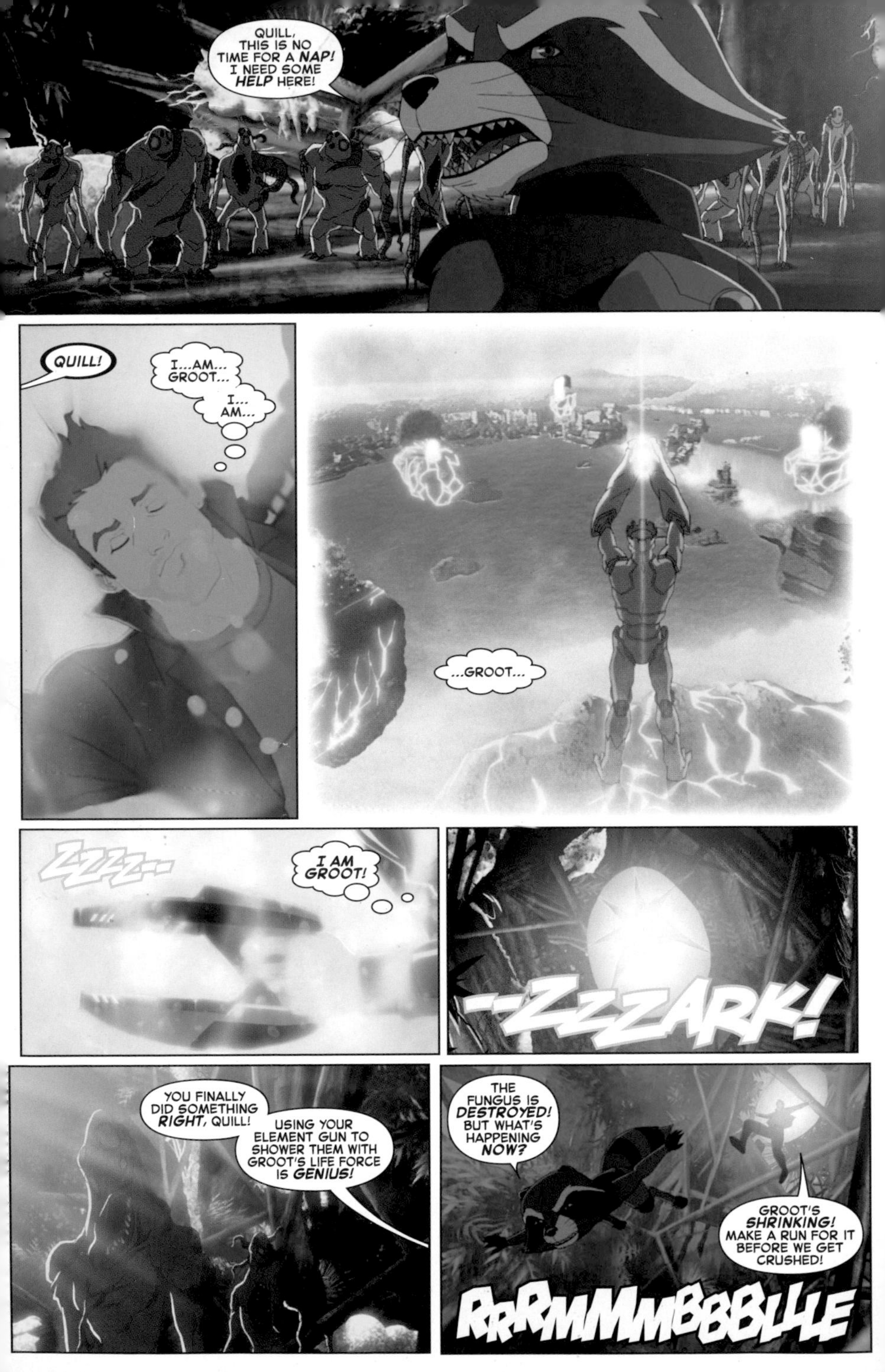
QUILL, THIS IS NO TIME FOR A NAP! I NEED SOME HELP HERE!
QUILL!
I...AM... GROOT...
I... AM...
...GROOT...
ZZZZ--
I AM GROOT!
--ZZZARK!
YOU FINALLY DID SOMETHING RIGHT, QUILL!
USING YOUR ELEMENT GUN TO SHOWER THEM WITH GROOT'S LIFE FORCE IS GENIUS!
THE FUNGUS IS DESTROYED! BUT WHAT'S HAPPENING NOW?
GROOT'S SHRINKING! MAKE A RUN FOR IT BEFORE WE GET CRUSHED!
RRRMMMMBBBLLLE

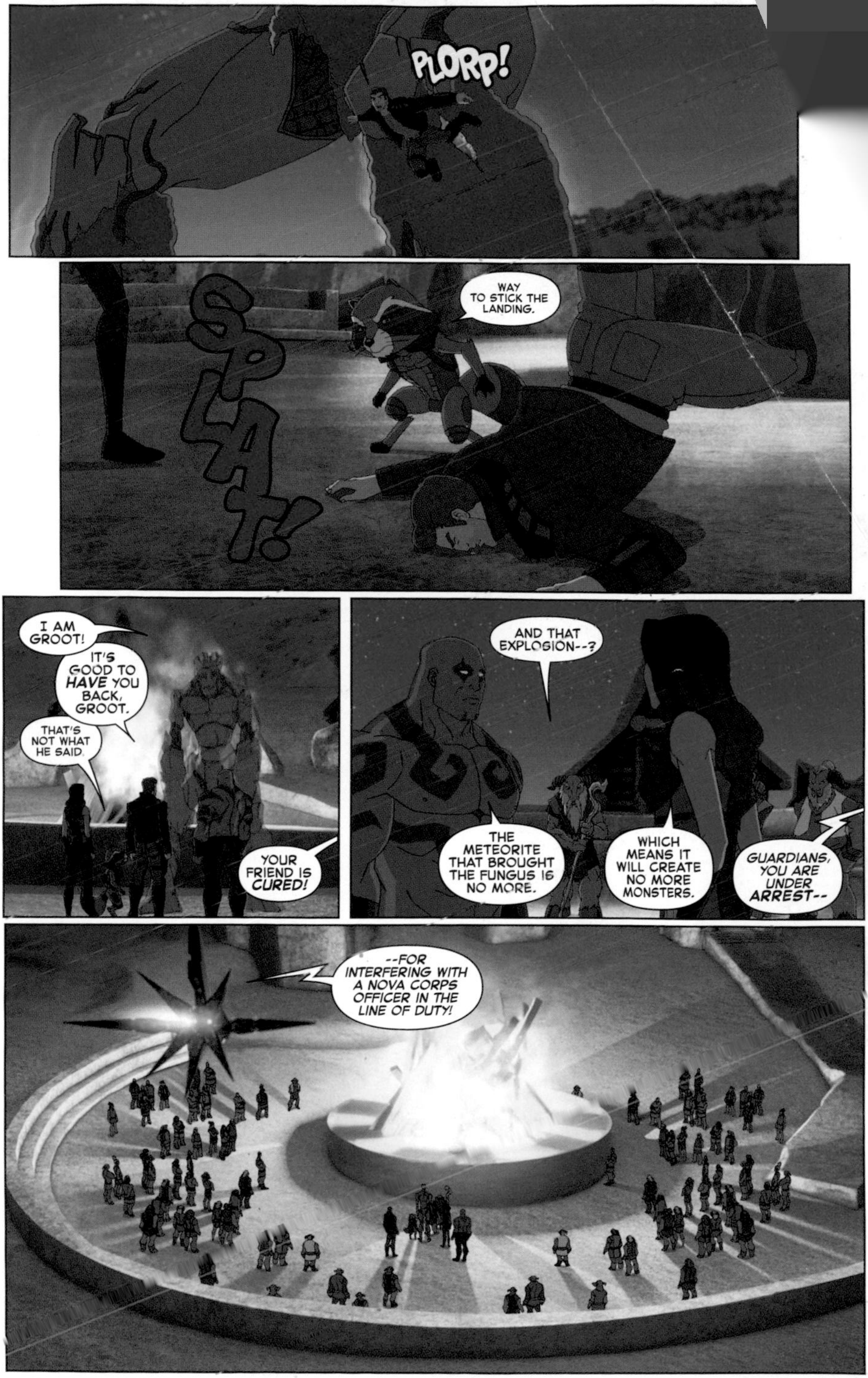
PLORP!
SPLAT!
WAY TO STICK THE LANDING.
I AM GROOT!
IT'S GOOD TO HAVE YOU BACK, GROOT.
THAT'S NOT WHAT HE SAID.
YOUR FRIEND IS CURED!
AND THAT EXPLOSION--?
THE METEORITE THAT BROUGHT THE FUNGUS IS NO MORE.
WHICH MEANS IT WILL CREATE NO MORE MONSTERS.
GUARDIANS, YOU ARE UNDER ARREST--
--FOR INTERFERING WITH A NOVA CORPS OFFICER IN THE LINE OF DUTY!

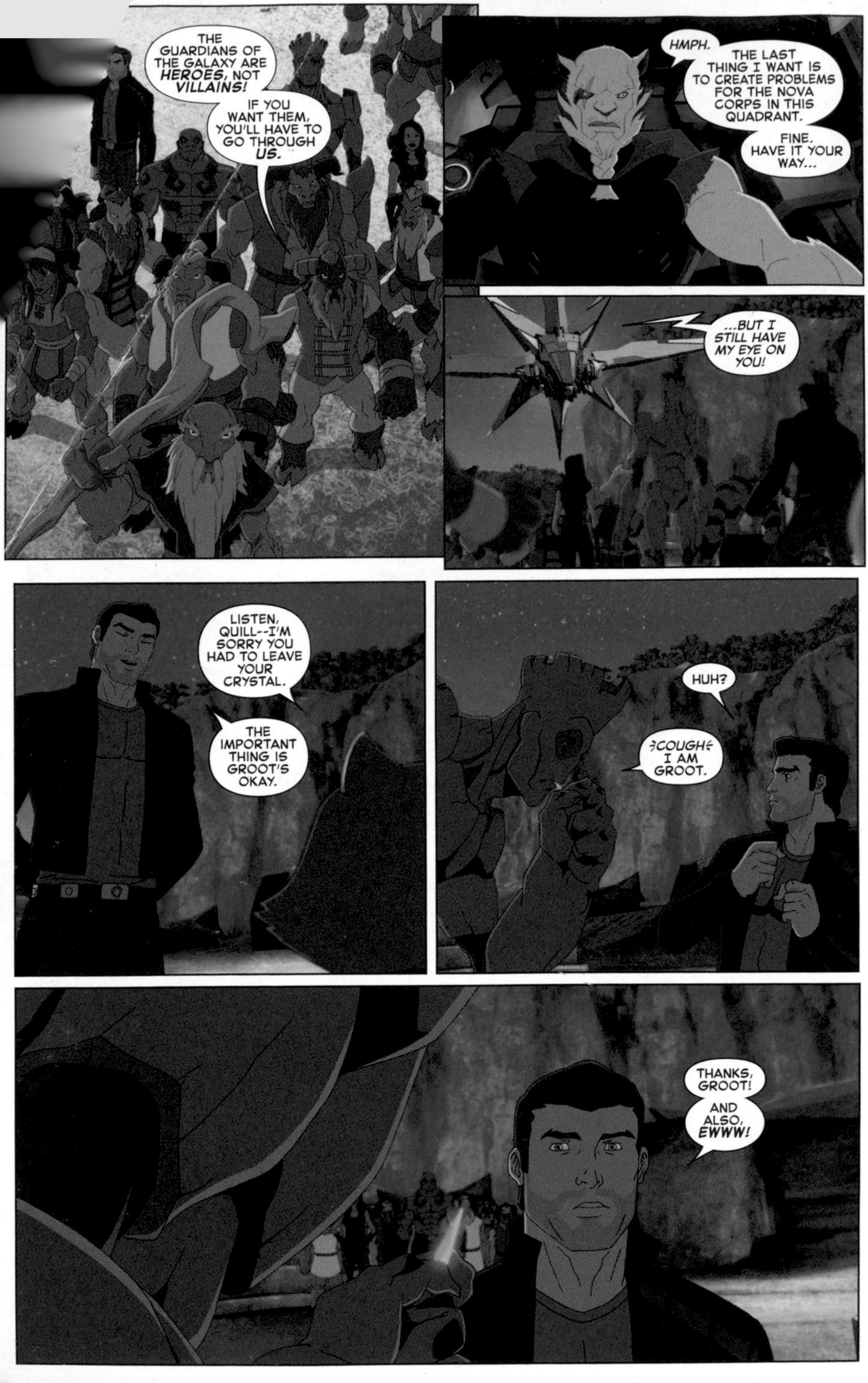
THE GUARDIANS OF THE GALAXY ARE HEROES, NOT VILLAINS!
IF YOU WANT THEM, YOU'LL HAVE TO GO THROUGH US.
HMPH.
THE LAST THING I WANT IS TO CREATE PROBLEMS FOR THE NOVA CORPS IN THIS QUADRANT.
FINE. HAVE IT YOUR WAY...
...BUT I STILL HAVE MY EYE ON YOU!
LISTEN, QUILL--I'M SORRY YOU HAD TO LEAVE YOUR CRYSTAL.
THE IMPORTANT THING IS GROOT'S OKAY.
HUH?
COUGH I AM GROOT.
THANKS, GROOT!
AND ALSO, EWWW!

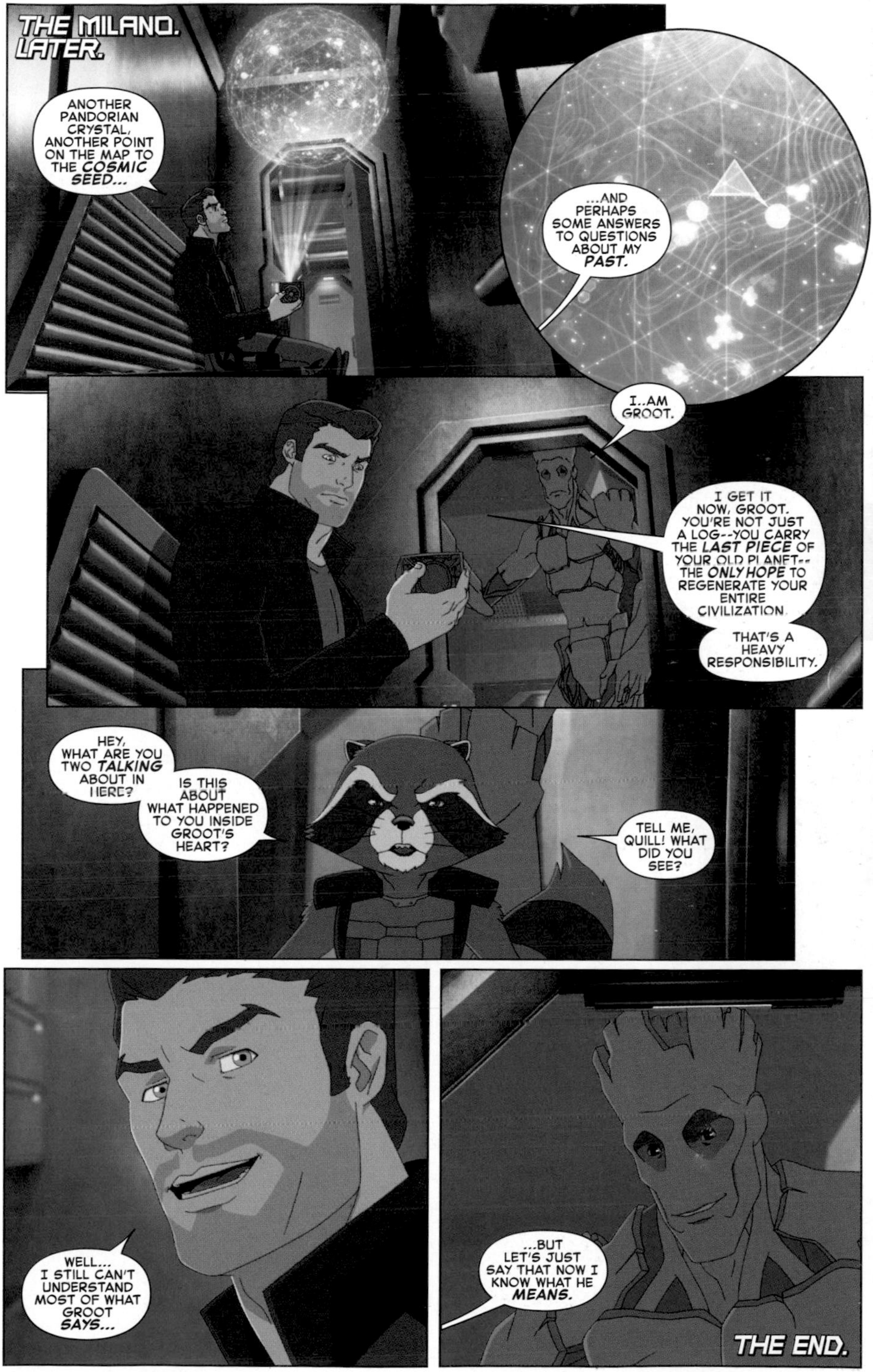
THE MILANO. LATER.
ANOTHER PANDORIAN CRYSTAL, ANOTHER POINT ON THE MAP TO THE COSMIC SEED...
...AND PERHAPS SOME ANSWERS TO QUESTIONS ABOUT MY PAST.
I..AM GROOT.
I GET IT NOW, GROOT. YOU'RE NOT JUST A LOG--YOU CARRY THE LAST PIECE OF YOUR OLD PLANET--THE ONLY HOPE TO REGENERATE YOUR ENTIRE CIVILIZATION.
THAT'S A HEAVY RESPONSIBILITY.
HEY, WHAT ARE YOU TWO TALKING ABOUT IN HERE?
IS THIS ABOUT WHAT HAPPENED TO YOU INSIDE GROOT'S HEART?
TELL ME, QUILL! WHAT DID YOU SEE?
WELL... I STILL CAN'T UNDERSTAND MOST OF WHAT GROOT SAYS...
...BUT LET'S JUST SAY THAT NOW I KNOW WHAT HE MEANS.
THE END.

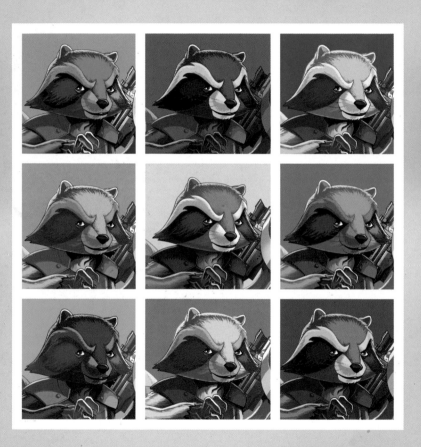

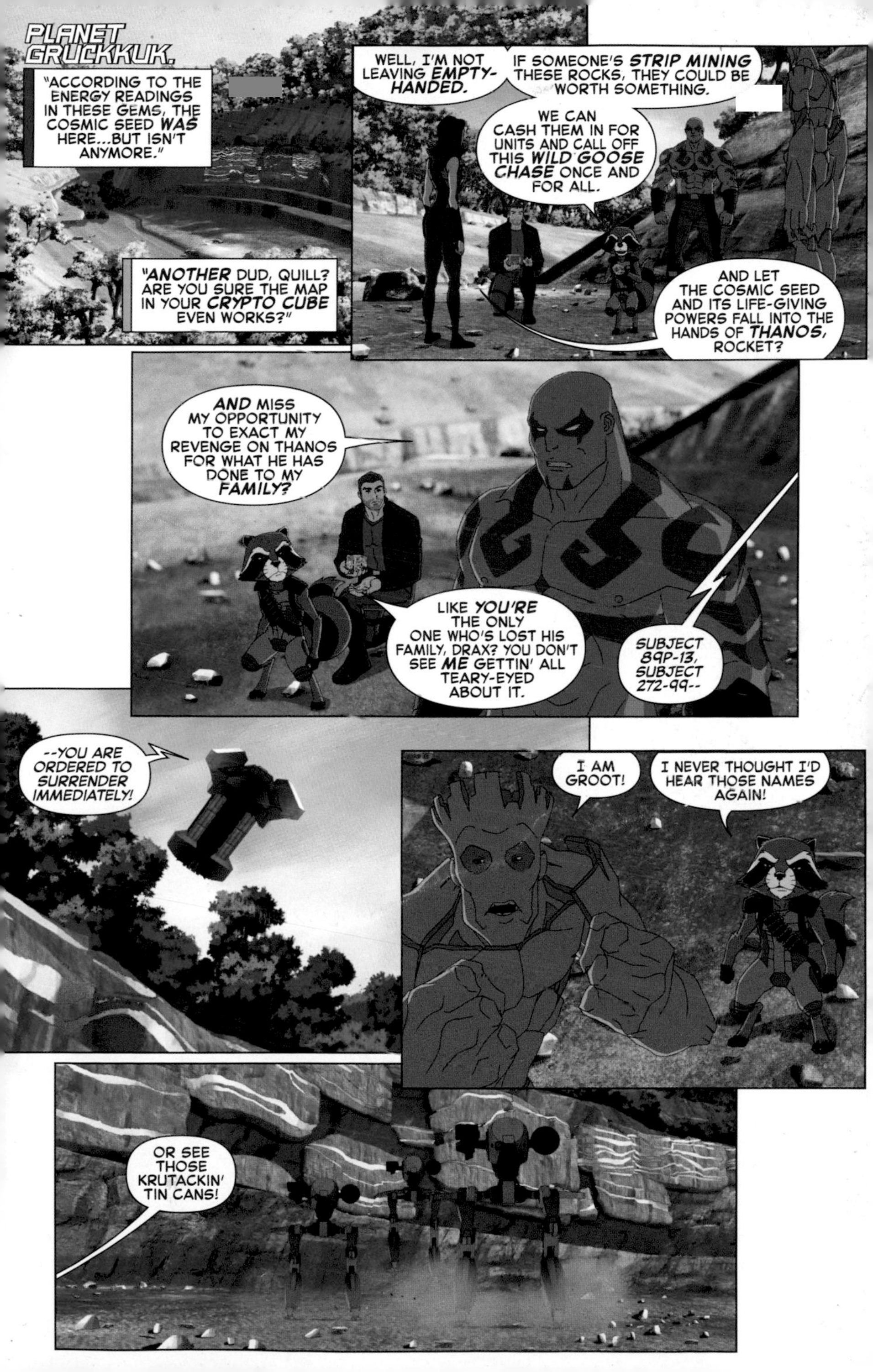
PLANET GRUCKKUK.
"ACCORDING TO THE ENERGY READINGS IN THESE GEMS, THE COSMIC SEED WAS HERE...BUT ISN'T ANYMORE."
"ANOTHER DUD, QUILL? ARE YOU SURE THE MAP IN YOUR CRYPTO CUBE EVEN WORKS?"
WELL, I'M NOT LEAVING EMPTY-HANDED.
IF SOMEONE'S STRIP MINING THESE ROCKS, THEY COULD BE WORTH SOMETHING.
WE CAN CASH THEM IN FOR UNITS AND CALL OFF THIS WILD GOOSE CHASE ONCE AND FOR ALL.
AND LET THE COSMIC SEED AND ITS LIFE-GIVING POWERS FALL INTO THE HANDS OF THANOS, ROCKET?
AND MISS MY OPPORTUNITY TO EXACT MY REVENGE ON THANOS FOR WHAT HE HAS DONE TO MY FAMILY?
LIKE YOU'RE THE ONLY ONE WHO'S LOST HIS FAMILY, DRAX? YOU DON'T SEE ME GETTIN' ALL TEARY-EYED ABOUT IT.
SUBJECT 89P-13, SUBJECT 272-99--
--YOU ARE ORDERED TO SURRENDER IMMEDIATELY!
I AM GROOT!
I NEVER THOUGHT I'D HEAR THOSE NAMES AGAIN!
OR SEE THOSE KRUTACKIN' TIN CANS!

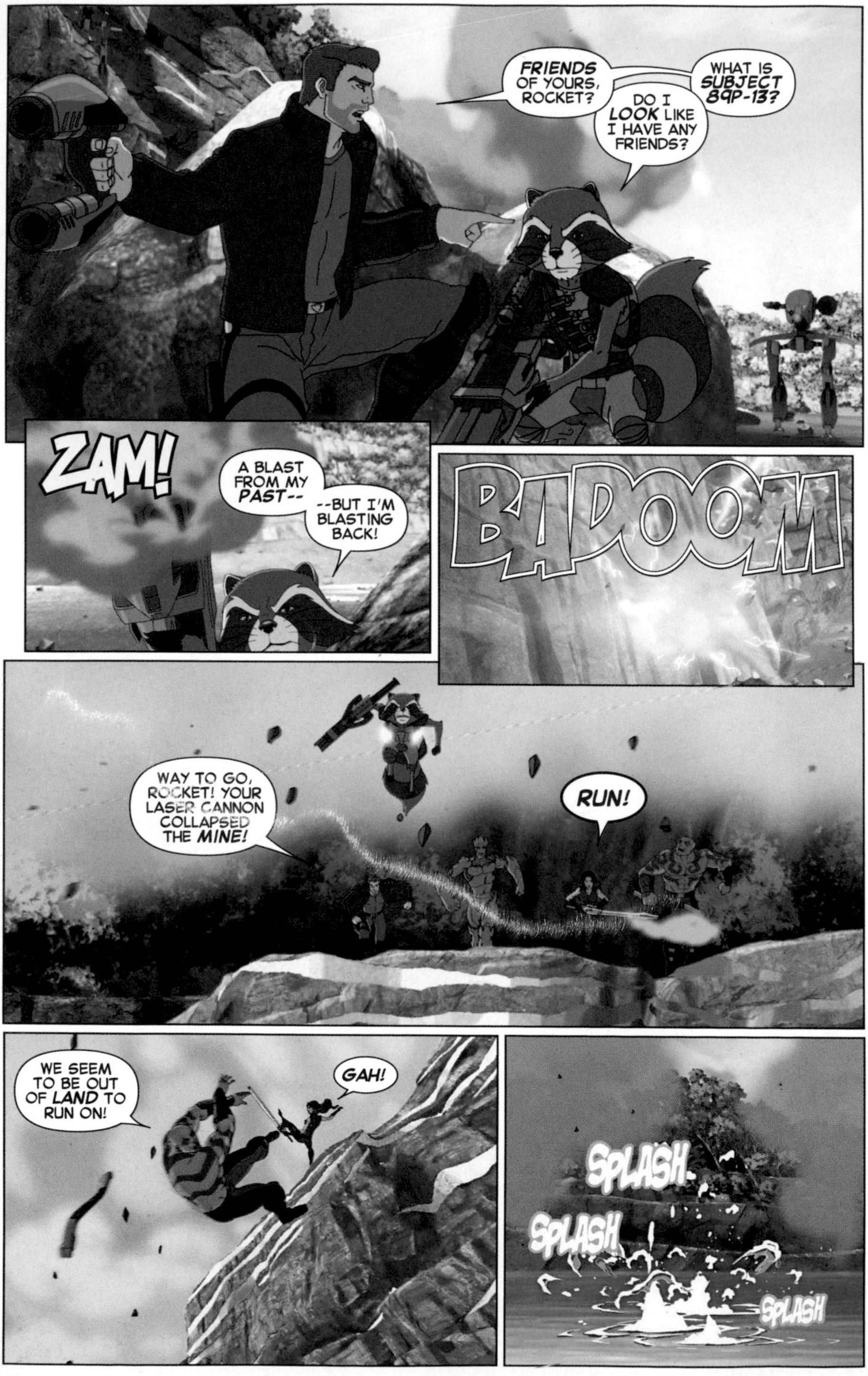
FRIENDS OF YOURS, ROCKET?
WHAT IS SUBJECT 89P-13?
DO I LOOK LIKE I HAVE ANY FRIENDS?
ZAM!
A BLAST FROM MY PAST--
--BUT I'M BLASTING BACK!
BADOOM
WAY TO GO, ROCKET! YOUR LASER CANNON COLLAPSED THE MINE!
RUN!
WE SEEM TO BE OUT OF LAND TO RUN ON!
GAH!
SPLASH
SPLASH
SPLASH

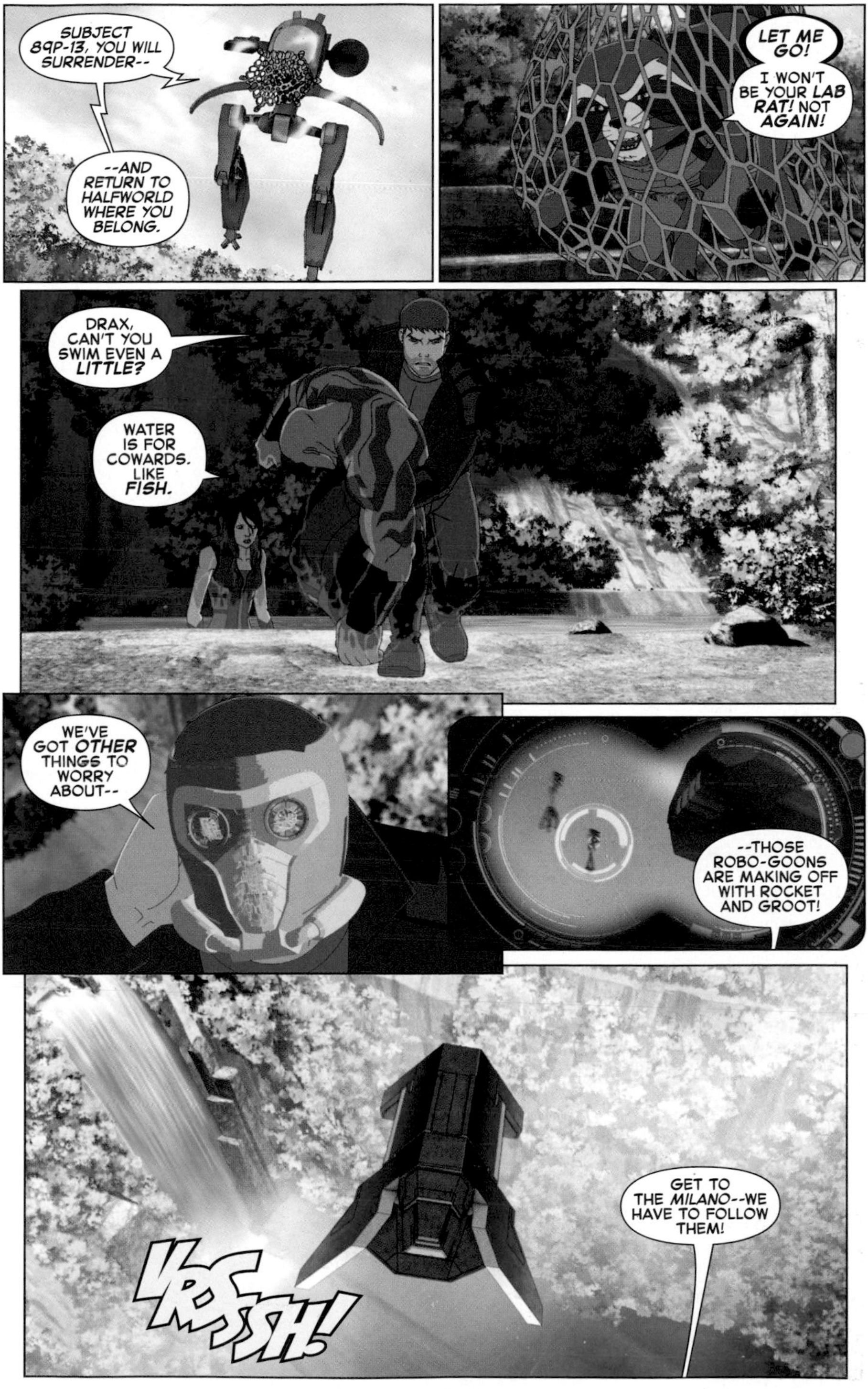
SUBJECT 89P-13, YOU WILL SURRENDER--
--AND RETURN TO HALFWORLD WHERE YOU BELONG.
LET ME GO!
I WON'T BE YOUR LAB RAT! NOT AGAIN!
DRAX, CAN'T YOU SWIM EVEN A LITTLE?
WATER IS FOR COWARDS. LIKE FISH.
WE'VE GOT OTHER THINGS TO WORRY ABOUT--
--THOSE ROBO-GOONS ARE MAKING OFF WITH ROCKET AND GROOT!
GET TO THE MILANO--WE HAVE TO FOLLOW THEM!
VROOSH!

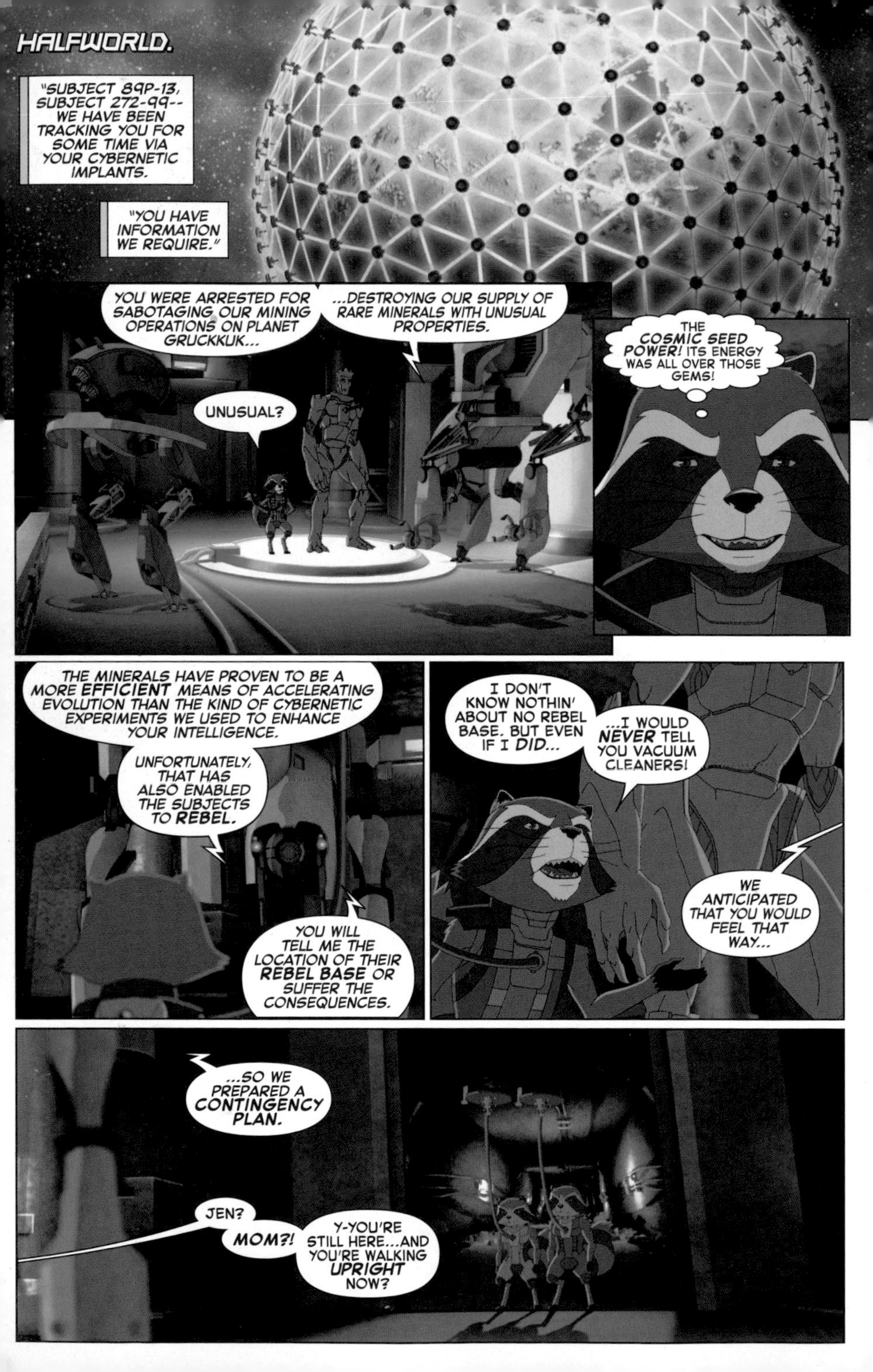
HALFWORLD.
"SUBJECT 89P-13, SUBJECT 272-99-- WE HAVE BEEN TRACKING YOU FOR SOME TIME VIA YOUR CYBERNETIC IMPLANTS.
"YOU HAVE INFORMATION WE REQUIRE."
YOU WERE ARRESTED FOR SABOTAGING OUR MINING OPERATIONS ON PLANET GRUCKKUK...
...DESTROYING OUR SUPPLY OF RARE MINERALS WITH UNUSUAL PROPERTIES.
UNUSUAL?
THE COSMIC SEED POWER! ITS ENERGY WAS ALL OVER THOSE GEMS!
THE MINERALS HAVE PROVEN TO BE A MORE EFFICIENT MEANS OF ACCELERATING EVOLUTION THAN THE KIND OF CYBERNETIC EXPERIMENTS WE USED TO ENHANCE YOUR INTELLIGENCE.
UNFORTUNATELY, THAT HAS ALSO ENABLED THE SUBJECTS TO REBEL.
YOU WILL TELL ME THE LOCATION OF THEIR REBEL BASE OR SUFFER THE CONSEQUENCES.
I DON'T KNOW NOTHIN' ABOUT NO REBEL BASE. BUT EVEN IF I DID...
...I WOULD NEVER TELL YOU VACUUM CLEANERS!
WE ANTICIPATED THAT YOU WOULD FEEL THAT WAY...
...SO WE PREPARED A CONTINGENCY PLAN.
JEN?
MOM?!
Y-YOU'RE STILL HERE...AND YOU'RE WALKING UPRIGHT NOW?

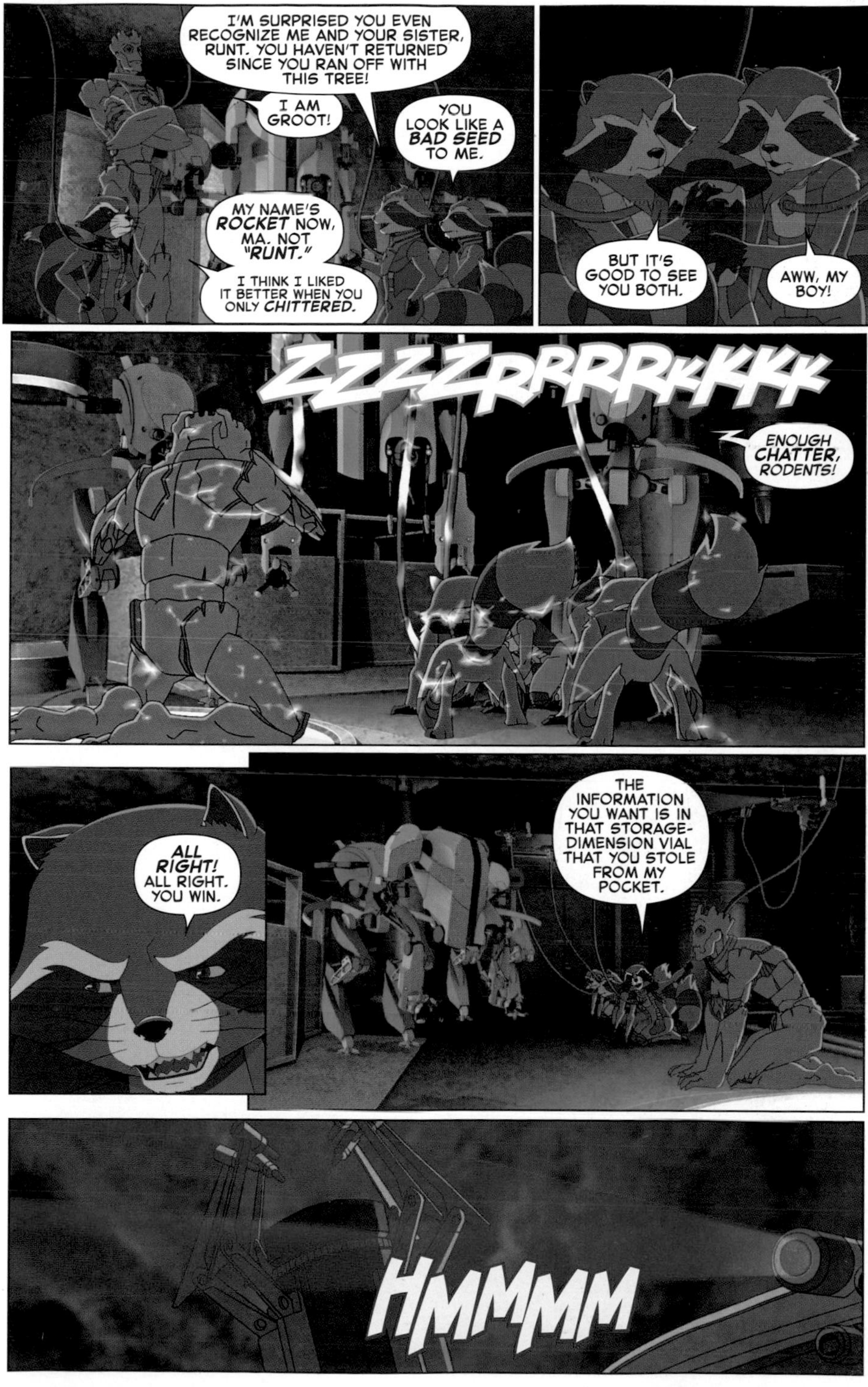
I'M SURPRISED YOU EVEN RECOGNIZE ME AND YOUR SISTER, RUNT. YOU HAVEN'T RETURNED SINCE YOU RAN OFF WITH THIS TREE!
I AM GROOT!
YOU LOOK LIKE A *BAD SEED* TO ME.
MY NAME'S *ROCKET* NOW, MA. NOT *"RUNT."*
I THINK I LIKED IT BETTER WHEN YOU ONLY *CHITTERED.*
BUT IT'S GOOD TO SEE YOU BOTH.
AWW, MY BOY!
ZZZZRRRRKKKK
ENOUGH *CHATTER,* RODENTS!
ALL RIGHT! ALL RIGHT. YOU WIN.
THE INFORMATION YOU WANT IS IN THAT STORAGE-DIMENSION VIAL THAT YOU STOLE FROM MY POCKET.
HMMMM

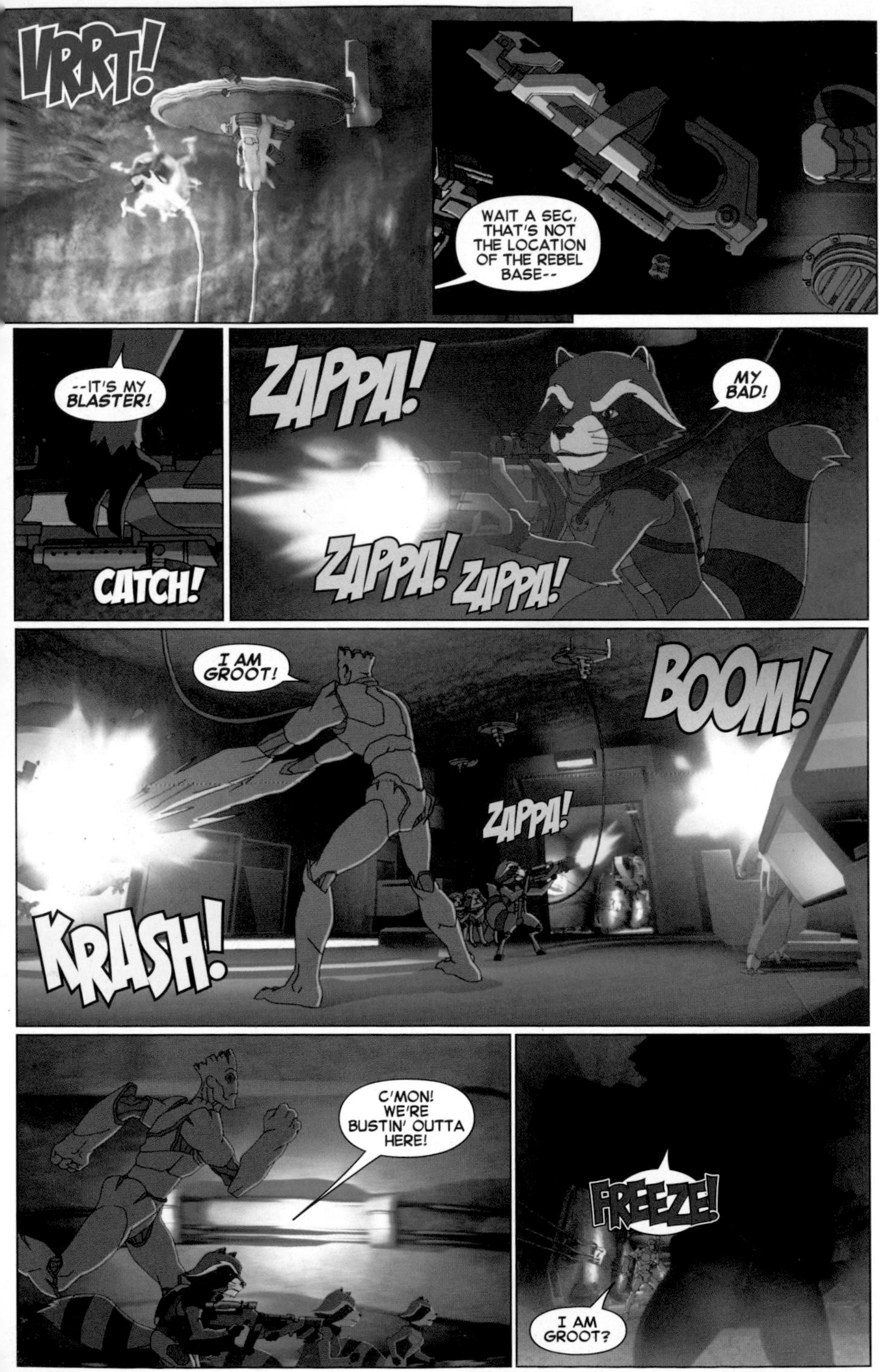
VRRT!
WAIT A SEC, THAT'S NOT THE LOCATION OF THE REBEL BASE--
--IT'S MY BLASTER!
CATCH!
ZAPPA!
MY BAD!
ZAPPA! ZAPPA!
I AM GROOT!
BOOM!
ZAPPA!
KRASH!
C'MON! WE'RE BUSTIN' OUTTA HERE!
FREEZE!
I AM GROOT?

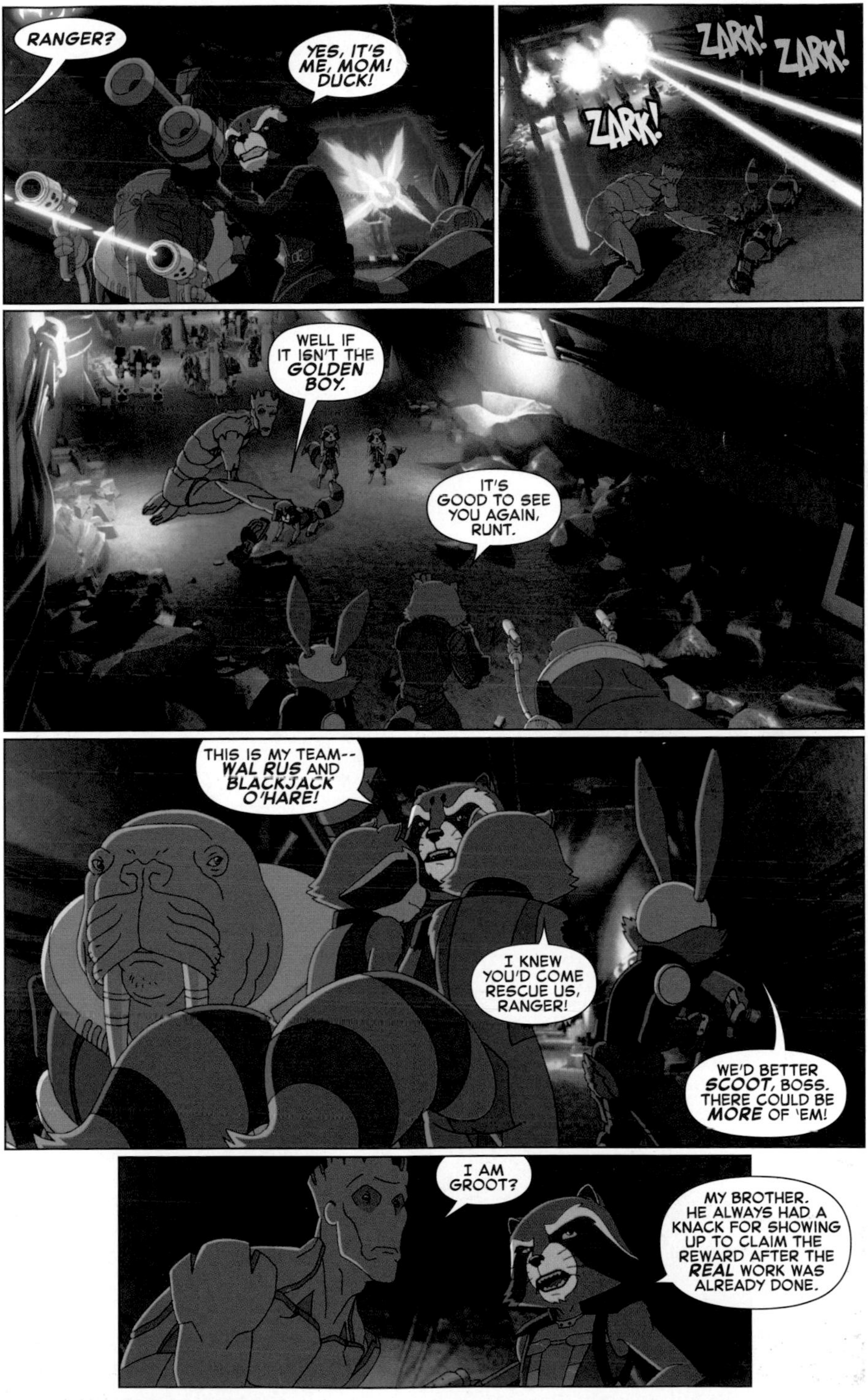
RANGER?
YES, IT'S ME, MOM! DUCK!
ZARK! ZARK!
ZARK!
WELL IF IT ISN'T THE GOLDEN BOY.
IT'S GOOD TO SEE YOU AGAIN, RUNT.
THIS IS MY TEAM-- WAL RUS AND BLACKJACK O'HARE!
I KNEW YOU'D COME RESCUE US, RANGER!
WE'D BETTER SCOOT, BOSS. THERE COULD BE MORE OF 'EM!
I AM GROOT?
MY BROTHER. HE ALWAYS HAD A KNACK FOR SHOWING UP TO CLAIM THE REWARD AFTER THE REAL WORK WAS ALREADY DONE.

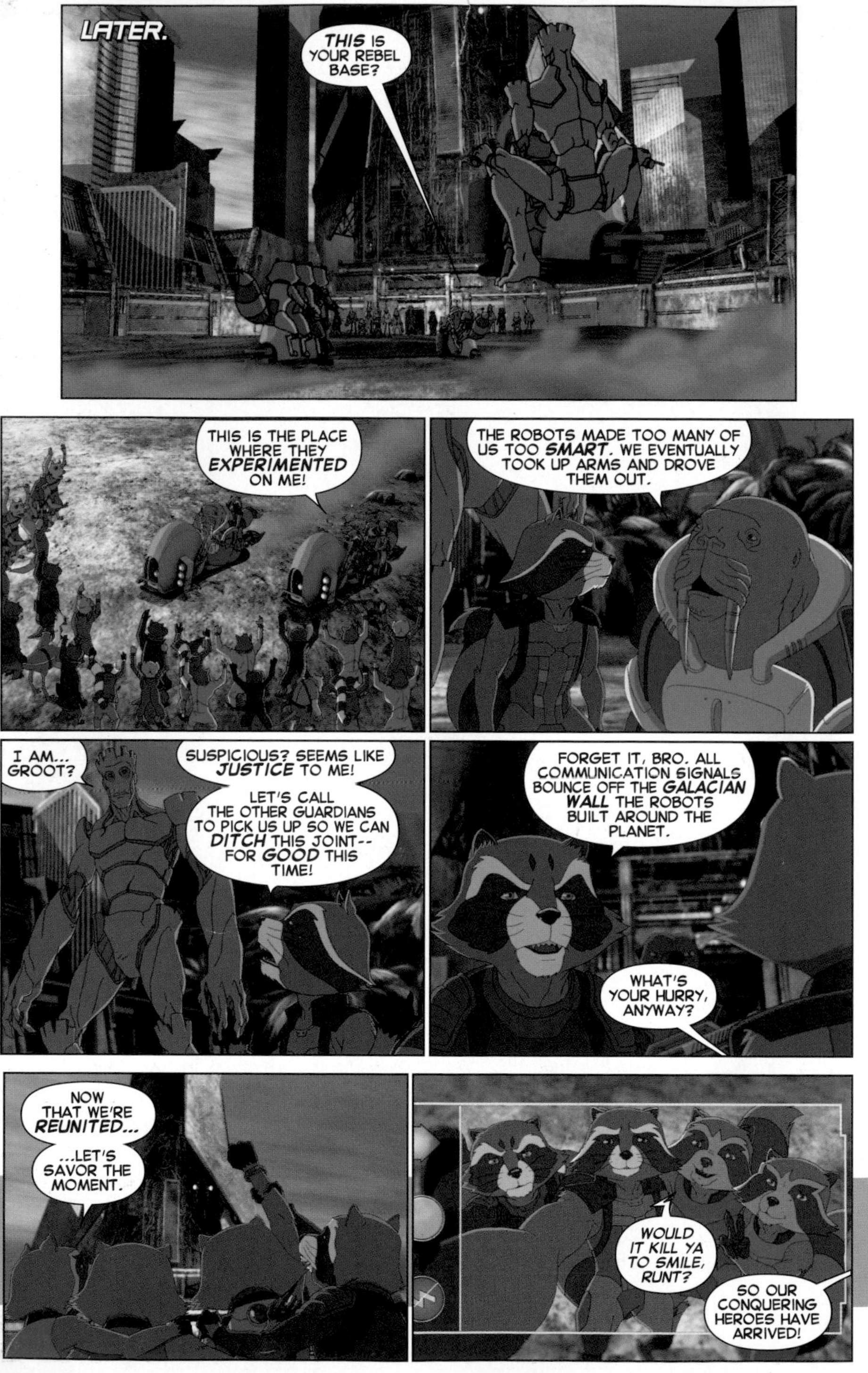

LATER.
THIS IS YOUR REBEL BASE?
THIS IS THE PLACE WHERE THEY EXPERIMENTED ON ME!
THE ROBOTS MADE TOO MANY OF US TOO SMART. WE EVENTUALLY TOOK UP ARMS AND DROVE THEM OUT.
I AM... GROOT?
SUSPICIOUS? SEEMS LIKE JUSTICE TO ME!
LET'S CALL THE OTHER GUARDIANS TO PICK US UP SO WE CAN DITCH THIS JOINT-- FOR GOOD THIS TIME!
FORGET IT, BRO. ALL COMMUNICATION SIGNALS BOUNCE OFF THE GALACIAN WALL THE ROBOTS BUILT AROUND THE PLANET.
WHAT'S YOUR HURRY, ANYWAY?
NOW THAT WE'RE REUNITED...
...LET'S SAVOR THE MOMENT.
WOULD IT KILL YA TO SMILE, RUNT?
SO OUR CONQUERING HEROES HAVE ARRIVED!

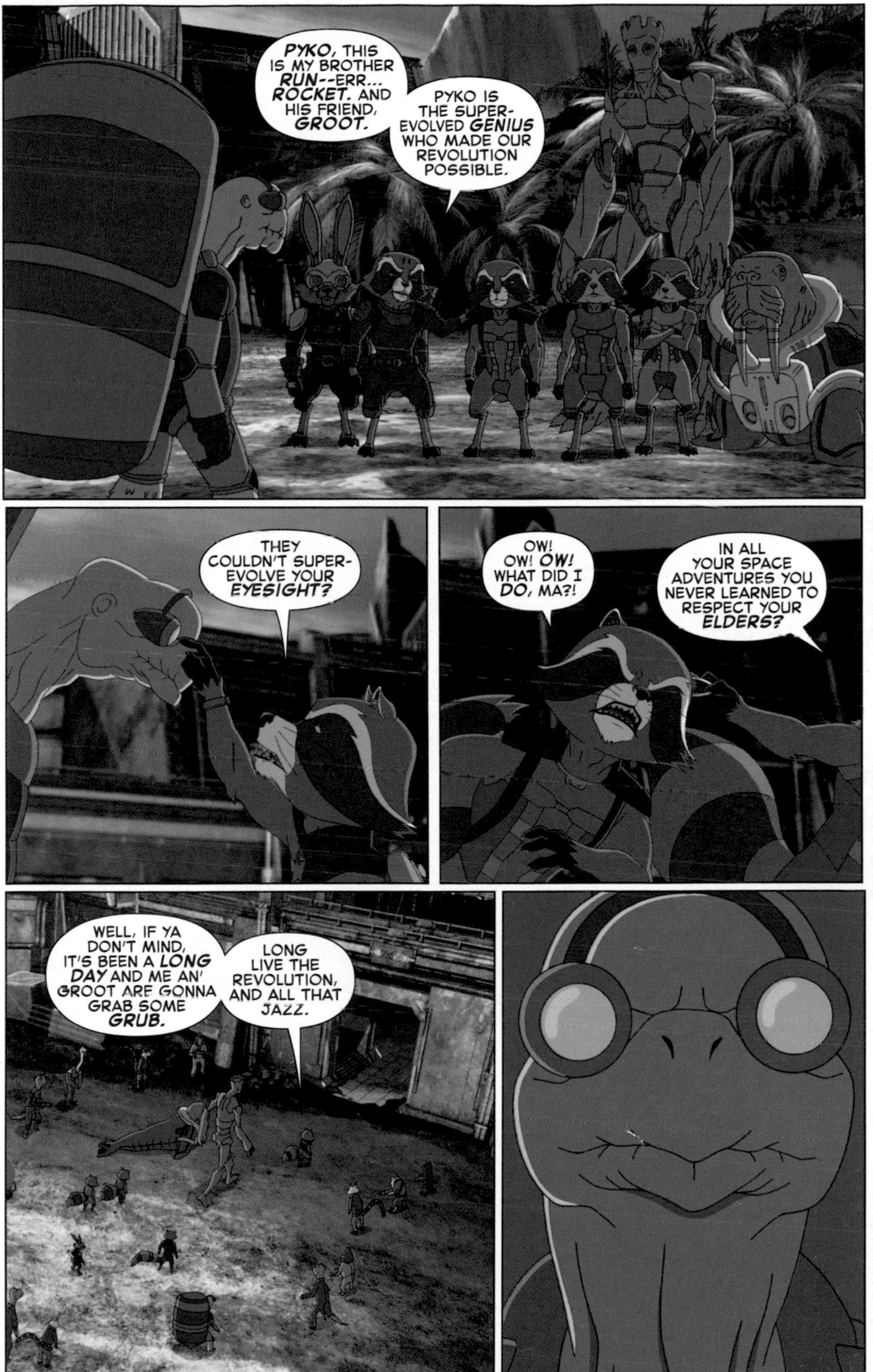
PYKO, THIS IS MY BROTHER RUN--ERR... ROCKET. AND HIS FRIEND, GROOT.
PYKO IS THE SUPER-EVOLVED GENIUS WHO MADE OUR REVOLUTION POSSIBLE.
THEY COULDN'T SUPER-EVOLVE YOUR EYESIGHT?
OW! OW! OW! WHAT DID I DO, MA?!
IN ALL YOUR SPACE ADVENTURES YOU NEVER LEARNED TO RESPECT YOUR ELDERS?
WELL, IF YA DON'T MIND, IT'S BEEN A LONG DAY AND ME AN' GROOT ARE GONNA GRAB SOME GRUB.
LONG LIVE THE REVOLUTION, AND ALL THAT JAZZ.

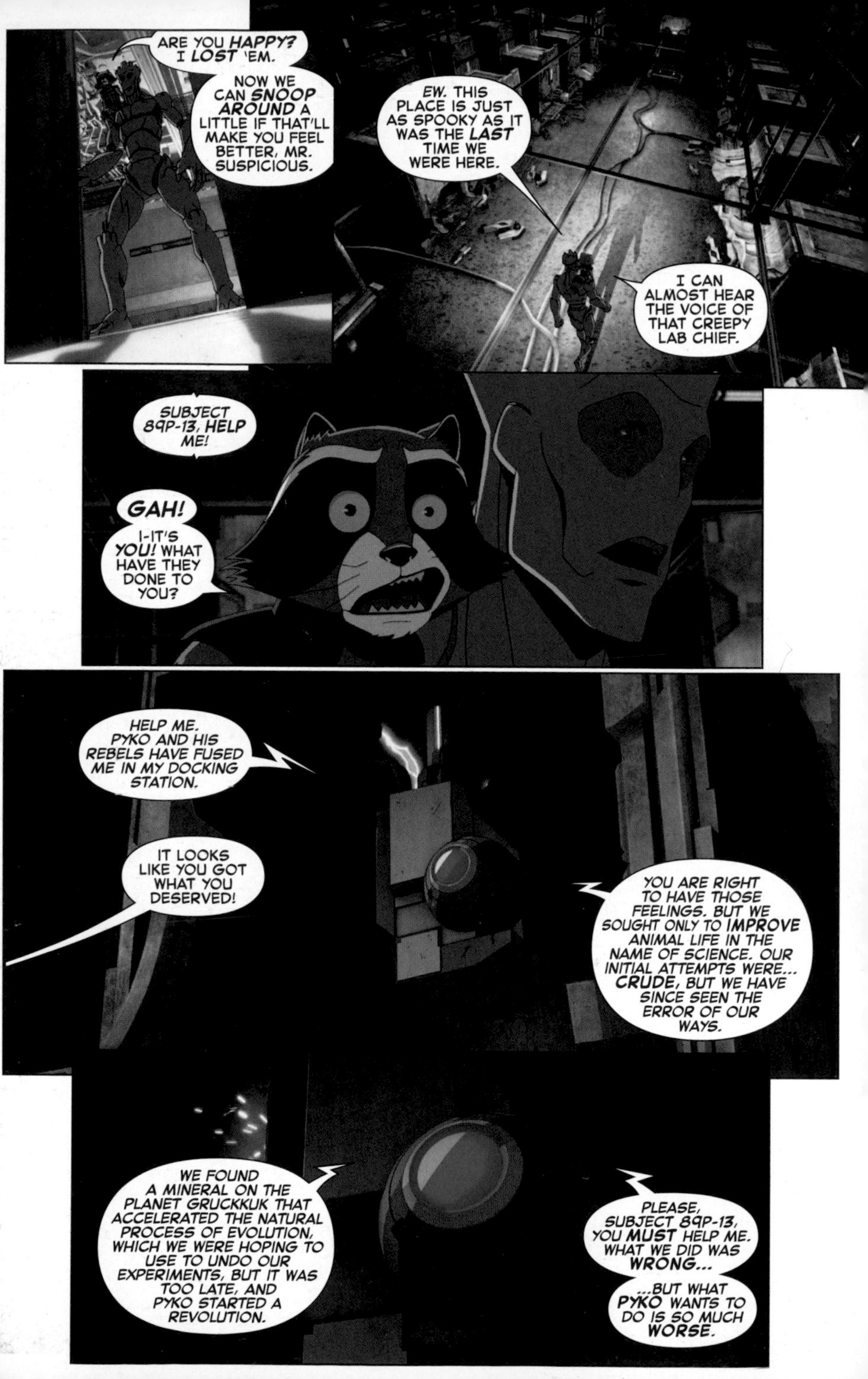
ARE YOU HAPPY? I LOST 'EM.
NOW WE CAN SNOOP AROUND A LITTLE IF THAT'LL MAKE YOU FEEL BETTER, MR. SUSPICIOUS.
EW. THIS PLACE IS JUST AS SPOOKY AS IT WAS THE LAST TIME WE WERE HERE.
I CAN ALMOST HEAR THE VOICE OF THAT CREEPY LAB CHIEF.
SUBJECT 89P-13, HELP ME!
GAH!
I-IT'S YOU! WHAT HAVE THEY DONE TO YOU?
HELP ME. PYKO AND HIS REBELS HAVE FUSED ME IN MY DOCKING STATION.
IT LOOKS LIKE YOU GOT WHAT YOU DESERVED!
YOU ARE RIGHT TO HAVE THOSE FEELINGS. BUT WE SOUGHT ONLY TO IMPROVE ANIMAL LIFE IN THE NAME OF SCIENCE. OUR INITIAL ATTEMPTS WERE... CRUDE, BUT WE HAVE SINCE SEEN THE ERROR OF OUR WAYS.
WE FOUND A MINERAL ON THE PLANET GRUCKKUK THAT ACCELERATED THE NATURAL PROCESS OF EVOLUTION, WHICH WE WERE HOPING TO USE TO UNDO OUR EXPERIMENTS, BUT IT WAS TOO LATE, AND PYKO STARTED A REVOLUTION.
PLEASE, SUBJECT 89P-13, YOU MUST HELP ME. WHAT WE DID WAS WRONG...
...BUT WHAT PYKO WANTS TO DO IS SO MUCH WORSE.

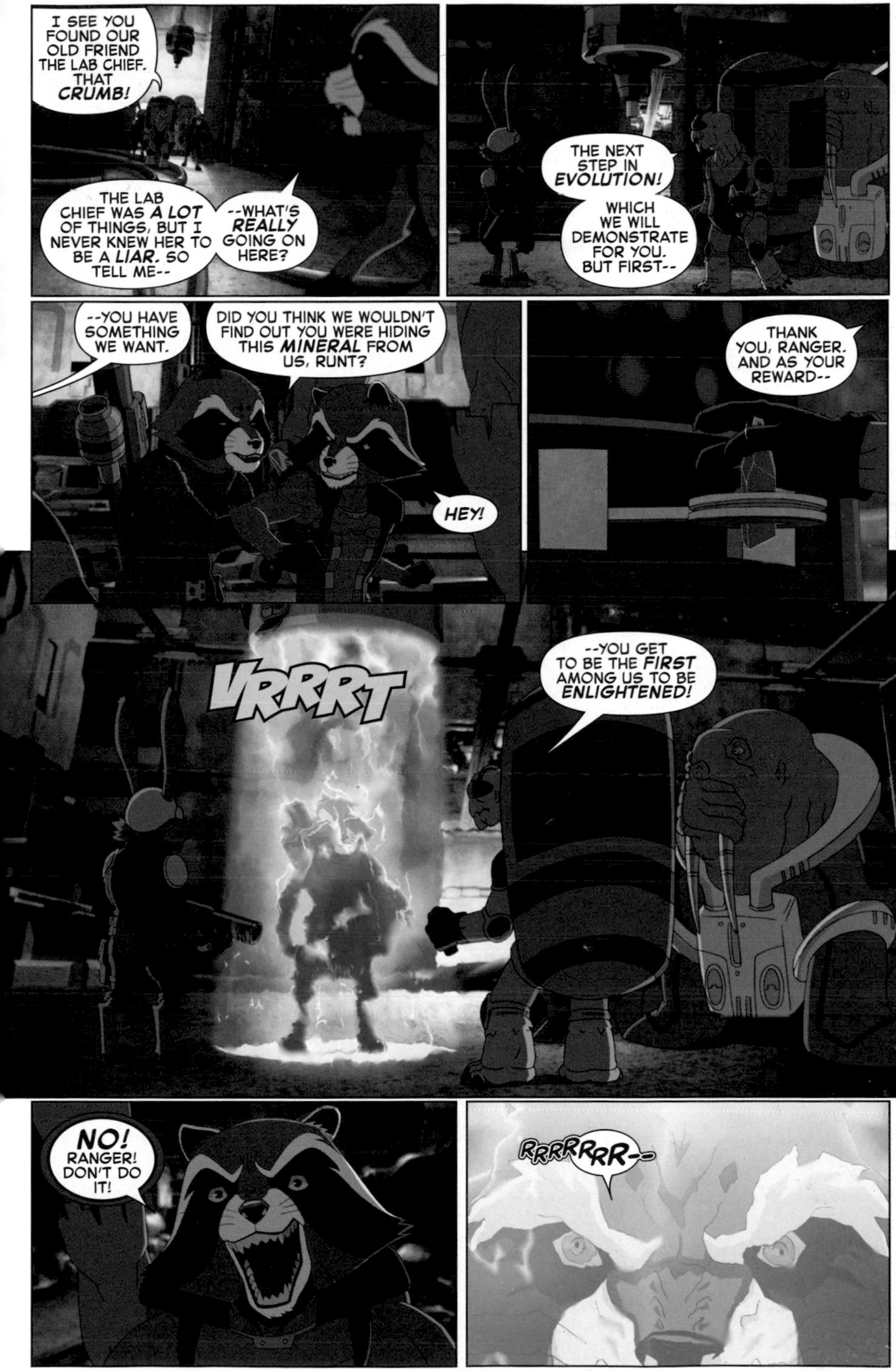
I SEE YOU FOUND OUR OLD FRIEND THE LAB CHIEF. THAT CRUMB!
THE LAB CHIEF WAS A LOT OF THINGS, BUT I NEVER KNEW HER TO BE A LIAR. SO TELL ME--
--WHAT'S REALLY GOING ON HERE?
THE NEXT STEP IN EVOLUTION!
WHICH WE WILL DEMONSTRATE FOR YOU. BUT FIRST--
--YOU HAVE SOMETHING WE WANT.
DID YOU THINK WE WOULDN'T FIND OUT YOU WERE HIDING THIS MINERAL FROM US, RUNT?
HEY!
THANK YOU, RANGER. AND AS YOUR REWARD--
VRRRT
--YOU GET TO BE THE FIRST AMONG US TO BE ENLIGHTENED!
NO! RANGER! DON'T DO IT!
RRRRRRR--

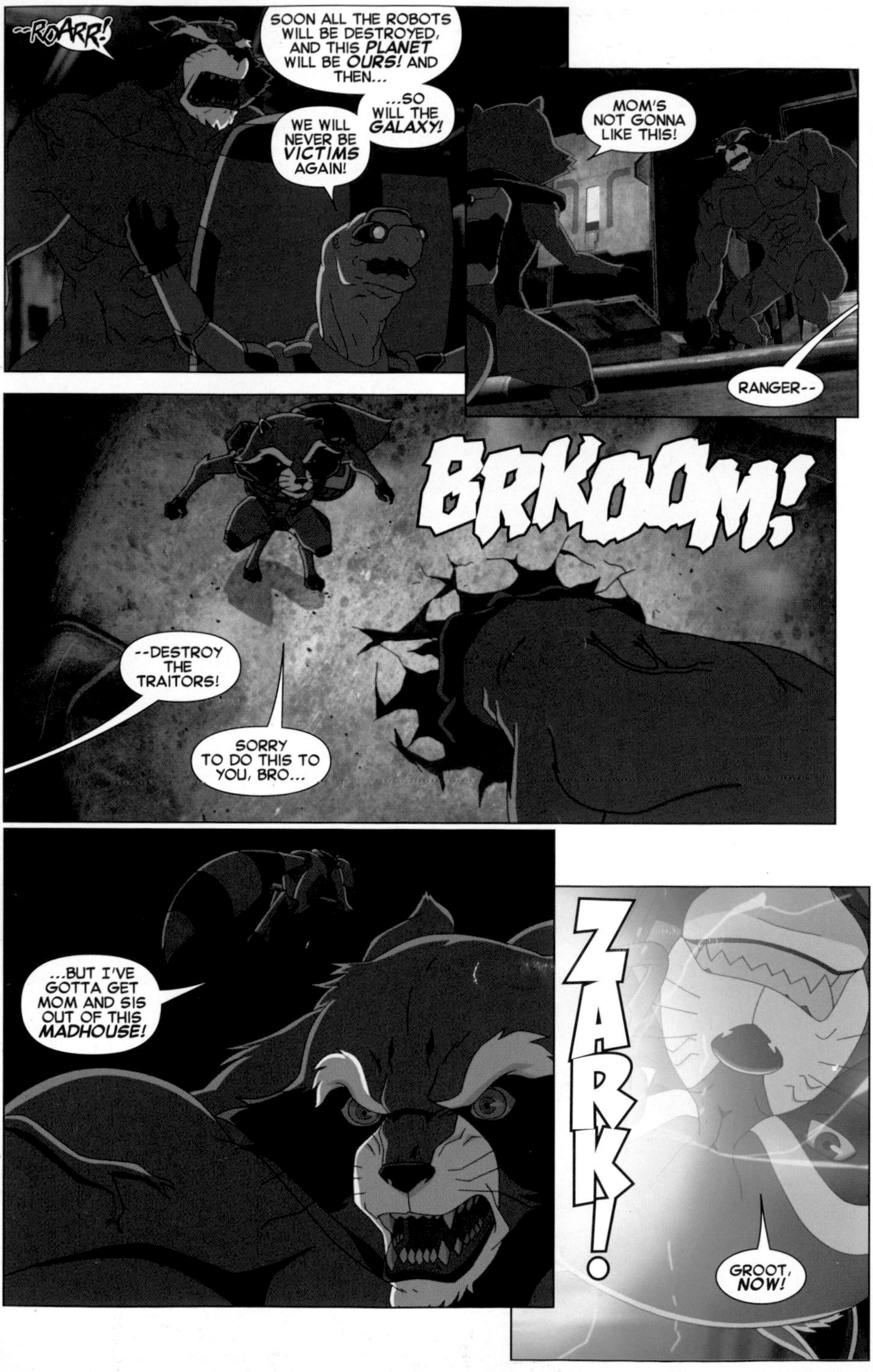
--ROARR!
SOON ALL THE ROBOTS WILL BE DESTROYED, AND THIS PLANET WILL BE OURS! AND THEN...
WE WILL NEVER BE VICTIMS AGAIN!
...SO WILL THE GALAXY!
MOM'S NOT GONNA LIKE THIS!
RANGER--
BRKOOM!
--DESTROY THE TRAITORS!
SORRY TO DO THIS TO YOU, BRO...
...BUT I'VE GOTTA GET MOM AND SIS OUT OF THIS MADHOUSE!
ZARK!
GROOT, NOW!

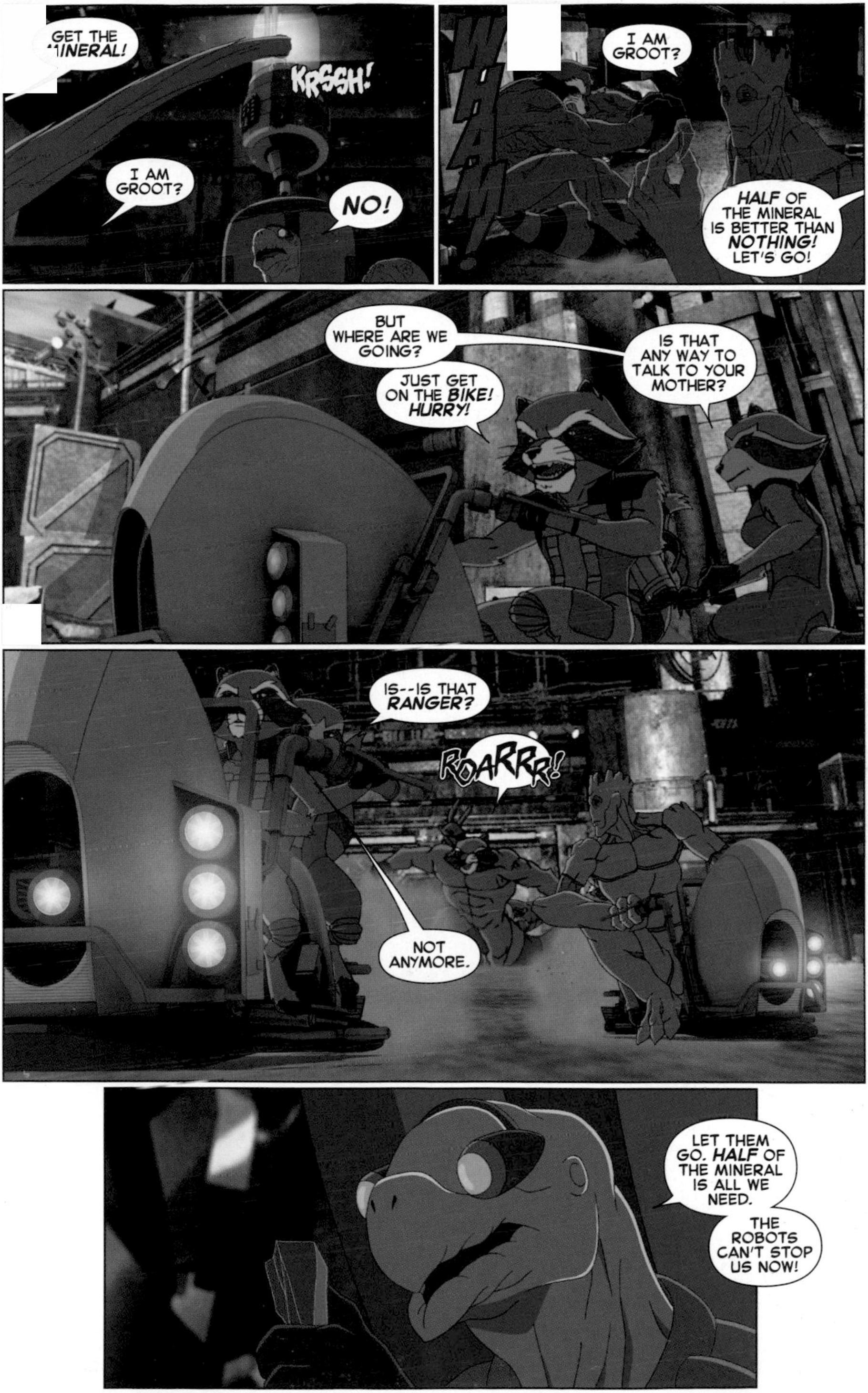
GET THE MINERAL!
KRSSH!
I AM GROOT?
NO!
WHAM!
I AM GROOT?
HALF OF THE MINERAL IS BETTER THAN NOTHING! LET'S GO!
BUT WHERE ARE WE GOING?
IS THAT ANY WAY TO TALK TO YOUR MOTHER?
JUST GET ON THE BIKE! HURRY!
IS--IS THAT RANGER?
ROARRR!
NOT ANYMORE.
LET THEM GO. HALF OF THE MINERAL IS ALL WE NEED.
THE ROBOTS CAN'T STOP US NOW!

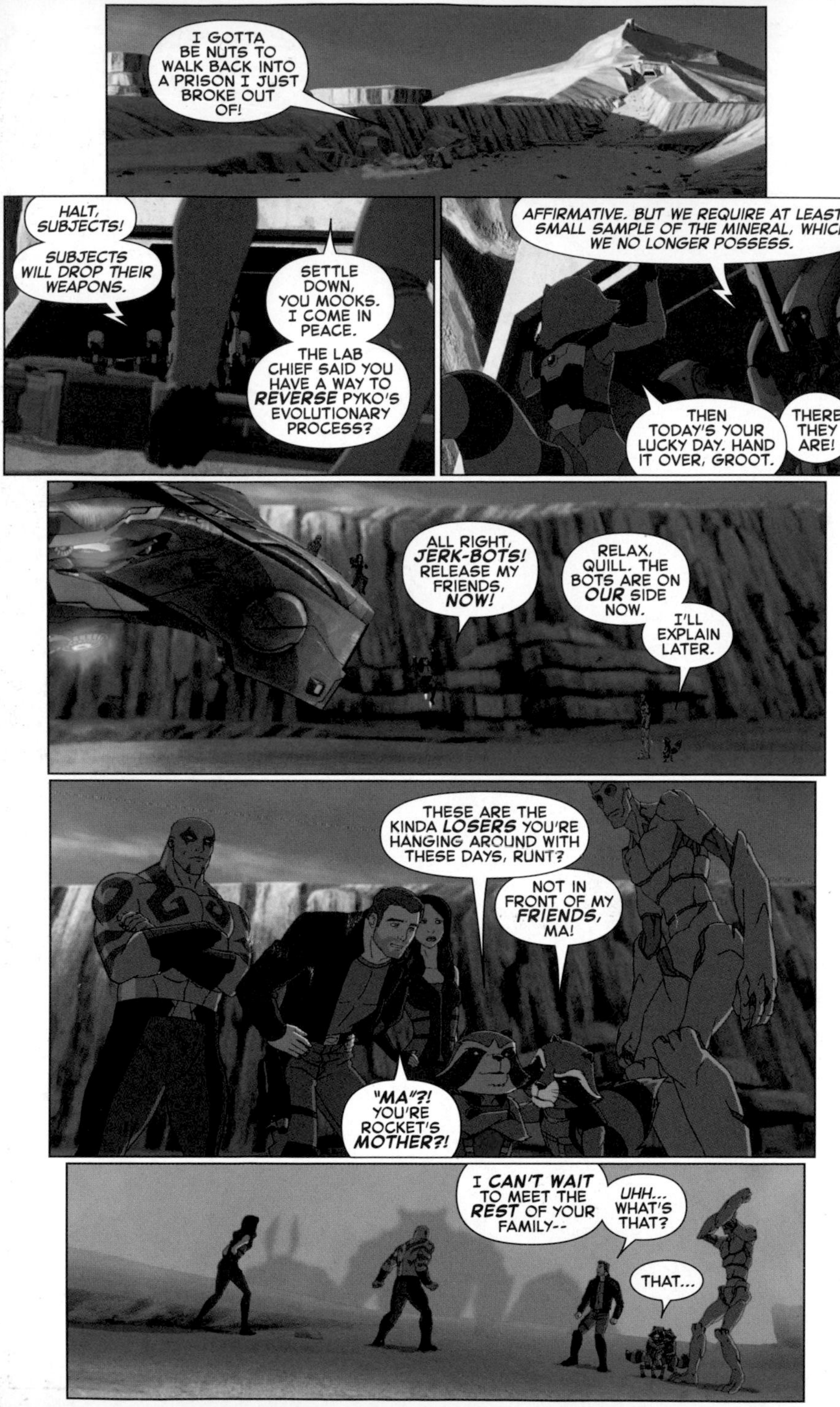
I GOTTA BE NUTS TO WALK BACK INTO A PRISON I JUST BROKE OUT OF!
HALT, SUBJECTS!
SUBJECTS WILL DROP THEIR WEAPONS.
SETTLE DOWN, YOU MOOKS. I COME IN PEACE.
THE LAB CHIEF SAID YOU HAVE A WAY TO *REVERSE* PYKO'S EVOLUTIONARY PROCESS?
AFFIRMATIVE. BUT WE REQUIRE AT LEAST A SMALL SAMPLE OF THE MINERAL, WHICH WE NO LONGER POSSESS.
THEN TODAY'S YOUR LUCKY DAY. HAND IT OVER, GROOT.
THERE THEY ARE!
ALL RIGHT, *JERK-BOTS!* RELEASE MY FRIENDS, *NOW!*
RELAX, QUILL. THE BOTS ARE ON *OUR* SIDE NOW.
I'LL EXPLAIN LATER.
THESE ARE THE KINDA *LOSERS* YOU'RE HANGING AROUND WITH THESE DAYS, RUNT?
NOT IN FRONT OF MY *FRIENDS,* MA!
"MA"?! YOU'RE ROCKET'S *MOTHER?!*
I *CAN'T WAIT* TO MEET THE *REST* OF YOUR FAMILY--
UHH... WHAT'S THAT?
THAT...

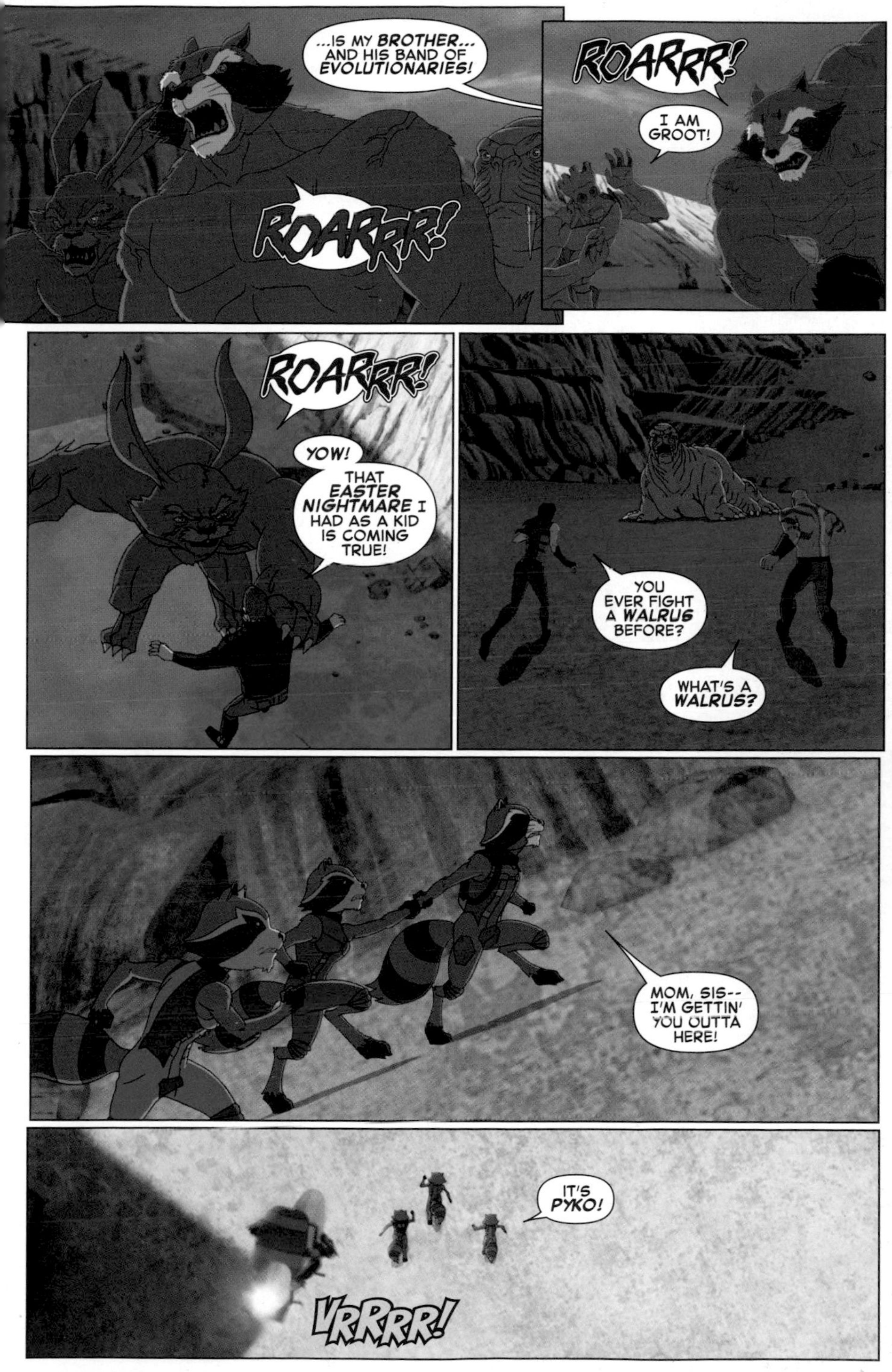
...IS MY BROTHER... AND HIS BAND OF EVOLUTIONARIES!
ROARRR!
ROARRR!
I AM GROOT!
ROARRR!
YOW!
THAT EASTER NIGHTMARE I HAD AS A KID IS COMING TRUE!
YOU EVER FIGHT A WALRUS BEFORE?
WHAT'S A WALRUS?
MOM, SIS-- I'M GETTIN' YOU OUTTA HERE!
IT'S PYKO!
VRRRR!

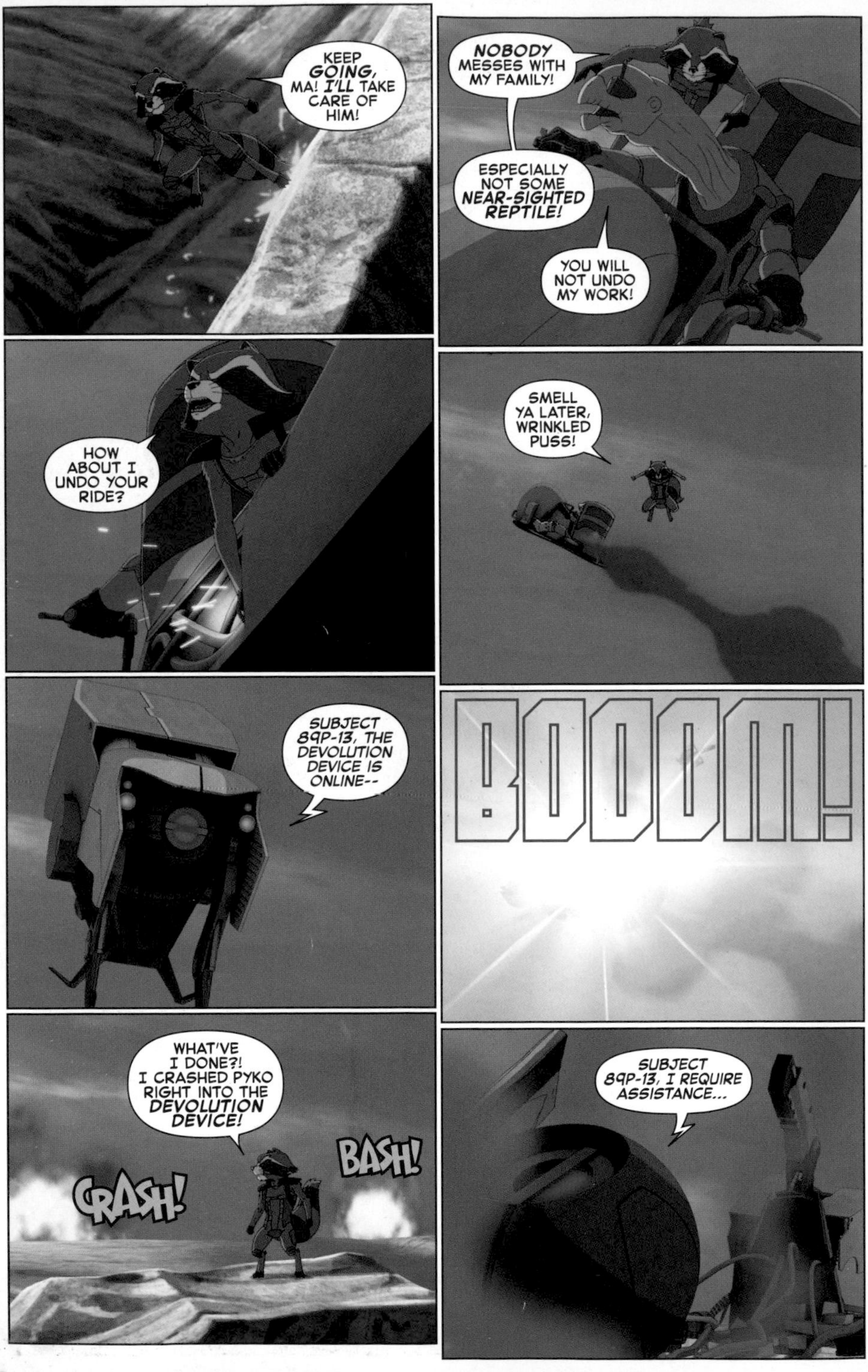
KEEP GOING, MA! I'LL TAKE CARE OF HIM!
NOBODY MESSES WITH MY FAMILY!
ESPECIALLY NOT SOME NEAR-SIGHTED REPTILE!
YOU WILL NOT UNDO MY WORK!
HOW ABOUT I UNDO YOUR RIDE?
SMELL YA LATER, WRINKLED PUSS!
SUBJECT 89P-13, THE DEVOLUTION DEVICE IS ONLINE--
BOOOM!
WHAT'VE I DONE?! I CRASHED PYKO RIGHT INTO THE DEVOLUTION DEVICE!
CRASH!
BASH!
SUBJECT 89P-13, I REQUIRE ASSISTANCE...

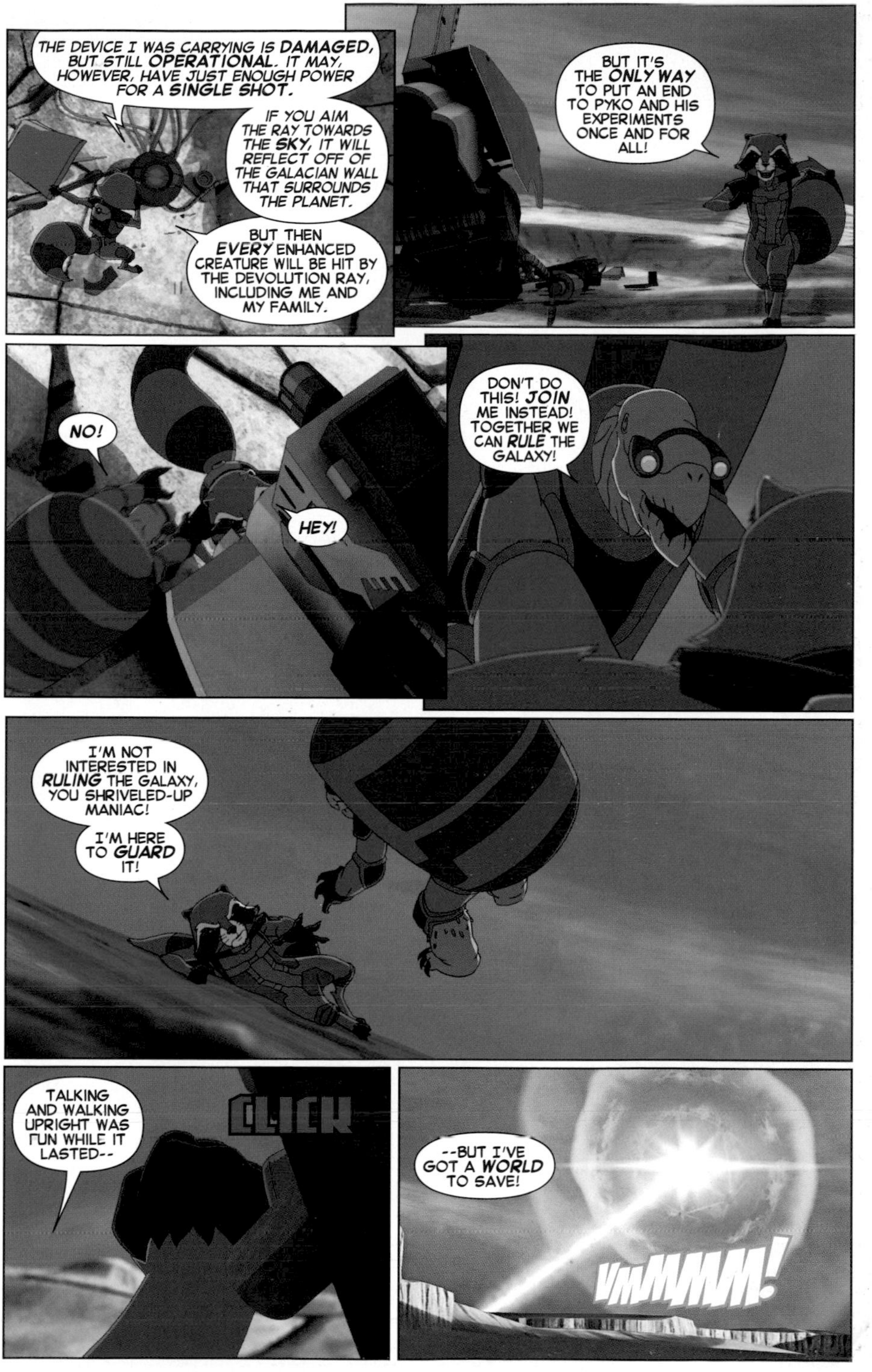

THE DEVICE I WAS CARRYING IS DAMAGED, BUT STILL OPERATIONAL. IT MAY, HOWEVER, HAVE JUST ENOUGH POWER FOR A SINGLE SHOT.
IF YOU AIM THE RAY TOWARDS THE SKY, IT WILL REFLECT OFF OF THE GALACIAN WALL THAT SURROUNDS THE PLANET.
BUT THEN EVERY ENHANCED CREATURE WILL BE HIT BY THE DEVOLUTION RAY, INCLUDING ME AND MY FAMILY.
BUT IT'S THE ONLY WAY TO PUT AN END TO PYKO AND HIS EXPERIMENTS ONCE AND FOR ALL!
NO!
HEY!
DON'T DO THIS! JOIN ME INSTEAD! TOGETHER WE CAN RULE THE GALAXY!
I'M NOT INTERESTED IN RULING THE GALAXY, YOU SHRIVELED-UP MANIAC!
I'M HERE TO GUARD IT!
TALKING AND WALKING UPRIGHT WAS FUN WHILE IT LASTED--
CLICK
--BUT I'VE GOT A WORLD TO SAVE!
VMMMM!

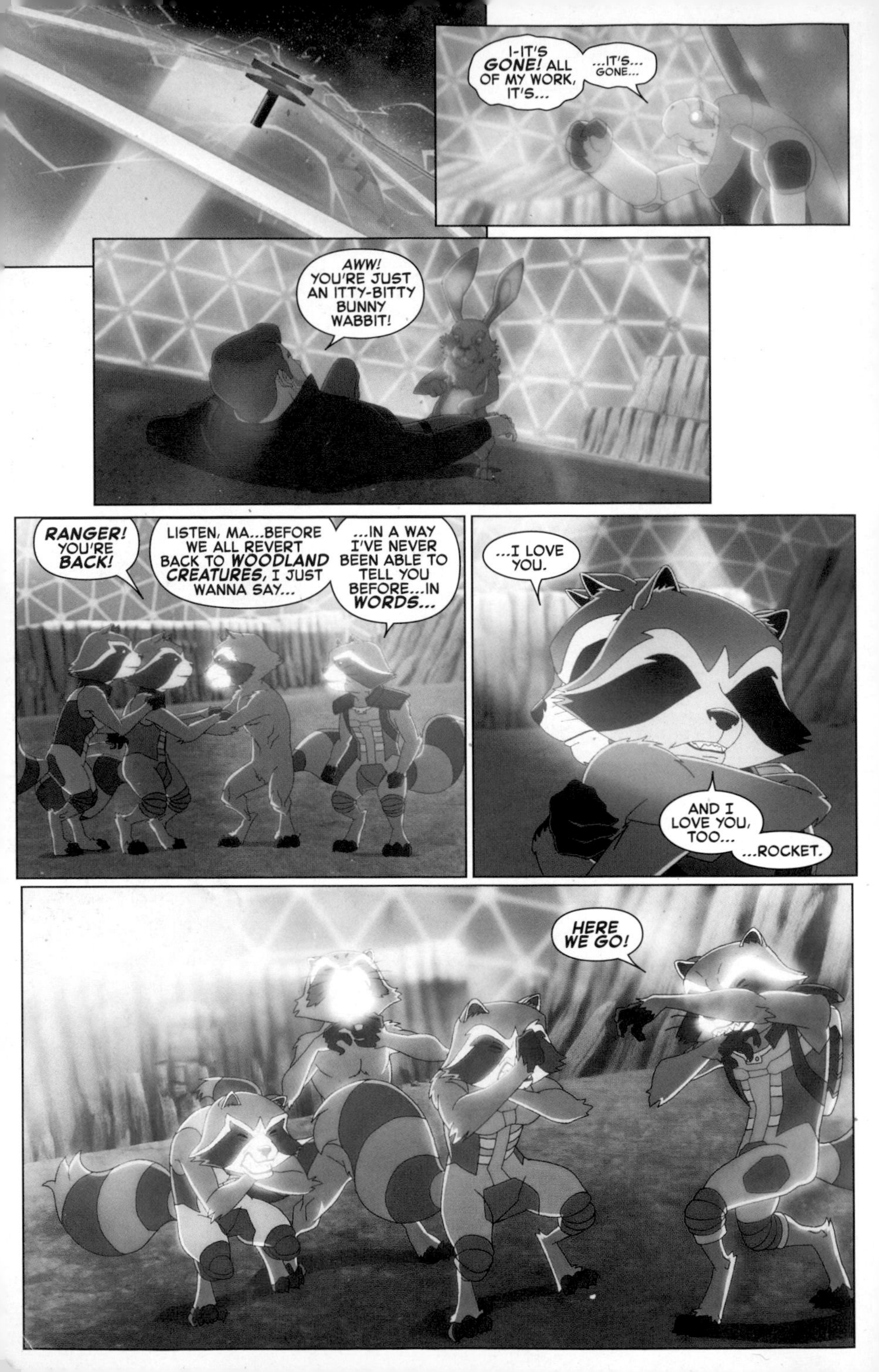
I-IT'S GONE! ALL OF MY WORK, IT'S...
...IT'S... GONE...
AWW! YOU'RE JUST AN ITTY-BITTY BUNNY WABBIT!
RANGER! YOU'RE BACK!
LISTEN, MA...BEFORE WE ALL REVERT BACK TO WOODLAND CREATURES, I JUST WANNA SAY...
...IN A WAY I'VE NEVER BEEN ABLE TO TELL YOU BEFORE...IN WORDS...
...I LOVE YOU.
AND I LOVE YOU, TOO...
...ROCKET.
HERE WE GO!

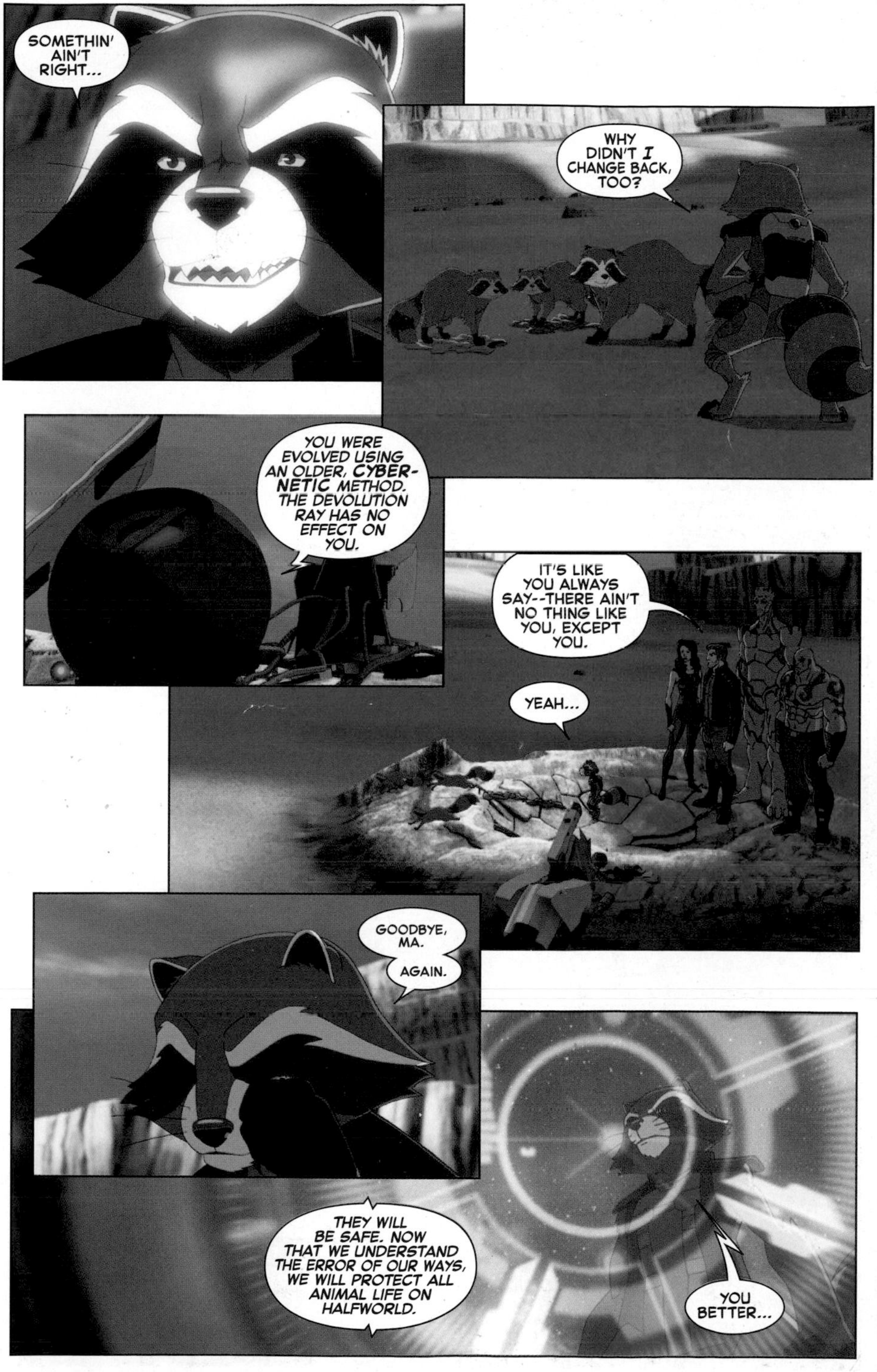
SOMETHIN' AIN'T RIGHT...
WHY DIDN'T I CHANGE BACK, TOO?
YOU WERE EVOLVED USING AN OLDER, CYBER-NETIC METHOD. THE DEVOLUTION RAY HAS NO EFFECT ON YOU.
IT'S LIKE YOU ALWAYS SAY--THERE AIN'T NO THING LIKE YOU, EXCEPT YOU.
YEAH...
GOODBYE, MA.
AGAIN.
THEY WILL BE SAFE. NOW THAT WE UNDERSTAND THE ERROR OF OUR WAYS, WE WILL PROTECT ALL ANIMAL LIFE ON HALFWORLD.
YOU BETTER...

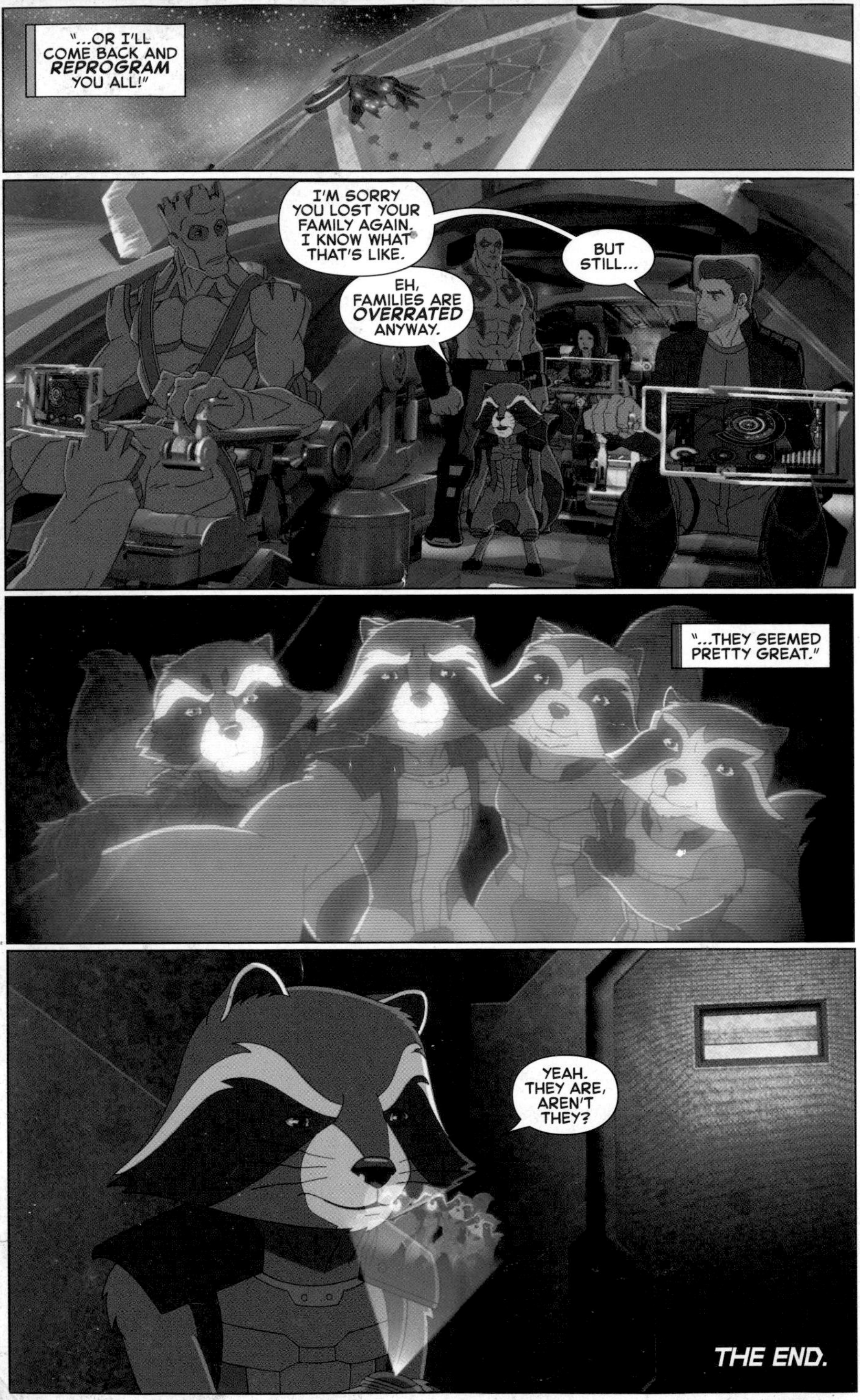
"...OR I'LL COME BACK AND REPROGRAM YOU ALL!"
I'M SORRY YOU LOST YOUR FAMILY AGAIN. I KNOW WHAT THAT'S LIKE.
BUT STILL...
EH, FAMILIES ARE OVERRATED ANYWAY.
"...THEY SEEMED PRETTY GREAT."
YEAH. THEY ARE, AREN'T THEY?
THE END.